Kings Series:

Mated To The Werewolf King

Alena Des

Inkitt

The Shock

Belle

"Come back here, Annabelle, right now!" My dad shouted at me as I ran out of the house.

They wanted to send me away from here. Werewolves lived in packs, secluded away from humans. Mine was in Chicago, a rather large pack with at least hundred members. Every one of us contributed to the enhancement of our pack which made us self-sufficient, with our own schools, entertainment centers, restaurants. That is why this wasn't just home to me, it was all I ever knew in my life.

"I'm not going to my aunt's place. I'm not going!" I yelled. I wasn't sure he heard me. The howling wind took away my words and carried them into the far distance. I didn't bother repeating them. They knew how I felt. I was going to stay right here where I belonged. Some might have called me childish, but I didn't care. Everybody and everything I loved was here. I would not let them take me to a faraway place where I would no longer be able to see my brother Sean, my best friends, Joshua and Danny, not to forget Gregory, the man I knew I was destined to be with. As I was running, I felt the familiar warmth seep into my skin, saw my limbs stretch, and felt the reddish fur wrap around my body like a thick blanket. Morphed into my wolf form, I sped towards my secret place. I had found this place when I was five and my ten-year-old brother, whom I found to be so annoying at the time, had driven me nuts by telling me how ugly I was, and how nobody loved me because they had found me at the border of the pack territory years ago. I had cared at the time, I was only five after all!

"Liar, you are a big fat liar." I had screamed at my brother, but I could not prevent the tears of frustration and hurt that came streaming down my cheeks.

"You are not my real sister. You should go back where you came from," Sean had replied arrogantly, his young face contorted in anger.

I had then run in the forest, and my brother had let me. After what seemed like hours of running, I had come to a clearing by the cliff, falling out of exhaustion. Waking in the middle of the night to a full moon in the sky looking down on me, I'd been mesmerized. The moon's light had almost blinded me, the fleeting shadows on its sphere had spoken to me silently, soothing my worries. Now I looked back on it, I'd imagined the moon to be mine that day, my secret friend, the mirror of my soul. Staring at it for hours, I had felt all my anger and resentment leave my body. Right then, I had heard them, the wolves howling in the night and knew they were coming for me. Unable to bear the thought of sharing this place with anyone else, I had taken off, not stopping until I knew I was far away, waiting for them to find me.

I was running there right now, to the place where I always found consolation when I was agitated. It always gave me peace as if I belonged there. Then I was shaken by another disturbing thought; dear Moon Goddess, leaving also meant I would be away from my secret place, how would I ever bear that? How was I ever going to be okay with all of this shit they were piling on me? I just wanted everything back as it was. I hated change; I absolutely loathed it.

"Belle, stop. Wait for me," hollered my brother.

I almost stopped. I knew he cared. Growing up had resolved our differences, and we'd become very close in time. The only annoying thing about him now was his over-protective manner. He was forever keeping me away from Gregory, his best friend, the hot son of the pack's beta, as well as all the other potential boyfriends. I was shielded from any slander, and insult against my small wolf because everyone in the pack knew that making me a target would mean confronting Sean. And nobody wanted to do

2

that, he was huge at 6 feet 10 inches and he was notorious for his rock-hard punches. A few pack members had already been the target of his silent fury which had the tendency to blow like a volcano within seconds, especially when I was the talk of the conversation. So, many preferred to keep away from him, away from me.

I did not look back; I needed to be away from everyone. But, I heard him morph into his large gray wolf behind me which meant that he would catch up with me in just moments. Unfortunately, my wolf form was pathetic; it was small, weak and slow. It had always been like that since the moment I shifted at 15. I never understood it; my father was the alpha of the pack, and my mother was the alpha's daughter. I should have come out better, it was so damn unfair! My parents had come up with a thousand explanations when I was young, just to stop my tears. But, none of it had ever made sense. In the end, father had said how I was perfect just the way I was.

Needless to say, soon my brother's gray wolf landed on my back bringing me to a sharp stop. I tried to use my paws to get away, but I was miserably pinned under his large form. I morphed back to my human self, and he let me get up. Weirdly enough, I was the only one with the talent to keep my clothes on while shifting back and forth. I turned my back as I heard my brother put on the clothes he'd carried in his mouth.

"We need to talk," said Sean.

"Sure, shoot away. But, know this, I won't be leaving home," I said in an angry tone.

"You have to, Belle. That is the only way," said my brother with a defeated expression.

"What is going on for Moon Goddess's sake, Sean? Tell me why I have to go".

"He is coming for you, and he knows where you are. You can't be here for your eighteenth birthday."

"What are you talking about? Who is coming for me?"

"I'll let father explain it to you."

3

"He has no intention of making any explanations, Sean. He is completely okay with the idea of just ordering me to go."

"He is scared, Belle. You're father's little pup. The idea of anything happening to you is scaring the shit out of him."

"You're talking bullshit! Who is coming anyway, another alpha?"

"No, he is not a werewolf. He is something else."

"C'mon Sean, you're pulling my leg here. There is nothing else," I said, shaking my head.

"There is so much you don't know, Belle."

"Then tell me. I'm done with knowing nothing." My voice was shrill; I was just losing it. I felt that the world I knew was soon about to shatter and I knew even my secret place would no longer provide me with a safe haven from my troubles. I feared that after I heard what Sean was about to tell me I was never going to be the same again. But, still, I had to know. The cat was out of the bag, and there was no putting it back.

"Well," stammered Sean. Nothing much worried my brother, so seeing him nervous like this made me more scared than ever.

"Spill the beans, Sean. It's ok," I said to him reassuringly.

"He is the Demon Lord."

"Excuse me?" I said laughing. Now I knew he was pulling my leg, all of this was a joke. What a relief! But, just as I felt the weight lift off my shoulders, every neuron in my head seemed to rattle. I would expect Sean to pull a prank like this, but would my dad be in on it? Absolutely not. As wonderful as he was, Dad was not known to be flippant at all. Ever. On the contrary, I was sure he was born without the humor gene. So, then, what did he mean by a Demon Lord?

"This is no laughing matter, Belle!" warned Sean, his eyebrows furrowed.

"Ok," was all I could mutter under my breath as I waited for him to crush my safe world.

"Do you remember that day when you ran away in the forest, and I got grounded for a week for taunting you?"

"Yes, of course, you totally deserved it. You made me furious; I hated you that day."

"Yes, of course," Sean said impatiently as if I was keeping him from making his point. "But, do you remember what I told you before you took off?"

"Hmm, let me see. You said I was ugly, and that nobody loved me. You were a real jerk back then. You know that? You made my life a living and breathing hell," I said.

I looked at Sean's eyes. Both of us were aware of what I was doing. I was delaying the inevitable by diverting from the topic and my brother was allowing it. He knew I needed some more time.

"What else did I say, Belle?" he then asked forcefully, letting me know that we could not waste time any further.

"Well, you told me that I was found in the trash bin or some other rubbish like that."

"Not the trash bin, Belle, the pack border."

"Whatever. It's the same stupid joke every old brother says to a younger sibling. You were simply jealous; I get it. No biggie," I said in a pretense calm demeanor while my heart was pounding fiercely in my ribcage. I knew what was coming even as I tried to deny it.

"That was no joke, Belle."

Shit. I was still unprepared for how much hearing it out loud hurt.

"That is why I was angry at you for a long time. I remember the knock on our door in the middle of the night that day. Dad was talking to his beta for a few minutes and then he left in a hurry. He was gone for a long time and then he came back with you in his arms. My parents started arguing heatedly. I had never seen them that way. I started listening to their debate. Mom wanted to keep you, but Father was worried. He was saying that there must be more to the story than met the eye. He said somebody surely would come back for you. I was just five, but I wanted to see what it was that we could keep. Whatever it was, I knew I wanted it. I rushed downstairs to help Mother convince him to keep it, to keep *you*.

Then I saw you bundled in a tattered gray blanket. You deserved so much better! You were so small and so fragile that I wanted to protect you forever. But I was scared. I feared you would be taken from me, from us, because you weren't ours. It took me a long time to accept that you *could* be ours. That was the day when all changed between us."

"Yeah, I remember. I was eight years old, and you had shifted for the first time. I heard the shatter of the bones as they cracked beneath your skin. You craned your neck, flexed your arms until your body phased into a massive canine shape. A blanket of fur sprouted from your thickened skin. Your eyes glowed amber, and your teeth sharpened into fangs just as the claws curled from your fingertips. In your wolf form, you lowered your head and ambled closer. You were such a massive beast in gray. I remember I'd stiffened as you'd been such a boorish prick until that time. Anyway, you buried your nose against my shoulder. I'd thought you were bipolar; you had not let go until I'd patted you."

Sean chuckled. It was nice seeing him relax again, even if I suspected it was to be short lived.

"Well I had turned into a massive wolf, what did you expect? I knew then I could protect you from everyone who meant you harm, and that changed everything." But then his face fell.

"Well, congrats! Your arrogance remains untouched," I said hoping to bring back his cheerful self again. I failed.

"Now, I am not sure anymore. I don't know what I'm up against."

"Sean, stop it! Who the hell am I?"

"We don't know for sure. There was nothing on you when Dad found you."

Apparently, I still had to wait for the revelation of my identity.

"Well, then, who is the Demon Lord?"

"He is the leader of demons, and he issued an ultimatum last week to King Blake to hand you back. He threatens with war. The king's been investigating into your whereabouts."

"Our king? A war?" I stammered. "Why should the Demon Lord start a war over me? What does he want with me? I am no demon for Goddess's sake. I do not even know what a demon looks like; I am sure it is not sightly. I am a werewolf, a pathetic wolf, what would he ever want with me?" I asked, frantically. I was taking short quick breaths; my hands were cold and sweaty. I was gasping for precious air. I felt like I was suffocating.

"You're hyperventilating. Take a deep breath and start counting down as you exhale slowly," Sean told me as he held me firmly. The Demon King, The Werewolf King, war, this was all too much. Ten, nine. Exhale. Eight, seven, six and exhale. I couldn't breathe. The last thing I saw was the back of Sean's hand fast descending upon me, and everything went black.

"Are you ok? Answer me, Belle!" I heard Sean's voice.

"What happened?"

"You were having a hard time breathing; I didn't know what to do so I knocked you out."

"What the hell, Sean?" I tried to get up as I rushed to feel the lump on my head. It was huge. Damn it. Unfortunately, fast healing was not one of my virtues. This would stay with me for a few days now.

"I am sorry. I really didn't know what else to do. Besides, you're a werewolf; you'll be fine."

"Gosh, I pity the poor soul who will be your mate," I said.

"Don't say that. I'm sorry, Belle."

"It's okay," I said. After all, it had helped. I was able to breathe again.

"We should go back home. Dad will be worried. I've told you all I know, and frankly, I don't think you can take more information today anyway."

I had to agree.

"You wanna shift?" asked Sean.

I morphed, with the egg sized lump rising glamorously on my wolf head. Lovely!

As we ran back towards home, I wondered what tomorrow would bring.

Too Late

Belle

When we reached home, my parents were waiting for us with worried expressions. I went upstairs in my wolf form, changed into a pair of clean blue jeans and a t-shirt, and put my red hair in a ponytail before I strolled down to face my parents. Sean was already in the living room. They all looked at me tensely as I threw myself into my favorite rocking chair in the corner and said, "Let's not talk about this anymore. That is seriously all I can handle for today."

They both looked at me intensely, their faces tense, worried. Dad opened his mouth as if to say something, but then I caught Mother pinching his hand, ever so slightly. Father closed his eyes for a few seconds, swallowing those unsaid words. "It'll be alright. We still have the time," Mother mouthed silently. He then nodded, his body slouched in defeat. He grabbed her hand tenderly and they left the room hand in hand. That was my parents for you! They were still madly in love. Sometimes I couldn't believe how they were still so engrossed with each other after so many years. One day, I wanted to be in love like that, which was only going to happen if the Werewolf and the Demon King left me alone to find my mate. A minuscule possibility, by the looks of it. I was likely to die mateless. I was better off coming to grips with this reality. My mission was to survive; I could do without love.

There was a knock on the door. Sean went to open it and came back with Gregory. Well, I probably was not going to live long enough to meet my mate, but I could still enjoy ogling Gregory, couldn't I, now?

"Hi, what's up, Belle?" asked Gregory, his eyes averting me as always. He was so very shy, in a very cute sort of way. He had curly black hair of shoulder-length and vivid green eyes with long eyelashes. I loved watching how he twirled the locks of his hair at the back of his nape, or how he chewed the inside of his cheek whenever he was nervous. He had a killer body, but he carried it with the uncertainty of a lanky teenager, hunching his broad shoulders, keeping his chin down. It was amazing, really, how insecure he was despite his amazing looks.

"What are you guys up to?" I asked him.

"Not much. We'll just watch a movie," he said, grabbing harshly at another curl of his hair.

"Can I join?" I asked, hoping this time Sean would let me. After all, I'd really had a lousy day.

Gregory sadly turned his head and looked at Sean expecting his normal rebuttal. Gregory was in Sean's circle of friends who followed his strict "hands off my sister" policy which included not looking, and definitely not spending time with me.

"Well, okay," Sean said, shocking both his friend and me.

"Cool, what are we watching?" I asked eagerly, but I really didn't care. I just wanted to take my mind off it all.

"The Lord of the Rings," replied Sean, as he took the first DVD in the series from its case and put it in the player which immediately projected the movie on the 75-inch flat screen.

I got up from the rocking chair, aiming to place my butt on the comfy leather sofa across the TV. I really loved this room; it was small, though cozy. The smell of vanilla from the two lit candles permeated my nostrils. There was something soothing about watching the movie in candle light. The flames flavored the room in thin yellow streaks while keeping the mysteries of the darkness. I tried to wiggle my way into the small space between Sean and Gregory, but my brother reverted to his old ways, scooting towards his buddy before I could even place myself. Well, so much for my subtle way of getting close to Gregory! I guessed there was only so much that Sean would allow, even under these circumstances. My butt still in the air, I reluctantly lowered myself next to Sean.

Watching a movie like this made me feel good, like today was any typical day. I was almost beginning to think that the impending doom was just a figment of my imagination, and I never had that conversation with Sean. I felt my eyes falling when it was sometime in the middle of the night, and Sean hurried to insert the last DVD in the series. I couldn't believe how energetic both he and Gregory were as the first lights of dawn danced and shimmered on the window glass; it must have been the alpha and beta blood in their veins. But, I also had the same blood, and I should have been as alert! Nope, I suddenly remembered. That thought woke me up like a bucket of icy water, and I shifted in my seat, straightening my shoulders. Sean suddenly paused the DVD and stood up.

"I'll make some popcorn. Don't start the movie without me; I'll be right back," Sean said, in a serious tone.

Men…He must have watched this movie a thousand times, and he was still watching it as enthusiastically as the first time.

When Sean left, Gregory looked at me fleetingly. His right eye twitched with nervousness.

Oww, he was so very sweet! Too bad he wasn't interested. The werewolf world was full of macho, arrogant men who were extremely possessive over females. All they did was order you around and act as if they were creatures possessing an ancient wisdom only inherited by men. You could understand why Gregory was such a rarity in my world. I moved closer to Gregory, wanting to know him better. Right then, Sean showed up with a huge bowl of popcorn, of course.

"Move back," he said as his eyes twitched with anger.

"Really, Sean?" I rolled my eyes but did as he asked.

I jumped in my seat at a big commotion outside. There were wolves howling, their paws circling the house. What was going on? And then I heard my father run down the stairs. Gregory and Sean rushed outside with him.

"What is going on?" I asked in vain, and then I caught hold of Mom whose beautiful face was taut with stress.

"He's here," she said with a shaky voice.

"Who? Oh, Moon Goddess, you mean, the Demon Lord?"

"No. The Werewolf King."

"Oh, then it's nothing. You got me worried for a sec there," I said, trying to lighten the atmosphere.

Dad suddenly rushed inside, his sad, delirious eyes looking for me.

"We're too late."

This was killing him, this helplessness. I couldn't bear seeing this despair on his face.

I had to be strong for all of us. I lifted my head high; I may not be his real daughter, but I was still raised as an alpha pup. I would act like one.

"It's okay, Dad. Let's go and meet the king then. Shall we?"

"I won't let him take you away from us. I swear to you, Belle," he promised.

But, this was one promise I knew he couldn't keep. Both of us knew it. The Werewolf King was the alpha of all the alphas and no one, including Dad, had the power to disobey him. In fact, if the rumors were true, he could bring down any werewolf to his knees with sheer brain power without ever lifting a muscle. The thought of it scared me. I didn't want to face him. I could happily spend my whole life inside the borders of my pack, not ever setting eyes on the Werewolf King. But, alas, life had other plans. I took a deep breath of air, and walked outside in a pretense of calm, as calm as my shivering legs would let me. Outside, Sean and Gregory had already phased into their wolf forms, while others slowly appeared in small groups, their movements fast, their soulful howls praying tribute to the Moon Goddess, asking for strength, bravery and victory. When they saw me, they immediately formed a circle around me. The transition to their role as loyal pack soldiers had happened so very quickly, their growls were now vicious, threatening, laden with a willingness to fight for me.

"This is all so encouraging my friends, but, back off before you piss me off," warned a very deep voice with a full timbre, belonging to a face I couldn't even see, as I was still kept in the protected cocoon of wolves. His voice, however, penetrated all my bones, muscles, and cells, turning my insides into mush. My heart rate rose to a rapid crescendo, and I had a hard time ordering my body to keep me standing. What was happening to me? What his presence did to my body and mind scared me more than the uncertainty of my fate. I felt dizzy. I swallowed heavily to shake it all off, his control over my body was alarming, it hit me like the unexpected side effects of a heavy medicine. I had to be strong. I had to remain standing. I had to....I no longer knew what I had to do.

"We will not give her to you," growled my dad.

"Step aside," the king shouted with a clear alpha command that could not be denied. Within seconds, all the wolves except for Sean and my father, who was still in his human form, scattered, their heads bowed in submission. The two were trying hard to resist the order with all their might. They kept struggling, trying to tolerate the explosive pain in their head with limited success. Dad had pressed his fingers harshly on his temples, and he was turning his head viciously from side to side as if to wrench away a bug firmly planted in its depths.

Damn it; the king was hurting them with some invisible power. So, the rumors were true! I couldn't bear seeing my family like this; I pushed myself forward with sheer determination.

"Stop it, stop it, please! You can have me. Just don't hurt them anymore," I cried out with exasperation. Sean howled, finally free from whatever was holding him captive in the throes of agony, but I saw my father collapse, his form still on the ground.

"Nooooo!" I screamed, running to his body, trying to see whether he was still breathing.

"He will be fine. Come to me, little girl. I'm losing my patience," he bellowed.

"I will kill you with my bare hands if anything happens to him, do you hear me?" I shouted with a boiling rage that was turning my insides out.

12

He howled with laughter.

I got up from the ground and started walking rapidly toward the monster. I would show him.

As wolves scattered from my way, and the path opened revealing his features and majestic form, I tripped, falling ungracefully face down. He stood out among the others, not only because of his size but, I was ashamed to admit, his perfection. His beauty was so disturbing, so unusual and so unfair that I was caught completely unawares. There was masculinity streaming out of his pores. He had the most daunting black eyes surrounded by clear, brisk eyebrows which, frankly, should have freaked me out, yet I could happily drown in their depths. His eyes were surrounded with the thickest eyelashes gifted to any mankind. He had a straight, symmetrical nose, surrounded by a strong forehead and a chiseled jawline. I nearly let out a sigh at the sight of him as I hastened my steps to get to what I thought at the time as my salvation. I desperately wanted to touch his body which was sculpted like a Greek god, with broad shoulders, a beautifully carved muscular chest and ripped abs. He was a marvelous chiseled beast. My perfect beast. What? I shook myself out of my stupor, scolding myself for my stupidity and weakness. He was the enemy, and I'd best remember it.

He looked at me deeply when I was within touching distance. His eyes were furrowed with rage.

"Who the hell are you?" he suddenly roared.

"I am Belle," I managed to say calmly, trying very hard not to show the turmoil of my emotions.

He stood silent for a minute. "You are coming with me, we are leaving," he said. He suddenly morphed into his humongous wolf, throwing me easily onto his back with a single hand which had already turned to a lethal paw. I heard Sean's mournful cry from afar, and before I was even able to mutter a word, I found myself almost flying in the air. The speed with which his wolf was running along with his selected warriors was beyond anything normal. The trees became a blur as I struggled desperately to hang onto his thick mane. If I didn't know any better, I would have sworn he had wings.

The Journey

Belle

I didn't know how I would survive this journey. My shoulders ached, my neck muscles screamed, and my hands were numb from trying to hold on to him. I knew if I fell off his back, that would mean some serious injury to me, especially with my impaired healing skills. He simply didn't care. After what seemed like an hour, the monster finally came to a stop, throwing me harshly off his back. I was so nauseated and dizzy; I simply collapsed on my feet. I stretched my hands, grimacing at the pain of waking my numb fingers.

"We will rest here. Get up!" he ordered as he put on a pair of black trousers to hide his naked human form.

I was overwhelmed by hysterics right then, an uncontrolled bubble of laughter erupted from my throat. The Demon Lord, this monster, my dad hurting on the ground, and hours of clinging to his mane all the while feeling I wouldn't survive it. It was all too much. I was rolling on the ground, holding my stomach and laughing, unable to suppress this cruel mirth attack. My stomach was hurting, but I simply couldn't stop.

"Stop. I forbid you to laugh," he bellowed, not understanding what was happening to me.

Forbid me to laugh? Oh, that was precious! I felt the anger surfacing again upon hearing those words, which, thankfully, was enough to end my hysteria. I managed to move my hurting limbs with an unexpected litheness and rose to my feet, pointing my finger at him threateningly as I approached him.

"Don't you dare tell me what to do, you arrogant bastard," I yelled, oblivious to how suddenly everything around us had come to an eerie silence. His warriors were looking at me in horror as if I had a death wish on my shoulders. I probably did, but I was too far gone in my second stage of hysteria even to notice.

His face curled in a snarl of rage, his lips now a flat line of anger. A muscle was ticking steadily in his cheek as he was trying to control his inner beast.

"You will learn to show me some respect," he barked as he seized me by the neck with both hands and lifted me high in the air, squeezing my throat so hard along the way I couldn't breathe. This was it; I had pushed the monster too much, and I was going to die. I was choking, my face turning blue as I struggled and writhed weakly in his grip.

"Keith. Let her go, you are killing her," I heard someone yell in the distance, but I was far too gone to care.

Just like that, he let me go, I fell on the ground, coughing and gasping for breath. He looked at my body with a look of disgust on his face as I lay down on the ground shaking and convulsing uncontrollably. He then turned sharply and stomped away.

"Are you okay?" asked one of his warriors with an unexpected kindness in his eyes.

I tried to speak, but nothing came out aside from a pathetic squeak. It sounded like a door with a rusty hinge.

"Don't try to speak," he said apologetically.

I nodded. The bastard had tried to choke me to death.

"You are dangerously impulsive, if I may say so. I suggest you control yourself before you push him too hard."

"He is a beast." My whisper came as a croak. It was all his doing.

"He is that," he sighed. "I'm sorry, I forgot to introduce myself. I am Xavier."

When I attempted to say my name, he stopped me with a hand gesture. "I know who you are. You are the mystery girl the Demon Lord wants," he chuckled.

Wow, this guy was actually nice. So, the king's warriors were not all evil like him. Good to know.

Right then, the monster had to come back and ruin it all again. His black hair was wet, small droplets clinging to his long strands and falling on his forehead. He must have taken a quick dip in the lake. I was unfortunately mesmerized by a water droplet that found its way into his muscular chest, streaking further down the long line of his torso, finally disappearing beneath his trousers.

He caught my gaze. He had the nerve to stare back at me.

That did snap me out of my daze.

Damn it; I was disgusted with myself for my impulsive attraction to him. I was undeniably and uncontrollably drawn to this beast who had no regrets for what he'd done. What was wrong with me?

I clenched my teeth in an effort to curb all the vile words that threatened to pour out of my mouth. I could only whisper anyway.

His calm demeanor ended just like that and he was his old self again, barking orders. "Wrap it up. We are leaving."

I turned to Xavier and touched his arm softly, my eyes silently begging him to be my new ride. Xavier shook his head with an apologetic look on his face.

Suddenly, Xavier's huge body was thrown into the clearing, his body crashing into the trunk of a tree with a loud thud. Even though he grimaced a little as he stood up, I was relieved to see that he was not injured badly.

"You do not touch anyone but me, and nobody touches you!" the king yelled with a rage that rattled the Earth.

"Fine," I said, and before I knew it, I was back on his mane again, clinging to him with all I had.

Thank the Moon Goddess, it only took a few minutes this time before he came to a sudden stop.

"Ouch," I whined in a whispery cracked voice, as I rubbed my ass which had landed ungracefully on the harsh ground after his abrupt halt. Before I knew it, I was forcefully pushed behind a tree.

When I was about to ask him what his damn problem was, his angry growling pinned me to my place. Then it all went crazy, with red eyed creatures swarming around us, all of them had spiky blonde hair, their skin slick with an oily substance that somehow seemed to glow.

I saw the monster take out a few of them with just a touch of his paws. I couldn't help but stare at the taut muscles twitching and stretching over his wolf chest as he battled these creatures whose existence I was not even aware of until a few minutes ago. I shook out of my stupor pretty quickly as one of them spotted me behind the tree. He stood ten meters away, grinning. When I thought I could outrun him, he had me pinned beneath the tree with his hand which stretched from where he stood. For the sake of the Moon Goddess, how was that possible? He gradually pulled back his overstretched limb as he walked towards me.

"Well... well," he said, drawling his words. Up close, he almost looked normal, except of course for the unnatural sheen of his skin. I was too stunned to move at first, but then when I was just about to phase into my wolf form to make my escape, a big jaw closed around his neck, ripping his throat open, and a greenish gel-like substance gushed into the air.

I saw his familiar black eyes before he rushed back into the thick of the battle. The king had saved me. But, after he had choked me, I reminded myself harshly, lest I forget it.

The place was bursting with these creatures who were not as fast or as strong as the werewolves, but they surely compensated for their lack of speed and strength with their ability to stretch limbs. Their hands and legs extended like flexible poles surrounded the torsos of werewolves like a tight blanket, sticking to their flesh. The wolves struggled to loosen their grip, often snapping the muscles that held the limbs. Quickly though, the forest floor became covered in green gooey blood and dismembered spaghetti limbs. None of the corpses belonged to the werewolves, thank the Moon Goddess. I looked around deliriously, my eyes instinctively searching for the king. There he was talking to Xavier in the center of this bloodbath. I sighed happily, unable to help myself. He seemed to be in complete and utter health, with only minor scratches on his perfectly shaped body.

I got out of my hiding place. I was curious to know about these creatures. Were they demons?

"Are you okay?" asked Xavier who left the king's side.

"I am. Are they…?" I asked, expecting him to finish the sentence. I noticed my voice was getting better, but it was still a struggle for me.

"Yep, demons," he replied.

"Were they here for me?" I asked hesitantly.

"Probably, despite the treaty."

"What treaty?" I asked.

"The treaty that keeps the peace between all species, except for the demons and witches, who hate each other's guts, of course. They are life-long enemies. Oh well, one can't have it all. We just let them destroy each other. It is quite fun actually," he said chuckling.

"What?" I exclaimed in my still croaky voice. "Did you just say *witches*?"

"Yes, of course. And then we have the fae, vampires, ifrits, nymphs and of course shadow spirits."

I was so stunned that I could not speak. The world I knew did not exist.

"So, do you know why the demons wanted me?"

"Not a clue, unfortunately. I am sure Keith will figure it out soon. It may seem improbable to you right now, but believe me when I say he is your best shot of survival in this world."

I snorted in an unladylike fashion, raising my eyebrow.

"That is enough chit-chat for today," my monster interrupted us rudely. "We are leaving. Unless, of course, you want to wait for the next demon attack?" he asked mockingly.

Asshole. He hadn't even asked me how I was. He didn't give a damn about me. If my survival rested with him as Xavier would have me believe, I was doomed.

A New Home

Belle

As the sun cast its vivid hues of oranges and yellows across the sky, slowly disappearing beneath the horizon, we finally stopped. And this time, I managed to stay on the monster's back. I certainly was getting better at this. That thought of victory evaporated when I tried moving my aching limbs. My arms hung from my shoulders like twisted branches, tight with overused muscles, yet at the same time, as brittle as glass, ready to be shattered with a brief touch.

A majestic castle loomed before us. I took hesitant steps towards it, trying to give life to my shaking legs, when I saw its gate open to reveal a gorgeous slender female behind it. From the joy on her face, I presumed her to be the mate of one of the warriors. She rushed towards us with her thick auburn hair flying in the wind. I sighed, thinking of *mates*. There was nothing like it.

As I stood there wondering who the lucky guy was, she threw herself at my beast, wrapping her legs around his waist and locking her mouth to his, kissing him as she thrust her hands into his thick black hair.

What the hell? I certainly wasn't expecting that. Who was she? I literally wanted to rip her heart out. To my utmost surprise, I found my hands balled into tight fists at my sides. With an apparent effort, I managed to unclench them. What was I doing? She was welcome to him. Why did I even care? But damn it, I did! I walked towards my new and only friend, Xavier, hoping he would quench my curiosity.

"Hey, Xavier," I said. "Who is the bitch?"

"The bitch is my sister, Zena," laughed Xavier.

Oops! I looked at his face with a silent apology, hoping that I hadn't offended him, the only ally I had in this strange foreign place.

"No worries. She is indeed a bitch," he smiled.

The bitch had finally left the king's mouth, now trailing a string of kisses along his jaw. Get a bed! I was nauseated just watching the scene.

The simple reality was that I couldn't bear watching their intimacy, for whatever reason I couldn't fathom. Oh, the Moon Goddess, what if they were mates?

"Behave," I heard my monster say as he finally put the girl down. To my utmost dismay, she continued hugging him.

"If you don't mind, I'd like to find my bed now. I'm quite tired," I said even though it was still way too early for that.

He sharply turned to me with the girl still clinging to him like a limpet. "Of course, your majesty," he said mockingly. His eyes pierced mine for a few seconds. Then he moved his hand to the girl's ass and squeezed as she pressed herself even closer to him.

A smile flickered in his dark eyes as he then said the dooming words that sealed my fate.

"Take her to the dungeon."

"What!" I exclaimed in shock. Was this a joke?

"C'mon, Keith. Is that really necessary?" asked Xavier.

Keith didn't even bother answering and simply continued making out with her, as if I was a fly beneath his boot, as if I didn't matter at all. My eyes brimmed with tears. But I held them back as I refused to cry in front of him. I wouldn't give him that satisfaction.

"I hate you!" I screamed as two of his warriors held me by my arms, dragging me to the dungeon. I tried to catch Xavier's eye as I was passing, but he wouldn't look at me. Poor Xavier! It wasn't his fault. He had tried. But the beast wouldn't listen.

As the guards were speeding away, half dragging and half carrying me away from sight, I looked back at him one last time. To my utmost surprise, he had finally pried the girl away from him, holding her at bay with his outstretched hand despite her sound protests and pitiful attempts to come closer. All the while, his eyes were unblinking, watching me with an undecipherable expression.

I still couldn't believe any of this as we descended the winding stairs to the dungeon. The dungeon was a small windowless cell with walls of brick that oozed damp. There dripped a foul moisture from the ceiling that stank of urine, blood and sweat. I wrinkled my nose in disgust, but there was no respite from this nightmare. I shivered in horror thinking of the past inhabitants of the room as the guards pushed me inside, shutting the dungeon door to leave me in pitch darkness.

How could he have done this to me? Being a werewolf himself, he should have known how devastating it would be for me to be trapped in a place like this. Our wolves were free spirits born to roam in the wilderness, wild and untethered. How was I going to survive this? Reality suddenly hit me as I threw myself on the dirty floor and it was when I felt the cold touch of wetness on my cheek that I knew I was crying.

After what seemed like long agonizing hours of sobbing in sheer panic, I finally fell asleep. Suddenly, the dungeon door opened, and Xavier walked in with a lantern, some blankets and a tray of food. I closed and opened my eyes a few times as I tried to adjust to the blinding light after sitting in the dark for so many hours.

"How are you, Belle?" he asked with a pained smile.

"How do you think?" I snapped at him.

"I'm sorry. He's beyond any reasoning. I've never seen him like this. He is not acting like himself."

"I don't care, do you hear me? Don't talk to me about that monster! I've been in this dark, damp and stinky hole for hours. All because of him! My father would have wrenched his black heart out if he knew what he was doing to me," I sobbed in exasperation.

In fact, there was nothing my dad could have done, and I knew it well.

"Does he know?" I asked pointing at the stuff Xavier had brought to my cell.

"Yes. It was his idea."

"I thought maybe it was you." I wanted it to be Xavier. I wanted to hate the monster with every fiber of my being.

"Unfortunately, betraying him is not an option Belle. He would know," he said, shrugging.

"Fine. I will have the lantern, and the blankets and the food because I need to survive here. But, I will not feel gratitude to him nor will I forgive him. Ever! In fact, I will hand myself willingly to the Demon Lord the first moment I see him. I refuse to believe that he can be worse than this monster," I shouted.

A shadow moved behind the dungeon door.

"Who's there?" I yelled.

After a few seconds of silence, he came out. The monster.

"What are you doing there, lurking in the shadows? Too afraid to show your face?" I asked in a derisive tone. I couldn't help it, goading him. Fury had long replaced any other emotion.

"I told you not to come out, man. She is pissed off, Keith. Rightfully so," said Xavier.

Wow, Xavier seemed too friendly with the monster. This was a huge blow! So far, I hadn't blamed him for my presence here. What a mistake! Apparently, he could have tried harder to get me out of here. He simply hadn't. I didn't know whom to trust anymore. The answer was no one.

"What do you want? Did you come here to gloat?" I said.

"It is your deserved punishment," the Werewolf King shrugged.

"Are you nuts? I didn't do anything" I exclaimed.

"Really?" he said, narrowing his eyes. "Do you think you can fool me? I know what you are doing. It won't work. And you are going to stay here until you stop doing it," he said in a disturbingly calm voice.

"I don't know what you're talking about," I said, exasperated.

"Fine, if that's the game you wanna play let's play it and see who will burn," he said, gripping me by the sleeve. I heard the loud slamming of the dungeon door as he dragged me up the stairs, into a long corridor that opened into a spacious room.

Denial

Belle

Once we entered the room, the monster abruptly let go of me, and I tumbled backward on the marble floor, having being deprived of the only momentum that kept my legs going. Directly across the hall stood a throne placed in the center of a raised dais supported by two forward and backward columns, each of which was sculpted with figures of vicious werewolves.

"Yes, I'm waiting. I don't have all day," he said folding his hands on his arms with a bored expression.

"Oh, please don't let me keep you away from your precious Zena," I muttered under my breath.

"Excuse me?" he said ferociously.

"You can just deliver me to my comfortable sleeping grounds in the dungeon and then you can go back to her," I said defiantly. I'd had enough of his boorish manners.

His arms suddenly lashed faster than a whip, seizing me by the arms, which had already started bruising from his impenetrable grip. I panicked, trying to break his hold, as I expected the second choking session to start. Xavier had warned me; I had failed to heed it. Then he jerked me harshly towards him. I had only a few seconds to register the feel of his body against me before his mouth was on mine, kissing me hard and sending jolts of pleasure down my spine. I didn't think. I just acted as instinct took over and I wrapped my hands around him, struggling to bring him closer to me. His hands pushed up my shirt, his hands gliding over my bare back, his fingertips lightly grazing my skin. I was burning up as his kiss became more frantic, deeper. His tongue was exploring my mouth in hunger, tasting my essence as it twined with my tongue. The deep rumble I felt in his chest made me shudder. I couldn't get enough of him.

And that is how it ended. One moment, I was in the throes of passion, and the next I was flying in the air, my back colliding with the harsh stone wall.

"What is your problem?" I screamed as I rubbed my bruised back. He was nuts. There was no other explanation.

"You've done it again. You make me want you," he said, running his hand absentmindedly through his hair in exasperation. "Why do I feel you are my mate? What are you doing to me?" he bellowed, losing his temper again.

So he thought I was his mate? Interesting.

"How do you know I'm not your mate?" I asked snapping in frustration. I didn't want to be his mate any more than he wanted me to be his, but his cocky attitude was getting to me.

"Because you're not even a werewolf," he grunted, his black irises shimmering dangerously.

"You're a liar," I blurted out, not caring that I was talking to the most lethal creature in the world. He roared in laughter, the sound of which irritated the hell out of me.

Aargh! How I wanted to rip his heart out even though I wanted to glue my body to his and stay there forever, basking in his scent. I was so mad that I wanted to show him how wrong he was. Soon, he would be sorry; he would kneel and beg for my forgiveness. The mental image of him on his knees made my lips twitch with amusement. I shifted to my wolf, I prowled and preened to show off my beautiful fur. He laughed even harder. I simply wanted to kill him. Yes, my wolf was small, but it existed. Why in the hell wasn't he on his knees then?

Conveniently, I phased back, fully clothed. Sean had always said the ability to shift like this was my unique talent. It didn't make up for my lack of speed and healing abilities as a wolf, but oh well it was still something, and it had its practical uses just like now.

"You've seen me. You can't deny I'm a werewolf."

"You don't have a wolf; all you have is an illusion. You're a witch," he said smirking.

Was he kidding me? "Of course I have a real wolf. Everyone in my pack will tell you that. They've all seen it," I said, resolved to set him right.

"Belle, I am the most ancient of werewolves. Your spell may keep your pack enthralled, but not me. Believe me; I see through your magic. Your wolf has no additional scent."

That did make me pause.

"What are you saying? I don't understand." I said hesitantly. I couldn't be a witch. How was that even possible? How could I belong to a species I didn't even know existed up until yesterday?

"So I'm glad we have covered that. Now, if you'll only stop enchanting me, we will get along just fine. Just make it stop," he scolded me.

"I am not doing anything. I don't know any spells. Heck, I haven't even seen a witch in my life."

"You mean, apart from yourself?" he mocked.

"Look, I'm not saying I buy into your story, but even if I am a witch, I am a clueless one. Where do you think I would even learn to weave magic? I've been raised among werewolves all my life, for Moon Goddess's sake."

"Fine. But we'll sort this out one way or another. First thing in the morning, we are leaving to visit The Wiccan Priestess, and once we do, we'll know who you are and how you can stop what you are doing. Until then, you must keep away from me. I will not allow you to manipulate me," he warned.

"Who is the priestess? How will she know anything about me?"

"She is the eldest witch on Earth, and she knows everything. She is a seer," he cut me off abruptly as if scolding an ignorant child.

"Xavier," he then shouted.

"I am glad she is still alive," Xavier said as he entered the room and winked at me. I looked away. Despite his charm, he wouldn't win me over so quickly this time.

"You are taking over tomorrow. The witch and I will be traveling to the Wiccan coven in the east. We may be gone for a few days depending on what we discover." Then he waved his hand shortly, "Take her to one of the rooms above for the night."

Thank the Moon Goddess, I wasn't going back to the dungeon. I needed to wash away this stench on me so badly, I could almost taste it.

I grimaced as I walked. My back, where I hit the wall, was still hurting badly.

"What's wrong with you?" he asked.

"It's funny you should ask since you were the one who threw me at the wall," I shouted.

"Oops! Lovers' quarrel." Xavier chuckled.

Keith and I both looked at him at the same time, narrowing our eyes.

"Shouldn't you have healed by now?" he asked.

"I have a hard time healing. It's always been difficult for me".

"Of course it has. That's because you're not a werewolf," he said, knowingly, and then he continued, "Just heal yourself with magic."

"I don't know how," I snapped.

Then he said something so surprising, so extraordinary, that I simply gawked.

"I'm sorry," he muttered.

"What's that?" I asked still not believing what I had heard.

"I didn't know, okay?" he said.

"Know what?" I pressed.

"That you couldn't heal. I will have to be more careful with you. You're just weak. It's not your fault," he said.

Asshole. He had to ruin it.

"C'mon, Xavier. Take me to my new quarters, will you? I've had enough of him for today," I said turning away from the monster. I would take Xavier over him any day.

"Hey, Xavier! While you are up there, tell Zena I will be in my bedroom, waiting for her," the king said smugly.

He was testing me. The bastard! I would not let him get to me.

"Witch or not, I can take down the bitch anytime I want," I said smiling as I left the room.

Getting Ready To Leave

Belle

I felt the splash of cold water on my face. I sat up in bed to see the bitch's cunning face.

"Sorry," she smiled sweetly, too sweetly for my liking. "I tried to wake you up, but simply couldn't."

Yeah, and pigs can fly.

"Keith is expecting you downstairs in ten minutes. He said, and I quote, 'she'd better not be late.' So, you should hurry," she said trying hard not to laugh at the water dripping down my face.

Ten minutes, huh? I bet you've been trying to wake me up for the last half an hour, bitch. What she didn't know was that it took me very little time to get ready. I was literally out of the shower in five minutes. I grabbed my faded t-shirt and my pair of jeans which I had thankfully washed last night despite my exhausted state. It wasn't as if I had a choice; the monster had dragged me here with just the clothes on my back. I hastily put my still wet red hair into a messy bun, and voilà, I was ready to meet the monster. I headed out the door.

I was a little anxious about this journey, I had to admit. I felt I was heading into the unknown. Who was I? And what did the Demon Lord want with me? Would the priestess help answer these questions? What if she couldn't? Worse still, what if she could? I was still skeptical about the things the monster raved about, and I was hoping the priestess would conclude I was no witch. But what if she didn't? What if I was indeed a witch? Was I brave enough to hear the truth? All these questions were spinning around in my brain, making my head hurt.

As I descended the stairs, I realized I had no idea where I was supposed to go. Hmm, this posed a problem. I started opening each door to find the monster, but there were too many rooms for my liking. After a few vain attempts, I gave up. The castle was simply too big.

I headed towards the throne room, one of the two places in the castle I knew about, the other being the dungeon. Needless to say, I had no intention of ever setting foot in there ever again. Well if you lose somebody, the best thing to do is to go back to the last place you've seen him. That was exactly what I was doing; I would wait in the throne room till he showed up. I congratulated myself for my sound logic.

I opened the throne room and as my bad luck would have it, it was empty. Not even Xavier was in there. I sighed in resignation. I stared into space for a long time as I waited for him. Bored of waiting, I paced back and forth for about ten minutes and then I was bored again. I traced my fingers over the stone walls, the columns holding the dais, and touched the padding on the throne. I opened the door from time to time and peeked outside, looking around to find somebody, but it was to no avail. After a few times of repeating this routine, I'd had enough. I was getting tired of just waiting for him, and there were no places to sit except… I looked at the throne. Oh well, I smiled mischievously. It was not my fault he was selfish enough to think of only his own comfort. I guess he liked everybody standing and bowing to him all the time. Not me. I sat on the lofty throne. I found it to be quite comfortable.

I bounced up and down in my seat like a naughty child, immensely enjoying this experience. I play acted a few hand gestures. I waved my hand as if giving a handsome warrior permission to speak, then flicked my fingers to show approval of what he said and held up my hand to silence the crowd, who was, in my wild imagination, cheering at my decision. This was way too much fun!

I must then have fallen asleep which was not surprising considering how the memory of the dungeon had haunted me the whole night yesterday, disturbing my sleep. I heard —distantly— somebody shouting, "I can smell her, she'd better still be there, or I'll not be responsible."

I suddenly jerked awake with the monster's roar as the door jolted open.

"Where have you been? Look what you forced me to do. Eventually, I had to come and get you!" he raged. His nostrils flared in anger; his eyebrows knitted together. His jaw was locked tight, stretching his facial muscles taut.

That did not disturb me in the least. After all, my idea had worked. He was here.

"We should have left the castle hours ago. I warned you not to be late!" he bellowed as undeniable irritation settled over his features.

Then he noticed I was sitting on his throne; he quirked his eyebrow disbelievingly.

I stood up fast. No need to play with fire.

"I was here, waiting for you," I said calmly.

"You were supposed to come to the breakfast room!" he said with a shaking voice, eyes wide with disbelief.

"Well, your girlfriend didn't exactly tell me where it was. I thought it best to wait for you here," I argued.

That shut him up.

"Damn it. We are leaving right now," he grunted.

I sighed, that meant I'd be skipping breakfast. I wasn't going to complain; he wasn't in the mood to listen.

As we headed outside the gate, Keith was giving instructions to his men.

Then Zena came running, throwing herself into his arms, her eyes misty with tears. "I don't want you to go," she pouted.

He kissed her loudly which made her giggle, her previous misery completely forgotten.

"I'll be back, sweetie," he smiled. Then his eyes caught mine as if to check my reaction.

I smirked. That should do it!

The monster could go to hell, taking the bitch with him.

Finally, he managed to pull himself out of her embrace.

"We are leaving," he said.

I cringed at the idea of riding on his back again.

"Well, perhaps I should shift, too," I suggested.

"You cannot shift," he said sarcastically.

I rolled my eyes. He was adamant in his belief. I had no hope of changing his opinion. Not without the help of the priestess anyway. The shifting had to wait, at least till the return journey.

"How about I walk then?"

"No," he said rudely and threw me on his back as he shifted.

As simple as that.

Day 1

Belle

We came to a stop in a clearing. Oh, thank the Moon Goddess! I threw myself on the grass, putting my arms under my head. I stretched my limbs for a few minutes and sighed. My stomach grumbled loudly, reminding me I hadn't eaten.

Keith frowned at the sound.

"I didn't have breakfast," I said, feeling the need to explain.

"Well, that was your fault now, wasn't it? After the prank you pulled, we didn't have the luxury of dallying around any longer."

"Prank?" I shouted. "That was no prank. If you had taken me downstairs yourself instead of sending your vicious girlfriend with a bucket of water, I would've known where to go."

"Belle, do not test me," he warned.

He was making me so mad; my blood was boiling.

I was the lucky recipient of all his dark moods. I took a deep breath to relax.

"We'll eat something here. I'll hunt. Do not disappear anywhere," he said, as if that was possible. Where would I go, I didn't even know where we were.

I looked around once he was gone. The valley embosomed thickets of oaks and jack pines, and the emerald verdure stretched lazily before me. I was trying to find something to appease my hunger until he came back. I finally spotted some thorny bushes ahead of me, and when I went to explore, I discovered a delicious-looking group of small blue berries dangling teasingly from the branches beneath all those green leaves and brown thorns. And, there were lots of them. Unable to tolerate my hunger any longer, I gobbled up the ripe fruits one by one, their sweet and plentiful juices running freely down my hands and my arms, staining my skin. After eating tons of delicious berries, I lay down on the grass, rubbing lazily my almost satisfied stomach. A cool spring breeze was blowing, ruffling my hair which was tickling my face. I spread my arms and legs wide on the grass as if to blend my body into nature. I was happy.

"Why are your hands blue?" Keith asked as his face appeared above me, ruining my blissful peace. He threw down a bunch of dead rabbits he'd hunted. He raised his eyebrows, obviously expecting an answer.

"Berries," I said pointing my finger towards the bush.

Once he saw what I was looking at, he became livid with rage, raising his voice high at me, "Are you crazy? I cannot believe you were foolish enough to eat poisonous berries. I told you to wait for me to bring food!"

"I was hungry," I said, and suddenly his words clicked. "Poisonous? Did you just say poisonous?" I stammered, my heart starting to beat fast. "How do you know they're poisonous?" I asked, trying to retain my calm, but finding it tough under the circumstances.

"Because I know the type," he said exasperatedly.

"Oh, shit! What is going to happen to me?" I asked, scared out of my wits.

"They are lethal for humans, but not for supernatural beings," he stressed. "And, thankfully you are the latter."

Whew! Thank the Moon Goddess, that was close. Apparently, this was not going to be that bad.

"So, I'll be fine?" I asked, nevertheless, wanting to be sure.

"No, not exactly," he said as ran his hands through his hair in frustration. "You will have red spots all over your body, and they will itch like hell. But you cannot ever scratch them."

"Why? What happens if I do?" I asked, not feeling so good anymore.

"You don't want to find out, believe me."

"Just tell me please," I begged.

"The spots will fill with acid. The only way to get rid of them is to squeeze them out and let the fluids discharge."

Definitely not okay.

"We have to stop and camp here for the day because this will be a long night," he said.

He skinned the rabbits and built a fire by rubbing sticks. He then tied the rabbits into short sticks. Meat was the favorite food in werewolf communities, but the digestion of raw meat in human form was often difficult. Hence, he wasn't taking any chances now, not with what was already coming. I rose to help, but he interrupted me with a hand gesture.

"Just lie down, it'll be ready soon."

I was scared. I wanted my parents; I wanted Sean. Instead, I had a monster to look after me and take care of the red spots, crazy itching, and possibly the acid and all that painful squeezing I was likely to face in the upcoming hours. While he seemed calm enough, it was evident to me that he didn't possess an ounce of sympathy in his bones. How was I going to survive the night?

Soon, the sweet smell of cooking meat filled my nostrils. He held out a roasted rabbit on a stick. I was still hungry, but my stomach was in knots. I couldn't imagine eating.

I sadly shook my head.

"You will eat," he ordered.

I reluctantly took the roasted rabbit and took a bite. In the time it took me to force just a mouthful down my throat, he had already devoured three rabbits. I felt an itch on my stomach, and my hand automatically went to the spot to scratch it. His hand halted the descent of my fingernails before they could do the job.

"It's happening," he said as he pulled up my t-shirt to reveal a few rashes that were already forming around my stomach area. "It's going to get worse," he said with a trace of sadness and regret in his voice.

In a few minutes, the rash began to spread, covering my whole body from my neck to my feet. I itched so badly that I wanted to scratch all the way to my bones. At some point, the itch became so overpowering that I completely lost it. My delirious hands seemed to have a mind of their own as they fought their way towards the red spots. He pinned my body firmly on the ground, one of his hands holding both of my wrists, his grip firm and unyielding. Frantic, I thrashed underneath him, kicking wildly with my legs to free my body. I had to scratch; I needed to scratch. I would do anything to scratch.

"Please... please...," I begged him.

There was a lot of compassion in his eyes as he looked at me. The monster did not budge. I started crying. He winced as if in pain.

"I want to scratch, please," I moaned.

"I know, I'm sorry...I'm sorry, baby. It'll be over soon," he whispered, his eyes reflecting sorrow as he brushed away my tears with his fingers and stroked my hair for what seemed like hours. He planted little butterfly kisses on my forehead, my eyebrows, my eyelids, my cheeks and the tip of my nose, then repeated the pattern all over again. All the while he murmured soothing words in a caressing tone until my shallow gasps finally evened out and my eyelids drifted shut, allowing me to fall into a deep slumber.

I woke up with the sun streaming onto my face. Slowly, I pushed away the haze of sleep that muddled my mind. I felt a heaviness on my chest. I realized with panic that an arm was draped over mine, holding me tightly. I focused my eyes and recognized the face so close to mine, Keith. Then it came back to me, all of it. The itch, my endless attempts to scratch, his counter-attempts to stop me. I frantically looked at my arms and was relieved to find the rash had all cleared up. I sighed. So, it was over.

I examined him as he was sleeping, my eyes flitting from his wide thin mouth to his perfect, straight nose. Last night, he'd acted so wonderfully. He was so very compassionate, gentle and loving. It was as if he cared; as if he finally believed we were mates. Or had I imagined it all? Was the memory just a figment of my delirium?

He opened his eyes slowly, blinking a few times, trying to focus. "Hi," he said. "Hi back," I replied smiling. We were face-to-face, little tingles were spreading through my body. My heart was doing a somersault in my chest. He leaned in towards me; I closed my eyes expecting the kiss. But, it never came. He cursed. I opened my eyes to see him pushing himself away from me in frustration while running a hand through his ruffled hair.

"I see that you are much better. We lost precious time yesterday because of you, first through your morning prank and then your sickness. So, let's get moving," he said reverting to his old monster self.

Day 2

Belle

After his unfeeling words, I climbed onto his back again reluctantly.

An hour of riding brought us into a clearing. He shook me off his back and walked away. The monster morphed into his human form, putting on his clothes.

"We are here, where the first test begins," he said.

I looked around, bewildered and confused.

"There's nothing here.

"What test?"

"No one can enter the Wiccan coven without passing some tests. As far as I remember there are either two or three tests, it all depends on Tessa's mood. She's a real eccentric," he said.

I didn't find this amusing at all.

"What kind of tests?" I asked.

"You'll see. Hurry. We don't have all day."

He took deliberate steps towards the middle of the clearing, and raised his fist in the air, shaking it back and forth as if knocking on an invisible door. And then, right before my eyes, a door emerged out of nowhere, unattached to any solid visible structure.

"Huh?" I was stunned.

"The door is invisible to humans but serves as a beacon to all supernatural beings who pass this way and seek the guidance of the seer," he explained.

"C'mon now, we have to be quick," he said, snatching my hand. "Once the door opens, we have only a few seconds to get in. If we miss it, we need to get another appointment from the priestess before we can try our luck again. And that, unfortunately, would take days."

As soon as the door opened, he jerked me towards the opening, pushing me inside. Okay, so if the first test was to get inside before the door closed, we sure had succeeded. Now, what?

It was almost pitch dark inside, I shivered.

"Are you ready?" he asked, still holding my hand.

"For what?" I asked surprised.

"For the first challenge, of course."

"I thought we were already done with the first challenge," I said, irritated.

"You mean the door?" he quirked his eyebrows. "No, that wasn't it."

"Hold tight," he said, and, without warning, he shoved me forward into a pit. We fell in what seemed like endless space, hand in hand, as I screamed. As we kept on falling, I thought there was only one way this would end: with my death. When I felt I was close to crashing and cracking my skull, an invisible force emerged beneath our feet, stopping us in midair, slowly descending us as if we were in an open elevator.

Once my feet hit the ground, I turned to Keith and started shouting, "Are you crazy? Why didn't you warn me?" My limbs still shook wildly from the experience.

He chuckled as if this was one hell of a great joke. "Would you have taken that step here if you knew?"

"Of course not. I'm not suicidal, unlike you!"

"That's exactly why I didn't tell you," he said smugly.

Asshole.

"What is next?' I warned him. "You'd better tell me this time. I don't want a repeat of that."

"Unfortunately, I can't say because I simply don't know. From here on, the challenges are always new. The witches always transfer our bodies to an unknown location, and then we do our best to get out of there alive," he smirked with the cockiness of a king. His eyes were dancing with glee; his face lit up with a huge grin. He was enthusiastic, like a little child who was visiting the playground.

Great! I wish I had inquired about this journey before I decided to follow him around so stupidly.

I looked around. We were in a cave. I had no idea why we were here or what was expected of us.

"Follow me closely; do not get lost," he said as he took the lead.

As if I would. I was going to glue myself to him. I had no intention of finishing this challenge, whatever it was, on my own.

Inside, it was dimly lit. There were gas lamps on the walls, casting large shadows before us as we marched. There was not a soul inside, and aside from the sound of our footsteps, the only other sound was water dripping to puddles in the cave. The moisture was clinging to the walls turning them to black. I brushed my hands through my curly hair which had already frizzed from the intense humidity inside. After walking another two hundred or so feet, the path divided into three tunnels. He took a left one; I had no clue as to why. I kept following him from a close distance. I could feel the temperature fall a few degrees as we ventured deeper into the cave. But although cool inside, the rising humidity offered no relief. My breaths were getting labored with each step. Just then, the tunnel got narrower and shallower. I was fine, being only five feet eight inches tall, but he had to bend his huge frame as he continued walking.

About two feet in, our torture was over as the cave finally opened into a large chamber with a ceiling that rose well over forty feet high, and stone walls that glittered with quartz crystals buried in their depths. We moved in cautiously, trying to prepare for the dangers that lurked inside.

A small bald creature landed on the wall, holding himself erect on the straight stone structure. How was that possible? Crawling on the wall with limber legs and arms, he was jumping from one wall to another, his eyes always keeping us within his sight. His face looked quite human with slanted eyes, but his teeth were crooked, and his body looked like that of a six-year-old child. Then, more of those creatures appeared, each one of them nesting in one of the walls, circling us like hawks.

"What are they?" I whispered, scared out of my wits.

"They are half-blood ifrits," he said as he watched them cautiously.

"Ifrits?" I asked in shock.

"Yes, only the pure-blood ifrits can fly. Others like these can walk on any solid surface, and jump well, but they don't have wings," he tutored me.

"What do they want with us?" I asked.

"I really don't know, Belle," he sighed. "If it comes to that, can you fight?"

"Sure, I'll shift."

"Oh no, not that again," he grimaced. "Just stay out of my way. Better still, go back to that shallow tunnel we came from and wait till I'm done."

"But, there are so many, are you crazy?"

"I can easily take them all. This is child's play," he said with an undeniable air of arrogance. "Don't you trust I can protect you?" he asked disbelievingly. "I am the king of the strongest supernatural species."

I sighed with exasperation. Men!

"Look, let's just go back to your castle and be done with this visit and the stupid challenges. This is nonsense." I turned around, looking wildly for some sign of a camera. "Hello? We are done. We want to go back," I shouted hoping that the witches were indeed watching us.

"Belle, it does not work that way. While the coven does provide free passage to us, the witches don't interfere in what happens afterward. This is quite real, and there is no turning back. Should we go back the way we came, the door will just open to new and more daunting challenges. We will either end up finding our way to the Wiccan coven by overcoming the challenges, or we will perish along the way. There is no alternative."

"Are you serious? Why the hell are we here then? Have you lost your mind, dragging us here?"

"I've done this many times. It's not a big deal; it's quite fun," he said surprised at my reaction while looking around to make sure the ifrits behaved.

I couldn't believe my ears!

"Besides, did you forget that the Demon Lord is after you? We need to know who you are, which I'm hoping will be the key to understanding why he wants you in the first place. Or, perhaps you wanna go with the Demon Lord, rather than stay with this monster?" he teased, throwing my previous words at me.

I shook my head.

"I didn't think so," he said "And there's also this thing we need to sort out," he said as he waved his finger at us. "This mate-pull," he said pausing. "I need it to stop."

"Whatever," I said, disappointed with his desire to be free of me.

Why didn't he want me?

In one shocking moment, the ifrits attacked, all at once. I crawled back to the narrow tunnel. But from where I cowered, I could still see the battle raging inside. I wanted to make sure that I knew when to help him, if he needed it, whether he wanted it or not. The thought of something happening to him made my blood run cold. I didn't even want to think about it.

Keith didn't bother shifting. Even then, he was a formidable beast with bulging muscles and unfathomable strength as he killed the creatures three or four at a time. Seeing him like this, I felt completely confident in his ability to get us through this challenge.

One moment I was looking at my handsome beast, and the next I was snatched behind my waist, my legs dangling in the air. I screamed, my shrill voice echoing in the stone tunnel, as I found myself flying in the hands of what I presumed to be a pure-blood ifrit. He carried me across the narrow tunnel, flying a few inches off the shallow ceiling. He was bumping me into one wall or another, my body in agony at the speed and force of each impact. Once he came to the intersection, he turned right to the central tunnel, which thankfully was high and spacious enough for him to fly without bruising me any further.

Soon, I found myself in another chamber, in the center of which stood a magically elevated platform holding a large golden chair. I was shocked; did these creatures also possess magic? There was an ifrit sitting on the chair with his wings folded behind his back. I assumed him to be the Ifrit King. He looked just like the half-blood ifrits I saw in the other chamber, except for his height. He was slim and very tall, with very long limbs in proportion to his body. What specifically drew my interest, however, was that his hands had extremely long fingers, as if he was suffering from Marfan syndrome, and palms glowing with some layer of blue light.

"Oww Dada, look vat I fond. I keep, plwese? She is vey pwety. Mine, dada? Plwese?" I heard my capturer say as he finally released me. I turned around sharply to examine him. Despite his baby-talking, he looked very much like his father with an adult-sized body. He was almost six feet tall, yet he was a child. How was that possible?

"Okay, Kathildon. But you have to take care of her."

"I vill dada. Tanks. I lov herr, vey lov herr."

For the sake of the Moon Goddess, what was going on in here? And where was Keith?

"Look, you don't really wanna do that," I intervened. I had to save my own life in here, so I would play all my cards until my monster came to my rescue.

"You see, I am here with the Werewolf King and he would not be pleased to know that you've captured his mate." He would be the first to deny that, but the Ifrit King didn't have to know that, did he now?

The Ifrit King looked uneasy at first with lines of worry crossing his features. But, after a few seconds of thinking, he said, "I don't think so. He has no business here. Besides, I know he

44

already has a mate, I saw her at the council meeting once. And she looks nothing like you."

Aargh, he was talking about Zena!

Before I could utter another word, his son grabbed me and flew me to a rectangular room with a wooden table and some chairs. Apparently, the ifrits were minimalists, with no carpets, cushions or comforts of any type.

"Naw, I feed ya," he smiled with his crooked teeth and disappeared.

I had to escape. I sped out of the room, not knowing exactly where I was going. I was running as fast as my legs could carry me, feeling the accumulation of moisture on my forehead and scalp along the way. As I was running, I heard his wings behind me. Despite all my efforts to speed up, he had easily caught up with me, his wings now flapping right above me.

He then landed in front of me with a heavy thud, his eyes angry, his fists clenched.

"Yu aye mine. Me dada say sov," he shouted with the vexed emotions of a child who had just dropped his ice cream.

Perhaps I could talk some sense into him. I always got along with small kids in my pack. I would use that talent now.

"Look, I would love to stay and play with you, but I need to go back home, okay? I have my own parents who are very much worried about me right now. Wouldn't you be sad if you were not with your dada?" I asked patiently.

Unfortunately, he was not like any wolf child I knew. He immediately pitched a fit, screaming and yelling like a spoiled brat.

"Noooooooooooo, yu aye mine. Naw, I vil punishhh yu. Dada punishhh me ven aym baad. Yu vey baad girrl."

I sighed, disappointed. Yep, the time had come to fight. He looked slim enough, and he was a child. I could take him down. I considered shifting for a second, but then I remembered the monster's mocking reaction and decided against it. Damn it; I was becoming shift-phobic because of him!

I drew my fist as Sean had taught me and hit him fast in his belly. He had a jelly-like body which immediately absorbed my fist, capturing and trapping it. I tried to pull it back using all the muscles of my arm, but it was useless. Slowly, his body pushed my fist outward, and I watched his hollowed-out abdomen fill in again in slow motion.

"Tat waz funn," he cackled loudly with glee. "Do it agayn plwese."

He was almost sweet as he chuckled like a child tickled mercilessly. Oh, by the Goddess, I was way in over my head with this creature. I realized then I couldn't hurt him. Not that I could, as my pathetic attempt had clearly shown. He was just a child, a spoiled one for sure. But still a child.

I drew my fist and hit him again. He laughed so hard as I waited to retrieve my hand.

"Ve gow naw. Me vey hunger" he said rubbing his stomach. He grabbed me easily as he lifted us in the air.

Once we came back to the same room, I saw several plates laid down on the table. When I saw what was on them, I gagged uncontrollably. He took one of them and said, "Iz my favorrite. Vey gud. Trry," and pushed it towards me. There were eyeballs rolling in some kind of a greenish sauce. My stomach wrenched, and a bitter taste of bile rose in my throat.

"Where did you get those?" I asked, disgusted.

"Thos aye humman eyess in demon blod sauce. Di best. Vey sweeet," he said innocently. And he grabbed one, the cracking sound of eating a crunchy eyeball soon filling the room.

Holy crap, they were *human* eyeballs!

He then frowned. "Iz no warrm," he said. He then raised his palm and the blue veins of light on the surface of his skin turned into a ball of fire. He heated the plate for a few minutes and then continued devouring his sweet confection.

"Wan som?" he asked cheerfully.

"No, thanks," I said trying very hard to forget the stuff on the plate.

"Vey gud wif more demon blod," he said as he took what looked like a ketchup bottle and squeezed more green thick liquid onto his plate.

"How do you find demon blood?" I asked curiously, holding my stomach. I didn't think the demons voluntarily donated any.

"Dada kil demon" he giggled. "Dada vey strong."

The peace among the species my ass! It was obvious everyone was killing each other in this world.

"Dont like your hed. It not pwety," he said pointing at my hair. "Let's burn tat," he said with a mischievous grin, turning his palms upside to bring the fire to his skin.

Oh, no! He wanted to make me bald like him.

"No, sweetie. This keeps my head warm," I said pointing at my red hair. " You see, otherwise I get very cold and sick. You wouldn't want me to get sick, would you, now?" I explained. That was the stupidest excuse I had ever heard of, but unfortunately the only one I could come up with on the spot.

"But aye nevey sick," he said pointing at his lack of hair.

"Yes, but you are a mighty ferocious warrior. I am just a weak girl," I said knowing full well how to boost the ego of a child who wanted to be just like his dad.

"Yess aym vey strong. Okay den," he smiled, happy with my answer.

I had to get out of here before this bloodthirsty, and yet innocent child, turned on me.

My monster burst into the room and with a cry of rage launched himself at the ifrit child. He lifted him high up in the air with one hand while circling the child's neck with his other as he tried to crunch his throat. The child made a strangled, groaning sound, his eyes full of fear and terror.

"Stop it," I screamed at Keith, jumping on his back, trying to hit his hands. "He's just a child, stop it!"

Keith looked at me, stunned. "What?" he said.

"He's just a child," I repeated firmly.

"Do you know how hard I've been trying to find you in this damn place! Do you know what I've been through?" he barked as he still dangled the ifrit boy.

"Well, I'm fine. Just let him go, he's scared."

Keith loosened his hold on the ifrit child, who fell onto the floor, crying.

I couldn't believe what I was about to do. I went to him on the ground, cuddled him softly. I kissed him on the forehead. "Are you okay?" I asked him.

He nodded his head. "But he huyt me," he said and hugged me. Oh, crap.

"My boorish friend is very sorry. He was just very worried about me, that's all. He didn't want to hurt you," I said soothingly. "Isn't that so, Keith?" I asked with a warning tone as I turned towards my monster.

Keith stood there stupefied, unable to comprehend my words.

"Keith, snap out of it!" I exclaimed. "Tell this sweet child that you didn't want to hurt him."

"What?" he croaked.

"Tell him you're sorry," I said, lifting my eyebrow threateningly.

He did not utter a word.

"You see, he is very sorry," I assured the child. "He is simply beyond words to express his regret."

"Dont gow plwese," he begged me. "Aye be gud aye promis."

"I have to go, but I'll see you again, I am sure. And when I do, you will be even stronger just like your dada, won't you?" I asked, again playing the ego card.

"Yess," he said, finally smiling.

"That's enough. We're leaving," Keith said while grabbing my hand impatiently, still not understanding what had transpired in that room.

Day 3

Belle

Keith grabbed my hand with a viselike grip as we ran away, hand in hand, from the ifrit child's chamber. I just followed him blindly as he seemed to know where he was going. Apparently, he had mapped out the ifrit dwelling while he was frantically trying to find my whereabouts. I chuckled at the thought.

After twenty minutes of strenuous tempo running, my breaths now coming raggedly, he suddenly pulled me to him, holding his hand over my mouth to stifle my gasp of surprise as he flattened my body against the stone wall.

"Who massacred the half-bloods?" roared the Ifrit King, a few feet ahead of us.

His men shuffled around, averting their eyes.

"You dimwitted assholes, you are all useless to me! My army is nothing but a hoard of idiots," he raged as he threw balls of blue fire randomly at the walls to blow off his steam. The fire tore bits of rocks as they hit the walls, sending them flying in the air like a meteorite attack. The avalanche of rocks rumbled as they bounced on the floor, thundering loudly in our ears.

Keith covered my body with his, to provide me with a hedge of protection as one of the fireballs flew past us, sizzling on impact as it hit the spot right above the wall. After a few minutes, the fireballs finally stopped.

"Why are you still here? Go find the culprit, you boneheads!" The Ifrit King ordered.

We peeked to see that the army of pure-blood ifrits had taken flight along with their king.

"Whew, that was close! Let's go," I said.

"This is it," said Keith.

Thank the Moon Goddess! I looked around, but my eyes failed to see anything resembling a door.

"Uhm. I don't see anything. Where is the damn door? Is it magical again?" I asked, unable to stop the question that had been circling in my head.

"It's up there," Keith said with a cocky smile as he pointed up.

"Where?" I asked as I followed the direction of his finger to the ceiling that did not exist.

"You mean? "I stammered.

"Yep, we are climbing all the way to the door."

"Shoot!" I shivered, suddenly haunted by the memory of that fall. "You mean that's the only way out?" I cried out in shock.

He nodded.

"This is crazy! Somebody should teach these witches 101 Inter-Species Diplomacy. This is so freaking unbelievable," I exclaimed.

He only laughed. I wanted to strangle him.

"How?" I cried as reality suddenly hit me in the face. There was no way I could do this.

"Just trust me, Belle," he said as he lifted me to his back, wrapping my arms around his neck, and my legs around his waist.

"Hold tight," he warned as he made his way up the cave. This was no way an easy climb. It was quite steep apart from the boulders that sometimes protruded from the side of the cave. But, he soon found a rhythmic pattern as he set his hand and foot into a tight crevice in the cliff, pulling us up and then repeating the process. I was mesmerized as I watched his upper arm muscles bulge just before each pull-up. Moon Goddess, help me! I found myself drooling over him, completely having forgotten about the direness of my circumstances. I was snatched from my daydreaming when he unexpectedly lost his foot, stepping on a cliff of shale that flaked off and crumbled under our weight. I muffled my cry on his back as his feet dangled dangerously alongside the cliff for a few seconds, his arm muscles straining with the burden of carrying two bodies. His face etched in concentration, he held on until finally he secured his foothold again.

I could not believe he thought this journey was fun. I wanted to kick him once my feet were on solid ground again. Thankfully, the rest of the climb was eventless, and soon enough we were facing that damn door that had brought the ifrits upon us.

I jumped off Keith's back quickly and hurried to the door. I couldn't wait to be out of this accursed cave.

"Wait, we need to walk out together, or we can end up in different places," he warned me.

Damn these witches! They sure had a twisted sense of humor. And he thought I was one of them? You had to be kidding me!

I waited as his warm hand enveloped mine again, sending shivers of pure bliss along my nerve endings. Then he opened the door, and I took a step forward. And just like that, I fell face down into the depths of what can only be described as chilled water. Getting over the shock, I kicked my legs wildly to reach the surface and coughed, trying to get rid of the water I had swallowed. I looked around to see where we were. In the middle of a fucking ocean, that's where! Short of flying out of here, we had no way of getting out. I wished we had taken the ifrit child with us.

"What now?" I shouted, resisting a tantrum as I shivered with cold.

"Well, let me think," said Keith, still calm. Too calm.

"The only exit must be way down there," he said pointing to the depths of the water.

"Are you kidding me? I asked disbelievingly. Then terror gripped me as I yelled hysterically, "How do you even know there is an exit? How do you know the witches are not trying to kill us? Nobody gives a damn about the peace treaty!"

"Chill down, Belle. It's all right. I've done this many times. It's going to be okay. I won't let anything happen to you," he said gazing into my eyes. "Wait here for me, let me explore first," he said, and he dived back into the blue water.

After what seemed like an eternity, he resurfaced, shaking the water from his face. "There is an entrance to a cave deep down there. Can you hold your breath?"

"As if I have a choice," I said.

"Okay then, follow me," he replied.

I took a deep breath as I plunged into the freezing water. The water took my breath away; my heart almost stopped beating when I felt its cold shock on my body. Colorful reef fish formed a welcoming committee around me, along with the coral foundation that harbored them and jellyfish floated around us in brilliant colors, but I was too pumped up with adrenaline to enjoy this sightseeing. We swam down, and down until I felt my chest tighten under pressure. Keith often looked back at me to make sure I was still behind him. On the right, we came upon some rock formations, and I felt a surge of relief when Keith finally pointed at an entrance just ahead of us. The opening of the cave was nothing but a narrow tunnel at the end of which was a door, like a bank vault. It quickly opened to a large chamber, allowing us to inhale precious oxygen to our lungs.

'Now, that wasn't so hard. Was it?" asked my monster.

Was he kidding?

"I am done. I don't care about who I am or what the Demon Lord wants with me. In fact, I will gladly hand myself over to him on a gold platter if only somebody ends this torture for me," I cried.

He didn't even respond. I launched myself at him, attempting to punch him in his arrogant face. He captured my wrists and held them over my head. Encircling my waist with his other hand, he pulled me harshly against his body. He then let out an animalistic growl as he captured my mouth in a frenzy. I welcomed this kiss; I craved it as his fingers trailed down to the curve of my hips, slipping lazily to my ass. I rocked my hips against him, causing a groan to escape his mouth. He was no longer restraining my hands, and I used this opportunity to grab onto his shoulders, digging my nails into his back as our kiss became more passionate. He eased away from my mouth, his lips trailing down to my neck and then up to my cheeks and mouth again.

"Mine," he growled. "You are mine."

"How sweet," said a voice. Neither the words nor the fact that we now had an intruder in the cave, however, immediately penetrated our haze of lust. He was the first one to come to his senses as he shoved me behind his back to face her, the beautiful white-haired woman who was standing behind a heavy stone door inside the cave.

Was the door invisible a moment ago or had we simply not noticed its existence? I didn't know.

"Tessa," Keith said, his eyes still glazed with passion.

"The priestess?" I asked turning to him.

"I waited for you to knock on the door, but I guess you were too busy to do so," said Tessa.

"I'm going to kill you!" I shouted. "I had to suffer through a deep fall, kidnapping, human eyeballs, fireballs, rock climbing, and a dive into the depths of the ocean, all because of you." I was unable to veil my anger towards this woman who simply thought she could charge such a high price for a simple visit to her precious coven and get away with it.

I felt my hair rise in the air, challenging gravity, standing proud and erect in all its glory. My eyes became sharper, more focused, as I locked them on the priestess standing right before me. I felt encircled by an undeniable heat in my body as veins of blue light started moving all over my arms in a snake-like movement.

"What the hell is happening to you?" I heard my monster cry out, his voice lined with concern. "Do something," he shouted at Tessa.

"Hmm. This is interesting," was all I heard her say as she stepped aside and gestured for us to enter.

The Visit

Belle

My eyes were mesmerized by the snake-like movement of the veins in my arms as I followed the priestess involuntarily. What was happening to me?

And how could I stop it? I had lost control of my body. My anger seethed inside me, breathing, alive like a ferocious monster. I felt my blood boiling like burning lava, bubbling against my skin.

"This is all your fault, witch!" I heard my throat emit a deep voice which I didn't recognize. It seemed to have burst from a source embedded deep within the hidden crevices of my body.

"That is indeed who I am," she said, gleefully. "I have to admit that I never got this reaction from any of my visitors. Child, you need to relax before you explode."

The priestess seemed unfazed and unmoved by the changes in me even though she was the sole target of my rage. Having been the oldest creature on Earth, she must have seen it all, I thought.

"You are not helping," I heard my monster cry. "You're making it worse, look at her!" he shouted in panic.

I realized then that I didn't feel the ground beneath my feet anymore. I was slowly rising above the ground. I looked around me in horror as I levitated. Oh, the Moon Goddess, help me!

Suddenly, I felt my monster's arms embrace me, anchoring me against his body. His eyes looked deeply into mine. A lock of hair had fallen over his forehead, and I was aching to sweep it back, but I literally couldn't move. My hands were not my own as fire erupted from my palms. Tears of panic flooded my eyes, rolling slowly down my cheeks. His fingers softly brushed them aside.

"Belle. You need to come back," he said softly, soothingly.

His familiar voice seemed to delve into my haze of confusion and bring a sense of sanity back to me. But I was still unable to snap out of this emotion, this rage that had enslaved my body! My body threatened to rise more, his strong arms straining to halt its movement while turning my burning palms upside down. Thankfully, the floor was marble, extinguishing my small balls of fire on the spot.

"Look at me," I heard him say. Then I felt his lips brushing mine softly. I didn't, literally couldn't, respond at first. Determined, he continued brushing small gentle kisses on my mouth, forcing me to submission. I felt lightheaded; my heart began to pound, a different kind of heat enveloped my body, pushing back the fury. I opened my mouth ever so slightly, but it was enough for his tongue to slide in, to stroke my tongue deliciously and awaken all my taste buds. I felt my body relax against him completely, his heat flowed through me, healing me, warming me from the inside out. He slowly pulled back, his stare meeting mine.

"Are you ok?" he asked, worried. Even though he looked completely unaffected by the kiss, I still had tingles all over my body.

Once his words clicked, I checked my body. My feet were on the ground and the blue veins on my arms had disappeared. I touched my hair which was now plastered to my face in frizzy waves.

"Yes," I nodded. "What was that?" I asked the priestess, no longer suffering from this indescribable wrath towards her. "Did I get infected by the ifrits? I posed in distress.

"That's it, isn't it? I've been infected. How can that be? I didn't even eat the disgusting eyeballs. I certainly had nothing to do with the demon blood sauce," I continued, my voice shrill, hysterical.

"Let's get inside my child, and have a cup of tea. Then we'll talk."

Keith grabbed my hand, determined to keep away my demons with his touch. The priestess took us to a comfortable and cozy living room with two armchairs and an overstuffed sofa with lots of cushions. The room was filled with a light touch of vanilla smoke coming from burning incense. The sun was throwing long shafts of light from the large bay windows which were rising to produce various patterns and shapes on the ceiling high above. One side of the wall was lined with wooden shelves harboring tattered scrolls and ancient books. At the other end of the room was a fireplace with a five- pointed star placed on its marble stucco.

I sat down on the soft couch, Keith's arms around my back, his fingers running softly over my back. His touch was doing crazy things to my libido; I restlessly shifted in my seat. Thankfully his fingers stopped once a child of around nine years old entered the room carrying a tray with three cups of tea and a plate of blueberry muffins.

"Ah, there you are, Katrina," said Tessa. "Katrina, you know Keith, and this is… " She paused, looking at Keith to complete her sentence.

"This is Annabelle," I said, irritated that she was addressing him instead of me. I took a deep breath; I didn't want the second episode of what I had experienced just because the priestess excelled in infuriating me.

"Thanks, you are such a wonderful child," I said trying to be friendly as I picked up my mug.

"I'm not a child," Katrina said in an enraged tone. "I am five hundred years old."

"Excuse me?" I asked politely, thinking I had misunderstood.

"Katrina is the Child-Sidha, the witch of all children," the priestess replied.

"Aha," I said as if it all made sense now. But, it hadn't. Not really.

"She chooses to look like a child," Keith explained.

"I see," I muttered. Whatever.

I had no idea why anybody would want to look like a nine-year-old child. Every child I knew wanted to grow up. But, apparently, the witches had the power to change their age. What a weird ability! I examined the priestess sitting across me on one of the armchairs, her white hair flowing loose at her back, unhindered by a pin or comb. She was extremely cute with violet-colored eyes surrounded by copious black eyelashes. Her fair white skin contrasted nicely against her black satin draped curves. She looked in her mid-twenties, and I wondered how old she really was.

As I started sipping my tea, I noticed how hungry I was and grabbed a muffin. I looked at it, looking at the shape and the texture. I shuddered remembering the human eyeballs when one blueberry popped up from the surface, feeling as sticky as the demon sauce.

"Now tell me who you are, child," she said, her eyes mirroring some ancient wisdom as they peeked at me.

What? I couldn't believe she had just asked me that.

"I thought you were going to tell us that," I said turning to Keith, with a hint of irritation in my voice. Are you saying you don't know?" I asked her.

"My child, I cannot know what you don't know. I am not a fortuneteller now, am I?" she chuckled. She was doing that too often for my liking.

"Tessa…" Keith said leaning forward to capture her eyes. "She thinks she is a werewolf. I feel that she is my mate. And the Demon Lord wants her."

"I see," said the priestess.

"I *am* a werewolf; I can shift. I've been doing it since I was fifteen," I said. "He just refuses to believe it."

"You were not a werewolf a minute ago. I don't even know what you were," cried out Keith.

"That was just the effects of a severe ifrit infection. I'm healed now; I'm my old self again."

"That was no infection," snapped Keith.

"Hmm," Tessa said. "Let me see your wolf then, child."

"Finally, somebody believes me," I said, throwing up my hands in exasperation. Perhaps she wasn't that bad after all. I phased out to my wolf form and then shifted back to my human one again.

"You certainly are no werewolf, child," chuckled Tessa.

Nope, I didn't like her.

"But that was a wonderful imitation of one," she said thoughtfully.

"I know she is a witch. She's weaving her magic on me since the first day I saw her at her pack. She's tricked me into thinking she's my mate," said Keith. "Can you help stop this Tessa?" he asked.

"My dear Keith. I've known you for decades now. I thought you'd be happy to finally feel the mate-pull. Why don't you think she is your mate?"

"C'mon Tessa. You just said she is no werewolf. You know we cannot mate with other species. There has never been an inter-species mating in the history of our kind. It's unheard of."

"True, true my friend," she said, then she went on, "Indeed she may not be your mate," she said, her eyes glazed with some unfathomable knowledge.

Keith's face made a despairing grimace upon hearing those words. I thought he would be relieved.

Her words had cut through me like little knives. I was not his mate, some other female was. It was as if someone was squeezing my heart. He was never going to kiss me again. He was not meant for me. I didn't exactly know how I felt about that, but it hurt.

"She may not be a werewolf, but she is also not a witch," continued Tessa.

"What? Are you sure?"

"Mmm," she nodded her head.

"What are you telling me? Is she a demon? Is that why the Demon Lord wants her?" asked Keith, his lips thinning with displeasure.

"Hmm maybe," Tessa seemed to ponder this for a few minutes.

I shivered in disgust. Just when I had thought it couldn't get any worse.

But then she said, "Nope, I don't think she is a demon either."

"Then what am I?" I cried with exasperation.

"I am not sure my child, not yet anyway. You should stay here for a few days. I'm sure all will be clear by then," she said.

Witches

Belle

Katrina took us to the guest rooms on the second floor. My bedroom had wooden floors and was painted in pale blue with splashes of paint all over the walls. There was a walk in closet in the right-hand corner that had hangers and shelves filled with clothing for the guests. Thank the Moon Goddess, I was going to have clean clothes tonight. I rushed to the bathroom as soon as Katrina left the room and started running my bath. Just when I was about to remove my clothes, I saw my reflection in the mirror behind the sink, and I gasped with horror. I couldn't recognize the creature looking back at me. I had huge dark circles under my eyes which were blood red from the lack of sleep over the last two days. My once shiny red hair was now hanging dull and lifeless all over the place, gathering in dark wispy tangles.

I winced. Keith had seen me like this, had kissed me like this. It must have taken him an enormous effort to do so. He must have done it just for the sake of snapping me out of that state. What a sacrifice it must have been! No wonder he had remained completely unaffected by the kiss. Of course he didn't want me as a mate. Heck, I wouldn't want me as a mate right now either. I felt victimized by waves of self-pity rushing over me like a powerful tide. Well, there was no use in wallowing in it. I just had to take a bath and sleep well, I told myself, and, voilà, I would be my old self again in the morning. I smiled, feeling more confident. After taking a long hot bath with scented oils and bubbles, I went to bed wearing a clean white nightdress and relaxed. Soon sleep overtook me.

I yawned and rubbed my eyes in the morning as I woke up, stretching lazily in the king sized bed. Life was good again! I found some black skinny jeans, thankfully my size, in the closet and put them on along with a red tank top. As I went down the stairs, I realized how hungry I was. I had been not only deprived of sleep for three days but also of food.

"Hello there," said a woman of my height with a cheerful smile as she was coming out of a room.

"Uhm… Hello," I replied back.

"My name is Alice. You must be Annabelle," she said.

"Please call me Belle. Everybody does so," I smiled.

"Well, Belle. You must be hungry, how about a hearty breakfast?" she asked.

"I'd say you just made my day." Finally, I had met someone I liked. Perhaps not all witches were as irritating as hell.

She took me outside to a beautiful garden with beds of beautiful roses, orchids, lilacs and many species of exotic flowering plants and trees. There was a large multi-tier fountain at the center, splashing merrily from a statue of a beautiful woman into a shallow basin, the bright sunlight creating a magical hue as splashes rippled the water. Looking out at the garden, I felt myself rejuvenated by its tranquil beauty and silence. I followed Alice to a glass-topped outdoor table where a large beautiful breakfast was set. I gazed at the exquisite chinaware and the variety of cold and warm dishes on the table including omelet, bacon and sausage, English muffins, cinnamon rolls and fruit, accompanied by hot tea and freshly squeezed juice. I used all my restraint not to attack the food in front of Alice.

"So, how do you feel after the spectacle yesterday?" asked Alice.

"Well, I think the infection is over," I replied as I started devouring the food.

She laughed heartily. "Aah Belle, you are a novelty."

"Well, I guess thank you," I muttered, embarrassed by the weird flattery. I couldn't help but feel I was missing something.

"Can you tell me a little about the priestess and the Wiccan coven?" I asked as I munched on a soft roll.

"Tessa, as you might have figured out, is the leader of our coven. She is the oldest, excepting her twin, of any species out there. She is around one thousand and one hundred years old."

I choked on my roll and started coughing. One thousand and one hundred years old!

"And yes, she loves playing jokes on others, which explains the visitation fee," she winked at me.

"I guess it gets pretty tedious once you are that old, and there is nothing to do but rejoice in the misery of others," I said sarcastically.

"She's not that bad. Actually, everyone likes Tessa, even your Keith."

"He's not my Keith," I said hastily feeling my cheeks redden.

"If you say so."

"I am not his mate. Even Tessa said so."

"Did she now?"

"Yes, she did."

"What else did she say?"

"She said I'm not a werewolf, a witch or a demon. Actually, she has no idea what I am. So you see, she is pretty ignorant for an all-knowing ancient priestess who is over one thousand years old," I said. Then I felt bad.

"I didn't mean to be disrespectful," I apologized hastily.

"That's okay. You see Tessa says a lot even if it seems as if she says nothing. You should hang on to her every word."

"Will do," I shrugged not believing a word she said.

I was so full at that time that I was unable to take another bite, so I lazily sipped my tea as I asked, "So how many witches are there in the coven and what kind of abilities do you have?" You see, I was completely unaware of the existence of witches until a few days ago," I admitted.

62

"Are you serious? Where did you live, among a pack of wolves?" she joked.

"Yep, that would be a correct assessment," I murmured.

"Well, we have one hundred and fifty witches, but they live all around the world. Only thirty of us live in this coven here, actually twenty nine now that Shea is gone," she said with an expression of regret and sadness shadowing her beautiful features. Remarkably, all the witches I'd seen so far were beautiful, even the child witch, Katrina.

"And then, of course, there is Tannon, the warlock. He lives in the Alps, in isolation. He only comes once every year or two."

"Who is he?" I asked curiously.

"He is Tessa's twin; that's who," she said dreamily. "And he is a balm for sore eyes," she sighed.

"Oh, we have the hots for him, huh?" I asked. "Wow, another ancient being just like Tessa… Unbelievable."

I was enjoying talking to Alice. I felt I could relate to her easily. My joy evaporated like water in the summer heat though when I suddenly remembered my best friends in the pack, Joshua, and Danny. I wondered what they were doing now. Were they thinking of me, worrying about me? Would I ever see them again?

"Why does he live in isolation?" I asked, trying to repress my sorrow.

"Well, nobody knows. Tessa surely misses him, especially after Shea disappeared."

This was the second time she was bringing that name up. "Can I just ask who Shea is?"

"She is, I mean, was, Tessa's daughter. One day she simply disappeared. And, nobody heard from her ever since."

"How come Tessa couldn't find her?" I asked surprised. "I'd have expected her to have some exceptional powers."

"Shea went to a place where only the Moon Goddess ventures," she said, as if that made sense to me.

I didn't probe any further. "So, do you have, like, some cool powers?" I asked my new friend.

"Of course. Watch and learn Belle," she winked as she began to chant some words over and over again until…well until nothing. Nothing happened.

She smiled. "Oh, your face was precious," she chuckled. "I only have healing powers. I can heal by touch, and I can do absolutely nothing else."

"Well, that's cool," I said. "What about the others?"

"Katrina is extremely powerful; she can control children."

"What do you mean by that?"

"She can have them do whatever she wants. She is like the mother of all children."

"Wow."

"Daisy is the one who does the teleporting for visitors. Basically, she can send you anywhere she wants. Others can do various stuff like lifting and moving or pushing objects. Oh, and Lin can control the weather. And Tessa can do pretty much what everybody is doing and then of course she can see some of the past and future".

"Amazing, your coven seems to be pretty powerful," I said, praising her.

"Thanks. But we are not warriors. Not really. Not in strength. Except for Tannon, of course. We mostly rely on magic."

"Well, that is more than enough," I said.

"I guess so," she replied.

"How old are you?" I asked Alice.

"Oh, I'm one of the younger ones," she said throwing back her black hair. "I'm only seventy years old."

"Wow, witches do look great for their age," I replied, smiling. It was true, she looked in her twenties.

"How about you?" she asked.

"I will be eighteen when… Oh wait, I already *am* eighteen. Yesterday was my birthday. I can't believe I missed it," I tried to smile, but my lips felt as if they were set in cement. It was the first time that I hadn't been with my family, sitting around a table, opening up presents, blowing the birthday candles and eating my all-time favorite chocolate chestnut cake. My life had changed dramatically since the day Keith took me away. And I couldn't seem to shake the feeling that I could never go back.

"Oh super cool," Alice said, feeling the dramatic change in me and trying to lighten up the atmosphere.

"We have to celebrate!"

"We have to celebrate what?" asked my monster walking towards us.

Running Away

Belle

"It's Belle's birthday, that's what we're celebrating," said my new friend Alice.

"How old are you now?" Keith asked.

"Eighteen."

He winced.

I didn't like that. Did he think I was too young?

"Well, celebrate it in your own time, we've got work to do," he snapped.

"Excuse me?" I said, my voice turning to ice. "I cannot celebrate it in my own time and with the people I love because you snatched me from them." I walked towards him threateningly.

"What do you think would have happened to them if I had left you there, huh my dear Belle? Did you ever reflect on that? You should be thanking me instead of cursing me. I am the reason why your family is still alive," he roared.

"What do you mean?" I asked incredulously.

"The Demon King knew where you were. I have no idea how, but that's the truth. He would have come for you. Without the alpha command to restrain them, your family would have fought him. And they would have lost, of course," he said nonchalantly.

"Are they okay?" I said in a panic.

"They are now. The Demon King knows you're with me."

"But what if he uses them to get at me?" I cried out, unable to stop the hysteria rising in me.

"Well my dear, he wouldn't."

"Why is that?"

"Because he knows my reputation," he said, smirking.

"What reputation is that?"

"My reputation of being a merciless king of course. I am not known to be driven by frivolous emotions or any other types of weakness ever. That is, I wouldn't give a damn about your family."

"You're an asshole," I said to him.

But at the same time, I couldn't help but think that probably in this case that was a good thing. It may have saved my parents from being used as a bargaining chip. Yet, I was still gripped by worry and fear for them.

"I have to be sure. I need to see them; I need to make sure they are okay," I said.

"That's out of the question. But you don't need to see them in order to know they are alive," he said as his eyes suddenly focused and his face became devoid of expression. This was how my father looked when he communicated with his pack members. The monster was talking with my dad. Wow, I didn't even know the alpha command worked from such a far distance. Apparently, it did.

"Tell them I am fine. I don't want them to worry about me," I tried to intervene. He blinked his eyes in frustration and patted his hand in the air to shush me.

A few minutes later, he turned to me and said, "They are fine. Just as I told you."

"What? Is that it? Are you nuts? Didn't they give you any message for me?" I asked as I was hungry for any news of my family.

"That's it, and no, I didn't wait for a message. And you'd better stop wasting my time. We need to see Tessa so she can end this thing," he said, his words full of derision.

He meant the mate-pull, of course.

"Not that again," I complained.

I looked one last time at the beautiful garden, inhaling the sweet fragrances of orchids and lilies aromatizing the air as I followed him back inside the house.

I saw Tessa sitting towards the end of the sofa, one leg lazily tucked underneath her, the other hanging over the side, reading a tattered tome.

"Hello, dearies," she said cheerfully as she set the book aside.

"Umm, hello," I replied back.

"How did you sleep, my dear?"

"Very well, thanks."

"Can we just stop the pleasantries and get straight to business? We've come a long way for answers. Do you have any?" asked Keith.

"Maybe," replied Tessa.

"And?" Keith persisted.

"I believe Belle is a hybrid."

"A hybrid? A hybrid of what?" asked Keith.

"I must say she has me intrigued. My best guess is she is a hybrid of a demon father and a witch mother. I don't know who her mother is exactly but performing an illusion like that requires great mastery only a handful of witches possess. And, well there is no doubt as to who she is after seeing her hair and eyes like that," she chuckled. "I'm sorry dear, but that can only have come from a demon father. It is hard to imagine any witch being tasteless enough to fall for a demon, but you know what they say: There's no accounting for taste. However, the blue veins and levitation do concern me, I have to admit."

"No way!" I shouted. "You're out of your mind. I've been infected; that's all. The ifrits did this to me. I was okay until yesterday. I will be okay again. All of this will go away, I am sure of it. And my wolf is real."

'If you say so dear."

"But inter-species mating? That's not possible!" Keith said, ignoring me.

"Maybe. Maybe not." Tessa said. "But, that does not rule out casual affairs now, does it? You should know better than anyone else."

Tessa's words were crystal clear, my beast had other women besides Zena, and they were not necessarily werewolves. Waves of anger consumed me. I tried to inhale deeply and exhale slowly, focusing on the Wiccan star across the fireplace and trying very hard to relieve the tension that suddenly seized my muscles. I had to accept the reality. He wasn't mine. He was never going to be mine.

"Ok, let's just say that I am a hybrid, although I am not accepting that as a fact. Why does the Demon Lord want me? Is he my relative? Perhaps my real father?" I shivered with distaste just thinking about it. I remembered my dad back in the pack, his eyes always bright with love and affection, he was the most caring father anyone could ever have. I just couldn't imagine replacing him with a demon father.

"Mayhap. The answers will all come in good time."

"And how and when will this mate-pull end?" Keith asked like a pestering child.

"Soon, your mind will be clear. Don't you worry, I can feel it. Very soon."

"Thank the Moon Goddess, it can't come soon enough!" he said, annoying the hell out of me.

"Now, if you excuse me, dearies, my old bones are aching, and I need to take my midday nap," she winked as she left us in the room.

"Is she real? There's no way her bones are aching," I muttered.

"I told you she's a real eccentric."

"I can't wait to get out of here. When do we leave?" I asked.

"We should wait for a few more days in case she decides to say something more concrete than 'maybe' and 'soon,' which is all we've had so far."

"Oh no, how are we going to get back? Don't tell me we have to go through more challenges," I cried out.

"No, the way back is a direct route to home."

Home. Was that even my home? I could never go back to my family, not unless I found out what the Demon Lord wanted from me. I had to stay with Keith. But for how long? I let out a sigh of frustration as answers evaded me.

I heard voices in the hallway. I was curious to meet other witches as well as Tessa, Katrina and Alice, so I hurried outside to take a look.

"I will send him straight to Siberia," a blonde witch said to those around her. They were in a circle, oblivious to my presence. Dressed in a casual outfit, they looked like a group of teenagers meeting after school.

"And then perhaps to the vampires' lair?" the same witch winked.

"Isn't that a bit too harsh, Daisy?" asked the one standing next to her.

Moon Goddess! This was the witch Alice told me about, the one who threw all the nasty challenges on our way here. She was stunning with her large innocent blue eyes which disguised the wickedness that lay in her.

She turned towards us, her slender hands sweeping her long, blonde hair back over her shoulders. A smile erupted on her face.

"Long time no see, Keith," she said. "Did you like my new challenges? I prepared them just the way you like them, fresh and dangerous."

"Loved them, very entertaining as usual," he teased back.

Nuts, they were all nuts!

She swayed her sexy hips seductively as she approached Keith.

"And who is this?" she asked pointing at me, her eyes examining me. I felt like a horse being appraised by an expert.

"I'm Annabelle. I'm with Keith," I said. Let her try to decipher my meaning.

"Is that so?" She raised one eyebrow.

"That is so," I said, rising to the challenge.

"I'm Daisy," she said with an insincere smile that failed to reach her eyes.

"I am thrilled to meet the witch who designed our challenges. That was so fun!" I said. Had she felt my sarcasm? "If you'll excuse me, I'd better find Alice," I said making a hasty exit.

To my utmost surprise, I found Alice in the kitchen making me a huge chocolate chestnut cake.

"How did you even know that was my favorite?"

"I asked Tessa. I just asked her to pick an image from your birthday".

"Can she do that?"

"Yes, I'm sorry if I intruded on your privacy. But, I wanted to surprise you. I swear, that's all the memory we dug into," she said tentatively, fearing my emotional reaction.

"That's all right. And you are right; I am surprised," I said, my lips curving into a smile.

"But wait," I exclaimed. "If Tessa has the ability to dig into my memory at birth and find out who my parents are, why is it that we still have so few answers? I swear she…"

"Chill down," said Alice. I withheld the words threatening to pour out of my mouth. Alice continued to explain, "She can't dig into the memories in your past because their traces have already been wiped clean. She can only pick out the memories from your recent years."

"Fine," I muttered, trying hard to calm myself.

The kitchen was customized with a bar and stools complimenting elegant black appliances and exotic granite countertops. Cherry-colored wooden cabinets lined the walls of the kitchen and the floors were covered in square terracotta ceramic tiles. Tucked into the niche in the corner was a double-doored stainless steel refrigerator. The high kitchen windows looked out at the terraced garden which I had seen and adored earlier. There was a breakfast room that flowed seamlessly out at the end of the kitchen to a beautiful window-wrapped kitchen banquette illuminated by sunlight.

My examination of the stunning kitchen was interrupted when Alice suddenly sprayed me with flour. The kitchen decor soon changed with our flour fight. I flipped a spoonful at Alice, but she ducked. Then, she threw the package at me. Puffs of flour fogged the air, falling on my hair, my eyelashes and my black jeans. Soon, we were laughing like two crazy teenagers, holding our bellies and swatting at each other. Once we were able to control our laughter, we looked around. The once spotless kitchen was now a huge mess. White powder glistened on the walls in the sunlight, and the tiles looked as if veins of snow had rained on them in an impetuous torrent.

"No worries! I'll just call Timothy."

"How will Timothy help us?"

"You'll see."

She disappeared from the room, and I found a sponge cloth and started cleaning up. Just when I was taking care of the countertop surface, Alice showed up with a blonde guy with a slightly crooked nose who had piercings on his eyebrows. The way he was dressed in black boots and leather pants made him look like a rock star. When she saw me wiping off the dirt with the sponge cloth with one hand while using another one to dry it, she stopped me immediately.

"No Belle. Don't touch anything. I've brought Timothy."

"It's no problem," I said as I didn't find it fair that he should clean up our mess. I also couldn't imagine him in that role; in fact, any minute now, I expected him to plug his electric guitar and perform a solo piece.

He smiled a boyish grin and muttered a few words as he flicked his hand over the kitchen. And, I found my mouth hanging open as I saw the kitchen return to its spotless state in a matter of few seconds.

"Magic takes care of everything," Alice said.

"Wow. That is indeed cool."

Alice then introduced us and I liked him. He was very funny, reminding me of my two best friends at the pack. I laughed when he spotted the cake batter, took a large spoon of it, and swallowed with great gusto.

"This is going to be the best cake ever," Alice said confidently. We sat around the kitchen until the baking was done. Alice then decorated the cake with chocolate and chestnut cream and shelved it in the refrigerator. I was grateful to Alice. She had made me feel at home.

As the night settled in, Alice congregated everyone at the dining room, and she set the cake in the middle of the table with candles.

"Is everybody here?" asked Alice before lighting the candles.

"Where is Keith?" I asked. I didn't see him around, and despite his rude comment in the morning, I still wanted him to be part of this celebration.

"I'll go get him," I said as I ran out of the room.

"Let me go with you. You wouldn't know where to look," said Alice coming after me.

I adored her.

We checked a few rooms, and they were all empty. Where was he? Just when we were about to check the garden, we saw a dim light coming from the library room.

"There he is," I said as I opened the door. And I gasped as my eyes focused on the silhouette of a couple making out on the couch. One of the guy's arms was draped over the woman, while the other was sliding up her mini skirt. The woman was moaning through their passionate kiss. She maneuvered herself in his lap just enough for him to caress the tops of her heaving breasts. Her head lolled back in ecstasy, she dug her nails into his back, raking them along his skin. It took me a few minutes to recognize the embracing couple. Keith and Daisy.

The couple were too immersed in each other to notice any presence in the room. Not until I cried out involuntarily.

"Oh, my Moon Goddess," I whispered as I felt unimaginable pain like thousands of pins and needles piercing my skin, my insides contracting. I almost doubled over from the pain in my chest.

"Belle, damn it," I heard Keith curse as he tried to control his ragged breathing.

I turned around, and I saw Alice's face contorted in pity. I pushed her aside and started running away, trying to put as much distance between me and the beast. I heard him call after me, but I

73

didn't look behind. My tears gushed like a spring. I went up the stairs to the second floor, with each step fading in and out of my blurred vision. I blinked my eyes to regain my balance as I ascended the third floor and then up to the attic. I heard his footsteps come after me, but I ran without stopping, my heart pounding like crazy, my breaths short and loud. I locked the attic door and stumbled on the floor.

He started pounding on the door.

"Please Belle, open up. I can explain," he said his voice etched in pain.

I couldn't speak; I was hollow inside, there was too much sadness, too much disappointment, all eating me alive. I knew it was stupid to expect his loyalty, we really had nothing going on between us, yet my stupid heart listened to no logic, and the enormous pain didn't subside.

"I'm not going anywhere until you open this door and we talk, Belle. If you don't open up, I'll kick the door down!"

He was going to break the door! It would only take one kick!

I forced myself to stand up. I had to escape; I would throw myself out of the window if it came to that. But I couldn't talk to him. Not now, not ever. Then I noticed a small wooden door almost hidden in the wall behind some boxes. I touched the knob, filled with an undeniable feeling that I was doing something irreversible, yet I seemed to have lost control of my hands. They felt odd, almost like alien appendages with a will of their own as they turned the knob. The door opened, and I felt an invisible force, almost magical, pulling me in, beckoning me. I walked in.

I heard the attic door break down with the beast's kick as I closed the door behind me.

Keith

Keith

"Belle, wait!" I shouted as I entered the attic. I rushed to catch her, kicking the old randomly placed boxes along the way to get to that door. But, what I saw when I got there was beyond imagination. The door, the one I had just seen Belle open and enter into, had completely disappeared. I kicked the wall relentlessly a few times hoping the hidden door would just yield under pressure. There was no visible sliding door panel, and I touched the wall surface looking for a seam or crack anywhere. I could still detect her now sweet aroma, a sweet aroma of citric, fresh and warm, hanging all over the hidden door as if to tease me. I drank it all in, her sweet perfume flaring in my nostrils.

"Belle," I shouted after her, daring to hope she would let me in from the other side, my voice easily heard from all over the coven.

It was as if my soul was trapped behind an impenetrable wall of despair and fear. I started punching the door over and over again, driven by frustration that threatened to suffocate me. Soon, the wall was stained with the blood splashing straight from my bruised and torn knuckles. I seemed oblivious to physical pain as my punches continued with no intermission.

"Keith, what's going on?" asked Tessa as she entered the attic with Alice.

"She's gone. Open the damn invisible door Tessa, or I swear I will bring this whole place down," I roared, my eyes burning with anguish and sorrow. All my muscles strained as I tried not to let out my beast which was so enraged, so hurt now that Belle was gone, that it only wanted to destroy everything in its path. If I did, I would be unstoppable, and there would be a bloodbath from which there would be no return.

"Oh, for the love of the Moon Goddess, gone where?" asked Alice in shock.

Tessa could see the state I was in, the inevitability of what they were facing should they fail to snap me out of this madness.

"My dear Keith, tell me just what happened, and I will help you," said Tessa, with a gentle assurance.

"She's fucking gone! And, I can't get to her because I can't seem to find the damn door. Just show me the door, that's all I'm asking. Where is it?" I asked.

Tessa looked confused as her eyes roamed around the room. Then understanding settled in her pallid face, her features contorted in a sudden rictus of pain. "There is no door there, Keith. There never was one," she said softly.

"What?"

"I mean, even if there is one, it is not one I can locate or open for you. Not even with magic. You don't know how much I wish I could," she said, her eyes dull, her cheeks as white as snow.

"Tessa, I am on edge here. Stop rambling with words, what do you mean you can't open the fucking door? What is going in here?" I barked.

"That door is the door of destiny, and it belongs to the Moon Goddess. No one but the person whose destiny calls is allowed to enter," she said, her whole body shaking like a leaf, tears slowly rolling down her cheeks. She remembered Shea, years back, using that door when she had stumbled upon it. Tessa had tried everything to get her back, she had tried the location spell, but there was no movement in the magical map she had conjured. It had remained as still as waveless water. She had then spilled her own blood on the altar on a full moon. Her blood was so ancient that once spilled in the moonlight, she could call out to anyone in the world. She had cried out her daughter's name, all in vain. Somehow, Shea couldn't hear her from wherever she was; her blood had failed to penetrate the magic that held her captive afar and masked her existence from the most ancient priestess on Earth.

Tessa had even brought Tannon home to see if he could be of any help, but his omnipotent wizardry had also been useless, silent against an unknown force. She had been frantic with the thought that Shea might be dead, so she had even appealed to the Dark Lord of the underworld to let her go. He had tolerated her interference the first time. After she had disturbed him a few times with the same request, he had simply lost it. "Leave me alone, witch. She's not here," he had shouted, unable to understand how she could even summon him, his whole body twirling in dark flames.

Tessa had been adamant in her search for her daughter until one day the Moon Goddess had appeared in her alluring beauty, her blue-black hair flowing around her without gravity, her skin so luminous that it glowed more powerfully than the sheen of a million moons in a pitch dark sky. She had floated around, draped in a silk of blue, peppered with specks of shimmering gold. She had a striking pendant on her neck, a gift from God, the only adornment touching her bare skin. It was said that the God blessed his twin daughters, the Moon Goddess and the Sun Goddess, with the gift of identical pendants except for their shape and the source of the power the pendants drew upon. This crescent moon shaped pendant, Tessa had noticed, was alight with blue, the color of cool moonlight.

"My dear child," the Moon Goddess had said, addressing Tessa with a deep, enticing voice, sweeter than honey. "You can find Shea neither with magic nor with will. She is now on a quest to find her destiny; she is on a path where no one else can trespass. Leave her be."

Tessa had begged the Moon Goddess to bring back her daughter, at least to allow her to talk to her. The goddess had smiled tenderly, raising her hands in the air, from which dissipated a faint red glow surrounding her like a gauze veil, spreading calm and peace to every cell and fiber of Tessa's body. She had then disappeared. Tessa had abandoned the search for her daughter that day, but she had never given up hope. Now seeing Keith's torment over the loss of Belle reminded her of her own loss and grief, inflicting new hurt upon old, unhealed wounds.

"That's how my Shea disappeared," Tessa said to me.

A wave of understanding hit me.

"You mean, Belle's gone like Shea?" I stammered. If Tessa, with her commanding powers, couldn't bring her daughter back, what chance did I have of finding Belle?

I didn't know how to deal with this pain. I had driven Belle to this, there was no one to blame but myself. Knowing that my fears were correct, that she was not my mate, I had simply snapped. Unable to deal with the power of the mate-pull, and too impatient for it to subside in time as Tessa had assured it would, I had tried to choke it out of my system, smash it to pieces, stamp on it, kill it brutally. My solution seemed perfect at the time, to throw myself into the arms of another woman. I didn't even like Daisy. She was an old fling, always entertaining and sexy as hell. And today, she was way too willing, way too persistent as she wove her spell of temptation around me with the expertise of a seductress. I had just let myself go, not because I was immensely attracted to her, but because I needed to rid myself of this clawing, excruciating need for Belle. It hadn't even worked; I had found myself imagining Belle's face, her alluring body, as I caressed and kissed Daisy. And that's when she had walked in on us. And that's why she had run. And that's why she had disappeared, taking the sun and the moon from my world, condemning me to a world of complete darkness.

"Why in the hell did you not demolish that wall once you lost Shea? Why would you keep it standing here to take more victims, to take Belle? Why?" I roared, trembling with uncontrollable rage.

"Because the door has not always been there Keith," she said with a deep sigh. "Its location continuously shifts; my Shea was not even in the house when it happened. She was in the garden. There is no escape from the Moon Goddess's call when it lures you. You should not blame yourself."

"But, I do. I hurt her," I said, disgusted with myself. I ran my hands through my hair in resentment. "And badly. I'm not even sure whether she will ever forgive me. And worse still, she could be in danger wherever she is, and I can't do a damn thing about it," I said, starting to punch the wall again.

"My dear Keith, stop tormenting yourself. Belle is an exceptional woman, and she can take care of herself. But, are you even sure she is your Belle? Perhaps, you should just let her go."

My punch froze in midair like a pack of arctic ice, and when I turned slowly towards Tessa, I was in a killing rage. I was slowly trying to pace my breathing, unable to halt the appearance of one furry paw which had replaced my long fingers.

"I don't give a damn about whether she's my mate or not, do you hear me? She is mine. Mine!" I bellowed, my voice loud and clear.

"Told you, it would all become clear very soon, didn't I, my dear? "she said in a half-chuckle, half sigh, forcing herself to find some humor in this whole situation.

Veins popped up in my neck, chest, and arms, tracing mountains of fury along my body. When I was about to lose it, I vaguely heard Tessa's hypnotic voice which penetrated through the haze of my rage. "Look, I know where we can get more information on Belle, and I think it's time for you to go on a quest," she said, blinking her eyes rapidly to snap out of her present trance, a trance she had entered a minute ago suddenly and unexpectedly.

"Quest? Where?"

"To the Alps in Switzerland of course. You need to visit the warlock, my twin brother, Tannon. He resides in the highest summit of the Monte Rosa. He will simply be thrilled to have you there," she said. Her eyes lit up with amusement. She was back to her old self again.

The Quest

Keith

I asked with a serious expression, "Why, what will I find there? What did you just see?"

Tessa sighed. When she entered into a trance, everybody knew, and without a doubt. The iris of her eyes would turn white, and the whites would turn into violets while her whole body became intangible, losing its solid mass. Everybody knew. Unlike what other species presumed, she did not frequently enter into a trance state, not unless the Moon Goddess wanted to gift her with specific information, just like now. Most of the time, she had hunches, or a highly advanced sixth sense, whatever you call it, which guided her and allowed her to guide others who sought her help.

"I want you to fetch some old scrolls for me. I suspect, one of them has vital information on Belle, perhaps even on her whereabouts. Wouldn't you like that now, my dear Keith? You see, all will be well in good time," she answered.

"Okay, how do I get there?" I asked impatiently.

"My dear, I will give the instructions to Daisy, and you should be there in no time."

Hearing Daisy's name made me flinch. My face twisted in dismay thinking I would have to see her again, and once more be reminded of what I had done to Belle. I deserved it, and much worse. I would get the scrolls, and then find Belle. And then, I would win her back. In that order. I swore to it.

"How do I get back in here afterward?" I asked.

80

"Oh, that should be easy. Tannon will send you back in here. Just make sure you don't piss him off," she said.

"That shouldn't be a problem," I assured her. "Okay, let's get rolling. We don't have a minute to waste," I said resolutely.

"Daisy!" Tessa yelled. Despite all their powerful magic, witches had not mastered the art of mind-linking with each other, weirdly a trait common in almost all other species. And Tessa could mind-link only with a handful of older witches, which included Katrina and Tannon, but not Daisy, who, despite being a powerful witch, was still too young to be included in that chain. Hence the yelling.

"I'm coming!" shouted Daisy. Her footsteps resonated as she rushed up the stairs. She entered the attic, eyeing me while swaying her hips, completely assured I would, once more, appreciate her display.

I didn't.

She asked, "What did I miss?" as she tried to comprehend the sudden change in me.

"Belle is gone, she found the door of destiny," explained Tessa.

"Oh, I see," she said, not understanding what the big deal was. She shrugged.

"As you can see, Keith is tormented by her loss," Tessa said, summarizing the gravity of the situation before Daisy triggered back the rage in me she had tried so hard to quench. Daisy was a powerful witch and a prominent member of this coven, but even Tessa often admitted that, most of the time, she was queen of the bitches.

"So, I am sending Keith to Tannon to fetch some scrolls for me. I'm too exhausted mentally and emotionally after this debacle to be of any help, so please take care of it."

"Sure, Tessa. No problem," she said, smiling.

"Follow me," Daisy pointed to me. She turned back and winked at me, swinging her hips dramatically a few inches off my face.

I followed her all the way to the door of the Wiccan coven. She paused at the door and moved her lips in silent chanting. A globe suddenly appeared in between her palms. The Earth, constantly turning around its axis, was colored in different shades of gray. Daisy continued her chanting until the globe finally came to a deadly still, and a black spot on its surface began to shimmer and shine. "Perfect. Ready to go. And, don't forget to say hi to that hunky warlock for me," she grinned as she waved her hand towards the door. "Enjoy the trip," she said, blowing me a kiss.

I grabbed the knob in a hurry to take off and opened the door. I found that I had not been transported to the warlock's house, or any other house for that matter. What had that witch done? Had she played me for a fool? Was Tessa in on it, too? If so, they would all be sorry for sending me on a merry ride when Belle's life may be hanging on a thread. I looked around to find some clue to my whereabouts. I seemed to be in a dense forest lined up with snow-covered pine trees. I began to climb the top of the nearest tree. I needed to see what was out there. When I got to the top, I looked into the distance, my eyes roaming for a hint of where I was or where I was supposed to go.

Everything was white, nothing but snow, snow and more snow. I climbed down and spotted some animal footprints filled with fresh snow, but still faintly discernible. I didn't know where they led, but that was my best shot. In the worst case, it would lead me to water, at least to a river of some sorts, which meant I would run into civilization at some point. I shifted into my wolf form and took off, following the trail. I barely stopped to hunt for food, running for a whole day. As the day fast turned into night, I passed a frozen river to the right, the light of the moon reflected off its snow-covered ice. I hoped I was now close to some village or town.

I tried to hang onto the remnants of my sanity as I thought of Belle, of whether she was alive or not. I was occupied by such grim thoughts when I was alerted to the scent of humans. I morphed into my human form once I spotted their fire. The three villagers, all between the ages of forty and fifty five, were huddled around the fire, consuming alcohol, roasting meat and singing loudly in merriment. I approached them carefully, considering the possibility that they might have guns. While I could heal from a gun wound, it would certainly lead to another delay, the last thing

I wanted or needed. Besides, I would then have to kill the humans, which was something I did not want to do.

"Hello," I addressed them cautiously as I walked into their camp.

"Ciao! Look we have a guest, Jonathan," one of the men hit the other lightly on the shoulder. It was obvious they were drunk.

"Si. You are right my friend. And who might you be, young man?"

"My name is Keith," I said, glad they could speak English. "I am looking for the Swiss Alps. Can you tell me how to get there?"

"Che? You mean on foot?" the third man asked, and there was so much guffaw that I was getting utterly annoyed.

"Yes," I said sternly.

"Man, you are in the wrong country," Jonathan said, wiping tears from his eyes. "Sei in Italia," he said. "I mean, you are in Italy, mio amico. Andate a nord... Yes, go further north to the border," he said, hooting with laughter again.

"Thank you, gentlemen, it was a pleasure," I said trying to control myself not to wipe off the smile on their fucking faces by ripping off their fucking jaws. I quickly shifted behind the trees and took off in a sprint.

Fuck you, Daisy! She had deliberately teleported me to Italy. She was a bitch through and through. Now it all made sense; she certainly hadn't liked being thrown off my lap when Belle had intruded. This was my punishment, all because she had failed to get my attention.

It would not take me long now. Being the Werewolf King, I was possessed with extreme speed. And I definitely could forego sleep. More importantly, werewolves were one of the creations of the Moon Goddess, along with vampires, demons, and witches, whereas the fae, nymphs, ifrits and the shadow spirits were the creations of the Sun Goddess. That's why it was the night and not the day, the moon and not the sun, which boosted my powers, enhancing my ability to sense, to heal, to run and to fight. I could already feel the energy of the moon surging through me.

So the border was in the north. Thank the Moon Goddess, I had been traveling in that direction since the beginning anyway. At least I wouldn't waste any time circling back. Above me towered the dark forest illuminated only by moonlight. The frost and snow-covered branches of trees swung over the white covered ground. The forest soon gave way to villages, towns and single houses with snow-piled roofs in valleys. After what seemed like hours of running, I reached the border as dawn poured forth in a flood of light. I continued my run until I spotted the Monte Rosa, which straddled the Italian-Swiss border. All I had to do now was find Tannon's place.

Gray jagged cliffs rose high in the Alps, cutting across the blanket of white snow sweeping across the mountainsides down into the valleys below. There were similarly styled houses lined up all over the valley, with walls of yellow stucco combined with a deep red brick. They all had steep hip roofs with double hung windows. I passed them without a second glance, soon reaching the bottom of the mountain. Despite the steepness of the mountain and strenuousness of the climb, I set up a fast pace until the summit. Streams of snow white foams beat against the rocks, and steep slopes glistened like white jewels under the sun. But, I was much too occupied with trying to detect Tannon's location to even notice the breathtaking view. I gazed around for a while, and at first didn't spot anything of interest. Then, I saw a huge rock formation protruding as a ledge five hundred feet below to the left. I grinned for the first time in days since losing Belle.

I ran down the mountain excitedly until I found the ledge. I was, however, perplexed by the scene that welcomed me. There were three identical cabins with heavy timber roofs on the ledge, placed in a U-shape, their backs facing the steep cliff. I was just about to walk randomly towards one when my instinct kicked in. Why build three identical cabins? That didn't make sense at all. I remembered Belle's ability to create a make-belief wolf. Then it clicked. Of course, two of these cabins were illusions. But, why put illusions if one could quickly check each one until finding the real one? Then I realized, one couldn't. But, how would the warlock prevent visitors randomly checking each house? It took me a few seconds to find the answer to that mystery. This was a life and death puzzle;

there was only one correct path I could take, and if I didn't…I would probably meet my death.

How was I going to find the right house? Of course, illusions were scentless. I knew that. I inhaled deeply. Tannon must have used a protection spell to mask all scents as there was no discernible odor around. But no magic was powerful enough to hide the odors from me, especially from this close distance. Werewolves possessed the best sense of smell. They had, on average, one billion scent receptors which were up to four hundred times more sensitive than a human's. Being the king of my species, my sensitivity was enhanced by at least ten fold compared to any other werewolf. I inhaled again, focusing on any odor that lingered behind the magic. This time, I could detect a very faint, almost non-existent, scent coming from the house on the right. But, what if the smell was conjured magically to confuse me? That surely was a possibility. I shrugged. Even if that was the case, I had to take the risk.

I took deliberate solid steps towards the house, knowing I had no other choice. If this turned out to be the wrong house, I had no idea how and when I would meet my fate; while I was walking or once I reached the house? My first step was followed by the second one which was followed by the third one. I relaxed. All in all, I seemed to be faring well, approaching the house without yet perishing. Then I finally reached the door. And I knocked.

Knock knock.

The Warlock

Keith

The door opened.

"You are late," Tannon said, a serious expression on his face.

I examined the warlock who was very much like Tessa in looks; he was also white-haired with striking violet-colored eyes. Like Tessa, his hair was straight and his long bangs cut straight across his broad forehead in messy layers. Just over six feet two, he was tinged with a light tan on his pale skin, with broad shoulders narrowing to well-muscled arms and legs.

"I didn't know I was expected," I answered.

"You were."

I noticed two things about the warlock: one was that he was stingy with words, said too little and then rather grudgingly. Secondly, most of the time he was rather emotionless, and at other times he was stern-faced, both of which made him strikingly different from his chatty and extremely cheerful twin sister.

I looked around. Surprisingly, the warlock lived a stoic life; this was no luxury house, but an almost bare wooden cabin with a stereotypically heavy, dark home décor. It was two storied with only a kitchen and living room on the first floor. The bedrooms were probably on the second floor. The light red of the kitchen cabinets, the small round table and the chairs around it punched the predominantly wooden furnishings and balanced out the dark shades used throughout the space. Two solid armchairs were placed across the large window overlooking the cliff. The wooden

86

stair railing on the left featured the motif of the Wiccan pentagram, which probably was the only embellishment in the cabin. The shelves and mantelpieces were devoid of any ornament except for the hundreds of books he had lined from one wall to another. There were throw rugs on the wood floors, and a large fireplace at the rear end, adequately heating the cabin, and lighting the room with a soft glow. The walls were completely bare except for a cane which looked like a medieval sword in its scabbard, hanging on the wall.

"Well, I was delayed," I shrugged.

"You are here because?" asked Tannon.

"Tessa sent me to pick up some scrolls." I was surprised the warlock didn't know my purpose of arrival given that he'd been expecting me. The whole Wiccan coven was beginning to get on my nerves. But I needed the smooth ride back to Tessa, so I would clamp down on my anger for now, even if it killed me.

"You shouldn't trust her," Tannon said calmly.

Did he mean Tessa? I had no clue the twins were antagonistic to one another. That was a shocker! Would he even help me now that Tessa had sent him?

"I meant the flower witch."

Could he read my mind? "What flower witch?" I arched my eyebrows in confusion.

"Lilac, or Rose or something like that."

"You mean Daisy?"

He nodded.

"How did you know I was delayed because of her?" I asked.

"I can read emotions. You were exasperated when you entered the cabin. I saw her image in red stamped all over you."

"I see." Weird.

"Well, the flower girl said hi to you," I relayed the message unwillingly.

The warlock shrugged, his face devoid of expression. Yep, he was definitely short with words and it was impossible to discern his emotions and thoughts. He was an expert in hiding them beneath a mask of indifference. That made it hard to find his weakness, I didn't like that.

Tannon brought some tea which he had already brewed over the wooden stove, and we sat down in two armchairs with a cup of hot tea in our hands, the sweet aroma of cardamom soon filling the air. The cabin was set at the edge of the cliff. Looking out the window and seeing only the vast sky extending into the infinite horizon, I couldn't help but feel as if we were stranded in midair.

"What's the deal with the identical cabins?" I inquired, trying to assuage my curiosity.

"They are traps for wanderers and idiots. The path to the other two takes you straight down the cliff." No chuckle accompanied that statement. I almost expected it. Again I was extremely surprised by the contrasting personalities of the twins.

"How many other visitors did you have here, besides me?" I couldn't imagine many species passing that test.

"None."

"None?" I asked, unable to believe this warlock lived the life of a hermit.

He nodded.

"How about Tessa?"

"She doesn't disturb me here."

Wow. I realized I owed Tessa a big favor for sending me here, or better still, attempting to send me here.

"Let's get you the scrolls you wanted."

I didn't see any scrolls on the shelves, so I was surprised when Tannon waved his fingers and a few scriptures appeared out of thin air and floated like feathers to land in his large hands.

"You should have these and get going," he said handing them to me.

"Can't you read them?" I asked, hoping he would. I didn't want to waste any more time with possible travel complications.

"I can." He paused. "But, I won't."

I was on edge with the warlock's persistent lack of explanations.

"Why?" I insisted. I had gathered that the warlock did not provide any information unless he was directly asked.

"Tessa wants it that way."

"Why?" I repeated, patiently.

"That means there is something in these scrolls I shouldn't see."

"Doesn't that make you curious?" Damn it! I just wanted the damn scrolls to be read asap.

"No."

Moon Goddess give me patience! I was losing it, but I remembered Tessa's words. It wouldn't do to piss the warlock off. Even if I failed to convince Tannon to read the scrolls, I still relied on the warlock for teleporting.

The cabin's wood floors started shaking, an ominous rumbling echoing from deep beneath it.

"What is going on here?" I shouted, taken aback as I instinctively jumped up, my paws appearing subconsciously to fight whatever lurked down there.

Tannon seemed undisturbed. He casually flicked his hand. His lapis lazuli carved cane, just like the tattered scrolls, flew in the air completely unsheathed from its scabbard, which remained on the wall.

"Nothing. Just the usual ruckus from the Underworld."

"What the hell man?" I barked.

Tannon thumped his cane a few times on the wooden floor and yelled, "Quiet!"

That was the first time I had seen the warlock raise his voice, even if it still sounded monotonic, almost mechanical.

As abruptly as the shaking had begun, it ended.

"They do not hear me otherwise," Tannon explained calmly, having caught the taint of surprise in my expression.

"Explain," I demanded.

"My cabin lies above the underworld of demons."

"Underworld of demons? Really, and?"

"I am the only one keeping them at bay. That's why I rarely leave here."

"How do you hold them here?" I asked, not understanding.

"By magic, of course. They just try their luck from time to time."

"But, sometimes you leave here to visit Tessa. Then what happens?" I questioned.

"My cane takes care of it," he said.

Conversing, or trying to converse with the warlock, I always came to the same conclusion, even if it beat my comprehension entirely. Tannon was the most tight-lipped being I had ever come across. I was also known to be taciturn, but I couldn't hold a candle to the warlock on being the man with the fewest words.

I looked at the cane, eyeing its handle which was made from a hawk's eye. I didn't quite understand how the cane could replace the warlock in his absence.

"How?" I asked again, forcing the warlock to appease my interest.

He whistled, and the hawk eye on the staff handle blinked. The eyes started moving forward, pushing their way out of the cane, along with the head and body of a large hawk. This sight captured my full attention.

"I created him. He carries part of my soul." He paused and then continued. "He is barely strong enough to secure the gate in my absence. But, he can uphold the magic for a few days, and he does a good imitation of me."

He clapped his hands. The hawk thumped the floor with his beak and then yelled, "Quiet" in exactly the same tone as Tannon.

"But, that means you leave part of your soul and power here when you are gone. What happens if your hawk dies?"

I was not surprised that Tannon chose not to answer.

"I see," I muttered. So, this was his weakness. And, nobody in the world knew, except probably for Tessa. I felt respect for this warlock who was solely burdened with such a huge task, which he accomplished with a reserved dignity.

"You can trust me," I said.

"I know," he answered.

I wouldn't trust anyone in his place. But, if what he was saying was true, Tannon could tap into my emotions. That explained the certainty in the warlock's voice.

Tannon whistled back, and the hawk went back to his place in the cane, his eyes now unmoving.

"Well, going back to the scrolls," said Tannon as if all was fine with the world. "I guess, I can read them. But, it will be at your own risk."

I jumped at his offer. "Sure."

I looked at the scrolls to see if it was written in any of the ancient languages he knew. But, there was no scripture on them. Absolutely none.

Tannon closed his eyes and concentrated, and one of the scrolls separated itself from the others, slowly rising to the air. It slowly unrolled in midair and began to change shape. A head appeared with all the facial features of a stunning woman, and the rest of the paper curved to create the figure of an alluring woman until we were soon looking at the miniature of the Moon Goddess herself.

The Moon Goddess's ethereal voice shook me to my core.

"The first of many hybrids
will be born,
possessing a part
of each and many
who stand dear to me.
She will be the fate
of many rulers,
but, will be claimed by
only one.
She will bring darkness
among my children,
but, then
the light will appear

once she decides.

Many will grieve,

but, with her marking

the pain will wither away

and finally

they will all be free

to seek their own destiny."

Once the reading was done, the Moon Goddess disappeared, as if she was never there, leaving in its place the old scroll which rolled itself back and slowly descended to Tannon's open palm.

"What was all that?" I asked, feeling that something of paramount importance had been said about Belle.

"It's a prophecy about the hybrid girl."

"Yes, Belle. What else?"

"She is your mate."

Whew! I was relieved. "Are you sure, because she's not a werewolf?" I asked, nevertheless, as this knowledge defied hundreds of years of old convention.

"It is ordained to be so by the Moon Goddess. With her begins a new era."

The mystery of the mate-pull was finally answered. She was my mate. Not that it mattered anymore as I had already decided she was mine. But a feeling of despair hit me upon these words as I remembered what I had done to her. I had hurt my beautiful mate with my lack of faith, with my own suspicions.

"How can I find her?" I said, standing up, too impatient to sit.

"Later," he waved his hand, as if finding her was a trivial matter. He continued, "That's not all about the prophecy. Now, I know why Tessa didn't want me to see this."

"Okay, why?" I pursued hesitantly, fearing the answer.

"She is not only your mate."

"Go on," I urged him, waving my hand impatiently.

"She's also mine," Tannon said with a stoic face.

"What the hell?" I growled, ready to fight the warlock for my mate.

"She is also the Demon Lord's mate, and the Vampire King's. They will all come for her."

That certainly explained why the Demon Lord was after her. I was about to go berserk; I was shaking with rage, my eyes burning red.

"I will kill them all. She is mine. Only mine. My mate," I roared.

"I don't want her; that is one less rival for you."

I was fuming. "You want me to fucking believe that? You slimy, manipulative son of a witch!"

"I can't be distracted. Not now, not ever," the warlock interrupted me nonchalantly, not reacting to any of my insults.

The warlock's words seemed to appease me. Tannon acted as if none of this mattered to him, not Belle, nor the fact that she might be his mate, his love, his own moon, his orbit in life. I was beginning to believe there was not a scrap of falsity in him. Moon Goddess, help me if I was wrong about the warlock.

"But, I may not resist the pull if I set eyes on her."

"What are you rambling on about, warlock?" I roared, seething in a rage all over again.

"Just don't let me see her. That's all," answered Tannon plainly.

"I will do that. Just remember your words. I don't want to have to kill you. But I will, if it comes to that," I warned, exhaling deeply to expel my tension. I indeed liked the warlock, and I hoped I didn't have to end this newly formed friendship by severing his head from his shoulders.

"Know this; she will be yours and yours only if you mark her before all the others."

"Good. I will mark her. It will be done as soon as I find her," I said with full conviction.

"But, it has to be of her own free choice."

"No problem," I said smugly. "And, I will kill all the others," I vowed.

"It may not come to that."

"C'mon man, out with the words, you are killing me here! I swear your whole existence gives a different meaning to the maxim, 'silence is golden,'" I said with a pained expression.

No, Tannon did not laugh. I hadn't expected him to.

"Once the marking is done, the mate-pull will dissipate for others," Tannon said.

"Great. That simplifies things a lot." I grinned from ear to ear.

"By the way, why did Tessa not want you to read the scroll?" I asked curiously. "Are you telling me she favors me over you?"

Tannon shook his head. "No, it's not that."

"Then, what is it?"

"We have a tight bond."

"So?" This didn't make one bit of sense. "Shouldn't she be helping you get your mate then?"

"Tessa doesn't like sharing," Tannon explained.

So the ancient priestess was possessive over the warlock. Whatever! I was not going to complain. I would use Tessa's jealousy to get Belle back.

"What else did the scroll say?" I asked, trusting Tannon more now that he had abandoned his claim on my Belle.

"She is given one trait from each of the Moon Goddess's children. Have you noticed any so far?"

Of course, I had seen strange happenings with her. How could I not? She had displayed mysterious powers just outside the door to the Wiccan coven. I'd been scared out of my wits seeing her like that.

"Yes, she can create an illusion of a wolf. And once when she was extremely enraged, her hair stood up, her eyes became red, and her body rose from the ground."

"Hmm, powers of a witch and demon? An illusion, you say?"

"Yes, Tessa thought she was a hybrid of a demon father and witch mother."

"The ability to create illusions is an extremely rare trait in a witch," Tannon informed.

Tannon's expressionless face did not reflect much of his thoughts, but it was obvious his interest was piqued.

"I also saw her throw balls of fire from her palms. But, isn't that the trait of an ifrit, a morning child?" I pried, trying to make sense of Belle's powers.

"Why, did she have blue veins?"

"Yes."

"Where exactly, in her palms?"

"No, not just her palms, but all over her arms."

"Don't say! Of course, that explains it," said Tannon.

Wow, that was literally the only time I had seen the warlock rattled.

"It explains what?" I was puzzled.

"The sudden movement from the Underworld."

"Why?"

"He's also coming for her."

"Who?" I asked, my voice chilling.

"You know who," he said, leaving it at that.

Belle

Belle

I heard the monster's anguished cry echo beneath the door. Then all was silent. I collapsed in a heap on the floor, feeling as though my limbs weighed a ton. I sobbed quietly, curled up on the floor. When my tears finally stopped, I felt nothing, just numb and vacant like a complete stranger in my own body. I slipped into a half awake state, vaguely aware of who and where I was. My memories of the past mingled with that of the present, creating new torments for my tattered soul. I no longer knew what was real and what was not.

I felt his lips move so slowly against mine, kissing away my tears, his fingers stroking my face with a gentle caress. Why was I crying? I didn't know; I didn't want to remember.

"Don't cry," Keith told me as he feathered more kisses on my face. "I love you, come back to me."

"Come back where?" I asked, my emotions whirling in a confusing jumble of love, pain, and anger. Why was I even angry, and why was the joy of his touch infected by a lingering sorrow? I held his rough face in my hands and leaned towards my monster. I wanted to bury this pain deep down in my memory, throw it in a bottomless abyss where it would never be disturbed and resurface again. I was going to drown it in the magic of his kisses. But before my lips found his, I felt the sudden, devastating loss of his body heat. He was no longer with me; I wanted to call out to him, tell him to stay, but it was as if my lips were numb, paralyzed.

Where was he? Why had he left me? I was losing the battle against this unknown sorrow and pain which were fast sweeping through my cells victoriously. My eyes looked for him in a desperate attempt to bring him back to me. I needed him; I craved him. My search for him, however, was in vain. Instead, all I could spot was a couple sprawled on the sofa a few feet away from me. I didn't want to look, but I was unable to tear my gaze away from the way their bodies entwined, the way their lips locked in a torching passion. I was mesmerized by the movement of the man's messy black hair brushing her skin as his face glided back and forth her neck. Who were they, I didn't know, but my heart started its rapid drumbeat in my chest, my breaths were quick shallow gasps.

Then he lifted his head and looked at me.

"Keith," I cried out.

For a second, I saw a flash of my own pain and sorrow duplicated in his eyes. Then he buried his head back in her neck again.

"Moon Goddess, help me please," I said as the anguish of this memory pierced my numbness, jerking me from my comatose state.

I couldn't stay here forever. I had to go back to the attic; I would ask Alice to help me get back to my pack without letting the monster know. It had to be Tessa; I couldn't bear the idea of Daisy teleporting me anywhere. I vowed that I would find a way out of this mess by myself without endangering the people I loved. I didn't need him. This thought made me feel better. I would not shed any more tears on the monster. He was not my mate, I reminded myself. When I found my real mate, it would all be different; I would be loved and cherished, I would be the orbit of his universe. I refused to allow the monster to taint my hopes and dreams of love. He was an asshole. And that was that. Yep, that made me feel better.

I pressed my ear to the door and listened. No sounds were coming from the other side. I was ready to go back inside and face this nightmare; I felt strong enough to do it. I turned the knob. It didn't budge. Damn it; it was probably stuck. Only the Moon Goddess knew when somebody had last attempted to use this door besides me, if ever. I tried to open it a few more times, but it was utterly useless. I decided I had to kick the door in; there was no other way. I gained momentum and kicked it hard, but it didn't open. And worse still, because I had been bracing myself to go forward, I lost my balance and went ass over tit on the floor. Nothing seemed to be working. I was getting desperate. I knocked on the door loudly trying to get somebody's attention. "Hello, is somebody out there? Please help me; I can't open the door. It's stuck. Hello?" I shouted. After twenty to thirty minutes of countless attempts to be heard, all I had done was acquire a hoarse voice. I would wait for somebody to find me. Eventually, they would look for me, wouldn't they? After all, they knew I was in the attic. That thought did make me think. Indeed why wasn't anybody trying to find me? Tessa, not even Timothy or Alice? What about Keith who was desperate enough to kick down the attic door, but not the one inside the attic? Nothing made sense here.

And then, I suddenly got it. This was probably the door of teleportation the coven frequently used, and I had accidentally stumbled upon it. This meant there was no way back in until I faced Daisy's stupid challenges. Did she know about it? Was she the one behind this? Of course, a thousand times of course. I couldn't imagine the lies she sprouted to others to explain my absence. And if Keith had tried to follow me, he must have ended up somewhere else. I wouldn't trust Daisy if she were the last witch on Earth. What was I going to do? Knowing her, she must have sent me to Siberia along with that poor soul she was joking about, and she must be howling with laughter now. Damn it! The situation was not good. This time, I didn't have Keith to carry me on his back as he climbed the cave or show me the way out of the ocean. Nope, this certainly did not bode well for me. I would need all the skills I had to survive this. I hoped to the Moon Goddess that they would be enough.

I started walking. Indeed, just as I expected, this was no closed room but a long winding tunnel. Thankfully, the lanterns mounted on the wall were automatically triggered, lighting upon the sound of my footsteps, so I didn't have to grope my way out of darkness. The tunnel finally came to an end. I took a deep breath as I opened the exit door, embracing myself to greet the freezing weather of Siberia.

I walked outside to a meadow of some sorts, and I felt the bright crispness of a spring night as I breathed in fresh air. I was not in Siberia. That, I knew for a fact. The valley beyond glistened with the splendid sheen of moonlight. There was a gentle wind, its sound soughing through the pine trees. The trees swayed as if they were dancing to its song, the leaves making a soft rustling sound. I embraced the spring landscape, with its lush yellow-green foliage smelling of honeysuckle. On my right, I heard the waves of the sea, washing and sliding softly on the shore. Yep, I was by the seaside, which was some small consolation. All in all, it could have been worse.

The meadow was quiet with a sleepy kind of stillness; a hush seemed to have descended upon everything. I walked a little, not knowing where I was going or what my challenge was. Then I slowly lay down on my back, the exhaustion of the day finally taking its toll on me. I lay there alone in the tranquility of the night gazing up at the bright, full moon serenely smiling in the cloudless sky, its pale beams dancing upon the deep waters. I was filled with a certain elation as I spread my body in the perfect stillness of the green grass. It was almost the same contentment I had back in my secret place in the pack. I gazed at the moon for hours, feeling its light embrace me in a blanket of warmth and love. The moon's light flickered as if in silent conversation, beckoning me. Before I drifted off to sleep, I vaguely heard someone's soothing voice, but I was far too gone to make sense of the words.

I woke up at dawn. The sun's beaming rays were dipping into the sea like myriads of lulling stars. Hmm, this challenge was turning out to be so not bad after all. I smiled thinking how disappointed Daisy was going to be. I didn't know I had spoken a bit rashly as I suddenly became aware of the weird rustling sounds ripping through the quietness of the morning like the loud clap of sudden thunder.

I looked around in panic, and what I saw was beyond my understanding. Incorporeal creatures were floating in the air dressed in black capes around me; it was as if the clothes on somebody's back had come to life, turning into a breathing being with no head and body. They were always moving, weaving around each other in a kind of aerial dance, their capes flaring out like open umbrellas spinning in a dazzling array. Inside each hood protruded a face so blurred beneath a veil of thick mist that it looked as if the goddess did not have the time to carve out their features, but instead had just smoothed them all out. Their long hair swam in waves around their hoods which were gliding smoothly in the air.

"Who are you?" I managed to ask boldly.

"We are what we are, we are the shadow spirits," said one.

There were at least seven of those creatures circling me, steadily narrowing the distance between us, trapping me in small bounded space. I had to make my move, or they would capture me. That was my last thought as they all suddenly rushed towards me.

The Chase

Belle

When they all came at me, I dived, rolling underneath them, and started running for my life, not heeding where I was going. I looked back to see whether I was losing them, but they were right there behind me, giving me chase with their black capes flying in the air. I knew I didn't have Keith's speed, but I was sure I could run for a long time; I was in good shape. Underneath my feet lay a beautiful soft carpet of fine grass with sweet smelling flowers all around me filling the morning air. The adrenaline put everything into slow motion as I could feel the press of my feet on the Earth, the crash of the grass and the flower beds at each step, the way my arms pumped back and forth, my calf muscles bunched and my thighs stretched. My breath was gusting out of my mouth in white puffs, misting into the crisp, cold morning air.

The meadow gave way to dense trees, their vibrant colors and chestnut smells helping to awaken my dulled, fatigued senses. I hoped to lose my tail among the swarm of trees marching towards me, lines of thick bark-made soldiers with leaf-clad outstretched arms. I did not slow down despite the tearing thorns of tangled vines and the thick drooping branches which seemed to do their best to impede my speed. My face was in cuts, my palms and elbows were bleeding from shoving aside the branches and vines on my way. I continuously jumped over the ground littered with torn branches, hollow logs, and driftwood. The run was taking its toll on me while all this ducking and jumping slowed me down. I stole a quick peek at the creatures behind me. They were close by, their airborne bodies passing straight through the solid obstacles. I didn't stand a chance in here among the dense trees. I knew they would soon catch up with me. I made a sharp turn to the right, heading straight to the sea. I wanted to believe the creatures would be deterred by water. Short of a miracle, that was my only remaining hope.

I cut across the trees, zigzagging my way to prevent my capture. I was using all the energy I had to reach the sea. My blood was running wild in my veins, directly pumping to my legs. I was pushing my legs faster with a force I didn't know I possessed. The sea was right there within my vision; I could even smell the salty fragrance sweeping in from the gentle waves, I was that close. Just when I thought I was going to make it, I felt as if someone punched me in the gut, my breath leaving me in a whoosh of air. I was flat on my face gasping for my next breath. What had happened? I had no time to think as I struggled to get up, trying to haul myself up on my elbows and knees. But it was a tremendous effort as whatever had hit me had walloped me enough to knock the wind out of me. My arms and legs were shaking with the effort of lifting my body. I managed to stand on bent legs, my arms clutching my stomach to ease the pain of the previous impact.

"I wouldn't do that if I were you. I'll just knock you down again," I heard one of them say.

Upon hearing those words, I started half limping, half running with the urgency of an animal about to be trapped. I had to get to the water and, with the help of the Moon Goddess, I would. I refused to give up.

But then I was seized by another piercing agony, this time right around my chest. It was as if my heart had stopped beating; my lungs stopped gathering air. Before I fell, I saw the creature emerge right out of my body, his exit agonizingly slow and painful right before my eyes. My last vision was of his black cape flowing behind him as he exited his temporary host, my body. Then darkness rose up to swirl me in its midst.

I woke up in a daze, blinking a few times to clear my vision. I realized that my wrists and ankles were each grabbed by a shadow spirit floating in the air. It was as if I was stretched in a torture rack, I felt the pain of my stretched limbs and struggled to break their grip.

"We are almost there, little girl. Stop fighting," said the one holding my left ankle.

I struggled harder.

"Do you want Kenneth to knock you down again, little girl? You were much more compliant in your faint state. Is that what you want?" he asked.

Were they kidding me? Did they think I would give up that quickly, allow them to take me like a ragged doll? I may not be able to stop them, but I would die trying.

"Damn it, stop it," said another shadow spirit as I squirmed, kicked and struggled relentlessly.

"As you wish," he said grinning maliciously. I saw the sleeve of his cape first brush and then move right through my right ankle in the blink of an eye. Pain shot through me, making my vision blur and my eyes water. I bit my tongue so as not to cry out, had he broken my ankle? It sure felt like it.

"Do you want more?" he asked innocently.

I shook my head. I had to be clever; I wouldn't live through another one of those transgressions. However they may be doing it, these creatures were inflicting the maximum pain on the body they succeeded in invading, even if temporarily. How could these spirits force their entry into my body? I had no idea. But they were doing it, and I wanted to avoid that pain at all costs.

"I'm glad you see it my way," he said smiling.

I wanted to kill him.

I prayed that this journey would be over soon. I didn't know how much more of this I could bear.

It was sometime mid-afternoon, the sun still robust and indomitable in the cloudless, blue sky lingering above. Its peacefulness seemed to mock my agony as I gazed upon it. Suddenly, the shadow spirits started steadily rising in the air, flying towards a looming hillside covered in red sand as if painted in blood. With the corner of my eye, I spotted an enormous glass house sitting at the top of the hill overlooking the sea. The land around it was cleared back at least one hundred feet. The great stone walls surrounding it from other sides were draped with flowering vines and green ivy and guarded by huge trees. The four shadow spirits that carried me slowly lowered me to the ground in front of the steps to a large mahogany front door. I lay there for a second, trying to massage my aching arms and legs.

"Get up," ordered the one who hurt me.

I did what he asked despite the ache in my limbs; I feared what he would do if I didn't.

I went to the door with four of my floating bodyguards while the rest of the shadow spirits quietly glided through the solid glass wall. I walked into a grand foyer with a magnificent glass chandelier hanging from the vaulted ceiling. There were wood winding stairs with a stainless steel handrail and glass paneled balustrades leading up to the upper levels. Inside it was hot with the glass walls trapping the light and the warmth of the sun. I was taken up the stairs to a small room by my captors.

"You will stay here," one of them said, handcuffing my wrists to the small bed in the room with his invisible hands. He locked the door behind him as he left the room. There were only a few sticks of furniture inside, a bare mattress, empty drawers, and an empty closet. I tested the handcuffs, but I was not strong enough to break them open. I could try picking the lock, but there was nothing useful on me to use as a tool. The chains were long enough to give me some mobility, and I was able to check the small adjoining bathroom, but it was also minimally furnished with the basic necessities: a toilet, a mirrored sink and a small tub. Finally, I curled my legs beneath me and closed my eyes trying to get some rest before finding the means to escape.

"Wake up beauty queen. Time to go."

I opened my eyes at first, not knowing where I was. Then, it all came rushing back to me, the shadow spirits, my capture, the pain of what they could do to me.

What I saw before me, however, was not a shadow spirit, but a normal man with a solid body and face.

"Who are you?" I asked hopefully. Perhaps I could convince him to help me escape.

"I am a shadow spirit," he said.

"No, you're not," I replied.

"Yes, I am," he said. "C'mon, let's go. He does not like to wait," he said as he uncuffed me.

"Who? Where are you taking me?"

"To Derek"

"Who is Derek?" I asked.

"You'll see," he said as he started dragging me outside the door.

I was surprised to see that it was already dark outside, I must have slept for hours. We went down the winding stairs basking in the moonlight and entered a colossal room with a spectacular view of the sea. The furniture was modern but fairly minimalist. There was a low divan set heaped with high cushions to one side of the room, its light color contrasting with the sedate warm autumn tones in the oriental carpet pieces. In front of the divan sat a large structured coffee table with a clean finish in steel. Colorful modern art lined the walls. Though the elegantly styled wall lights were dimmed, the moonlight was streaming in through the glass walls, casting a bright silver light inside.

I saw the back of a man sitting on the divan as my guard pushed me inside the room.

"She's here, Derek," he said.

The man turned his head. Wow, he had a square jaw, light brown expressive eyes, a high forehead, and shoulder-length brown curly hair. His every move was touched by a gentleness I hadn't been expecting.

He gestured for me to enter.

I walked to the divan and stood there looking at him.

"Please sit down," he said pointing at the seat next to him. The guard disappeared, leaving us completely alone in the room.

"Are you the Demon Lord?" I asked him.

The Demon Lord

Belle

He flinched upon my question; regret etched all over his beautiful face.

"No, I am not."

Thank the Moon Goddess for that! I was relieved, this was likely a mistaken identity case that should be easy to resolve.

"Who are you?" I asked, feeling more relaxed now.

"I am the leader of the shadow spirits."

"But! But how? You don't look like them," I stammered. What was going on, first the guard in my room and now him? They looked perfectly normal to me.

"You mean I'm not bodiless?" He smiled. "But, I am."

I simply didn't get it.

"We are the children of the Sun Goddess. We all get to be like that under the sun, we lose our solidity, and we amass what you might call unusual powers with the magic of sunlight," he explained. "I heard you got a glimpse of our abilities yourself. I'm deeply sorry for that. I wish it hadn't come to that," he said sincerely.

"You mean all shadow spirits are normal at night and get freaky in the morning?" I asked stunned.

"Normal at night and freaky in the morning? Exactly!" he repeated my words. His features lightened and a smile tugged at the corners of his lips. Then he became serious. The intensity in

106

his brown gaze as it settled on me made me uncomfortable. It reminded me of the black eyes of my own beautiful monster. And it bugged me that I still thought of Keith even as I sat across from this gentle soul.

I squirmed in my seat as my imagination wreaked havoc on me. What did this man want from me?

"Belle," he said. "I hate to do what I have to do."

Holy crap! That didn't sound reassuring at all.

"You are here because I made a deal," he said in exasperation. "A deal with the devil."

That sounded ominous.

"You see, I would never hand a lovely girl like you to him if it weren't for Jason. If it were one of my men, I would leave him be; he could deal with the devil's torture. But not him. He is only three years old for Sun Goddess's sake," he said, cursing at the injustice of it all. "I looked everywhere for him, but he was already gone. He is my only brother, my only family in the world. What was I supposed to do?"

A devil who likes torturing small kids?

"I don't understand," I muttered.

"I'm mucking things up. What I mean to say is that he kidnapped my little brother. He won't let him go unless I deliver you to him."

"You mean?" I tried to finish the sentence a few times, but couldn't. It was as if my saliva was stuck in my throat.

He averted his gentle eyes.

"The Demon Lord."

Here we go again. It was always back to the Demon Lord. There was no escape.

"I see," I murmured. "What does he want with me, do you know?" I asked, preparing myself for the worst.

"Look, I really don't know much," he said with a pained expression. "But, he's on his way here. I'm sorry."

"What about your brother? Will he be all right?"

No child should have to suffer torture; it was abominable. I hated the Demon Lord already.

"Yes, he's bringing Jason with him for the exchange."

Hmm, an exchange...Me for Jason. I guessed that was fair.

"I'm glad he'll be all right," I said, trying to be brave, desperately fighting the fear coursing through every fiber and neuron in my body. I had to clear my head and find a way out of this. But, there wasn't any. I couldn't escape and, even if I could, I wouldn't. The Demon Lord was keeping a three-year-old child hostage, and only the Moon Goddess knew what would happen to him if he failed to get his hands on me. I wouldn't do that to him. I had to face the Demon Lord. Only then I would try to escape. Yep, that sounded like a sound plan.

"You must be hungry," said Derek as if everything else was fine with my world. "I'll ask for some food." I saw his eyelids droop a little as he communicated with someone.

I hoped eyeballs were not on the menu.

A teenage girl entered the room carrying a large tray of food. There was an assortment of food on the tray: chicken wings, curry rice, potato salad, and some pita bread. The girl had a rather boyish appearance with her short curly blonde hair cropped just above her ears. She set the tray on the large coffee table and asked, "Anything else Derek?"

"No, thanks."

I realized how famished I was as I piled some food on my plate. There was no reason to starve myself just because I knew what was awaiting me, a nice dose of the Demon Lord and his infamous torture.

I felt Derek's eyes on me.

"Sorry, I didn't mean to stare," he said embarrassed. "It's just, you're not what I expected."

"What did you expect?" I asked. I started eating as I waited for his reply. The food was excellent.

"Someone far less innocent. How old are you?"

"Just turned eighteen."

A brief flash of surprise crossed his face, but he just nodded.

I took a spoon of rice. Mmm, it was bliss. As weird as shadow spirits might be, they sure knew how to cook. I had to ask them for some recipes.

"So you said you didn't have any other family. What happened to them?" I asked.

"I lost my mother at childbirth when Jason was born. It was just Jason, my father and me after that. But father was taken from us last year when several underworld demons somehow managed to open the gate."

"Excuse me?" I asked coughing, unable to swallow my bite.

"Underworld demons? What gate?" I realized sadly that I was not close to catching up on this strange world. Every day felt like watching a never-ending BBC documentary.

"The underworld has been closed off from the surface since...well since almost the beginning I guess. They are the disowned children of the Moon Goddess, and hence are bound by no rules or anyone."

Disowned children? What must have they done, I wondered. Wow.

"How did they manage to open the gate, then?"

"Nobody really knows. But the incursions happened everywhere that day, underworld demons traveling in groups were spotted all over the world. My father, at the time, was going to the council meeting with a team of elite shadow spirits. They were attacked at night when they were at their weakest. Kenneth and a few others returned with my father's body the next day. "

"I'm sorry."

He nodded.

"What happened to those underworld demons?"

"We hunted them. The council meeting was rescheduled to convene the following week. I took my father's place. The leaders of all species decided it would be best to go demon hunting. The shadow spirits came across at least ten. Overall, we managed to clean that mess up pretty well. But, of course, I lost my father and the shadow spirits lost their leader."

I didn't know what to say. What was there to say?

"Look, none of this is your fault," said Derek, holding his head between his hands, his eyes closed tightly. "Damn! I can't do this!" he said suddenly throwing up his hands in exasperation. He stood up, pacing the room in a frenzy. "I'll find another way to save Jason. I'll get you out of here, I promise."

"But how?" I asked as I started munching on another spicy chicken wing. Could I possibly take the food with me to the Demon Lord's den, I wondered.

Abruptly, Derek closed his eyes with trembling hands clenched at his side.

We heard the loud engine of a helicopter as it hovered around the house.

"Damn, damnation to hell. He's already here," he said suddenly grabbing me by the elbow. The food on my plate got scattered everywhere, ruining the spotless divan. But before we could get out, the door opened. How had he come so quickly when I could still hear the hammering sound of the chopper's rotors?

Derek pushed me behind his broad back, shielding me from him.

"Where is she, Derek?" I heard The Demon Lord ask. I was yet to see his face.

"I'm losing my patience here. You want your brother, don't you?"

"There has to be another way. I'm not giving her to you," Derek said.

"Is that so? Then perhaps you want to hear him scream?"

The agonizing scream of a little boy filled the room. He was the devil incarnate!

I pushed my way forward. I wouldn't let him torture the little boy. Derek's shoulders had slumped in defeat, his face a mask of grief and pain as he unwillingly let me go.

"I am here," I said.

After that scream, I was expecting to see Jason in the room. But, instead, all I saw was him.

"Where is the boy? I asked defiantly.

The man standing before me was like none of the demons I saw before. He was certainly not the way I'd imagined him. His short spiked dirty-blonde hair contrasted nicely with his devilishly mischievous red eyes. One corner of his mouth inched up when he saw me, enough to reveal a small charming dimple. What was most surprising about him was the exceeding and touching air of childish innocence on his face which defied his alleged devilish nature.

I took a step towards him, ready to face my fate. Based on the absence of the screaming boy, I assumed he could torture by thought. When would he torture me? Would it hurt too much? Would I scream? I didn't know.

"My love, finally my long deprived eyes have gazed upon your alluring beauty. My blood soars high at your sight; my eyesight blurs from your lustrous sheen. I have craved for you so deeply; my hunger is as high as the moon in the sky."

Huh?!

New Mate

Belle

"Come on, love. Let's go home."

"Home? I'm sorry, I don't understand?" I said.

He smiled. "Sorry, love. Of course you don't. I haven't properly introduced myself, now, have I? Where are my manners? I'm Lasarus, the Lord of the demons. I am your mate."

I gasped. Derek gasped. That was a shocker. Keith was not my mate. He had been right all along. Tessa, too. Apparently, Lasarus was.

Wow, how to digest that? I shouldn't have been surprised really, after all, I was alleged to be half demon. Still, I was surprised as hell. Being the mate of a torture loving Demon Lord wasn't my idea of joy. He wasn't bad looking; that was for sure. I could definitely get used to his looks even if the sparks I had for Keith were, as of yet, missing. I guess those would come in time. My body and heart would accept him once he marked me. How did a demon mark his mate? I had no clue. I was in a world of unknowns, and I was scared.

I caught Derek's face wincing in sympathy. But, he wouldn't intervene now, nobody would, not between mates. He held his hand to me, and I took it. Yep, my heart did beat faster upon the touch of our skins. There was something there. Was I indeed mated to the Demon Lord?

"The boy?" I asked.

"No worries, my men are delivering him as we speak, love."

Suddenly, the door opened, and a small boy with curly brown hair just like Derek's ran inside the room followed by two shadow spirits. His face reflected fear when he spotted Lasarus, but Derek caught him in his arms, holding him lovingly in his strong embrace.

"Are you okay, Jason?" asked Derek tossing Jason's hair, the raw edge of emotion seeping through his voice.

The boy nodded, wrapping his skinny arms fiercely around his big brother's neck.

"I didn't cry. I promise. I was very brave even when he broke my pinkie finger," the little boy said. "But look, it's already mended," he smirked, waving his little finger back and forth.

"Of course you were. Sure it did." Derek said proudly. He looked at Lasarus, daggers shooting from his eyes.

And he had every right. The devil had broken a three-year-old child's finger! He had no soul, what was I going to do?

"Blah blah, can we cut all this emotional crap, please? He was always screaming and he got on my nerves. What matters, in the end, is that the little brat is delivered to you. And, I have my beautiful mate. The exchange, in my opinion, is complete. It was great doing business with you, Derek. Till next time, adieu!"

Derek was barely holding it in check.

"Let's take our leave now, love," Lasarus suggested.

"Derek, it was nice meeting you," I said.

Derek just nodded his head in acknowledgment.

Lasarus squeezed my hand, his iris now ruby red. Wow, he was getting jealous! It was really time to leave.

I saw Derek toss his little brother in the air making him laugh as I exited the room with my devil mate.

We passed the foyer guarded by shadow spirits and left the house. Outside I heard the buzzing sound of the helicopter. We clambered aboard, and I grudgingly allowed Lasarus to belt me. The helicopter's rotors whirled for a quick takeoff. The night breeze played over my face and I inhaled the fresh air until the front door closed. Entrapment. That's what I felt. The engine roared into action, the rotor blades gained speed, blanketing us in clouds of whirling dust. I wanted to be part of the dust particles, and just float away. The helicopter took to the grey sky leaving Derek and all the shadow spirits behind. My world closed in around me; I was having difficulty breathing.

Lasarus was sitting next to me, his arm draped around my shoulders, his hands brushing so slowly back and forth at the top of my arm. He leaned in close, his lips stopping just short of touching me. I tensed and turned my head to look out the window of the helicopter, not really knowing what else to do. Outside, I saw the glistening blue sea shimmering in the bright moon, the waves splashing against each other with the night wind as if to display my inner turmoil. This was not good. How was I going to survive this?

I closed my eyes feigning sleep, breathing slowly. I hoped he would let me be, until at least this journey was over. He blew a frustrated sigh and shifted back to his side. When I was just about to thank my luck, I suddenly found my head cradled in the curve of his arm, his muscled shoulder now a firm cushion beneath my head. I had to inhale his scent with my face pressed against his chest, it was not unpleasant, but it was also not the intoxicating smell of my monster. Damn it; I had to stop making comparisons or I would only be inviting misery. I shifted uncomfortably, trying to minimize contact with him. But, it was in vain. After hours of a torturous journey with my body stiffened into a mummy-like state, I felt the helicopter descend. I opened my eyes, tired of keeping them closed for so long. The helicopter squatted atop a relatively flat plateau where up ahead a half mile away stood a large four-storied house surrounded by other small outbuildings. I was surprised to see that we were actually on an island.

"Welcome home, my love," the Demon Lord said as he unfastened my straps and took my hand walking outside the helicopter.

"What is this place?"

"This is the demon island. You'll be completely safe here, with me."

Mmm, safe from whom I wondered? So far, he'd been the only one I'd been trying to escape from, and now he had me. There was no one else hot on my tail. So I had no clue what he was talking about.

There was a slight chill in the air and I shivered with cold, but mostly with fear and shock.

He glanced at me and asked, "Cold?"

"A little," I said.

"Then let's get you inside, love," he said, and to my utter amazement he lifted me up in his arms and started walking. Then, other demons came outside to greet their lord.

"What is the situation?" Lasarus asked a demoness as he entered the house.

"No news from Tessa," she said.

Tessa? Why would they have news from her and why was Tessa in contact with them? What was going on? Did Tessa know I was here? Did Keith?

"Later," he said, and waved his hand. "My mate is in dire need of rest. Have some food brought to my room."

My room? Did he just say my room? Was I going to stay in his room? Along with him? This was dire news! I hoped he didn't have marking or mating in mind; I certainly wasn't ready for either deed.

He carried me up the stairs at an agonizingly slow pace as if he savored every moment of it, his skin touching my skin, his breath mingling with mine, his fingers grazing my legs. It was pure torture for me. On the last floor, he turned the knob on one of the two rooms and nudged it open with his foot. Inside was a master suite, lavishly decorated in warm earthy tones. He walked around the suite, steadfastly carrying me in his arms. There was an adjoining bathroom, a large living room with exotic Italian leather furniture, and a dining set overlooking the sea. There were also white marble stairs, streaked faintly with gray veins, leading up to the terrace.

After the mini tour, Lasarus laid me on the soft bed and was soon on top of me. Before I could even mutter a complaint, I found his lips descending towards mine and I managed to turn my head towards the side just at the last moment, letting his lips touch my neck instead. This was going too fast for my liking, and it was time to set up some ground rules with my devil mate.

He didn't seem to mind the new destination of his lips as his tongue continued its exploration along my neck and collarbone. I heard his breath, raspy, excited. His fingers were not idle either, finding the skin between the bottom of my T-shirt and my jeans, softly brushing it. I had tingles all over my skin. I didn't know how to stop him.

"Look," I said, turning my head towards him. He seized the opportunity, and this time I felt his warm breath on my face. I tried to push his arms away, but he was too strong. The knock on the door was music to my ears as he sighed in frustration, cursing. He finally got off me.

"Come in," said Lasarus.

I was relieved for the moment. Lasarus's touch was not repelling, no, it was far from it. His hands did not ignite the fire I felt under Keith's touch, but they made my heart beat fast. I enjoyed it. No, my problem was not that. It was far worse. I felt I was betraying Keith every time Lasarus touched me. It somehow felt wrong to be allowing him liberties with my body. I knew that was the most irrational thought. Keith had done worse first with Zena and then with Daisy. And Lasarus was my mate, nobody would lie about that. There would be no gain. So, we were meant to be together as ordained by the Moon Goddess. Somehow it didn't matter. What had Keith done to me? Why couldn't I get rid of this need for him, not even under the touch of my real mate? I didn't know, but it disturbed me.

A demoness and a child demon, probably a mother and her son, entered the room with their hands full of food and drinks. The demon boy who entered the room was about twelve years old. He looked so cute with his blonde hair standing straight up as if shaped by a ton of gel and hair spray, his arms glowing beneath a sleeveless shirt. The boy was carrying a tray of food which he laid down on the dining table in the adjoining room while the demoness was about to set up some cutlery, plates, wine glasses and two bottles of wine.

"No, put them all on the terrace," said Lasarus, smiling with a wicked gleam in his eyes as the boy and the demoness changed their direction, taking the trays upstairs instead.

Apparently, Lasarus was planning a night of seduction under the moonlight.

"Thank you," I said to them as they were leaving. It was time to start getting acquainted with all these demons who were soon to become my extended family in a weird sort of way.

"Let's dine," Lasarus said as he took my hand, helping me rise from the bed.

We went up to the terrace holding hands. The terrace view blew me away; there was a breathtaking view of the whole island and its four seas spreading in all directions. It wasn't that late apparently as the moon was still high up in the air, bright enough to light the terrace. There was a nice table set up with wine, and all sorts of crazy good-smelling food. I was still full with what I had at the Shadow Spirits' place, but I could certainly have some wine to relax my overstretched nerves.

He held my chair as I sat down to gaze at this magnificent view. He poured wine into our glasses and then raised his glass and saluted, "To us!"

I felt my lips stretch in a tight smile as I raised my glass in a similar motion.

He sipped his wine as he piled up all sorts of food on a plate and handed it to me. There was no way I could eat all that, but I took it anyway.

"I have a gift for you," he said smiling.

"Mmm. What is it?" I asked unable to bear the silence any longer.

"I have your family here."

What? Could it be true? I whooped with incredulous delighted joy. I was exuberantly happy.

My parents were here; Sean was here. I suddenly felt as if a ton had lifted off my body. I could do this with their help. I knew I could. Everything would be all right I thought as I sipped my wine, finally enjoying its taste.

Reunion

Belle

"Where is my family, Lasarus? I can't wait to see them," I said, taking a huge sip from my wine and then getting up from the table, unable to wait for dinner to be over.

"I love the sound of your voice as my name rolls off your lips," Lasarus said with an intense expression that I couldn't look away from. "Say it again."

Wow, it would be hard to rein in his passions.

"Lasarus," I said. He was my ticket to my family, and I would not do anything to endanger that. If he wanted to hear his name then I would say it a thousand times. And then some more.

"Come, love, let's go and see your family," he said, smiling.

His warm hands embraced mine as we descended from the terrace. We exited the building into the chilly night. I put on the jacket he gave me as it was getting colder. We walked a quarter mile or so past a few houses and then we stopped in front of a white house. I was so excited that I couldn't hold it in. I had missed my family so much. Stopping in front of the house, I knocked on the door. After what seemed like too many minutes for my liking, the door finally opened.

I couldn't believe my eyes.

The man who opened the door was Gregory wearing his flannel pajamas. His hair was messy, his eyes unfocused. It was evident he'd been sleeping. I couldn't believe he was also here; he must have come with Sean. I was so happy that I threw myself at him, hugging him. How I had missed everyone in my pack. It seemed ages ago when Gregory, Sean and I were last watching The Lord of the Rings together, unaware of how my life was about to change radically.

"Hi Belle," he said shyly, embracing me awkwardly.

"Where is everyone?" I asked, looking around in a frenzy.

"Everyone?" Gregory asked surprised.

"Sean, and my parents. Where are they? Are they sleeping?"

Gregory looked restless, shifting his weight from foot to foot.

"Uhm. Well, they're not here," he said while averting my eyes.

"What do you mean?" I asked, not comprehending his words. "Are they in a different house?"

"No, they are back in the pack," Gregory muttered, clearly uncomfortable.

"But," I uttered, completely confused. I turned to Lasarus and said, "But, you said my family was here."

"Yes, right in the flesh. You are looking at him, love," he smiled.

The smile was irritating as hell.

"You lied to me. Why would you do that?" I asked him, my voice chillingly cold. "You said my family was here. Obviously they're not." I desperately tried to control my temper.

"I did not lie, love. Gregory is here, isn't he?" he said, a little surprised at my reaction.

"Is this your understanding of a demon joke? Because, let me tell you, it is quite tasteless. As much as I like Gregory and I am thrilled to see him, he is not really family, is he, love?" I mocked him enunciating each word slowly as if speaking to someone of limited mental capacity.

"But, he is. He is your family, your only living relative in fact. He is my gift to you," he said, his lips curling into a wide smile.

"What are you talking about for Moon Goddess's sake?" I said, scowling at him.

Gregory was incessantly shuffling his bare feet on the plush carpet as he stared at the floor. What in the blazes was going on?

"Gregory is your brother."

I was silent. There was nothing to say to this nonsense.

"Love?" he said raising his eyebrow.

I wanted to take the word love and stuff it back in his mouth; I was so not in the mood for his endearment now.

"He's not my brother. Sean is. He is Gregory's friend; your demons must have brought the wrong guy. It's an understandable mistake," I said finally making sense of what was going on.

Lasarus softly held me by the elbow and led us inside as Gregory stepped aside from the door. This was the second time I had this feeling, this mounting uneasiness, this prostrating fear that I was on the verge of some discovery I neither sought nor wanted. I was still trying to get over the first one, the one about my adoption. I definitely wasn't ready for another.

Gregory turned on the lights. I was surprised to see that it was quite messy inside, with some tossed clothes on the floor and the sofa, and leftover food strewn across the coffee table. Gregory hastily tried to clear up some space for us on the comfy looking couch as he threw his crumpled sweatshirt and a few magazines into the far away corner. Gregory living in this disheveled state was new to me. Granted I had never been to Gregory's house, but he had never displayed any sloppiness whenever he was in ours, which I had to admit was quite often. Was this a side of him I didn't know or had something happened to put him in this state of mind, I couldn't decide.

Gregory sat across from us, his eyes fixed on a spot on the carpet, his nervousness oozing from all over his body. He was mechanically biting the inside of his cheeks and cracking his knuckles, the sound of which was reverberating in the glaring silence.

I crossed my legs, waiting patiently for someone to offer some explanation. Looking at how Gregory was still avoiding eye contact, it would have to be Lasarus. I turned towards him, "Well, I'm waiting," I said.

"Gregory is your twin brother."

The news shattered me.

"Excuse me?" I was having difficulty digesting this news, for sure. How could Gregory, our pack beta's son, and at the same time Sean's best friend, be my twin brother? This was possible of course, but very improbable. There had to be a misunderstanding.

"I was found and adopted by the pack's beta four years after you were," said Gregory.

I delved into my childhood memories but I couldn't falsify that information, I was too young to remember. I thought I knew him all my life, but I didn't remember much about my very early childhood years.

"You were adopted, just like me? How?"

"I lived among the demons for four years, and then they left me at the pack border."

"But even if that is true, that means you should be my age. I don't understand; I thought you were only two years younger than Sean."

"I was an early bloomer, they didn't know my age, and I looked much older. They thought I was six, or seven."

"But, why would you do that? Why not simply tell them the truth? More importantly, why not tell me the truth?" I asked completely puzzled.

"Love, we sent Gregory to keep an eye on you until I could come and fetch you and we didn't want them to suspect the two kids the pack recently adopted were related," he said.

"Why? Keep an eye on me? For what, I don't understand. And why didn't you simply come and fetch me if you knew who I was? Why send Gregory instead? And why all the secrecy and lies?" I was getting irritated with the many unknown parts of this puzzle. Damn it; it was as if I was part of a conspiracy theory. What was going on here?

"Uhm. Well, love, you weren't safe until you were eighteen years old."

"Not safe?" I was getting frustrated. "Damn it, Lasarus. Just start from the beginning, I need more than the bits and pieces of information you are giving me. Who am I? And who is after me?"

"You are the daughter of Balan who was once one of our top commanders."

"Once?"

"Yes, unfortunately, your father is dead. And so is your mother who died giving birth to you and your brother."

He continued. "Your father stumbled upon your witch mother when he was on a mission for me. Your mother was by herself, far away from her friends and family. Apparently, they fell in love; nobody knows how. Balan brought your mom along with him on his return. He wanted to mark her and make her part of the demon family. I told him that it was not acceptable. Inter-species mating, especially with a witch, our number one enemy, was not acceptable. It was not. Not at the time," he said checking my reaction.

"So he took your mother and went into exile. We didn't hear from him, not until he came back a year later fatally wounded carrying Gregory in his arms. Your mother had just died. He said he was being followed and he had barely found the time to leave you with the werewolves."

"Who was following him?"

"We do not know exactly as he died before telling us."

"Why did he take Gregory with him and leave me instead?" Was I the unwanted child? Did demons not care about their daughters?

"He knew you'd be safe there. Because of the prophecy."

"What prophecy?" I asked.

"Belle, you are the first hybrid child on Earth and you are mated to me which makes you a target for my enemies. That's the first news Balan gave me or else I would not have accepted Gregory among us, nor would I have come after you."

I wish he hadn't. My life was perfect once, and now it was a big mess I didn't know how to fix. I surely didn't want him as a mate. And I wanted to be back in my pack.

"This sounds a lot of gibberish to me, how do you even know it is true? How did Balan know it was true? What is the source of this information? Is it Tessa, the eccentric priestess? Because I'm not sure of the verity of her tales," I said. I was also careful to refer to my blood father as Balan. After all, he was just a name to me.

"No, Belle," he laughed. "But, I'm thrilled to know you share my feelings when it comes to that witch."

"Lasarus!" I warned him. This was no laughing matter, for Moon Goddess's sake.

"Yes, back to your question, it's no tale. The source is the Moon Goddess herself. Apparently she appeared when your mom was just giving birth to you. She assured your mother you were special and warned your father to protect you until you were eighteen years old."

"That was one question I had in mind; I never understood how you knew I was your mate."

But, was it even true? I kept my suspicions to myself. What if I wasn't his mate? The thought gave me a flicker of hope. But then I couldn't deny the intensity of his emotions, the tidal wave of longing and desire, absolute need and hunger I saw in his gaze all the time. The devil was in love with me; that was no lie. So it was probably true that I was his mate. Good or bad, eventually, I had to come to grips with it. But I was angry, I couldn't help it. The Moon Goddess should have chosen a willing victim; why did it have to be me? I almost wanted to stamp my foot with the injustice of it all.

"I never doubted it. A perfect mate created by the Moon Goddess just for me," he said smiling charmingly. "And a half witch at that, just to drive Tessa crazy," he was laughing. "No, love. I was thrilkfdsaled with the news."

He certainly looked happy.

"Can you imagine all the things we can do in this world, side by side? The reign of demons is coming." Lasarus seemed pretty satisfied with his own sick mind. "I waited till you were eighteen to get you. But you were not with your pack. Imagine my shock when the king of the werewolves fetched you away, refusing vehemently to give you back. He kept my rightful mate away from me," he said as his eyes became bright red, his hair standing like a picket fence, swinging slowly like it was brushed with a puff of spring breeze. "I will kill him just for that offense."

I shivered as his solemn vow pierced my heart. Keith, dead? No, I just detested the thought. Besides, no one was allowed to kill him. Only me at those times when he drove me crazy.

"And here you are, with me. As it was always meant to be."

Yes, apparently so.

"So you spied on me and betrayed the pack, the only family who raised you and loved you? Your father, your alpha, and Sean who trusted you?" I asked Gregory, suddenly aware of all the ramifications of what they'd been telling me.

Gregory kept his silence, still not looking at me. I was getting angrier by the minute. The shy boy I liked in the pack was my twin brother who had lied to everyone. He was nothing but a traitor. He should have let us know; he should have let me decide my fate. But instead, he had manipulated all of us with his secrets and lies.

"Love, it was all for the best. They are not your family. I am, and Gregory is. You should forget about them. You are starting a new life, with me, with us. You are a powerful demoness; you are one of us now."

I didn't want to be. But I kept my silence.

"C'mon. It is late. Time for bed. You'll have more time to see your brother tomorrow. Now it's time to pay more attention to your mate," he winked.

Time for bed? I certainly wasn't looking forward to that despite my exhausted body and mind. I reluctantly got up, once more looking at Gregory before I left. I didn't know how I felt about him. Could I even trust him if it came to that? I didn't know. I would let it go for tonight, just for this evening. Now, I had other things to worry about, like how to keep my mate at bay.

I followed Lasarus outside, embracing the cold night. The night's chilly air was refreshing against my body. I breathed it deeply into my lungs like a man drinking alcohol to drown his fears. I walked hesitantly, wary of what was to come.

Rapprochement

Belle

We headed for the bedroom with Lasarus enthusiastically taking up the stairs and holding my hand tightly. As I had suspected, he expected me to sleep with him in the same bedroom. And I would be lucky if he had only sleep in mind.

"Do you expect me to sleep here with you?" I asked with a straight face. Time had come to have that conversation.

"Of course. That's what mates do," he answered cockily.

"I understand, but all of this is too new and sudden for me. I need more time," I said with a determined face. He needed to know I would not bend, or else I was in trouble.

Faster than I expected, he gripped my face in his hands, his lips settling on mine. I felt his tongue press into my mouth, seeking entrance. With an astounding determination, I clenched my lips tight, denying him what he so wanted. He started kissing a wet trail along my cheeks, and my eyes, and I found his hands reaching for the button of my jeans, trying to undo it. I slapped his hands away. He then maneuvered one of his hands into my jeans and I hit him in the face, hard. He stopped and touched his cheek which was now as red as his pupils.

"Belle, don't do that ever again," he said, his words clipped and cold. His eyes were glittering with anger, getting redder by the minute.

I was scared, but mate or not, I would not yield to him.

"Then next time listen to me. I said I needed more time." My voice had hardened to steel.

"Fine, then go and find your own room," he hissed, pushing me outside the room and closing the door on my face.

Thank the Moon Goddess! If he thought he was punishing me for my disobedience, he was wrong. I was heartily relieved. The problem now, though, was finding a place to sleep. I didn't want to open the doors in the house randomly just to find a demon inside, waking up from his sleep fuming mad at my rude intrusion in the middle of the night. Nope, that wouldn't do. I would have slept on the floor if only it weren't chilly. And asking Lasarus for a cover was not an option. My feet carried me down the stairs, and I found myself out in the street. Subconsciously my feet carried me forward until I was standing in front of the white house again. I knocked on the door and patiently waited for him to answer.

The door grudgingly slowly opened to reveal a sleepy Gregory. His eyes widened in surprise and recognition.

"Step aside brother. I need a place to crash for tonight," I said, yawning, struggling to keep my eyes open. It was better my traitorous brother than my devil mate. It had been a long night, and all I wanted was to feel the touch of a soft mattress beneath my body.

Gregory stepped aside and closed the door without saying a word. He showed me to a spare bedroom with an adjoining bathroom. He left some clean towels, an extra toothbrush and one of his long t-shirts on the bed.

"Goodnight," he said as he closed the door behind him.

I threw myself in bed, relaxing on my pillow, the fabric cool under my cheek. Sleep claimed me within minutes.

I woke up in the late morning feeling much better. I washed my face, cleaned my teeth and walked bare footed towards the kitchen still wearing Gregory's shirt that hung down nearly to my knees. He was in the kitchen sipping coffee and reading a book; he looked up when he heard me enter, his eyes hesitant.

"Morning bro," I said. It was almost weird how easily I had accepted him despite not forgiving him as of yet. I guess that's what life does to you by putting you between a rock and a hard place. He was not Sean, but still, he was my twin, that should count for something.

"Morning," he said. He rushed to get me a plate and a cup, almost spilling his coffee on himself. There were blueberry pancakes on the table and my favorite syrup. I just helped myself, pretending I had the semblance of a normal life.

As I was eating, I looked at him, and I suddenly winced at a memory of ogling my own brother, my twin, for Moon Goddess's sake. What was I thinking? I shivered with distaste. Yuck!

"So, spill," I said as I bit my pancake.

He looked very uncomfortable, shifting in his seat and not uttering a word.

"Look, bro," I said. "I still haven't forgiven you, but I'm willing to try, so you better give me something. Does Sean know who you are? Did he ever suspect?"

"No. Nobody knows. I left just after you did. I haven't seen anybody from the pack since then."

"So I guess you can do an illusion of a wolf too, since you had everybody fooled, including Sean."

"So had you," he said almost in a whisper.

"The difference being I had no idea that I was performing an illusion, dear brother. I believed myself to be a real werewolf." I shot back at him.

He nodded, keeping his silence.

"Why did you do it? Everybody loved you in the pack: your father, your friends, especially Sean. He adored you. And all this time you were just spying on them, on me."

"It wasn't like that. I was protecting you as well."

"Protecting me from whom?"

"Look, there are things you don't know. They are better unsaid for the moment."

"I love this. All of you are hiding beneath this secrecy you conveniently refuse to reveal. I'm bored of you acting high and mighty! For what? For ruining my life? Protection my ass!" I shouted.

"Belle, it is not that simple. And it is not a farce," he said. "Look, Lasarus can protect you far better than your father or Sean. You have to believe me. This is all for your own good."

"Whatever." I shrugged my shoulders. "I don't like him, and I certainly don't want him."

"He is your mate," he said as if that meant something to me.

"I don't care."

"You should know better than that being raised among the werewolves. You can't deny him."

"I know that. Damn it! But I don't have to like it," I said crossing my arms.

"You'll get used to him in time. He's not that bad."

"Lovely, that changes everything. I am already looking forward to the ride," I replied sardonically, rolling my eyes. "Don't you miss them? The pack, your father, Sean?"

"I do," he said. "Of course, I do. But I am not a werewolf; this is where I belong. And once you were gone, I didn't have a reason to stay."

"Of course you did. If he'd only let me go I'd be there in a minute. Werewolf or not, I belong with them."

"He will never let you go, Belle. Don't even try; you'd only hurt yourself."

"We'll see," I said and left it at that.

"What do you do here all day?" I asked out of curiosity.

"I'm just settling in here among the demons. This house apparently was Dad's. It was a mess when I first came in; nobody had touched it for years. I've been doing lots of restoration and cleaning up since then. This was the best I could do in a short amount of time. I still need to paint outside the house."

That explained the mess inside.

"You've done a good job."

"Thanks."

"But then what? What will you do afterwards?"

"Are you the one doing the spying now?" Gregory smiled.

"Maybe," I grinned.

"Frankly, I don't know. Probably Lasarus will assign me some demon work."

"What do demons do?" I asked prying.

"The same things werewolves or witches do. Some human jobs and investments to earn money and then some demon business like protecting the island, infiltration of enemies, inter-species diplomacy, fighting, I guess. The usual stuff."

"Human jobs?" I asked. "You gotta be kidding me, who would hire a red-eyed spiky-haired demon?"

"Haven't you ever heard of the colored lens, dear sis? And spiky hair is all the fashion nowadays," he said grinning.

It was too funny to contemplate and I laughed heartily. I certainly needed a little happiness in my life.

"What happened last night?" he asked concerned.

"Well, he wanted to get to third base, and I wanted to keep him at zero," I said. "It was a battle of wills, and I won, but then I lost my bed, so I came knocking on your door."

"I see." He paused with a stern expression on his face. "You should be careful Belle; I'm not sure how long you can keep him at a distance. He is really not known to be a patient demon."

"Can I stay here till then?"

"Yes of course. This is also your house."

"But what will he do to you for putting a roof over my head?"

"I'm a big boy, Belle. I can take care of myself," he said, giving me a glimpse of the boy I liked at the pack.

"Okay, bro. Let's get to business. Where do we start?"

"Start?" he asked amused.

"With the house paint, of course. Pay attention." I said smacking him playfully on the head. "But I do have a minuscule bit of a problem," I said grimacing.

"What is it, Belle?" he asked, worried.

"I don't have any other clothes nor do I have any money to buy any."

"We do have money, Belle. Whatever our father had is ours now. We can go shopping on the island."

I jolted with the sound of footsteps behind me.

"That sounds lovely, I'm sure. But I'll be the only one to take my mate shopping if that's what she desires."

I turned back sharply to see Lasarus dressed in a black suit, black shirt, and a silver tie, all of which contrasted nicely with his dirty-blonde hair. We hadn't heard him enter the house, let alone the kitchen. He looked handsome, I had to admit.

"I've been looking for you. I'm glad to see you had your cozy brother-and-sister chat," he said. "But I hope you do know that it was for only one night," he warned.

"Why don't you get dressed, love, and we can get going?" Lasarus said.

There was no getting rid of him. I dragged my feet to my room to change, cursing along the way.

"Shall we?" He offered his arm when I came back and I reluctantly took it. Did I have a choice? Not really, not yet anyway.

I looked back at my twin, his face like a stone. The only thing that gave him away was one clenched fist.

The Ball

Belle

Lasarus held me tightly as we walked, and all the while a black SUV with dark tinted windows followed us from a close distance. I turned my head and looked back cautiously a few times.

"Don't worry, Belle. It's just the driver following us to take us to the island's downtown center, or to the plane should you wish to shop somewhere else. You are safe, you are always safe with me," he said, fixing his eyes on me again, his gaze frighteningly intense.

How those words mocked me.

"I see. It doesn't matter to me. I just need a few jeans and shirts." I paused. "And some underwear of course," I added, a little embarrassed.

"Then I shall enjoy shopping with you immensely. I shall have a few suggestions myself," he said with a wink, his meaning crystal clear.

Damn it! This was all Gregory's fault. He should have prepared me for this my whole life, instead of presenting me with a fait accompli.

"On second thought, we shall go to Paris," the Demon Lord said whistling to the driver behind. "You'll need a beautiful dress as I just decided we shall celebrate tonight with a huge gathering and a ball afterward where I'll present you to all the demons on the island. It's time they were introduced to their future queen."

Lovely, just lovely. I felt trapped like a helpless animal. Panic gripped me like the claws of a steel trap, reminding me that there was no way out.

"Fine," I said as I pulled away from him and turned back and walked towards the black car.

I opened the car door. As I sat down, I noticed with relief that the interior of the car was unexpectedly large. I placed myself at the far edge, just next to the window. He caught up with me in a few seconds, lowering his huge body next to me despite the whole vast space, putting his arms around me and squeezing me tight against him.

The ride was not long. Soon we were on the runway where his private jets and helicopters were parked. We headed to a middle-sized plane, where a pilot was waiting for us. The plane took off immediately.

"Uhm. How long is the flight? I don't even know where we are," I said trying to get some information from him.

"It's not long, only a few hours. And I will keep you suitably entertained."

Nope, he had no intention of telling me our location.

The plane was luxurious with its plush carpeting, extensive bar and kitchen areas, a comfortable looking sofa, two coffee tables, large leather upholstered seats and a personal cabin stewardess welcoming us aboard.

"Would you like something to drink?" asked the demoness.

"Belle?"

"Just coffee with half and half milk and no sugar please." I turned to him. "I'd like to visit my family in the pack," I said hesitantly as I was sipping my coffee.

"That can be arranged. Be nice to me and I'll be nice to you," he said as his hands started roaming my shoulders and arms, his eyebrows arching with a silent question.

I clenched my teeth but allowed him free access until his hands started feeling me beneath my shirt. I slapped his hands away. "Behave," I warned him.

He laughed, the devil. "Ok love, tonight then. When we are completely alone in our bedroom."

Then he let me be, thankfully. I had no idea how to fend off his advances tonight but I would think about it when the time came. Right now, I was happy with small victories.

To my utmost delight, I discovered a small entertainment room in the plane which provided me with the excuse to be alone for a while. There were books of all genres on the shelves and some recent and classic DVDs. I found The Lord of the Rings DVD, remembering the last time I was at home. I put it on, not really watching the scenes but reminiscing about the time I spent with my parents; a life enjoyed living among my pack and the pain of imminent separation from everything I knew and loved. I let the silent tears roll down my cheeks as I thought of them all. As the movie was coming to an end, I felt the plane descend. I went back to my seat to find Lasarus speaking on the phone. He sounded so enraged that I took a step back in alarm.

"Find them, unless you want some heads to roll tonight," he shouted. Then, he put a patently contrived smile on his face upon seeing me as he hung up.

"Did you have fun?"

"Yes, thank you. It was great. How about you? Is everything all right?" I inquired.

"All is fine. Nothing to worry your pretty head about. A few glitches, that's all. Nothing I can't handle."

"But about what, Lasarus? And I have no problem worrying my pretty head about it given a choice."

"My mighty pretty demoness! How elated I am that you are my mate. I thank the Moon Goddess every day for this beautiful design of hers."

Well, at least one of us was happy. That should be enough consolation for the Goddess.

"Aren't you?" he asked.

"Aren't I what?" I asked pretending not to understand the question.

"Aren't you happy with me as your mate?" he asked as he leaned in towards me.

It was either lie, which I wasn't very good at, speak honestly and be a target for his rage, or let him kiss me and forget about the question. I decided the third option under the circumstances was probably the safest.

His lips were warm on mine, lingering ever so softly with the touch of a butterfly. We were interrupted by the bumpy landing as we bounced in our seats a couple of times and heard the screech of the wheels making contact with the tarmac of the runway. I smiled at another small victory.

Then I realized he had never answered my question. Instead of me averting his question, he had successfully evaded mine. The devil! I had no choice but to question Gregory when we got back. I hoped that blood ran thicker than water.

Once we got out, Lasarus put on his Ray-Bans to hide his pupils from the humans. The day turned out to be exhausting with him taking me to every luxurious boutique all around Paris, buying me a thousand things I didn't need. He simply didn't listen.

"We want to try the black strapless dress and the high-heeled designer shoes. Bring also a black strapless bra, matching panties, and stockings," he ordered the sales girl who was busy ogling him. The customers were also examining him like he was first class merchandise. I didn't care, which was weird in itself. Why wasn't I jealous? Was something wrong with me? Granted he was a handsome man, but he didn't set my heart racing, not like Keith. Nope, I wasn't going to even think of him. He was eons away, in another lifetime, in another world. And I was still mad at him!

I took the satin dress, the black strapless bra, and the shoes the woman brought and went to the dressing area. The sleek black gown had a sexy low back hugging all my curves at the right places.

"Belle, come out."

I walked outside, barely able to take small steps given the tightness of the dress and the high-heeled shoes.

He was silent for the first time, not even his usual endearment escaping from his pursed lips.

"Leave us alone," he said to the saleswoman as he walked towards me.

He took off his sunglasses, his eyes glowing with the color of blood red, a fire burning in their depths. His iris was darkening with yearning, his gaze devouring every part of my body.

"Tonight, I will enjoy taking this dress inch by inch off your body," he said, his voice thickened with passion nearly beyond my comprehension.

When Hell freezes over, Lasarus!

I turned around and walked back to the dressing booth in baby steps to take the wretched dress off before he gave in to his passions.

When I got out of the dressing booth wearing my jeans and shirt, I felt much better.

He was paying the cashier, not only for the dress and shoes, but also for a few more items that were already packed, the contents of which I was yet to see.

The weather was beautiful in Paris despite a soft breeze. Just after lunch, we went back to the plane and I conveniently dozed off all throughout the flight.

When we got back to his house, he introduced me to two bulky demons. "Belle, meet your new bodyguards. As of tomorrow, you'll go everywhere with them, even to your brother's house," he said.

"But, why?" I asked annoyed.

He didn't answer, as usual.

"I had all your clothes taken to our room. Be ready at eight; the party starts then. I have some business to attend to. "Till then," he said kissing my hand like a gentleman.

I only had two hours left. I looked at all the packages piled up on the sofa. Out of curiosity, I opened the ones he had bought secretly while I was dressing. It was a variety of the tiniest, skimpiest lingerie made of the finest silks and laces, in predominantly black and red. If Lasarus thought I'd be clad in these sexy outfits tonight, surely we had another row coming.

I decided to take a quick shower, after which I lay in bed still in my robe, staring at the ceiling and just contemplating my situation. It all seemed so very hopeless.

The door knocked. Lasarus wouldn't knock, so who was it?

"You can enter, " I said as I rose from the bed clutching my robe tightly at the front.

A demoness of about my age entered with a large briefcase, some bags and a blow-dryer in her hand.

"I'm here to do your hair and makeup," she said meekly.

"Thanks," I muttered.

After an hour of pulling, coiffing, gelling and pinning my hair, she threw her hands in the air. "I give up. It does not stand up. I am dead; he will kill me slowly," she said desperately.

"Uhm, what are you trying to do?" I asked, perplexed.

"He told me to make your hair stand up like a demoness, but it is so soft, it just falls, I just don't know what to do."

"Of course it does. Is he delusional? There is something called gravity." I sighed in exasperation. "Look, just do something nice with my hair and makeup and don't worry about him. I'll make sure he doesn't hurt you," I assured her.

"Do you promise?" she asked pleadingly.

For the sake of the Moon Goddess, she surely wasn't serious, was she? Why would he hurt her for something so trivial and at the same time so unachievable? Nevertheless, I nodded just to stall her rising hysteria.

At five to eight, I descended the stairs in Lasarus's arms; his eyes were glued to me and his hand tightly clasped my waist. My hair was now loosely piled up in a half-bun with a few tendrils escaping to frame my face in wispy curls. Thankfully, he had not uttered a word about why it didn't stand up.

To my surprise, we went outside and got in the black car which took us to the center of the island where a huge crowd was gathered in their best clothes, waiting for our arrival. Small demon children were placed upon their fathers' shoulders to get a better view, others held their parents' hands, enjoying the giddiness and jubilation of the festive air. Adults were humming a song, the words of which I couldn't catch. Lasarus took me to the high platform that was erected on heavy spruce poles. Tossed like sparkling confetti across the sky, the stars blinked above us while the full moon blessed its children with its magical light.

We walked towards the platform and stood to face everyone. The audience hushed.

"Dear all, today we stand here to celebrate the arrival of Annabelle among us, my mate as blessed by the Moon Goddess herself. I present to you all, your future queen," he announced proudly.

A loud cheer erupted from the crowd, chanting, "Anabelle, our queen."

I forced a smile on my face, waved at them, extremely uncomfortable with so much attention pivoted on me.

I was in over my head; everything was moving so fast and I didn't feel as if I belonged here among them, or with Lasarus for that matter.

Lasarus nudged me. "Love, we now take our leave. As we speak, there is an indoor party at our place for the aristocracy."

"Aristocracy?"

"Yes, the first generation of demon families."

Whatever.

We got back in the car among the rallying crowd and went back to Lasarus's place which was now fully occupied with guests dressed elegantly for the ball.

As we entered the house, I saw Gregory wiggling his finger at me, beckoning me.

"Excuse me," I said to Lasarus, unlacing my fingers from his. He arched his eyebrow questioningly.

"I want to talk to Gregory for a few minutes."

He nodded. I walked towards Gregory as fast as I could, given the damn shoes.

"What's up?" I asked.

"They are here. We need to save them," he said.

"Who?" I asked, an impending panic sending prickles of uneasiness down my spine.

The Rescue Mission

Belle

"Save whom? Who are you talking about," I asked impatiently.

"Sean, Joshua, and Daniel. Lasarus has them imprisoned in the dungeons below," Gregory said.

"What?" He clamped his hand over my mouth to halt my upcoming scream.

"You need to get a hold of yourself if you want to help them escape," he warned me.

"Why are they even here?" I stammered. "There must be a misunderstanding. I'll just tell Lasarus who they are and he will let them go," I said confidently.

"He already knows."

"What do you mean he knows?" I whispered, disbelievingly.

"Belle, he already knows. He doesn't care about your old family ties. On the contrary, he wants to destroy them." He sighed. "Look, every minute is of the essence, Belle. Lasarus is not known to be lenient towards his prisoners."

Oh, the Moon Goddess, what did he mean?

"What are you saying, Gregory?" I asked.

"They are being tortured, sis." He supported me as my trembling legs threatened to give out.

"No! Take me to them, now!" I said to him. There was no time to waste, my brother and friends were being tortured.

"Look, we cannot go now, not until the party is kicking. And they are alone in their cells for the time being. We need to be careful if we want to pull this off. Lasarus cannot suspect what we are about to do."

My hands were shaking so badly.

"Belle, is everything all right?" Lasarus asked as he suddenly appeared, putting his hand on my back. I flinched uncontrollably. I could not believe he was inflicting pain on the people I loved while touching me at his will. This was so damn sick!

"Isn't your sister the most beautiful demoness ever?" he asked Gregory, his eyes glimmering with pride and triumph.

"Yes, of course she is," replied Gregory stiffly.

"Come, love. Let's dance. Everybody is waiting for us to initiate the first dance," he said taking me by the hand, dragging me to the dancing area.

It was a large ballroom which was not surprising given the size of Lasarus's house. There were too many rooms to count. The house was also connected to another wing. There were demon waiters dressed in white shirts and red pants, handing out an assortment of hot and cold appetizers on trays as well as alcoholic drinks such as cocktails, champagne, red and white wine, whiskey and brandy. I needed a drink so badly and I gazed longingly at the passing trays, but I needed all my wits tonight if I wanted to pull off this rescue mission.

Lasarus held me firmly by the waist with one hand as his other hand seized my hand gently. We waltzed through Andy William's 'Moon River' around the ballroom. I hated being in his arms right now. I just wanted to rip his face off. I was spinning and rotating on the wooden floor as if all was well with my world when my insides were churning, my chest aching as I struggled to hold back the tears. I was so worried for my brother and friends that I stumbled a few times, barely keeping my balance on the dance floor.

After the song ended, I couldn't bear it any longer. I was about to leave him with an excuse to go to the restroom, but I saw Gregory shake his head vehemently, telling me silently to continue the dance. We danced for two more songs; then we started walking around, chatting with the guests. Lasarus introduced me to everyone as his mate and the future queen of the demons. I just wanted this farce to end as I pretended, smiled and made small talk with all the guests whose names I didn't even pay attention to.

After another hour of meaningless wandering around the ballroom, greeting everyone with Lasarus by my side, forced to listen to incessant demon politics and bickering and stupid demon jokes, I finally got the signal from Gregory who nodded his head. Lasarus was heatedly engaged in a debate on how best to get rid of all the witches in the world when I excused myself for a breath of fresh air and slowly made my way outside the ballroom.

"Where are the dungeons?" I asked Gregory who was waiting for me outside.

"C'mon, follow me. They're down in the west wing."

We followed the long glassed passage to the west wing on the first floor and then descended the winding stairs three floors below the ground level. I ripped my dress up to the knee and got rid of the shoes to provide myself with some mobility. It was getting damper and colder beneath my feet as we went down, the thickening musty air getting harder to breathe. Each level was lit by a white fluorescent light on the ceiling. As we approached the level of the dungeons, Gregory pointed at two guards on duty. They were sitting at a table, eating celebration dinner, chatting loudly.

How were we going to get rid of them, I had no clue. I turned to Gregory, pointed at him and mimicked howling, I pointed at myself and imitated opening the door. His face lit up in understanding, and he grinned. I counted silently, and when my finger was at three, he had already shifted. His wolf was a lot larger and meaner looking than mine, that's why he was to distract the guards while I would find some means to open the cells. His wolf eyes looked at mine one last time, and then he raced past the guards letting out a deep scary growl.

The guards scrambled to their feet and ran after him.

There were several steel doors along each wall. I knocked on the first one to hear a girl shout from inside, "Fuck you. Leave me alone!" I knocked on another to hear another curse. The dungeon was like a five star hotel fully occupied for the season. Wow, Lasarus surely had a lot of prisoners. I stopped knocking on the doors. Instead, I started calling out to the inhabitants, "Sean, Josh, Daniel? Where are you?"

Some muffled shouts came from the third door on my right. I hurried there and shouted their names again.

"Here. We are here," came a weak voice. It was Joshua. Thank the Moon Goddess! Now, all I had to do was break this cell open. How hard could it be? I immediately searched the table where the guards were previously eating to find the keys, but there was nothing. I went back to the cell, rattled and rattled the handle, but it wouldn't open. The cell door looked sturdy so breaking it down was not an option. But I still tried it out of desperation and, as expected, it didn't even budge. The guards could be back any minute now, and I was at square one. I knelt down on the dirty floor, trying to see through the keyhole. What I saw pierced my heart. I was unable to spot Sean, but both Joshua and Daniel were shackled on the wall, their faces almost unrecognizable. Their eyes were swollen and half shut, their faces bruised and cut. I rattled the door again. "Just open, damn it," I shouted in anger, mad at my inferior rescue plan and operation, angry at my failure to help out my friends. I heard footsteps and I realized with dismay that it was already too late. I sat down on the floor, desperate and defeated, but unwilling to leave despite suspecting how this would all end, with me locked in the cell as well.

"Get up sis, I have the keys," said Gregory.

I looked up; Gregory had a key chain with four or five keys dangling from it.

"How?" I asked elated but perplexed at the same time.

"I knocked the guards out. We have a few hours at most to get them out of the island," he said pointing at the cell.

I hugged him tightly and gave him a big kiss on the cheek.

"Come on. We should hurry," he urged me. He kept watch while I started inserting all the keys into the hole one by one until eventually, the cell door clicked open. I pushed it open and walked inside with Gregory tagging behind me. It was a cold, damp cell with stone walls and floor and no windows. There was a small bulb on the wall, sticking from an old loosened wire, dangling almost to the floor. I looked around, but Sean wasn't inside. A glimmer of hope filled me. Perhaps Gregory was mistaken and Sean wasn't on the island.

We went to Joshua and Daniel's side. They looked up and forced open their swollen eyes. Their shirts were torn, their torsos bloodied. What had they done to them?

"Belle," muttered Daniel. "Hello red bird, we missed you," he said, barely audible.

Red bird. That's what Daniel always called me, ever since our first encounter. The first time we met, I was seven. I was following Sean around secretly as he met with a blonde human girl in the woods and I had climbed a tree, placing my butt on the far edge of a side branch, hiding beneath a dense cover of leaves. The peeping session had been utterly unfruitful. The branch I was sitting on had creaked and groaned loudly under my weight spooking the timid girl. First, Sean had looked around, trying to get a scent, but he was too excited with his first make out session to care. In the end, Sean had seized her hand and they had taken off. But I had gotten stuck there on a cracking branch, unable to move, lest it broke, or even call out for help. He and Joshua, best friends at the time, were hunting birds with make believe arrows and shafts when they had spotted me sitting immobile on the branch waiting for the catastrophe to happen.

"Look, a big bird, Josh. It's the biggest I've seen," I had heard Daniel point at me.

"Where, Daniel?"

"Right there, high up on the tree. Do you see it?"

He had squeezed his eyes, trying to make sense of the figure behind the leaves.

"Help," I had then shouted. "I'm stuck here."

They had started laughing. "It's a girl," Daniel had said. "A girl stuck on the tree." And then they had laughed more.

"Are you gonna help or what?" I had asked in a panic as the branch beneath my weight cracked some more.

It was then that Daniel, the most agile of the two, had climbed to my branch, his chest flattened on the branch while his legs were firmly anchored around the trunk of the tree. He had held his hand to me and said, "Grab it." I was so scared at the time that I had just looked at his face. "Come on now, catch it, or we'll both fall," he had repeated. As I grabbed his hand, the branch had finally given in, breaking at the midpoint, leaving me dangling in the air holding onto Daniel's hand for life.

"I won't let you fall," Daniel had said firmly, one hand holding me by the hand, the other seizing me by the elbow and slowly switching his grip from my hand to my elbows and repeating the process until he held me firmly by both armpits. Then in one swift motion, he had jerked me up until we were both sitting on the healthy part of the branch. "Look what I've found," Daniel had said grinning to Josh when we came down, pointing at my red hair. "A red bird."

And that's how I had gotten my nickname from Daniel. Now, looking at them, I couldn't believe these were my friends renowned for their cheery and humorous disposition. And, of course, their loyalty. And that's why they were here, probably to rescue me from the clutches of the Demon Lord. I felt so guilty; it was all my fault that they stood here in front of me, broken and tattered beyond recognition.

"Come on sis, focus. We need to find a way to open these shackles."

"Can't you break them?" I asked hopefully.

"I'll try," Gregory said.

His muscles tensed as he attempted to snap them off. I was getting desperate when I heard Lasarus.

"What's going on here, love?"

A Deal With The Devil

Belle

I turned back sharply, an indescribable anger taking hold of my body.

"This is all your fault, you imprisoned and tortured my friends," I shouted as I felt my eyes get sharper as if the lens on a binocular were adjusted. I felt my hair rise and a warming heat envelop my body. I slowly rose up in the air, my eyes ignited with an abysmal hatred and my heart pumped boiling blood through my veins.

He was shocked, but not in horror. His devilish eyes were twinkling with joy and pride. I noticed a few guests had followed him out of curiosity and were crowding behind him to see the commotion.

"I present to you, my queen, in all her glory. A real demoness," he said proudly, turning back to the small audience, making sure everyone had seen the highlight of the ball.

I was extremely mad. I opened my hands and arms, breathing out fire from all my pores. I threw a fireball right at him. He dodged, surprised for the first time. With a speed I hadn't seen coming, he stretched his arm almost a hundred inches until he could hold the door handle in his grip from afar, dragging it with him as he closed the cell door behind him.

He shouted before we made an attempt to open the door.

"I have Sean, your fake brother, love. You'd better cooperate with me if you want to see him alive."

"Where is he?" I screamed, getting angrier by the minute. If he thought I could control this thing, he was wrong; Keith was the only one who was able to help me. Everything Lasarus was saying and doing, on the other hand, was making it worse.

"Belle, I'll make a deal. I'll let your brother and friends go the moment I mark you. I give you my word. If you want to earn their immediate freedom, then I suggest we do it tonight, love."

"Leave," I growled, the words coming with a voice unfamiliar to me.

"I guess you need some time to think," he said.

I heard footsteps and shuffling skirts as noises and voices beneath the door dissipated until there was only deadly silence.

"Open the door," I said to Gregory who was extremely surprised by my transformation. I gathered he had not gone through a similar one himself. Lucky me, I must have gotten the best of the demon genes.

Gregory opened the door. Everyone had left, including Lasarus. I turned to my friends who were watching me intently, their eyes scrutinizing my new appearance with the interest of a curious child.

"You are indeed a red bird, one who can obviously fly," said Daniel as he curled his lips into a grin and then grimaced in pain. "Owww. That hurts."

I went to his shackles, holding them in my heated hands until they cracked under pressure, freeing them. I did the same thing with those on his feet. Then I repeated the process with Joshua.

"Take care of them while I blow this steam off," I said to Gregory who was utterly silent but nodded.

I went for a walk, or rather for a float, as I glided down the hallway opening my arms, allowing small balls of fire to hit the stone walls. I let the cool damp air expel the heat from my body gradually while breathing in and out slowly, deeply and rhythmically. I circled the damn sub-basement at least twenty times, coming across, many times, the still bodies of the demon guards Gregory had silenced earlier. I felt my body temperature cool off and my feet slowly touch the ground. I definitely preferred

Keith's method of curing me. It brought an immediate response and was definitely more enjoyable.

I went back to the cell. Gregory had taken the guards' half-finished food and drinks which he was slowly hand feeding to my friends, bite by bite, sip by sip.

"We can't leave the island by ourselves, they won't let us," he said.

"I know," I admitted facing the inevitable. "I have to accept the deal. Besides, he has Sean."

"I'm sorry Belle. I should never have let you be captured by him," he said mournfully.

"It's okay, bro. I'm not sure it could have been avoided anyway. As you said, he'd never have let me go."

Gregory didn't deny my words which, we both knew, were all true.

"Don't worry. They're werewolves; they'll heal quickly," he assured me.

"I really hope so." I cracked a smile.

We helped Daniel and Joshua get up, grabbing them around the waist, holding their weight as much as we could as we half limped, half walked, out of the dungeon. Climbing the stairs was a real challenge, I felt sweat drip down my forehead as I struggled to brace Daniel's weight on my shoulders. It was a strenuous journey as the demons let us walk out of the house, not holding us back nor helping us as we headed for Gregory's house. The relief we felt after we made it to the house and lifted them to Gregory's king sized bed was huge and we grinned like little kids who'd accomplished a lot.

"I have to go back there. I need to find out where Sean is, make sure he's okay," I said.

"I'll come with you," said Gregory.

"No, you stay here with them. Make sure nobody comes to hurt them. " I swallowed. "Make sure they are healing."

"But" he objected.

"No buts. I'll be okay. He won't hurt me; you know that."

148

He nodded his head in silence.

I went back to Lasarus's house, my feet felt like lead with each step, but I kept pressing forward.

The ball was disbanded, the guests were all gone, the staff hurrying to clean up the mess.

I saw the demoness who had greeted us the first time I stepped in this house.

"Where is he?" I asked, my meaning very clear.

"My queen," she acknowledged me. "I'll take you to him." Apparently everybody had heard about my little freak show.

We took the stairs to the first floor and we walked till she paused in front of a door and knocked.

"Enter."

"Lasarus, your mate is here to see you," she said.

"Great," he said cheerfully. I entered the room. It was a meeting room. He was sitting around a table with a few of his demons, looking at some documents which he hastily rolled and put aside when he saw me.

"Leave us," he ordered his men. The demons shuffled their chairs, moving hastily, all muttering, "my queen" as they passed me by.

"Belle, I'm glad to see you. I already missed you," he said intensely, rising from his chair. "Have you thought about our deal?"

"Where is Sean? I demand to see him."

"All in good time, love. What is your answer?"

"Fine, you'll have me, mark me, whatever you want to do. But, I want all of them out of the island tonight, and they are to be escorted only by Gregory."

"Done, Belle. Whatever you want. I'll do anything for you," he said coming closer, his hands softly brushing my face. I drew back.

"When the marking is done, you'll feel the same aching need and hunger I have in my veins for you. You'll see," he said, his eyes blazing with fire.

149

"We'll see, won't we, mate?" I said sarcastically. "Now, take me to Sean."

"No. You'll not see him. I don't want him talking to you, muddling your brain. That's my last offer," he said with an edge of steel in his voice.

"Damn it, Lasarus. You are making it terribly hard even to like you, let alone love you."

"It will happen, Belle. Soon. You'll see. Tonight you'll be mine, and you'll be crying out my name in ecstasy. Then, all will fine as it was always meant to be".

I shivered with distaste.

"Why did you do it?" I asked him in a hushed tone.

"You mean capture and imprison your friends? They were snooping around my territory. I had every right," he said angrily.

I winced. I remembered his phone chat on the plane to Paris. He'd been sneaky, secretive. I didn't know he was talking about my brother and friends at the time.

"They are your past, Belle. You'd better accept that. There is no return for you." He paced a little in the room and then faced me angrily, "Your friends violated their rights as visitors the moment they stepped foot on my island, secretly hatching plans to snatch you beneath my nose" he bellowed. "I didn't kill them, did I now? I was quite lenient under the circumstances. Any other prisoner would have been long dead for trying to steal my mate."

"Should I thank you for only torturing them? Their faces and bodies were beyond recognition. I don't even know what you did to Sean," I screamed at him.

"Love, it was just an interrogation, merely a tickle for supernatural beings such as them. I needed to know what their plans were, how many people they had brought with them et cetera. They will be okay; no permanent damage is done," he said brushing away his actions as though they were of no consequence.

I wanted to damage him permanently.

"Say your goodbyes. You didn't eat much tonight; I want you here in half an hour, ready to dine with me, all willing and malleable. Then, only then, will I send my driver to pick them all up. They will take off tonight from the island along with Sean, and that will be the end of that. But know this Belle, if they ever set foot here again, I will show no mercy. So, if you love them, you'd better convince them of your sublime happiness here with me."

I banged the door as I left in anger. I headed for Gregory's place. I had to convince my friends to exit the island and not ever come back. It would be a challenge.

A Tug Of War

Belle

"Belle, you have to come with us," said Joshua. "This is completely unacceptable; your father is crazy worried about you. He does not even know the Demon Lord has you, you know."

"How did you guys even know?" I asked, curious.

"We didn't. When Gregory left, Sean suspected foul play. We didn't expect him to be part of it, of course. We thought he was in danger or something. We followed his scent until we found ourselves on this island. Then to our utter shock, we saw him settle comfortably here among the demons. We've been spying on Gregory for a few days now. And we were doing just fine hiding ourselves up until yesterday."

"What happened?" I asked.

"When we saw you here with the Demon Lord, Sean flipped out. I mean he seriously lost it," Joshua explained.

"We thought Gregory was a traitor. Sean wanted to kill him," said Daniel, averting his eyes from his host.

"Yeah, he simply became uncontrollable. We were unable to restrain him. He threw himself at Gregory. That's when we got discovered. We ran away, but eventually they found us," Joshua added.

Gregory flinched. "I know. I'm sorry."

"Look, what is done cannot be undone. Do you know that Gregory and I..." I said leaving the sentence half-finished as I looked at their faces expectantly.

"Are twins?" said Joshua. "Yes, we know. Gregory told us all about it. However Sean probably still thinks the worst of him since he is yet to hear his side of the story."

"Where is Sean, why were you guys split up? How come he wasn't in the same cell with you?"

"The Demon Lord thought he could get credible information from us by interrogating us separately. Not that we said anything, but the bastard tried hard, I have to give him that," said Daniel, recoiling at the memory. "Anyway, we didn't see Sean after we were taken to our cells."

Damn it. This wasn't going very well.

"Guys, you have to take Sean and leave here."

"We are not leaving you behind," said Daniel, determined.

"Look, I'm sorry for what he has done to you, and I'm not going to justify his behavior. But, he's my mate for better or for worse. I'm slowly molding him for the better. We may be arguing a lot, but you know what they say, there is a thin line between hate and love." I placed a contrived smiled on my face.

I didn't give a damn about the devil, but I had to make sure they didn't know that.

"Belle, you can't be serious," said Joshua.

"But, I am. I'm happy here, and speedily getting used to the demon life. You saw me, I fit in quite nicely with my gorgeous spiky red hair, right?" I joked. "Look, Lasarus's driver will be here soon, so I guess this is goodbye," I said with tears in my eyes.

"Aren't you going to see Sean?" asked Joshua, surprised at my weird behavior. He knew how close I was to Sean. The 'old me' they knew would never let the opportunity to see Sean slip by. It was tearing my heart right now not to do so, but I had no choice. Not really.

"No, Lasarus and I had a bad row as you guys witnessed. I don't want to make it worse. He's rather jealous of Sean," I said. "But I will come and visit you guys quite soon, I promise."

What must they be thinking of me? I was acting like a selfish bitch. But their safety was more important to me than their good opinion. And, thank the Moon Goddess, my friends were nodding in silent resentment. So, I had pulled it off. That was the only thing that mattered.

Gregory told me he'd be back as soon as he escorted them home to the pack. I thanked him and left reluctantly, heading back to Lasarus's house.

I looked for Lasarus in the house. I wanted him to send the driver immediately before he changed his mind. But he was nowhere to be found. I stopped a demon on my way and asked, "Excuse me, where is Lasarus?"

"He is at the dungeons, interrogating, my queen," the demon said.

If he was torturing Sean a little more before he sent him on his way, I was going to rip his heart out. I ran to the west wing, descending the stairs as if I was in a race. Even the guards couldn't stop me as I rushed towards the only open cell door, horrified with the scene that I was witnessing.

There was a girl who had slumped towards the floor despite the shackles that kept her half-standing. Her head hung down, a cascade of dirty blonde hair covering all her face. She was moaning in pain, at times screaming. Despite Lasarus not touching her, fresh blood was constantly pouring from the deep wounds that seemed to appear out of nowhere on her arms and legs. I didn't know how he did it, but he was mind-torturing her!

"Stop it!" I yelled.

My yell ended his concentration, giving the poor girl a breathing space. He turned to me in anger.

"Do not meddle in my affairs, Belle," he said, his temper barely controlled.

"My goodness, look at her. How can you do this?" I asked unable to comprehend the extremity of his meanness. "Who is she? What has she done to deserve this?"

"She is the niece of the Fae King. She just lost her usefulness to me when Derek found you, that's all."

Huh? Was he crazed? I looked at him in disbelief. "What does this have to do with Derek, or with me?" I asked, stunned.

"I captured her so that the Fae King would search your whereabouts and deliver you to me."

"I don't understand! I thought you kidnapped Derek's little brother for that?"

"And the niece of the Fae King, a boy related to the Ifrit King and the brother-in-law of the Nymph Queen."

"Oh my goodness! Are you telling me you captured and tortured all of them so that they would all go searching for me?"

"But, of course. I diversified the risk by making sure that every morning child was on your trail. I didn't bother with the night children, of course. They wouldn't have delivered you to me no matter what".

"And why is that?"

He didn't answer.

"Why don't you just let them go? You have me now, for Moon Goddess's sake."

"Well, for one I'm punishing their kindred for failing to find you."

"Are you crazy?" I shouted. "How could they all have found me?"

He shrugged. "That's the beauty of it, they couldn't, which gave me the freedom to torture the rest," he laughed. "It's so much fun."

"Just let them go, please," I begged.

"Belle, you already used all your bargaining chips for your friends. I suggest you let it go, especially when your friends and that fake brother of yours are yet to depart my island," he said in a warning tone.

Damn it; he had me cornered. I had to let it go for now but I vowed that later I would find a way to free all of them. But the least I could do for this poor girl, for now, was to get Lasarus away from her. So I said, "Well, I thought we were having a cozy dinner?" as I raised one eyebrow.

"We are, Belle," he replied, taking the bait.

"Okay then, why don't we both get freshened up for the night? After all, it's a special evening," I said trying to act sexy, but fearing I failed.

"I believe my mate's right," he said to me, easily lured by my bait. "Let's go then," he suggested, his voice reflecting a sudden rush of enthusiasm.

"And what about the driver?" I reminded him.

He chuckled. "Yes, love, I will send him right away."

"Lock it up for the night," said Lasarus to the guards as we left.

I didn't relax, not until I heard him instruct the driver to get Sean, and then head for Gregory's house.

We went up the stairs together. "I need to get ready," I said.

"Love, I'll be waiting downstairs as soon as you're ready, I'm rather impatient tonight," he said, winking at me.

I hastily locked myself into the bathroom. I would take my sweet time.

"Wear the red mini dress and surprise me with the lingerie," he shouted outside the bathroom door in a rich, seductive voice. And then I heard him leave. I sagged against the wall, letting warm water cascade down my exhausted body. I closed my eyes, wondering how I got to this point of being mated to a creature I absolutely abhorred. I was dreading the upcoming night, but he had me trapped for good. I felt very helpless; I needed a damn miracle.

I went down the stairs in a red mini dress with sleeves billowing to my wrists. With a slit in the front, it was made of a stretch fabric that clung to my body and left little to the imagination. The plunging neckline clung seductively over my bust. Wearing red platform heels to match it, I felt like an alien in my own body. He was sitting at the beautifully set dinner table in the fancy dining room, patiently waiting for me. His eyes roamed over my body as I walked hesitantly to the seat next to him.

"Have they left?" I asked him. I didn't need to elaborate; he knew what I was asking.

"Yes. They took off ten minutes ago, just as I promised you. He smiled. "You look simply gorgeous. I'm very pleased."

156

As if that mattered to me. The waiter filled our wine glasses and started serving the appetizers. Despite the fantastic food, each bite tasted like chaff as the lump of fear and anxiety in my throat grew larger by the second.

"How will you mark me? I asked, shivering in distaste just imagining that.

"We'll just share some blood, then we'll chant some words, and it'll be done; then you'll bear my name on your wrist as a tattoo," he said as he grabbed my wrist and brushed the tips of his fingers back and forth as if tracing the unseen letters of his name.

It was when the waiter came to bring the main course, roasted salmon with a sweet sauce of honey and walnuts, that it happened. My miracle.

A demon entered the room in a frenzy, his eyes searching for Lasarus.

"What is it?" Lasarus asked, raising an eyebrow.

"We're under attack."

Lasarus scrambled to his feet immediately. "Who?" he asked.

"The morning children. It seems they've made a pact."

"How many?"

"Hundreds of them."

As he was leaving the room, he turned to me and said, "Go to our room, lock the door, do not come out until I come and get you." Then he left in a hurry.

That was my cue. I took off the shoes, tearing my dress as I ran up the stairs to grab some suitable clothing which would not hinder me for what I had in mind. I dressed hastily as a mixture of panic and unrestrained excitement charged my body with adrenaline induced alertness. I then headed straight for the dungeons. The two guards were sitting at their mini table as always, chatting. They rose to their feet when they saw me.

"The island is under attack. Give me the keys! Lasarus told me to lock myself in a cell until he came back to retrieve me. Apparently that's the safest place for me to be right now. And he asked you to go up there and help fend off the attack. He needs every abled demon to protect the island," I said, faking a panicky voice.

They stood immobile for a few seconds, uncertainty clear on their faces. But they didn't have any reason to doubt the words of a future queen, did they now? As I hoped, one of them gave me the keys and said "The last cell on the left is empty. Then they both left hastily.

Only the last cell was empty? I had loads of work to do. But thankfully I'd done it.

I started opening each cell door, finding unfortunate victims inside, each one in a worse condition than the other. Somehow I had to break their shackles and, without a key, it would be a struggle. I had been unable to come up with a good excuse to ask the guards for the shackle keys which probably were hanging around their necks. But this time I had a plan and I hoped it would work. As I opened the last occupied cell, I gasped in shock. It was the ifrit child, Kathildon, the king's son. I couldn't believe it. His eyes lit up when he saw who I was.

"Iz yu. Yu here tu sav mi? Plwese?"

"Yes, of course, I'm here to save you. Can you fly once we get out?" I asked, my heart squeezing at seeing him like this.

"No. He is vey baad demon. He cut me wings agayn and agayn."

"How did he capture you? Where was your dada?" I asked as I took off the bobby pin from my hair, straightening it and inserting it in the keyhole of the shackle.

"Ay waz wanting demon blod sauce. Ay was alone. Dada vil be angry. Tey hit me and tie me. Ay want dada," he started crying.

"It's ok, Kathildon. Your dada is here. I'll take you to him, be brave now" I said, as I continued pricking the key, going by feel until I finally heard the click that released the lock. I repeated the process with the other shackle. Thankfully, Kathildon was able to walk.

"Wait for me outside the cell. As soon as I free the others, we'll leave," I told him.

"Okayyy," he said, smiling.

158

I went to another cell; it took me only a few seconds this time to free the man from his shackles. He looked much worse for wear, though; he'd probably been here much longer than the ifrit child. The man collapsed on the floor as he was released from the shackles that kept him chained to the wall. I helped him up as his eyes tried to focus on me. I really hoped the other prisoners were in better shape or else getting them all out would turn out to be a problem. I dragged him out of the cell and left him in a heap on the floor as I repeated the process for the others. As I suspected, there were more prisoners in the cells than just the hostages taken from the morning children. As I was helping the poor girl tortured earlier, her eyes found mine in silent gratitude. Soon they were all out, some in a condition to walk and some barely hanging in there. But, all I had to do was get them out where their kinsmen would be able to find them. I hoped their relatives would give haven to the others as well. We left in a group of ten, helping the weak ones and making our way steadily up the ground floor. I was at the back of the group, making sure nobody was left behind.

It was too easy to escape, everyone was busy partaking in the chaos outside. The house looked almost deserted. Outside was a scene from the movies, pure-blood ifrits were flying and throwing fireballs at the demons who were fighting their way in among the rest of the morning children. The extremely blonde creatures with doll-like faces, whom I assumed to be the fae, were fighting with swords, attempting to hack and cut the demons who were much too athletic to be killed. With their extended limbs, the demons were knocking down the swords while avoiding any skin contact with the enemy. I saw a demon behead a beautiful woman, her head rolling down on the ground next to me, her eyes lifeless, staring back at me. It was then a hand slapped over my mouth trapping my scream as another came to the base of my neck, slightly squeezing. I heard somebody whisper, "Hello, mate." Then it all went black.

The Underworld

Belle

I opened my eyes to a world of blazing fire all around me. I couldn't move my hands nor my feet. I realized I was chained. Was it Lasarus, had he flipped after realizing I freed the prisoners?

"Hello, I see you are finally awake," said a voice that did not belong to Lasarus.

"Where am I? Where is Lasarus? I want to speak with him." I could barely speak. My lips were extremely dry and all my limbs ached from the stretching. I was panicking, what was going on?

"Lasarus?" he asked. "My dear brother cannot save you, little mate."

"Your brother?"

He had shoulder-length black hair unlike Lasarus's blonde locks, and his skin was extremely dark, almost the opposite of Lasarus's luminescent tan. How did he know I was Lasarus's mate? But, more importantly, what did he want from me?

"Yes, his twin brother to be exact."

Apparently twins were quite common these days.

"What do you want with me?" I asked.

"I don't care about you despite what you might believe. I don't give a damn about you, mate. But I want to end Lasarus, and you are the means to do that," he smiled maliciously.

"Mate? I'm not your mate." I said, confused.

"Oh, but you are, little mate. You are," he grinned.

I didn't know twins shared mates; that was news to me! Damn. One psycho wasn't enough; I had to have him too.

"Okay, even if that's the case, why am I chained here?"

"You are chained here because whatever I do to you will hurt Lasarus," he explained. "In the end, I will destroy him."

"Destroy him?" I asked.

"Yes, little mate. I'll kill you, but first, he will know the pain of your torture." He roamed towards me, red flames surrounding his body, the heat moving closer at each step. "I will cut off your fingers one by one, burn your skin, torch your hair and send all your parts to him to savor."

Oh the Moon Goddess, he was mad. I screamed as he came at me.

"Scream, little mate. Scream your heart out," he said as he raised his sword. The last thing I saw was its descent towards me after which I felt an excruciating pain. I saw my thumb fall to the ground like a block of wood, the ground soaking the blood as it poured from the severed nerve fibers. Blackness enveloped me.

I woke up in pain; my body was shivering despite the flames all around me. I was in shock; it didn't take long for me to realize why. Oh, the Moon Goddess! My thumb was severed, I was losing ample blood. With my impaired healing abilities, I would not survive this torture. I was going to die here at the hands of a demon incomparably worse than Lasarus.

"I'm glad you are awake, little mate. I was bored of waiting for you," he said as the sword descended again, I couldn't even scream as I was thrown into another darkness.

I was in oblivion, content to stay there where he could no longer hurt me. Keith was here in the room with me. Obviously, my brain had conjured him to give me some peace. He was standing right in front of me, his hands folded across his bare chest, jeans low on his hips, his beautiful abs all on display. He was absentmindedly looking out of the window into the deep cliff lying below.

"Keith," I cried out. I was so happy to see him one last time.

161

"Belle," he said, suddenly turning his head, stunned. "Where are you? Just tell me where you are and I'll find you. No matter how hard, I promise. Just tell me," he pleaded.

"You can't find me. I'm in hell," I said. "This is hell," I cried, tears rolling down my cheeks.

"Belle, what do you see around you? Who has you? Is it Lasarus?" he asked.

"No, his twin has me. I want to die." I said, defeated. "No, don't go," I yelled as Keith's face and figure suddenly faded, leaving me all alone in the darkness. I couldn't hold on to him, not even in my dream. I woke up, the pain pouring out of my every cell, freshly reminding me of why I kept blacking out. I closed my eyes immediately, I didn't need him to know I was awake, I would not survive another hacking of his. The pain I felt was so severe that I wanted it all to end. I tried to listen to the sound of his movements, but I could only hear the crackle of the flames all around me. I cautiously opened my eyes and then I saw Lasarus's twin grinning.

"Did you think you'd fool me?" he asked as he raised his sword again.

The sight of the sword and the knowledge of what was coming triggered something in me, a boiling, unstoppable rage. I screamed and screamed, my voice reverberating all around me. My hair whipped up, and my eyes gained focus. Flames like his surrounded me; he was looking at me perplexed, his sword yet to complete its full plunge. I rose up in the air, only the metal chains holding me in my place. I forced my mobility upwards as I continued rising, the heat around my body twirling like angry tornadoes, spinning faster and faster. I felt the chains break as I finally rose high into the air.

"Not so fast," he said coming after me, finally overcoming his shock. I felt the brush of his fingers on my arm as I took off in the air. When I looked back, he was coming right after me gliding in space as smoothly as me. So this was a demon skill inherited from this side of the demon family, and I had no advantage over him. I flattened my body, opened my arms and mimicked the flight of a bird. Not only was I untrained in this, but I was in a land unknown to me.

It was desolate, just flames, some mountains with their tops blown off and restless lakes of fire with boiling, seething masses of red-hot lava nurturing their depths. Where were the inhabitants of this place? Was I all alone with him in here with no way out?

I turned left, I was flying so fast I almost crashed on an arch with a sign written in English that read, "Welcome to The Underworld, your discomfort is crucial to us." This was also written in several other languages, most of which I couldn't even recognize. Apparently, they were expecting guests from all over the world. How ironic!

So, I was in the underworld. I looked back; he was coming right after me. I flew straight and saw a humongous castle-like structure built on an outcrop of conical rock rising steeply from the ground. The gloomy structure looked scary with its glassless windows and blackened walls; it was almost high enough to reach the sky. Some demons were wandering around the perimeter, while some were posted on top of the randomly placed columns, remaining immobile as soldiers on duty, as if they were guarding an invisible cell.

"Catch her," I heard him shout as the demons scurried to capture me in the air. I saw several balls of fire hit me in the face; I flinched, expecting to be scorched, but nothing happened. It was like I was immune to the fire. Thankfully, the pain of my severed fingers had also dimmed to a low throb and the blood at the severed ends was clotting. I had to escape at all costs. I dodged to the right and left, blocking attacks from all angles, but so many of them kept coming. I felt one of the demons punch me on the shoulder while another grabbed me from the back with a viselike grip. Then the evil twin came grinning, raised his fist and hit me, knocking me out cold. My last thought before I closed my eyes was that I would wake up with more severed fingers.

My focus was fuzzy as I opened my eyes a few hours later. I was in a cage small enough that I couldn't even move. There were other cages around, some of which were hanging from the ceiling, dangling helplessly in the air. It looked like a dimly lit underground tunnel, and despite the ample heat in the underworld outside, it was cold inside. I touched my face, expecting a huge lump and, yep, it was there. Not that there was much to enjoy in my present state, but I noticed with elation that my two severed fingers were back in their place. I turned my hand around and counted my fingers just to make sure. But how had this happened? I knew not. There was no way I could have healed myself that fast. In fact, I had enough contrary experience in the past to show me I couldn't. Was I able to recover more rapidly in the underworld? I had no clue.

I looked all around me, at the creatures trapped in the cages just like me. None of the creatures I saw so far in the underworld, including those in the cages, looked like your typical demon. For one thing, their hair was hanging down, and everything about them was dark. Their hair and skin color stood in stark contrast to the bright colors that defined most of Lasarus's demons who were known to have red eyes, shiny white skin, and blonde hair. Had the underworld darkened their features? It was weird. Looking at the caged demons scared me good because soon I would be like them, forgotten here like a piece of trash. It was as if life had already abandoned their bodies, their stares hollow and meaningless. What had they done to deserve this? What had I done? The abysmal fear of the future made my teeth chatter and my body shake uncontrollably.

"Hello," I called to them, to anyone.

"They can't hear you," I heard the evil twin say. No, no, no, no! He was here, and I wasn't ready for another torture session.

"You see, little mate, you surprised me with the demonic act. I didn't expect that. That changes things a little bit. Now that I know you can heal yourself and melt things, things will not be as fun."

He was insane!

"But not to worry, I put you in a cage where bars are made of a special steel and copper mesh; it is expressly tailored for you."

I had no idea what he was talking about. He smiled when he saw my blank expression.

"Hasn't Lasarus taught you anything?" he asked. "Copper neutralizes the powers of demons. Or is it that he doesn't trust his own mate? This is rich." he said, his eyes twinkling with mirth. "The light demons lose their ability to heal, focus, and stretch their limbs while the dark demons lose their ability to create fire and fly.

I have to admit you are a weird combination of the two so it has the capacity to do, well, almost everything. Anyway, now this cage will turn you into a human being," he explained. "Let's test that shall, we?" he said as he sent a ball of fire my way. I wasn't able to dodge it given I had no space in the cage to move. It hit me in the arm, burning me so badly that all I could do was scream.

"Yes, it certainly works. Rest a bit for tonight. We'll start anew tomorrow," he said winking at me. Then he turned back and said, "Oh, by the way, Lasarus already received your gifts; your precious two fingers. We'll send him some more tomorrow, won't we?" He laughed heartily as he left.

Tears were rolling down my face; I was in pain, but there was no reprieve from it. I had no painkillers, no antibiotics and no way to heal myself, not that I knew how. I closed my eyes, seeking solace in my dreams. In the middle of the night, I woke up to find my body shivering. An infection had set in, extending up the entire upper arm where my skin was turning into one mass of putrid flesh. My face was permanently contorted in excruciating pain and a shrieking cry bellowed within every inch of my consciousness. I feared I would not survive the night.

Opening The Gate

Keith

I ran to Tannon's room, opening the door without even bothering to knock. The warlock was relaxing in bed, nicely tucked under the covers reading a thick old book by lamplight. He bolted upright, suddenly startled by my unexpected entry.

"She is in hell. She's in fucking hell," I shouted, pacing the room in abysmal frustration, unable to remain still. "Where is that? I have to get her out, man," I said, punching the wall.

"What are you talking about?" asked Tannon calmly. "And, please stop punching my walls."

"She reached out to me from wherever she was. Who the fuck is Lasarus's twin? How do I get to her?" I asked, enraged.

"Lasarus's twin did you say? He is the lord of the underworld. But that's not possible."

"What's not possible? She freaking told me he has her. She wouldn't lie," I insisted, narrowing my eyes.

"No, I meant she couldn't have reached out to you, not with just the half-witch blood circulating in her body. The only two creatures who can do that are Tessa and me, and then only by sacrificing a few drops of the ancient blood pumping in our veins. Even Shea couldn't do it."

"Belle's done that. I don't know how, but she did it."

"Perhaps it was only a dream," Tannon said cautiously.

166

"Look, it was no dream. I wasn't even sleeping; I was looking out the window thinking of her when she suddenly appeared in my room looking utterly forlorn," I cried. "It was real; I know it. It was her," I said, my exasperation knowing no limits.

"Keith," Tannon said patiently as if talking to a small child.

"Damn it, man, I was not hallucinating. It was her; I'm telling you. Are you gonna help me or will I have to tear the whole gate to get to her in the underworld?"

"It's not that easy. You do not realize the ramifications of opening that gate. There is more to it than her safety or your future happiness for that matter. If thousands of the underworld demons manage to flood from the gate, we will be unable to…" He didn't finish the sentence. This was the most I had heard him explain about anything in the few days I'd been staying here. No matter what he said, I wasn't giving up. In the last few days, we had tried a few things to track Belle's whereabouts, but all had been futile so far. This was the best and only clue I had since she disappeared on me.

"I'm not asking you to keep the damn gate open. I just need a few seconds to get in and out. That's it."

Tannon was silent; he seemed to be thinking on it. He hadn't rejected the suggestion outright, and I was happy just for that small concession.

"I don't know."

"Tannon, she is in the underworld! Who knows what she's going through! This is shit, I'm doing this with or without your help," I said as I turned around to exit the room. Tannon's voice stopped me.

"It cannot be done from here. This is the center of the gate's force. Any crack from here will have a domino effect spreading to the rest until the gate stands no more. If this is to be done, it has to be done at the end section, and then only for a limited amount of time."

"I understand, that's fine with me." I nodded. "How do I get there and what do I do?"

"I will come with you to open a small crack and keep watch to make sure no dark demons pass through it until you get back."

"Thank you. I owe you one. A huge one."

"I want her to be safe just like you," Tannon whispered. "Even if I can never be with her."

I understood. "What will happen here? Will you bring in Tessa?"

"No, I'm the only one possessing the magic to hold the gate. I will leave my hawk here; he should be able to manage it for a few hours."

I was now grateful for the hawk's existence. "Ok, let's go. We don't have any time to lose. Just the idea he has her wants me to destroy everything on my way. I'm barely holding myself," I voiced.

Upon his words, Tannon called on his cane which came flying from its place on the wall from the first floor. He then chanted a few words to change the hawk into a solid being. They descended the stairs together, the hawk nestled firmly on Tannon's shoulder. The hawk then flew and took its place in the middle of the room, remaining completely immobile as it stood to wait.

"As you know, we need to enter the door together," Tannon reminded me.

Before I could even ask, "what door," a brass door emerged in front of us. Tannon opened it and we both walked forward as the door closed behind us.

I was surprised to find myself in a vast desert. It was a long distance from the snowy Alps in Switzerland. Were we in the Middle East or perhaps Africa?

"The Sahara," Tannon replied to my silent question.

We walked side by side on the shiny sand. The sun was lifting over the horizon, splashing across the intrinsic patterns of the dunes. Walking steadily, powdery dust billowing at each footfall, all I could see were the mountains of plain sand closing in on us. There was not even one blade of verdure in sight. We trudged through thick sand for some time as the desert got hotter and our shadows became shorter.

"Is the gate that long?" I asked, unable to see the end of it.

"Yes, unfortunately, that is why it's really hard to prevent cracks forming here and there from time to time which bring the underworld demons to the surface."

"Is that how the underworld incursions happened last year when we were heading for the council meeting?"

"Yes," answered Tannon.

I had been surprised by the news at the time. The meeting had been delayed when some species had encountered underworld demons traveling in small groups. I had heard the leader of the shadow spirits had been killed by a vicious attack at night. I'd been sorry to hear that as he was known to be a decent fellow, really honest, brave and straightforward. His elder son, Derek, had taken over afterward, coming to the meeting convened a week later, and had asked the agenda of the council meeting to be changed to underworld demon hunting. My men had not come across any so I'd forgotten all about that incident since then.

"How about now? Is that how this demon captured Belle?"

"I don't know, probably," Tannon said. "He must have found a weak spot in the gate. It needs checking," he said tiredly.

"Why didn't you explain it in the council meeting, Tannon, last year? Why don't you now? Everybody thinks this is the Moon Goddess's doing, that she allows her disowned children to visit the Earth occasionally when she feels reminiscent of the past," I urged. I thought it would be easier to prevent demon incursions if all the species acted on it in unison.

"I don't trust anyone with the knowledge. The Moon Goddess herself gave me the power to protect the gate, insisting that I keep it a secret. If the contours of the gate are revealed, it would enable the possibility of someone greedy exploiting its weakness or making a pact with the underworld. And that would be a disaster."

I remained silent. It was after all a possibility with many species wanting to harness more power. The peace treaty was extremely fragile. As Belle had once said, every supernatural being was hunting another. Damn it! That reminded me of Belle. I had to get her out, and once I did, I would make sure she never left my side again.

"They can feel my magic. I don't want to alert them to my presence before it's due. We'll walk a little bit more," Tannon explained.

"That's no problem," I said, though I felt the sweat trickle down my spine.

Tannon stopped.

I tensed.

"We are at the end section of the gate," said Tannon raising his hand and circling it in the air in a rapid tempo as though to mimic the span of a fluttering fan. Then, a huge transparent wall emerged, rising to the sky all the way to the back and the front as far as the eye could see, cutting them off from the other side of the desert. It was a majestic sight to see the beams of light shooting above them then slam into the wall which reflected a dark, barren land on its other side, lit only dimly by random flames towering in the air. Despite the transparency of the wall, the two sides were like the opposite sides of a coin. The underworld looked like an entirely new world, cut off as cleanly from the desert like an apple bisected in perfect symmetry under a razor sharp knife.

"They can't see or hear us. But, they may be able to feel us," said Tannon.

I nodded in understanding.

Tannon approached the wall, his hand moving along the solid structure as he kept walking, trying to detect the ideal spot for opening the gate. I watched him in silence, restless, his blood boiling for any action that would take him to Belle. I managed to keep still, afraid to interfere and ruin Tannon's focus.

I saw Tannon pause, his hands brushing across the same spot on the wall a few times, his face etched in concentration. His hands checked a large perimeter around it just to find their way back to its center again.

"This is it," he said.

"Okay, let's do it. I'm ready," I said in approval.

"What's your plan?" asked Tannon.

"Simple. Move in, find her, and get out. How hard can it be?" I asked mockingly.

"I can only give your three hours. Afterward, I will seal the door and leave the two of you to your fate which, as you can imagine, won't be fun," warned Tannon.

"I understand."

"Do you still want to do this? You may be locked in there forever."

"Well, at least I'll be locked in with her," I said with a weak smile.

"Okay, move as fast as you can once the door opens."

"Thrilemundo anestro khetrusne thesmus. Lastra bildes lastra denistro lastra seismus. Dontra!" chanted Tannon.

I could see a slight narrow crack opening around the spot where Tannon was weaving his magic. It was not yet big enough for a person to squeeze through, so I inched my fingers down its length to open it wider as the crack grew longer under Tannon's spell. I looked back at Tannon gratefully one last time before I disappeared into the unknown.

Searching For Belle

Keith

I felt the heat of the flames as I entered through the gate, trying to find my way among the billowing clouds of smoke and fog. There was a heavy stench in the air as if this land was home to thousands of decomposed bodies. I dashed around the patches of flames, making my way steadily deep inside the underworld. This was a dismal place, distant and almost quiet except for the sound of burning flames here and there. No trees, no animals. No other beings. It was also extremely dark, with black clouds like midnight, pressing upon us from the sky, creating a feeling of claustrophobia. Though I was running at full speed, I was yet to see a demon. I was getting impatient, after all, I was racing against time. I noticed a herd of blue shades following me from a close distance. I could feel their breath against my skin, but they were yet to take action.

"Show yourselves," I yelled, hoping I could get some answers from them.

The shades continued casting their almost ghostly shadows all around me, the air around me continually vibrating with their heavy presence. I felt their invisible energy; my skin tingled, the hairs at the back of my neck stood on end. I suddenly felt an inexplicable dose of depression and restlessness settle over me, making me question my sanity. It was as if a dark blanket had been dropped to envelop me. I just wanted to retreat into its folds and let it bury me in its depths. I wanted to stop and go back but I pushed on with sheer pure determination. After some time, I felt the air around me change for the better; it was as if the smog surrounding my heart had finally dissipated. I no longer felt the presence of the shades, and I looked back. Their bodies were gliding left and right, but unable to move forward. There seemed to be an invisible border or an impenetrable wall that appeared to hold them back. I surged forward, happy to leave these dark energy forces behind, when I heard one of them speak.

"Wait."

I turned back despite wanting to ignore the voice and its owner with every fiber of my being.

"Help me, and I will help you," I heard it say. The voice surprisingly belonged to a female although the owner looked nothing like one. With a constant blue energy pulsing around it, the shade was shapeless and looked gender neutral.

The others rustled around restlessly and then dispersed like ants as if to avoid any role in this scheme.

Could I trust this mysterious dark force? Did I really have a choice?

"Okay. I need help finding a girl with red hair and blue eyes. Her name is Belle, and your master has her. How do I find her?"

"First, you need to promise to take me with you to the other side."

"I'm not sure I'm allowed to do that," I admitted.

"Do you want to find the girl or not?"

"Yes, damn it!"

"You cannot find her without my help. You would not even be able to locate the entrance. You will be distracted by illusions. I can give you instructions on how to get there."

"Why don't you just show me the way?" I snapped.

"I can't. I'm now allowed to cross from here."

"Then how do you know the way? How do I know you are telling me the truth?"

"All the tormented souls first enter inside to pay repentance for a hundred years. I was one of those. After a hundred years, the souls are given a choice. Either they can become an umbra like me and lose their corporeal body to roam the outskirts of the underworld for an eternity, or they can drink from the Fountain of Lethe, in which case they lose all their memory and humanity, but keep their corporeality. Then they become the new guards and tormentors for the master. That's probably where the girl is."

"Where?" I shouted.

"In the underground cages along with the tormented souls. Now do you understand why you need me? You cannot find her, not without my help."

A burning rage surrounded me. My whole body vibrated with fury, my muscles tightened. My sweet Belle was in the underground cages. I was going to kill them all. But, first, I had to get there. Tannon was probably not going to be happy with what I was about to promise the shade, but it didn't seem as if I had much of choice here.

"Just tell me how to get there. And if you lie, I'll kill you."

"I won't. I want to get out; I have to get out."

"I'm listening. Be quick with it," I said.

"Once you cross the threshold, go straight ahead in this direction for about twenty minutes. Then you will see a large flame, around which you will see three smaller ones. It's the sign of Lucifer. You need to go inside the large fire, it will not burn you, it's just an illusion. The smaller flames though are real. The only way to find the entrance from here is to go through the fire. Or else you'll be wandering around in the underworld aimlessly. That's also how you get back."

"And then what? Where are the underground cages?"

"He's coming. I can say no more. I have to go," said the shade in panic.

"Just tell me where she is, damn it" I cried out.

"I can't. I've said enough," the shade said as it turned around to leave.

"Okay. But you'd better be here when I get back or else I'll leave you behind." I warned the shade as I pressed on forward. Twenty minutes of continuous running and I was getting desperate just when I came across Lucifer's sign, exactly as the shade had described it. The huge flame in the middle was a seething, burning, consuming force that any sane creature would surely want to avoid. I didn't trust the shade. I would survive the burning but the time required for healing would delay me considerably, a scenario I didn't relish. When I took the step that would finally engulf me in flames, I seriously expected to be burned. Just as the shade had said, it was cool inside though I could still see the massive flames surrounding me. Taking the last step which would get me out of the illusionary flames, I found himself standing in front of an arch with a welcoming sign to the underworld. This was the entrance, and the first step was complete. Now I should be able to find Belle or, at the very least, spot some clues as to her whereabouts.

As I entered through the arch, I saw a big dark structure majestically rising to the sky. There were demons around perched like birds on top of steep columns. I could spot ten demons at the very least just watching from above. I needed to capture a demon, but how? Walking in undetected was not an option. Oh well, in that case, it would have to be bloody.

I took off to the entrance of the dwelling which only took me a few seconds with my extreme speed. Nevertheless, I was sure a few demons at the very least had seen me. In fact, I was relying on it. Indeed, I detected their horrific scents as five of them floated in a herd to my hiding place.

"I saw something, I'm sure of it," a demon said.

"We have to let the master know," another confirmed.

I waited to hear the sound of their feet on the ground before I emerged out of my hideout.

"No, you shouldn't. It's bad telling on people," I said as I shifted.

Then I attacked. Within one second I had ripped the heart of one demon, letting his blood splash all over me, while my other held another by the throat, thrusting him high in the air as the demon, in vain, tried to secure his freedom. I snapped the demon's neck, my sharp claws piercing his jugular vein, the demon's sticky blood oozing from my fingers. Then there were three. I turned to them, growling and hissing. The demons circled me in the air, closing in on me from the above, their heads touching, and their bodies spread in the air like newly blooming flowers. I waited for the three to attack at the same time. When they did, I grabbed one's head, tearing it off from the rest of his body, then hit another with the back of my paws sending him viciously to the ground. Before he could get up, I killed him with a kick to the throat. Then there was one, and I needed him alive. As the last demon was making his escape, I held onto him from his feet.

"Not so fast, my friend. We need to talk. Where is the girl?" I asked as I shifted back.

"What girl?" asked the demon, playing the dumb.

"You really don't want to do this," I said as I broke the demon's ankle while I silenced his shriek by clamping my other hand on his mouth. "I can go on forever, you have many body parts to break and organs to shred," I said calmly.

"I can't. He'll torment me forever."

"How about I give you a clean death then, huh? Does that sweeten the pie?"

The helpless demon nodded in a reluctant consent.

"Where is she? Or do you need another reminder?" I asked as my hand circled his other ankle.

He shook his head. "She's there in the underground cage, locked up beneath copper bars."

"Take me to her."

"I can't walk. You broke my ankle," the demon complained. "I can fly, though."

"And you think I'm gonna let you fly? Hell, no! I'll carry you, just tell me where we are going, smart ass."

"The cages are down where the columns are."

"Come again?" I asked.

"The columns are an illusion, a gift from Lucifer himself. You walk inside each column to find that they are stairs going down to the tunnels."

"But demons are sitting on top of them, how can they be an illusion?" I asked, not believing a word he said.

176

"They are not sitting on the column; they are just immobilizing their bodies in the air."

Wow, these demons had a thing for security, that was for sure. I couldn't imagine why as I didn't expect they had many unexpected visitors, if at all any.

"Why so many tunnels?" I said, again rather suspiciously.

"Each one goes to another section in the underground from A to Z. Azazel, the master, is very keen on being organized."

"In which section is she?"

"She is at L section for Lasarus."

"Is there another way out of the underground tunnels once we get in?"

"No."

"First, show me where the L column is."

"It is right in the middle. " he said pointing at a column placed in the midst of it all.

Right! It had to be the middle column where I would be open to detection from all sides.

I looked around, thinking hard. I nudged the bodies on the ground with my foot, looking for a corpse in a relatively better condition, preferably with the head still intact. Damn, I should have known better than to shred all of them to pieces. Perhaps the demon with the ripped out heart would do? But then, the blood all over him would give me away. What to do? I was in luck as just then I saw a demon exiting the building in slow movements. The demon was perplexed to run into me, his eyes widening in their sockets. Before he could do anything, I had already snapped his neck in a clean move.

"This shall have to do," I declared as I held both demons at the back from their collars and walked slowly towards the column, my huge body hidden beneath the bodies of the two demons, one dead and one alive. The darkness helped hide the details from the guards' watchful eyes, details such as one demon's feet not exactly being on the ground or that the other's head was occasionally falling to the side, at least until I supported it again with his hand. Thankfully, no guard paid us much attention.

As I was about to enter the L column head on, the guard became alerted.

"What's going on, Zepar?" he asked. "Why aren't you in your place?" He then looked at me and said, "Who is he?"

Well, I was spotted. This wasn't good. I urged the demon to answer as I squeezed his neck.

"We are heading for the girl's cell. The master sent a healer to look at her condition. We were just showing him the way."

I winced in agony. They were torturing Belle?

The guard's eyes scrutinized me. "How come I haven't seen him before?" he asked, pointing at me.

"I'm new, but I'm the best healer the master's got," I stated. I didn't know how things worked in here and was giving him basic bullshit.

"We don't usually need healers here," the guard said derisively. Then he examined me again. "Your newness shows, you don't yet look like a demon. It's weird how the master trusts a newborn," he said, his voice a little suspicious.

This was not going well. I was getting ready to shift, when the guard finally said, "Oh well, be quick about it then."

Whew, the guard had bought the bullshit!

As we entered inside the illusionary column, I let the corpse collapse on the ground.

We descended the winding stairs down to the last floor. We ended up in a long tunnel which branched out to smaller tunnels along the way.

"Where do we go?" I asked, impatient to get to Belle.

"There is an orderly labeling system here. We just need to get to 'La.' The master arranged every section in here as a library. It is strictly forbidden to misplace tormented souls."

Fuck his master, fuck this red tape business! I was on edge, the intense need to get to Belle driving me insane.

Thankfully, we got to 'La' pretty quickly as it was the first adjoining tunnel on the right. What I saw went beyond anything I had ever seen in my life; there were hundreds of cages dangling in the air with tormented souls occupying each cage, their bodies remaining still, lifeless.

Then we went searching for 'Las' which was another agony in itself. I was slowly shifting back and forth, hair on my skin mixing with the emerging fur, nails curling to claws and then uncurling, as insurmountable anger was taking hold of my body. I couldn't bear the idea of Belle in a cage like this.

We turned right when we came across the tunnel with the label 'Las". It took us more precious minutes to get to "Lasarus."

I dropped the demon on the ground, as what I saw took my breath away.

"Belle," I cried.

The Escape

Keith

I could not believe it, my Belle was in a damn cage, thrashing around helplessly beneath the bars.

"Belle," I cooed.

She was talking incoherently.

"I want it. No! Give me that. Don't take it away. It's gone, where is it?" she said.

"Belle?"

"No, no! Please," she begged.

I grabbed Zepar violently by the collar, shaking him. "What have they done to her?"

"I don't know. I really don't know," he said, scared out of his wits by my spiked rage.

I let him go in frustration which was followed by the dull thump Zepar's body made as it hit the ground.

"I don't suppose you have the key to this monstrous thing?" I asked the demon, pointing at the cage.

Zepar shook his head.

I gripped the bars with both hands. With a growl, I applied pressure on the bars, twisting and bending them, my muscles straining as I finally wrenched them apart. There was so little space in the cage that her body was crouched. She was bleating piteously in her delirious state. I was furious, the beast in me wanted to be

180

let out. I took a deep breath and, slipping my hand under her legs, I lifted her carefully into my arms and carried her out of the cage. She was saturated in her own sweat, and her body was burning with fever. What had happened to her? I recognized her evident pain in the quick flinch of her body after my contact with her arm. I cursed under my breath, wincing at her moan. It was then that I noticed the yellow pus on her arm, the swell of her skin and its fiery red appearance. I softened my hold on her. "I'll kill him for this," I growled, fury causing my powerful body to tremble. I barely held onto my anger as I walked with her in my arms towards the stairway. I would unleash that anger, but not yet.

Zepar was meekly following me, floating in the air.

"I'll be right back, baby," I cocooned Belle in my arms as I softly placed her body on the ground.

"Take care of her while I'm gone," I warned the demon.

Zepar nodded his head vehemently.

I then took the stairs that would take me outside.

"What's going on? Are you done?" asked the guard outside.

"No, far from it," I thundered as I allowed my beast to take over. I knew I was transitioning to the berserk stage this time; I felt the extreme rage flowing through my veins like molten lava. While I was always a dangerous beast when I turned into my vicious wolf, I was the beast of all beasts in my berserk mood, which was, in fact, triggered very rarely. I had found myself at that stage only a handful of times in my lifetime, each time my mind had been blank once the deed was done. I had almost entered that stage when I lost Belle to the accursed door at the coven, but Tessa was able to hold me back by giving me a treat, the quest. There was no limit to the havoc I could wreak or the number of enemies I could kill once I hit that mood. My berserk stage was seconds away, seeing Belle like this had made that inevitable.

"What the hell?" the guard cried before he attacked. The remaining guards became alerted to the situation when they heard the sounds of fighting. I didn't care; on the contrary, I relished the physical fight to cool off my boiling blood. The last sane thought I had was of Belle as I saw the others fly towards me. Then I went berserk. I didn't remember anything about the fight as I later looked at the mess I had made on the ground: ripped off organs, smashed faces, torn limbs, blood spurting forth copiously from severed bodies. The desolate ground was completely painted with the color of vibrant green. I had killed all the guards. Knowing this made me feel much better.

I descended the stairs that would take me to Belle. When Zepar saw me, my skin smeared with blood, my eyes still unfocused from the haze of madness, he crouched in the corner, shaking in his boots.

"Give me your shirt," I ordered.

Zepar took off his shirt, trembling.

I cleaned myself up as much as I could. When I was about to lift Belle into my arms again, I heard the demon speak, his voice shaking in fear. "What about me? You promised." It was evident that when it boiled down to a choice of quick death versus an infinite torture session with the master, the demon had a clear preference.

I turned back to him, just nodding my head, still unable and unwilling to form any words in my present state. I walked steadfastly towards the demon, stopping one step away from him. Zepar took the last step, bowing his head in submission.

"Are you sure this is what you want?" I asked, finally able to speak. "What will happen to you once I do this?" I had no clue what happened when dark demons died again.

Zepar nodded. "I will cease to exist," he said.

Whatever, it was his choice.

I made it quick, as promised, and the lifeless body of the demon fell silently on the ground. I grabbed Belle's body. We exited the tunnels easily as there were no guards left to tell the tale outside. I started running. I didn't know how much time I had left but assumed it to be just over an hour. We would make it, and then Tannon would heal her and everything would be just fine. I was sure of it.

Thankfully, she had stopped struggling in my arms. Her eyes were open, looking at me. The frenzy that had possessed her seemed to sink into the labyrinth of a feverish confusion which made her less wild and restless. Or, was it my presence that seemed to soothe and calm her? Did she know I was here, that I had come for her, that I would take care of her now? I hoped so. I kissed her softly on her hot forehead as I came back to Lucifer's illusionary flame. I hesitated for a second, afraid to endanger her. What if it was no longer an illusion? What if they were alerted to my presence and discovered the bloody mess I left behind? What if Azazel had the power to alter Lucifer's illusions? It took every ounce of strength I could muster in my body to move forward towards the flames with her still in my arms. The need to protect her was so strong that it overrode any rational thought, such as this being the only damn choice. My step was small, hesitant at first; my plan was to retreat fast in case my leg burned. Thankfully, the illusion seemed to hold. I then rushed forward with full force. I still had the time but I wanted to take no chances with the gate. I wanted Belle out of this place, and I wanted it fast. I would then start anew with her; I would make it up to her for everything she had to suffer.

Once I came out of the flames, I didn't stop running until I came to the threshold that separated the edge of the underworld from its inner parts. Where was that damn shade? I would leave with or without her, that was for sure. I wasn't waiting for anyone. I felt her presence right next to me as emotions of desperation, sadness, and helplessness suddenly swirled inside me.

"Stop it!" I shouted as Belle's sudden moan tugged at me.

"Stop what?" asked the shade.

"The darkness you bring with you. You're like a deadly virus; I won't have it. She's already suffering," I warned the shade, barely holding onto the faith that Belle would make it. I felt as if she was dying, as if she was about to draw her last breath in my arms. The feeling of desperation gripped the fiber of my being, making my vision blur. She wasn't faring any better, big tears were dropping from her eyes, rolling gently down her cheeks. Her eyes, once feverish, now looked dejected. The muscles in my legs seemed to turn into mush at each step. When I had entered the underworld, I had found some reprieve from this darkness as the shades were withheld at the threshold. But now the desperation that surrounded me surged forth, viciously taking a crack at my once impenetrable veneer as it exploited my fears and worries for Belle.

"That's my burden, I can't help it," said the shade sadly.

"Then keep your bloody distance!" I roared. Belle began to struggle in my arms. The damn shade was getting to her. My lips brushed hers like a butterfly fluttering over her lips. "Shh, baby. It's all right. You are safe now. I'll never let you go," I said as I attempted to soothe her fears. We had made good on time, and we were almost there. I could see the wall stretching a hundred meters ahead of us. We would make it.

"Tannon," I shouted. "Where are you?" There was silence.

My eyes frantically searched for the gap in the wall. Where was the opening in that damn gate? "Tannon!" I yelled again. I didn't care who else heard me.

The crack had widened enough for my huge body to pass, and a gap that large should have been visible. Had Tannon narrowed the opening afterward to reduce the number of demon trespassers? I didn't know but hoped it was why I couldn't see it.

I put Belle on the ground and walked towards the wall. Despite the transparent outlook of the wall, it didn't reflect anything from the other side. I put my hands on the wall, searching for what my eyes failed to see. Then, I cursed at what my fingers felt: a fracture in the wall. I crouched down on my hands and knees to examine the small fragments of the chipped wall which stood scattered on the ground. I just stood there, unable to come to grips with the reality. It was so unacceptable that I shook with the ramifications of it. This was where the crack had been; there was no denying it now. Tannon had sealed the gate before the allotted three hours, condemning us to a life of eternal hell!

"Damn you, Tannon" I shouted as I looked at my beloved who lay helplessly on the ground. How was I going to save her now?

Tannon

Tannon

As soon as Keith disappeared from the magically opened gate, I took a war stance; I stood solidly, my legs apart, my body tense. I fixed my eyes on the opening while I held the cane firmly in my hand, ready to fight any demon who attempted to cross from the other side. The sun was high up in the air, burning my skin. I still didn't know why even tried to open the gate which I'd made it my life mission to guard. My brain rebelled at the thought of what I was doing, but my instincts screamed at me to save Belle. Was it because she was also my mate? Or was it something else? I didn't know. When the first hour passed peacefully, I began to relax. I thought perhaps this would not be so hard after all. Then I heard their voices.

"Hey, look at this. The wall is cracked open! Tell the master!"

"You're right. We can all get out," the other said.

I would have to go in. I squeezed my body through the opening I had created with my own hands.

"Hello boys," I called out to them to get their attention. They were not demons; they were energy forces. I had heard about them but had never seen anyone like them before. I examined them with the interest of a scientist. Their presence fascinated me. I lived for knowledge, my thirst for it knew no depths but unfortunately I didn't have much time to study them. There was a vapor of darkness hanging around the two forces, spreading thinly as they floated in the air. The darkness around them was stretching to envelop me, which is when I flicked my cane around a few times and chanted "thondra" to disperse the vapor. The moment it evaporated, the shades bent over in agony, their screeches of pain turned into a pathetic whimper until their bodies of energy first became immobile, and then vanished into thin air.

This was an interesting finding. I had no clue that the darkness around them was their life source. Good to know. I stepped outside again, preferring the sunlight to the dark gloominess inside. Another half an hour passed without a notable event, but then I heard a crack in another section of the wall. The wall was weakening, causing fragmentation in other parts. This was what I'd been afraid of from the beginning. Now that the process had started it would get much worse with each passing minute. I went to examine that section. I closed my eyes, a look of stern concentration on my face.

I shifted the cane back and forth in the air like a spider weaving its net and, soon enough, the crack in the wall began to fill in slowly until it disappeared completely. Then I went back to check the original opening, the gap that was barely big enough for Keith to pass now had widened to one and a half times its original size. I really hoped that Keith would come earlier than expected, and we would all be done with the underworld once and for all. I closed my eyes again. The gap in the gate narrowed considerably as I chanted, but did not close altogether. I preferred it that way, opening the gate from scratch without dismantling the whole protection spell was an incredibly difficult task, and I didn't want to risk the whole wall collapsing all at once. I hoped I wouldn't live to regret this decision.

In the next hour, I saw several more cracks forming along the wall, and I had to end the life of five more energy forces which came at me all at once. They circled me, rotating around their orbit faster and faster. Too late I realized, their weird dance sped the cumulative vapor towards the center where I stood. When it was about to hit me, I hesitated, my cane paused in midair. That hesitation cost me; I personally experienced the influence of their power when thoughts of the darkest corners of my mind surfaced, bombarding me with unimaginable fears and doubts. "No!" I yelled, flicking the cane, which felt like it weighed tons, and uttered the vital word which was as hard as if it rolled from a swollen tongue in my mouth. Then I voiced the chant more forcefully until all the shades disappeared.

All in all, I couldn't complain. In the end, if Keith had managed to find Belle, all this effort would be worth it. What would happen when I saw Belle? I had warned Keith to keep her away from me, but now that would be inevitable. I had to deal with it somehow; there was no other way. I didn't have any room in my life for a mate when I was destined to guard the gate.

Suddenly, I was seized with an indescribable pain. It was like a hole had opened up in the middle of my soul, and my cane flew out of my hand and landed on the ground twenty meters away from me. I rolled on the ground, out of breath trying to understand the source of this pain. Who was powerful enough to bring me to my knees? I turned my head to find the origin of this magic, but the desert stretched on around me with no one in sight. The pain was so excruciating; I felt I was going to lose consciousness. I tried to crawl on my hands and knees, but with each step, I felt terrible agony throughout my body. What was happening? I didn't know, but I had to get to my cane before all went black. I felt I was dying; my magic was fast leaving me like dust particles dispersing in the wind. A feeling of desperation seized me; I would fail Keith and Belle but, more importantly, I would fail the Moon Goddess.

I crawled up one step more just to simply lay there, exhausted and almost concussed. A few minutes later, I tried to get on my knees again. With sheer determination, I took a baby's crawling step and then another and another until I felt the cane was within my reach. I cried for the first time in a thousand years. What would happen if I lost my consciousness before I sealed the door? What would happen to Keith and Belle if I did? What would Tessa do once I was gone? I extended my heavy hand and clutched the cane firmly, pulling it towards me with all my might. Unfortunately, I was no way done. I still had to seal the gate.

"I'm sorry, Keith," I muttered under my breath. I searched my magic deep down, drawing upon it like water from a dark well, and chanted, "Thatcha kendist granh. Manthra yur manthra dankki." Every magical word took its toll. I could no longer stay awake. I was exhausted and numb from pain. I commanded my lips to form the last three words, "Manthra gruns sin." Nothing happened. I punched the ground feebly in pent-up frustration. Not only the gate stood open, but I felt the whole wall was cracking. My magic was wavering, how would it even hold after I lost consciousness? I used my last bit of energy and magic to shout once more the last three words that would complete the deed, "Manthra gruns sin." The last thing I saw before my body gave up the fight was the slow sealing of the gate.

***

Tessa screamed with an anguished cry as she felt her twin's life and magic fading. "Tannon!" she cried. Then she fainted…

Trapped

Keith

"What's going on?" asked the shade after witnessing my tormented outcry.

"Nothing much, we are fucking stuck here, that's all," I said furiously.

"But you promised," stammered the shade. "We made a bargain."

"Shut up," I bellowed. "Do you think I planned this? She's fucking sick, can't you see that? Do you think I wanna be here? That I want her to be here, huh, do you?" I punched the wall over and over again, but I couldn't even make a dent on its surface.

Belle would die; I would not be able to save her. She couldn't heal herself and I couldn't heal her. I deserved this; this was the Moon Goddess's punishment for hurting Belle, for denying she was mine. An eternal life in the underworld would be nothing compared to the anguish of losing her. And I would lose her, it was a fact, how else could it end? I felt as if the doors of my own private hell and damnation were closing in on me, consuming me, eating me from the inside out. I was losing it. I suddenly shook from my haze. "Keep your distance, or I'll kill you," I shouted as I realized that it was the shade who was poisoning my mind and muddling my brain. Self-doubt was the last thing I needed right now if I wanted to save Belle. And, I needed that damn shade far away until I found a way out of this situation.

The shade began to whimper in a far away corner. That suited me just fine. I bent on the ground next to Belle. Her face was hot to the touch. I examined the spreading infection with dismay. The swelling on the arm was getting worse. She was tossing on the hard ground, groaning and moaning. I didn't exactly know what to do, but I had to do something. She couldn't heal herself, that much I knew. I could think of only one thing, and I hoped that it would work. I half shifted until I felt my sharp paws emerge, then I cut the wrist from the inside out using my claw thumb, and then held it to her mouth as blood dripped from it. When she turned her head, I held her head firmly, pressing my wrist to her mouth, forcing my ancient blood into her bloodstream. She wiggled trying to get free from my grasp, but I was relentless, not stopping until she swallowed large doses of my blood.

"Just take it, baby, C'mon now. A little more," I soothed her with a caressing tone.

She looked at my face in confusion but continued to drink my blood. Then she closed her eyes, her body simply exhausted from fighting the infection. I sat down next to her, gently slid my arms under her sleeping form, and lifted her. I placed her head softly on my chest while wrapping my hands around her. Holding her like this, her body nestled within my enfolding arms where it belonged. I felt my heart give a thud and a stream of warmth filled me. I placed my chin on top of her head and a feeling of protectiveness swelled inside me as I felt tremors shake her weak body. "It's okay. You'll be fine, just fight it," I begged her, as if she could control what was happening.

"Damn it," I then said in frustration. I had to come up with a plan; we needed to survive in here until I found the means to get them out. Hanging out here on the outskirts seemed to be our best option so far. It was rather isolated but, most importantly, the wall was here, our only way out of this hell. The Dark Lord of the underworld would be after us as soon as he discovered the dead demons and found Belle gone. We needed to hide somewhere. Having the shade as an ally didn't seem such a bad option anymore as she would know where to go and we could get help from her friends, if she had any of course.

"We need a place to hide," I said.

The shade was crouched in the corner, cradling herself like a baby. She looked up. "What?" she asked, her voice shaky.

"Where can we hide? They'll be coming for us. I need her safe."

"We can hide in the caves, but…" she said, pausing.

"But, what?"

"But, eventually they will find us."

"Not if I can help it. I will die before I let anything happen to her, and I'm pretty hard to kill."

The shade got up hesitantly, wondering what to do.

I understood her hesitation. Tagging along with us no longer had its rewards; we were as good as stuck in here. Needless to say, the risks of being a traitor were as great, if not greater. I waited for her to decide. She bowed her head in thought. When she finally looked at me, there was a touch of determination in her eyes, even the dark aura around her had lightened with the gleam of a hidden spirit.

"Have you decided?" I asked a little impatiently. Every minute we wasted out here in the open put us all in danger.

"It's this way," she said as she took the lead.

"What's your name?" I asked.

"I'm an umbra. We don't have names here."

"What was it before?" I insisted, exasperated.

"Shana. It was Shana."

"Shana it is. I'll follow from a distance to protect her." I didn't finish the sentence. I didn't have to. She knew what I meant. She nodded.

We followed a trail along the wall, then we bore left to arrive at rock formations alongside the rugged mountains that jutted up into the black sky with flames all around us.

"There is a cave a little higher up, but its entrance is hidden by other rocks, so it may be harder to detect."

"Fine," I consented. I shifted. I needed my full strength to secure Belle's body with one arm while climbing with the other.

The entrance of the cave was low and the many boulders scattered around its entrance kept it well hidden from the prying eyes below. It was our best option for now.

Inside the cave it was dark. While I had good sight in the dark, I was glad Shana's blue energy lit it reasonably well as we explored the inner parts as I didn't want Belle to be scared. The narrow winding passage led us to a high arched vault. This was also the dead end, which was bad news. Should the demons find their way to the entrance, we would be fully trapped here. I lay Belle on the ground; she had been sleeping the whole time on the bumpy ride, and I was getting worried. I touched my hand on her forehead; it felt cool. I frantically looked at her arm; the swelling seemed to have disappeared; the infected flesh seemed to have turned into standard color and there appeared to be no trace of decay in the healthy tissue that replaced it. I pulled up her shirt to feel the skin on her stomach, to look at the flush of color on her body. Was I fooling myself in thinking she was healed? As my large hands splayed on her belly, I was slapped across the face.

"I told you no, Lasarus," she said.

"Belle! Are you okay?" I said, worried, not heeding the slap.

"Keith? Is that you?" asked Belle, as her hands moved to my face, her fingers touching and probing my facial features in the darkness.

"Yes. I'm here."

"But how? Oh, the Moon Goddess!" she cried as she remembered. "Where am I? Lasarus's twin, where is he?" she said in a panic as she tried to sit up.

"It's okay. You're safe now. He's not here. But, we are still in the underworld," I explained regretfully. I felt her hand clutch my arm tightly in fear. "I'll find a way to get you out. I swear it," I promised, holding her. I didn't know exactly how to behave around her. I wanted to hug her, kiss her senselessly. But we hadn't parted at the best of terms, and she had no idea about the prophecy. She didn't exactly know I was her mate along with all the others. And, after denying her so many times, how could I even claim her as mine now? That would sound so dishonest. How could she ever believe my sincerity? I felt extremely helpless. I would have to give her more time to forgive me and grow to love me.

"How are you here? What happened?" Belle asked. "The last thing I remember is the cage and *him*," she said shuddering with the memory.

"You came to me. You told me you were in hell, that Lasarus's twin had you."

"What? But that was a dream. How is that possible?" she asked, astounded.

"I don't know. Tannon thought that was impossible, too. He said you wouldn't have the abilities to pull such a clever trick," I said. "But I convinced him otherwise, and he opened the gate of the underworld for us. And here I am."

"You came for me?" asked Belle, slightly surprised. I didn't like that at all.

"Love."

"Don't you dare call me that!" snapped Belle.

That made me wince. But, one thing was sure, my Belle was back with all her fury.

"Look, I'm sorry for what happened between us," I apologized, as a loud helpless growl escaped my lips. "You didn't let me explain. I ran after you, but you just disappeared."

Belle cut him off. "No, I mean I don't want to hear that cursed endearment in my life ever again. Lasarus said it enough times, believe me. That should last me a whole lifetime, thank you very much. Find your own damn endearment," she said. "And your belated apology and explanations can wait a little longer, at least until we are out of here."

Upon hearing the demon's name again, I remembered why I was slapped in the first place. "Lasarus, what the hell did he do to you? Were you with him? Did he touch you? I'll kill him," I bellowed.

"Calm down, wolf boy," Belle said. "I'm more scared of that devil's twin than either Lasarus or you right now." Then she noticed the shade's presence who was timidly watching us from the corner. "Who are you?" Belle asked, surprised.

"I'm an umbra," she said as if that explained anything.

"Her name is Shana," I explained. "I don't exactly know what she is, but she's with us. Just stay away from her," I warned.

"Why?" asked Belle, narrowing her eyes.

"Because she is cursed with some darkness. It will affect you," I replied trying to explain it as simply as I could.

"I see. Hello, Shana," Belle said to the shade, smiling. She looked as if she had no idea about this darkness thing, but she let it go.

"Thank you," murmured Shana.

"How did I heal?" asked Belle, suddenly remembering the fire ball. "Did I heal myself?"

"You can't heal yourself, did you forget, baby?" I said. Was she having gaps in her memory, I wondered.

"I actually did when he cut off my fingers."

"He did what?" I said, breathing deeply in and out. "I'm going to torture him for eternity, cut off all his parts one by one and then repeat this cycle until the end of life." I got up to pace like a grizzly bear in a cage. He had hurt my mate badly; weirdly his own mate too. My beast wanted his blood. I wanted it now. But my priority was to get Belle out of this hell. I would be patient; revenge would have to come later.

"Then how did I heal?" Belle asked again.

"I gave you my blood."

"Yuck! You fed me your blood?"

"Well, it worked, didn't it? That reminds me, I should feed you some more."

"No, I'm fine. Really," said Belle, as she held her hands to hold me off.

"Belle, you've been starved, infected, fevered. This is the only way I can keep you strong and healthy."

"But, I feel fine, okay? I swear I'll drink it if I get worse," she assured me quickly. "So why are we here, why can't we use the same gate to get out?" asked Belle, agitated.

"Because it's closed. And we are cut off with no way to communicate with the other side."

"But, then, how will we ever get out?" asked Belle, trying very hard not to cry. She bit the inside of her cheek rather brutally and swallowed continuously but one tear just slipped beneath her control and found its way down her cheek. The possibility of being caged and tortured again simply terrified her, no matter how brave she pretended to be.

"We'll find a way, just trust me," I assured her as I moved to wipe the tear away, my fingers brushing her cheek tenderly. I was churning inside with the instinct to love and protect her. Damn all the waiting and the subtleties of flirtation! My arms had a mind of their own as they closed around her. I then tipped up her chin and lowered my mouth towards hers slowly, giving her plenty of time to push me away. She didn't. My lips teased over hers and I feathered them with the softest caresses. It was her who put a stop to my praiseworthy efforts of going slowly as she suddenly grabbed my head, her fingers clutching my hair while she yanked me towards her and parted her lips with a ravenous hunger to meet the thrust of my tongue. The kiss suddenly went wild, a raw hunger claiming us both. Her taste was so sweet, so intoxicating that I groaned helplessly, I couldn't get enough of her. I ached to touch every inch of her delectable body. It had been too long; I wanted her too much. I had denied myself too many times. No more; she was mine! The need to mark her was so great as my lips traced a path kissing and nipping at her flesh along the hollowness of her neck, steadily moving towards the pulse fluttering beneath my fingertips. But I pushed back that urgent primal need; the moment was not right. We needed to talk first. But not now, I thought rather quickly. Now I needed more of her.

My lips slanted over hers again as I kissed her fiercely, devouring her with rough sweeps of my lips and strokes of my tongue which drove her into submission, her body quivering with the desire I unleashed in her. It was almost as if I couldn't kiss her long enough or deeply enough. My efforts to kiss, suckle and taste her were frantic; I was simply helpless against the frisson of heat passing between us. Our moans mingled in the cave. She also wasn't making it easy on me as she moved restlessly against me,

195

her fingers relentless on my body, her skin feverish against mine. My control was on a razor edge.

Footsteps echoed in the cave. It took a few seconds for my brain to function. I immediately let go of Belle, pushing her behind my back as my unquenched passion still pounded the blood through my heart. I'd done it again; I had lost touch with the whole world when she was in my arms. I cursed at letting my guard down in the enemy territory when I needed to keep her safe. I saw the entrance of the vault suddenly fill with at least twenty creatures all with swords in their hands. Damn my passion!

"Umbra, you did a good job bringing them here," said one of them, moving forward. He held himself with the confidence of a leader.

I turned to Shana with a murderous look. That timid, innocent looking shade had betrayed us!

"I will kill you first," I vowed, glaring at Shana, my eyes blazing with fury.

The Resistance

Belle

"I would ask the rest of you who you were, but I see no need to be on a first name basis here as I intend to kill you all," growled Keith, one of his hands keeping me safely tucked behind.

"That would be foolish. We're on the same side here."

"And what side is that?" said the one in the front.

"The side against Azazel."

"Who the hell are you?" asked Keith.

"We're the resistance," he said.

"Explain," ordered Keith.

"Azazel has an alliance with Lucifer. One in every five souls that go to hell are sent here to be punished and then turned into dark demons unwillingly. Lately, a lot of supernatural creatures are being intercepted from Earth and forced to drink from the fountain of Lethe to forget their identities. They are not even demons! We try to free tormented souls from the cages, but it is a challenge. He's got hundreds of newly born dark demons every year, all willing to do his dirty job. We fight to overturn his rule."

"What?" croaked Keith, stunned.

I was trying to wrap my head around all that was being said in here, but I was as shocked as Keith. Newly born demons, a pact with Lucifer, kidnapped souls! This was all too much.

"Are you telling me you're fighting against Azazel, here in the underworld?" Keith asked.

"Yes."

"And how many have you got in this resistance force you claim?" inquired Keith.

"Almost three hundred. We'd be much higher in number if some of the umbra joined us. We've been trying to convince them for some time now. They live here on the outskirts because they have refused to do his bidding. But their loyalties lie with him. They are all mindlessly scared. I'm glad you changed your mind," he said, smiling at Shana.

"I didn't know where else to bring them," stammered Shana.

Okay, so this was not a betrayal. Keith's whole body was still tense and alert, but he had stopped restraining me. That was good because the heat of his body was making me woozy, and I was having a hard time coming back from the unbridled passion I felt a few minutes ago. I moved forward to see the faces of the rebels. Indeed, some of them didn't look like dark demons at all. The one who'd been talking so far had curly brown hair and the one behind him could easily mingle with Lasarus's team.

"Are you a shadow spirit?" I asked, addressing the one doing the talking.

'Yes, I was kidnapped. How did you know?" he said as his features softened.

"You look like Derek," I said. Thank the Moon Goddess I stopped myself before I said more as my monster growled beside me. "How do you know Derek?" Keith blurted out, all his muscles tensing.

"Well, he was the one who captured me for Lasarus."

"I'll kill him," he murmured, his voice too low to be heard. But I caught it.

"I'd rather you don't do that. I happen to like him."

He tensed even more. The muscles in his jaw flexed as he fisted his hand through his hair. "He's not your mate," he said.

"Neither are you," I stopped him. "Can we do this later?" I said to him sweetly. What was wrong with him? He was acting all crazed.

He punched the cave wall as if gut wrenching emotions assailed him. He angled his head towards me, his eyes hot with overwhelming helplessness and frustration, but didn't push further. "Fine, we'll save this conversation for later, but *sweetheart* we will have it," he said.

When we turned to the rebels, they were all watching us curiously.

"So, I'm Oliver. And if you are ready, we should get going, it's not safe here," the shadow spirit said, his eyes mischievously twinkling. Great, we'd made a spectacle of ourselves!

"Where?" asked Keith as he grasped my hand firmly. He had immediately transitioned to his warrior mood, all his senses sharpened and on alert.

"We have an underground city. We've been digging and carving it for years. Azazel does not know its location. We'll be safe there. It's close by."

An underground city in the underworld, was I the only seeing the irony here?

"Sounds good," Keith said. He turned to me. "Babe, I'd better feed you some more blood, I'm not sure you are strong enough to travel as of yet."

Was he kidding me? No way was I going to take his blood again. "I'm fine. I can even float," I joked. And just as I said that my body started rising again as if triggered by my command. This had never happened before; my demonic state had always been uncontrollable, appearing out of nowhere when my emotions were overwhelming. In fact, I had been extremely enraged on the three occasions it happened, yet I didn't feel angry now. Not even a bit.

Keith, who had only seen me once like that, had panicked and was trying to hold on to my legs.

"It's okay, Keith. I'm fine. I can come down, see?" I said as I lowered my body down.

"How?" asked Keith with a mixture of surprise and worry evident on his face.

"I don't know. I guess I must have had enough practice by now," I said. In fact, I was mighty proud of myself.

"Who are you?" intervened Oliver, narrowing his eyes. "You're not a tormented soul, are you?"

"No, I've been kidnapped. Just like you. By *him*." I said, shuddering at the thought of pronouncing his name.

"You have the powers of a dark demon, yet you don't look like one," he said perplexed as he focused on my red hair. "And if you are a dark demon, then what were you doing on the other side and why did Azazel have to kidnap you?"

"She doesn't owe you any explanations," Keith bellowed.

"It's okay, Keith. They need to know. I'm his mate. I think he kidnapped me to torment Lasarus, who also happens to be my mate," I said, trying to explain everything as succinctly as possible. I looked at Keith to see his reaction. After all, it was the first time he was hearing this, that the Demon Lord who'd been after me was actually my real mate. There was not even a flash of anger or surprise on Keith's face. He was simply unaffected. I couldn't believe it; the bastard didn't seem to care at all. The kiss we shared a few minutes ago hadn't meant anything to him; probably I was a convenient replacement for Daisy or Zena. While he didn't care that I was mated to the twin demons, the thought of him finding his mate made me want to smash the bitch's head on an imaginary wall. I had to stop feeling this way about him.

"This is not good news," said Oliver. "He'll be looking all over for you. He won't stop until he has you." He formed a tight circle with a few of his comrades. They bowed their heads and spoke in hushed tones.

"We need to understand where your loyalties lie. Don't you want Azazel as your mate? Is it Lasarus you want?" Oliver inquired finally.

Keith growled deeply, his chest heaving with the effort to control his rage. Then I heard him punch the cave wall, again. What was wrong with him; one second he was acting all indifferent and the next he was punching walls, acting like a complete beast.

"No, I don't want any of them. And Azazel only wants to use me as a way to hurt Lasarus. Believe me, I know."

I looked at Keith. Now he had a satisfied smirk stamped on his face.

"We decided we can use your existence to our advantage. Having you with us will rattle Azazel's nerves, and he's bound to make some mistakes. Besides, we need someone like him," Oliver said pointing at Keith. "So, we welcome you both to the resistance. What do you think?"

"As if we have a fucking choice, we are stuck here in the underworld with no way out," Keith replied.

"Good, I'm glad you are following 'the enemy of my enemy is my friend' policy," chuckled Oliver. "Now, come with us. We need to get out of here, fast."

We got out of the cave. As the others were climbing down, I just floated next to them. For the first time, I enjoyed my demonic powers. Keith, however, was continuously checking up on me as if I was a baby bird who had just flapped its little wings for the first time to begin its venture into the world. Oliver entered another cave down the hill, its small entrance, blocked by a huge boulder, was almost indiscernible from the outside. Everybody except me had to squeeze their bodies through that small opening. We followed him inside until we came to a dead end. Oliver's hand moved inside a little crevice on the cave wall, pressing a hidden switch. And moments after that, a part of the stone wall moved a couple of feet inwards, and then slid to one side exposing a secret passageway. Wow, how cool was that? We continued walking behind the rebels as Keith held me firmly by the elbow. Oliver pressed another switch from the inside, and the cave wall closed back in. As we walked inside, I could not believe how big this place was. It was a multilevel intricate tunnel system with many cave-like rooms, connecting passageways and stairs. The tunnels were lit with torches, and there seemed to be some ventilation system as I had no trouble breathing. There were tons of rebels inside, some of which were running errands, some of which were lazily sprawled in the cave rooms. Others were talking, laughing in the passageway or on the stairs with the knowledge that they were safely sealed inside within this elaborate subterranean city. There was a hush as they noticed us appear with Oliver.

Oliver turned to us and waved his hand around as he said, "This is the resistance." And then he turned to the rebels and introduced us. "We have three newcomers. Two of them are from the outside. And their names are…"

"Belle and Keith," I said noticing Keith had no intention of talking, his firmly sealed lips and frowning eyebrows could easily attest to that.

"Great. And we also have our umbra friend here. Let's make them all feel welcome among us." We heard welcoming mutters from all around us as curious eyes observed our every movement.

"Let me take you two to your room for the night so that you can rest for a while. Then, we'll talk in the morning," Oliver said as he took Keith and me to an open cave room. The earthy smell of the cave filled my nostrils. The clay coating the walls formed a thin dark curtain around us. I couldn't believe we had a room to ourselves, even if it was completely bare inside except for one blanket. We were safe; that's all that mattered at the moment. A few minutes later, a demon brought us some sandwiches, and that was the best food I tasted in a long while. I couldn't believe they had a self-sustaining system here with food and everything.

"Belle, can you contact Tannon the way you contacted me?" asked Keith as we finished eating. "As nice and cozy this place might be, we need to get out of the underworld. We can't stay here forever; this is not our fight. And for that, we need Tannon."

"I don't know how," I said in desperation. "I don't know how I managed to contact you. I was sleeping at the time."

"Then try it tonight. Concentrate on it, and maybe it will happen."

"Okay," I muttered, not believing I had the power to contact anyone.

"We need to talk. But not tonight. You need to rest now, you've just healed from your infection," Keith said. His eyes were intense with a leashed emotion I couldn't readily decipher.

I simply nodded. He was right; I felt exhausted. How were we going to sleep with one blanket, I had no clue. But soon it all became clear as Keith spooned me from behind and spread the blanket on top of us. I was glad to share his body heat, but another kind of heat soon enveloped me as he wrapped his hands around my waist and buried his face in my neck, smelling me. I could feel his searing hot breath pouring over me as he pulled me closer. His fingers brushed lightly on my arm, tracing small circles. Damn, I wanted him to kiss me so badly. I kept reminding myself that he wasn't my mate, but I didn't care. It was him I wanted. It had always been him. I wanted to turn my face just a little towards him so our lips would meet. Silent tears rolled down my cheeks, but I didn't turn. There was no future for us. I forced myself to be immobile in his arms. He let out a deeply disappointed sigh; then his fingers became still. But, my torture didn't end, not even when I heard his soft snores behind me. My heart betrayed me as I was attuned to his every breath, and I stayed awake deep into the night. Finally, my eyes became heavy, and I drifted off to sleep.

I found myself in a dark room.

"Tannon," I asked. "Are you there?"

There was silence.

Tasks

Belle

I looked around, trying to find my way in the darkness. I advanced cautiously, step by step till my hands encountered the rough surface of a wall.

"Tannon, are you there?" I shouted in the darkness. I couldn't reach him. I touched the walls in the dark and went from one side of the room to another like a blind person just to feel for the openness of a doorway, but this was an enclosed four-wall room with no doors or windows for that matter. I slapped the walls on each side, trying to find a light switch, but there was none. This felt too much like being caged in the underworld, and I recoiled at the memory, a dread settling over me at the possibility of going through that again. There was no way out. I was trapped here, and I felt the grip of a deadly fear grab my heart, holding me firmly in its clutches.

"Tannon, please answer me," I yelled, trying to hold onto the remaining scraps of my sanity. I beat the walls over and over again until I could feel my hands bleeding as warm liquid dripped down my fingers. I was immune to the pain, fear dominating over any other emotion. "Please, is there anyone out there? Please, just get me out. Tannon?" I shouted desperately.

I screamed and screamed for hours. I was stuck in here where nobody could ever find me. I collapsed on the floor, defeated.

I woke up suddenly, drenched in my own sweat, my chest heaving and my throat raw and dry. I was confused, not knowing where I was. Then I felt his arm which was slung across my chest. It all came back to me. I was with Keith. His hand was wedged firmly in between my breasts, and his leg was thrown across mine. Thank the Moon Goddess, I was in the underworld. I never thought that one day this would be a consolation for me. What had that been all about, the dark room? Was that simply a nightmare, or had I lived through all that? I didn't know. But whatever it was, I was glad it was over.

I tried to get up but Keith moved a little closer to me, if that was possible, and buried his face in my hair as his hands caged me tighter. Leaving without waking him up would be an insurmountable task as our limbs seemed to be intertwined. Defeated, I simply lay in his arms, just enjoying his scent and warmth. A little gasp escaped my throat as his lips suddenly started nuzzling my neck. "I'm sweaty," I said, trying to pull away, but that didn't stop him from running his tongue all over my skin. "Hmm, yummy," he said as he continued licking my neck as if it was some savory dish. I had trouble breathing. His hands on my chest were not idle either. He palmed my breasts over my shirt, then he pushed it up impatiently and pulled aside the cups of my bra, his fingers searching for my nipples. He brushed his thumbs back and forth across them which soon became extremely sensitive under his tender ministrations. It felt amazing; I couldn't help but let out a moan in pleasure. All the while his lips never left my neck, traveling up my jaw, his tongue incessantly licking, probing. I yearned for this, for him. This was pure agony. I turned my head, my previous resolution to resist him all forgotten as his lips finally found mine. His lips devoured me, hard and fast as if he wanted to eat me alive. He flipped me on my back and was now on top of me. I pressed myself against him as our lips stayed connected, and he rumbled deep in his throat. My hands feasted on him, exploring his back and chest. I couldn't get enough of him, of this! It was as if I was consumed by fire from the inside out, and he was my only salvation. I pulled up his shirt and rubbed my hands on his gorgeously flat stomach. It was then he lifted his head with a start, removing those heavenly lips from mine. I grunted in protest like a starving kid whose food was just taken from her. He stopped me as I tried to yank him back, lifted himself on his elbows and looked at his belly, now sticky with blood. Panicked, he seized my hands and looked at my knuckles which were bruised and bloody.

"What the hell happened to you?" he barked, his voice audible at least a mile away as he touched the torn skin on my knuckles.

I gasped in shock. I hadn't been attuned to the pain up until now, not until he had pointed it out to me. Indeed, my hands were bloodied and, unfortunately, I knew why. My goodness, last night had not been a nightmare, it had all been real.

"How is this fucking possible, I was with you the whole night," he said, obviously enraged at himself for failing to protect me. Then he grasped me again desperately. "Did somebody hurt you with magic? Is it Oliver? He's so dead," he said as he suddenly sprang to his feet, his action too fast for me to even attempt to stop him.

"No, Keith. It wasn't him," I shouted after him as I pulled back my shirt. He stopped and turned back to me.

"Then, who?" he asked as he knelt down again next to me. "Who was it, babe? You don't have to be scared," he said.

"It wasn't anybody, Keith. It was me. I did this," I said. He looked at me, confused. "I was trying to reach Tannon last night, just like you told me."

"And did Tannon do this to you?" he bellowed, disbelieving at Tannon's tenacity.

"No, of course not. I couldn't even contact him, but somehow I managed to trap myself in a dark room and I couldn't get out. This was me trying to beat down the stone wall," I said, trying to make light of the situation. "I thought I was stuck in there, but then somehow I got back in here. I figured it was all a nightmare, but apparently it wasn't."

"Damn it, I don't understand what's happening to you," he said, frustrated. "I'm venturing into uncharted waters here with you. I don't know how to help you, and it's driving me insane."

"It's okay Keith; there's no harm done. But, what will we do about Tannon? Perhaps, I should try again tonight," I said, trying to be brave even though the idea of finding myself in that dark room again, all alone and with the risk of not getting out, filled me with utter dread.

"No, absolutely not," replied Keith. "We'll find another way. We can't risk you being trapped somewhere in your dream. I wouldn't even know how to get you out," he continued.

"But, there is no other way, is there? You said it yourself; he's our only way out of here."

"I said, no," he replied.

Before I could say anything else, Oliver stood above us. "Oh, I'm glad you lovebirds are awake," he said. "If you are ready, you should eat something and then we'll assign you to your new tasks. We all pull our weight here, you know."

"Of course," I mumbled.

"She will only be doing things that won't endanger her," Keith explained, not happy with the idea I would be expected to do anything here. "I'll do whatever needs to be done for both of us to get us out of here."

"I understand," smiled Oliver. "And I'm glad to hear that as we certainly need someone with your skills. My men tell me that the mutilated bodies you left Azazel have already been discovered and he has rolled a few heads himself to mete out punishment. The rumor is that he's looking all over for you both," he said.

"Whatever," uttered Keith as he helped me up. Then we followed Oliver to take the stairs down one level which led to a long room carved out as a kitchen with a large stone table and two long benches. There was milk, bread, and cheese on the table.

"Where does all this food come from?" I asked surprised.

"We steal it from Azazel of course. It's not an easy task, I assure you. In fact, that's exactly where we'll need your help today, Keith. We need to replenish our supplies."

"I don't understand. How does Azazel grow food in here? It all looks, well, so barren."

"You're right on the spot, my sweet," Oliver said jokingly.

Keith growled. "Keep your damn compliments to yourself."

"Chill out, man. Anyone can see she's yours. We don't step on anyone's toes here, not if we want to stay united as an organization. We have rules here; that's the only way we stay alive."

I was perplexed. Oliver knew very well that I was mated to the twin brothers, yet he insinuated I was Keith's. Worse still, Keith didn't seem to dispute that, which, now thinking on it, was utterly strange. He'd always been in a hurry in the past to deny our bond at every chance, but now he seemed to relish doing the reverse, stamping his non-existent ownership of me whenever he could. What had happened to him, and what did all this mean? I didn't know. I had to be patient till that much-awaited conversation to find out.

"So, the food …Where did you say it came from?" I asked Oliver, reminding him of the question to ease the tension in the room.

"Nobody knows how the system runs here. I suspect it might be Lucifer sending routine supplies. After all, he was the one who helped Azazel build this place after he was disowned by the Moon Goddess. But, that's why stealing is the only option for us. There is no other way to get food here. They guard the storage better and better every day, but we find innovate methods to get in and out without being detected," he said proudly.

We ate fast; the food was simple but good. Now it was time to earn our keep.

"Tell me what I can do. I'd like to help," I said as I heard Keith curse next to me.

"Great, I can put you on rear guard duty. You seem to have impressive abilities."

"No way, why don't you fucking put her on display instead? I told you she has to be safe. Whatever you'll have her do, she has to be indoors at all times. That's the stipulation."

"Keith, I am not helpless, for Moon Goddess's sake. I have been surviving on my own for some time now."

"Need I remind you of the condition I found you in? You almost died in my arms. No, thank you very much, but you will be safely tucked inside or else they can all forget about my help."

Oliver didn't even ponder on this for a second. He needed Keith more than he needed me. "No problem, Belle can assist in the kitchen."

Keith seemed to like that idea. Very much. He smiled. But, I hated it. My only use in the resistance against the evil twin who had tortured me over and over again was to be a kitchen maid, how lovely! Needless to say, there was nothing I could do about it.

"Aysha," Oliver shouted, and a woman came running from an adjoining cave room.

"Yes? You want something?" she asked.

She looked rather stout and damn scary with a stern expression.

"Meet Belle, your new assistant. She'll help you in the kitchen."

"Finally! Feeding you greedy creatures is a challenge with so little staff at my disposal. I never understand why you keep allocating all the new recruits to guarding and fighting anyway. You need food to be able to do any task; any fool knows that!" she complained.

Damn it! I was gonna hate it here!

"Okay, pretty girl. Let's start toiling for our food," Aysha said.

"Can I clean myself with some water before I start any kitchen tasks? I don't think I'm even hygienic enough to prepare food," I asked hopefully. Surely they had some water here; I drastically needed to wash days of dirt and sweat off my body.

"We have an excellent well system here. The water is ice cold, but you can certainly clean yourself," Oliver said. That was the best news I had in a long time. "I believe we can also spare you some clean clothes, although they'll be extremely simple," he said.

Wow, my day was certainly getting better. The idea of wearing clean clothes was sweeter than a slice of cherry pie right now.

We went down two floors where it was much colder. The underground city was so huge, I wondered how anyone found their way down there. Oliver took us to a large vault in the middle of which stood a well and a bucket next to it.

"We have a good drainage system here; the ground is shaped like a flat cone so you can just pour the water over it. Excess water will automatically be accumulated in the ditches at each side which are specially sloped down to allow the flow of water to the pipes that take it to the lower layers of the underworld.

It was simply incredible what the resistance had built here in the middle of the underworld as they fought Azazel. "Great, thanks," I said, thankful.

"I'll leave you two to it, and I'll bring you clean clothes in a minute," he said.

"Uhm, there is no door here. Can you keep watch while I wash?" I asked Keith.

"Sure thing," he said grinning.

"Don't you dare look," I warned him. I didn't like that smirk on his face at all.

He pulled a full pail of water from the well and poured it into the bucket. He then left, his eyes twinkling with merriment. "Call me if you need any help with anything and I'll be there within seconds," he said, winking.

Would I ever? I thought about heating the water with my palms but the pale was plastic and heating it from the top would have taken too much time. Fearing Aysha's reprimand, I gave up on the idea immediately. I made sure Keith was gone before I took off my clothes hastily and started washing myself with the soap standing next to the bucket. It was so damn cold. Goosebumps sprouted up all over my naked skin. When I poured the water to rinse the foam off my body, I lost my breath, my body now completely benumbed by the coldness of the water. I bit my lip, tasting my own blood to restrain my squeal. I knew full well that he'd be here the moment he heard me cry out, and that certainly would not do.

I clutched my dirty clothes to hide my nakedness as I shouted, "I'm ready, can you throw the clean clothes this way?"

"Are you sure you don't want me to bring them? They can get wet, you know?" he chuckled.

"I'm sure." Bastard. He threw a black shirt and long tights in the air and I caught them before they hit the wet ground, putting them on quickly. Then I washed my underwear and my dirty clothes. Unfortunately burning them was not an option as we lived in a world of scarcity here. I hung them around the well. "Now, it's your turn," I said, and he came grinning, his eyes automatically darkening as they locked on my set of black underwear.

"Nice," he muttered under his breath.

"I'll leave you," I said.

"As you wish," he replied, his eyes beaming with untamed fire. "Belle…" he whispered as I was leaving.

"What?" I croaked. I was seconds away from accepting his unsaid invitation.

Pressed into that fraction of a second was so much raw emotion, so much unspoken thought that the air between us felt thicker. "Nothing," he said as he turned around and drew a bucket of chilling water from the well, pouring it all over him, clothes and all.

An Ordinary Day

Belle

"Work on the meat," ordered Aysha. "Smack it with the flat side of the knife and make sure the meat is flattened to an even thickness everywhere," she instructed.

Moon Goddess, help me, I was going to kill Keith. I started pounding the meat with a vengeance.

"Not so hard, you will make it too thin," reprimanded Aysha.

I was counting under my breath. I was that close to triggering my demonic powers and unleashing them all on Aysha. There were three more females in the kitchen with me, none of which looked like dark demons. I hadn't even had the chance to talk to them and ask their story as Aysha was ruling the kitchen like a battle commander, incessantly breathing down our necks to do this and that.

Keith entered the room as I was seasoning the meat with herbs and spices I couldn't even tell from one another.

"This becomes you," he said grinning.

"If I were you, I'd skip dinner. I think I might just poison you," I retorted.

He grinned. "I'm leaving with Oliver and his men to raid the storehouse. I'll also check on the wall in case," he said, pausing. We both knew that was a long shot. "Well, anyway, so I'll see you later," he said as he kissed me on the lips.

"Okay," I muttered still not knowing where I stood with him. Him being like this was all new to me.

"Are you coming, Keith?" asked Oliver.

"Coming," he shouted as he gave me another quick kiss. "We'll talk tonight," he whispered in my ear, as his hands played with my hair. "There is so much that needs to be said," he murmured as he wrapped a few tendrils of hair around his hand, touching it with a gentleness that set my heart racing. "I'm looking forward to it, baby," he added as he leaned in towards me. I could feel his face close to my neck, his molten breath fanning across my skin. I held my breath as he inhaled my scent ever so slowly, ever so deeply, savoring it as if he was memorizing it. I was so pliable under his hands. My body swayed forward of its own accord, so expectant, so damn needy. Then he withdrew from me mercilessly, and left me, just like that, all flustered and wanting more.

I let out the breath I'd been holding and my face flushed beet red when I realized everybody had witnessed that scene. "I'll be right back," I said to Aysha, and rushed out of the kitchen, hearing her mutterings like an old witch echo behind me. I followed Keith and the others, tiptoeing from a distance behind them.

"So?" asked Keith as they went to a meeting room to discuss the plan. Since none of the cave rooms had a door, I stayed behind, gluing myself to the wall a few steps back to listen.

"Don't know yet. The storehouse lies inside one of the hollowed mountains. There are at least thirty demons guarding it from the outside. Being inconspicuous is vital for us. We don't want to draw attention to our raids. If they swarm this place with demons, we'd be done for," replied Oliver.

"So what are our options for getting in?" Keith asked.

"There are two doors, both of which are well guarded," Oliver suggested.

"Demons on the ground or in the air?" asked Keith.

"They shift in between."

"How many demons inside?"

"Not many, only a few that are tasked with organizing and shelving food."

"What about entering from the top? The mountains I saw on my way to the center didn't have a top, could we climb down that way?"

"Yes, it would not be easy, but it could be done."

"How high up do they guard it up from the air?"

"Not too high," said Oliver.

"That seems our best bet. How did you do it before?"

"We dug an underground tunnel that took us directly inside, and we transported the food easily back that way. But in our last raid, the tunnel collapsed. Not only did we lose ten of our best men, but the rumble made the dark demons suspicious, and they increased the number of their guards."

"Why don't we just open the tunnel first? That seems to be our best option for staying inconspicuous," commented Keith.

"We can't. We're too low on supplies, and the damn tunnel keeps caving in every time we dig," said Oliver, frustrated. "In fact, I want to place you in the tunnels starting from tomorrow on. We can certainly use your strength in cleaning the debris."

"Fine," Keith said. "Belle, sweetie, aren't you done listening yet?" he asked.

Shoot! Did he just say my name or did I imagine it? I didn't move from my place, hoping I'd misunderstood.

"Belle, come here, baby. Your lovely ears will fall off."

Nope, I was caught.

I walked in slowly like a guilty child whose hand was caught in the candy jar. "How did you know?" I asked, surprised.

"Did you think I wouldn't recognize your scent?" chuckled Keith. "What are you doing here, curious cat? I thought you were busy preparing that meat for me?"

"Well, I wanted to see what you guys were up to," I said raising my chin.

"Now, you've seen it, you should go back to the kitchen, sweetheart. We don't want you shirking your duties now, do we?" asked Keith, holding back on his laughter.

"I'm not shirking my duties. I believe I can be more helpful than just chopping meat, that's all," I said, grinding my teeth.

"And how is that so?" Keith asked with an expression of fake innocence.

Unfortunately, I had no clue. They didn't need me to raid the storehouse; they probably had many strong rebels, all with more experience and skills than me. I kept my silence.

Keith chuckled. He extended his hand and I took a step towards him to take it. He pulled me to his chest, wrapping his arms around me from behind, and gave me a little squeeze.

"So, okay where were we?" he asked Oliver, as he held me close, his chin resting on top of my head, completely undisturbed by the fact that I had just interrupted their meeting. "If you ask me, we go in with as few men as possible, none of whom should include dark demons. We'll certainly blend in better if we camouflage ourselves and climb to the opening at the top, then simply climb down that way. Preferably we'll go in a group of four or five, and we'll leave five or six of us behind, somewhere close by, in case things go bad."

"Okay, Keith. Let's do this."

"How will you carry so much food between so few of you?" I asked perplexed.

"We'll carry as much as we can," said Oliver. "And if this works out, we'll repeat it once every week until the tunnel is opened."

"Okay, then let's get rolling," said Keith. He kissed me softly on the neck. "See you later. I'm looking forward to sampling that meat when I get back," he said grinning.

As he was leaving, I called after him. He turned with a questioning look, I ran into his arms, and just hugged him. "Be careful," I said, slightly nervous. It was the first time I had initiated anything between us. I didn't know how he'd react. His hand came under my chin, and he tipped my head up toward his, his eyes penetrating deep into mine as he lowered his lips and pulled me into a quick passionate kiss. Then, he ended it, as quickly as it had started. He pushed back my hair, bringing his lips to my ear and whispered, "Always, Belle-mine." Then, he left.

Belle-mine. That endearment alone was enough to turn me into a puddle of jelly. I was his Belle. His. Did he mean that? Being in the underworld didn't sound ominous anymore, I could live here. Sure the food was simple, and the water was cold, but I was free from Lasarus as well as Azazel who had no idea where the underground city was. The best of it was that I had Keith all to myself even if I wasn't his mate. I smiled as I hurried back to the kitchen. I would work in the kitchen, and he would work in the tunnels, we'd simply be like a conventional human couple retiring to our cave room after a full day of exhausting labor, and then we would make out numerous times in the non-privacy of our room. Why not? I sighed happily as I arrived at the kitchen to a screaming Aysha.

"Where were you? Do you think you can go away whenever you want? No, this won't do. I'll tell Oliver that this won't do."

"Look, I'm sorry. It was an emergency. It won't happen again," I apologized grudgingly.

"It'd better not." Then thankfully her attention was taken away from me. "No, Henna not like that. I told you a thousand times; you should gradually stir the flour into the milk. You've made lumps, you stupid girl," she shouted as she looked at the stuff in the boiling pot.

On second thought, the kitchen wouldn't do. The rest of the dream was all right, though. I sighed in frustration as I went back to flattening the meat.

Salvageable?

Belle

Keith and Oliver left the cave and the underground city with huge empty sacks in their hands. I couldn't help but worry about him as I aided in the kitchen the whole day, pounding meat, cutting potatoes, and preparing lots and lots of sandwiches.

"Sasha, take some sandwiches to the rehab center. Take the new girl with you," Aysha ordered.

My name was the new girl, how sweet! Well, I didn't know what or where the rehab center was, but I was thrilled to go anywhere that would take me fast out of this kitchen.

"Okay," muttered Sasha as she took twenty to thirty of the hundreds of sandwiches we'd prepared and put them in two bags.

"Let's go," she said. I had no clue why I was asked to go. Sasha seemed perfectly capable of carrying the two bags herself, but I was not gonna complain as I cheerfully left the sight of my new torturer, Aysha.

"So, what's your story? What species are you?" I asked Sasha. Finally, I could talk to her without Aysha's reprimand.

"I'm human," she said. "I was kidnapped along with my brother."

I had underestimated the extent of the problem here. Azazel was also abducting humans who, were likely the easiest prey for the dark demons who somehow made it outside.

"Is he here with you?" I asked.

"Unfortunately he didn't make it," she said bitterly.

I didn't probe any further. "I'm sorry," I said, not knowing what else to say. Poor her! As a human being ignorant of the existence of all other species, let alone other worlds, this probably was a complete horror for her, one that she could only imagine seeing in movies. On the other hand, I could completely relate to her. I couldn't help but feel that we were not really that different from one another.

We went one floor down to the level lying between the kitchen and the well. We walked along a narrow aisle, took the path winding to the right, and crossed a small bridge to arrive at a round chamber. It was darker in there. Inside the dark chamber, my eyes had difficulty adjusting to the lack of light. It took me a few seconds to understand what I was looking at. There were ten to fifteen of them sitting on the floor, some of whom were in a fetal position, whimpering pitifully, others looking blank in space. Three others were pacing back and forth from one side of the chamber to the other rather impatiently.

"Dresner, George, Wendy," Sasha greeted three of the rebels who were massaging the limbs of two creatures who were lying limp on the ground, moaning.

"We brought lunch. This is Belle," she said introducing me.

"Hi," I muttered, still not grasping what I was seeing.

"Hi, Belle. I'm Wendy. You're just in time," said the female rebel who seemed to be in charge as she pointed at the bags.

"What's going on here?" I asked, unable to hold back my curiosity. What exactly was this place?

"These are the tormented souls we saved last week. We try to rehabilitate them here before they are fit to join the resistance actively. It takes a long time; you can imagine the state they are in physically, mentally and psychologically after being caged for so long."

Oh, the Moon Goddess! These were the poor souls who were hanging in cages all around me when I was imprisoned myself. I had only stayed in that cage for one night, and I was so highly fevered I didn't remember much of it. I was still haunted by the little I did remember. I couldn't imagine what they'd been through.

"But how did you save them?" I asked.

"We have rescue missions, but we can't undertake them as frequently as we want. The last mission before this was six months back. It's really hard infiltrating the prisons under Azazel's nose and getting anyone out," Wendy sighed.

I felt an overwhelming guilt consume me. I had forgotten all about these poor souls. I was eating, showering and kissing Keith with no consideration for anyone else but myself since I'd been saved, completely ignoring the torment of others who were still in the clutches of pain and despair. I would do anything to help from this point on. And not even the fires of hell would stop me.

"Tell me how I can help," I said, determined.

"You can help us feed them for one. We need help attending to them all. They'll be ready in two weeks, but till then we need all the help we can get."

"Two weeks? I don't understand how can they heal that quickly and without professional help?" I asked, stunned. How could anyone get better that fast with what they'd been through?

"We are the professional help, Belle. All of us here are vampires," Wendy said, amused.

They were the first vampires I had met in my life. I examined them thoroughly, but nothing looked typical in their physique. Nothing jumped out at me as a common vampire trait.

I had no clue what she meant by professional help. "Excuse me?" I asked, hoping for some clarification.

"It's not the ideal method but surely it works under the circumstances. We reset their minds. They are all really vulnerable at this stage and their minds are unprotected, so it's not a biggie. But, it all takes time as we don't want to wipe out everything, turning them into vegetables. It's also not just a mental problem you know. They haven't been using their limbs for so long. We need to prepare their bodies as well."

"Reset their minds?" I repeated, stammering.

"Yeah, we do mind control, we help them forget the bad memories. But, the problem is some of them have done atrocious deeds themselves when they were alive, and hence their journey to hell in the first place."

Hell? I remembered Oliver mentioning a pact between hell and the underworld. Did that mean these creatures were all dead?

"What are you saying?" I asked, unable to comprehend her words.

"Well, not all of them can be rehabilitated in the way we want them to be. We work with them over and over again but, in the end, we can save only some."

"The rest?" I croaked

"Are eliminated of course," she said with the indifference of someone who's seen too much death and destruction. "Yes, my dear. A lot of them won't make it, but it's still worth it, you know? Not to mention that they also help increase our numbers," she said. "Needless to say, we also prevent them from joining Azazel, one way or another. It's so much harder to change their loyalties once they are demonized," she said, sighing.

I had a good idea what she meant by elimination. I guessed it was still more merciful than being caged. But then again, I had no idea what happened to them once they were eliminated. All of this was giving me a headache.

"How are they even demonized?" I asked.

"They are forced to drink from the fountain of Lethe, but what pours from the fountain is not water, dear Belle. It's a special liquid with a mixture of Lucifer and Azazel's blood to signify their alliance. The moment anyone drinks from that they turn into a dark demon, completely forgetting about their past and who they were. It works perfectly in creating a continuous supply of soldiers for Azazel's loyal army." She continued, "You see he sort of does what we do, but in a much more efficient way as he takes away their identities completely and we don't."

"But, what if the creature was previously a witch or a werewolf?"

"Nothing remains of who they were. They cannot shift or use magic anymore. That's the deal. I'm sure Azazel would have loved to have all their skill set at his disposal, but alas you can't always have what you want," she said.

I stayed with Sasha to help feed these creatures who were as feeble as new born babies. I cut the sandwiches into small bites, forcing their jaws open to put them inside. They then seemed to chew it under Wendy's command. Once we were done with the feeding, Sasha stood up. "C'mon let's go. You don't want to make Aysha angry. She can be meaner than anyone," she said.

"Was she one of the tormented souls?" I asked.

"No, she was a human being like me, captured outside of her town. Oliver rescued her before she drank from the fountain," Sasha replied.

"I want to stay and help here," I said.

"Belle," warned Sasha.

"Look, I have to do this. I'm sure Oliver would be okay with me helping here instead of the kitchen," I reasoned. "Besides, we already prepared so many sandwiches. You don't really need me there."

Of course, there was still the cleaning part. I hoped she would not bring that up. She didn't. And thankfully she left without another word.

I sat next to Wendy, massaging the arms and legs of one of the tormented souls as she began her session of mind control.

"Tell me your name,"

"Swarna."

"Swarna, I want you to go back in time, to a time when you were just a kid."

The session went on like that for an hour, Wendy interrogating her relentlessly. She was once a werewolf living in the east territory; she had a loving mother, an affectionate father, and two close sisters. She had a boyfriend and although he wasn't her mate, they seemed to love each other. Her sisters had all left the pack, but they lived close by and often visited. She had one best friend, Lana, who had been mated since she was eighteen and they often hung out as couples, going to the movies together, playing golf and dining. She was working in a jewelry store selling stuff she made herself. Everything about her seemed utterly normal. So what had gone wrong?

Wendy finally asked the question I was itching for.

"Tell me what you did to go to hell,"

"I murdered her, the bitch," she spat with a vengeance I didn't expect from her.

"Who did you murder, Swarna?"

"Lana and him, of course," she spat, saliva dripping from her mouth.

I recoiled reflexively, stopping the massage immediately.

"Is she shifting?" I asked.

"She can't shift, she's too weak for that," Wendy assured me.

After a day spent at the rehab center, I no longer knew what to feel about any of these creatures. Swarna had murdered her best friend and her mate because of pure jealousy, another one had massacred a whole town of humans and drank their blood. None of them were innocent, could they be salvaged, I had no clue. Was it even worth trying?

"Get away from her right now," bellowed Keith, suddenly emerging at the chamber step as I was attending Swarna.

I turned around to find a furious Keith, Oliver trailing right behind him in panic, carrying the sacks of food they'd stolen on his shoulders.

I blinked in confusion, not understanding why he was so mad. Seeing me remain immobile, he took large strides to where I was kneeling, and grabbed me by the hips, throwing me over his shoulder as he stormed out of the room.

"Keith, what are you doing? Are you crazy?" I shouted in vain. With each step, my upturned face bumped against his back and I could see my red hair streaming towards his legs. Put me down," I screamed as I thumped at his thighs with balled up fists.

He didn't stop, not until he came to the kitchen. "This is where you'll be, and this is where you'll stay," he said, his eyes blazing with fire.

"No, I want to help at the rehab center," I said, raising my chin stubbornly. "I can do some good there."

"No, that's out of the question. You'll do good in here by preparing food."

"I don't want her," bitched Aysha who had heard our conversation. "She's lazy and undisciplined."

"Shut up," yelled Keith, and, to my utter delight, Aysha cringed back in fear and disappeared out of the kitchen.

"Why?" I asked trying to remain calm, but I was fuming inside.

"They are evil creatures from hell who are dangerous and uncontrollable. Do you think for a second that I'll allow you to be exposed to that kind of danger?" he bellowed.

"Wendy is exposed to it every day, and so are George and Dresner. Why not me?"

"Belle, anyone can see they are fucking vampires with lethal fangs. They are strong and dangerous creatures themselves."

Not anyone could see it, obviously. How did he even know they were vampires?

He was breathing heavily, trying to control his rage. "Look, they can take care of themselves, but you can't," he murmured.

He made some sense, but I wanted to do this. I needed to do this. As Wendy had stated, even saving one was all worth it.

"You are not making sense. They'll take care of me too. It's not as if they'll sit back and watch if I'm attacked," I said, not relenting.

"I said, no," he stressed as if talking to a small child. "And that's that."

Obedience was not my strong suit. "I didn't ask you," I said as I grabbed a sandwich and left the kitchen. I needed to be away from him.

"Belle, come back here," he said coming right after me. He grabbed me by the elbow and turned me around, keeping me in his viselike grip.

"Belle, don't cross me on this," he said.

I raised my palms which, by now, were bursting with orbs of flames. He looked at me, startled.

"I suggest you let me go if you don't want a taste of my killer beams of fire," I warned him, wiggling my fingers. "And, as you can see, I'm not as helpless as you think."

"Belle, please," he pleaded.

"Keith, let me go," I yelled.

Frustrated, he loosened his fingers. I ran away from him as I closed my palms to kill the flames. I certainly was getting better at this.

I didn't stop as I passed our cave room. I wandered in the underground city following passages I had never set foot on before, looking for a place where I could be all alone. Finally, I found a small uninhabited room. Needless to say, there was no blanket inside which meant I would probably freeze at night. I didn't care. I ate my sandwich and lay on my back on the clay-like cave floor, staring at the ceiling for hours, tracing the movements of a bug which made me think about how it had gotten here in the first place. Was that even a bug, or a dark demon turned into a bug? Tired of overthinking, I finally fell asleep.

I woke up to a warm body snuggling up behind me, an arm at my hip. I yelped in panic.

"Shh, it's me," he said.

"Keith?" I asked puzzled, confused. What was he doing here?

"I don't want to fight anymore. I just want to sleep with you," he said as he wrapped the blanket around us.

The warmth from his body and the blanket wrapped around me fast. I sighed in contentment as my frozen body finally defrosted.

"How'd you find me?" I asked through my sleep-haze.

"Your scent, Belle-mine, it will always take me to you. Now sleep," he said as he planted a chaste kiss on my neck.

224

I was angry at him last night but, submerged in the bliss of his arms, I no longer remembered why. I went back to sleep, warm and cozy and content.

"I love you, Belle-mine," I heard him whisper, but I was far too gone to distinguish dream from reality.

The Tunnel

Belle

"Belle, are you awake?" Keith asked.

I was, but I kept my silence. Now that the morning had come and the warmth of his body had left me, I was back to being angry at him.

"We need to talk, don't you think?" he asked, trying to reason with me.

I didn't stir.

"C'mon, baby, I know you're not sleeping."

How could he know? He was bluffing. I chose to remain still.

"Look, nothing has changed, I still don't want you going to that rehab place," he said resolutely.

That did it. I rose to my feet in a matter of seconds. "I don't care, do you hear me?" I snapped at him.

"They are not to be trusted. And none of the dark demons in the resistance are, I've told Oliver, too. Can't you see that? For one, they've all been in hell. The demonized ones, on top of that, have all been put to Azazel's servitude by drinking his blood. You can't break the bond of blood. None of those creatures can ever be salvaged. Do you understand, none!"

"You are the most cynical being I've ever come across!" I yelled. "The resistance seems to be functioning just fine."

"For now, yes, but till when?"

"You are nuts," I told him.

"It all seems fine now because, like Oliver, most of the rebels who happen to be kidnapped from the other side of the gate are not dead, and certainly are no dark demons! All the others in here are bad news, including those souls in the rehab center, trust me I know. And I won't allow you to throw yourself in their midst without me to protect you."

"Those in the rehab center are not dark demons, Keith. They've just been saved from that fate by the resistance." I said angrily. "After all, that's the whole purpose."

"They are zombies brought back from hell. What part of it seems salvageable to you?" he asked impatiently. "Damn it, Belle. You can't go back in there."

"Again, I didn't ask for your permission. You're not my dad, you're not my brother, and you certainly are not my mate. You are nothing to me," I screamed, unable to hold back my anger. I wanted to take back the words the moment they were out of my mouth, but it was already too late.

His face flinched as though he was slapped.

"Fine, I see you are not in the mood to discuss things civilly. I'll be working in the tunnel all day long. Hopefully, that will give you enough time to blow off your steam," he said as he left the cave room.

Damn it! Now, he was making me feel bad. It was all his fault! Yes, he was sexy as hell, and he could turn my brain and body to mush with a single touch, but none of that changed the fact that he was still an arrogant, overbearing, self-absorbed brute! I stomped my foot in exasperation. He wasn't going to intimidate me, and he wasn't going to make me feel guilty, I decided. I was going back to the rehab center.

I made small sandwiches in the kitchen to take with me and I headed to the center, ignoring Aysha's cocky smile behind me.

"Hi guys," I said to the trio who had already started their daily routine. "Hope I'm just in time for breakfast," I said as I took out the sandwiches I'd brought.

"Lovely to see you," smiled Wendy. "We weren't sure you'd be back here after that mate of yours forbid it last night."

"Oh, he's not my mate."

"If you say so," said Wendy as she shrugged.

As we worked the whole day, stretching limbs and soothing minds, I became more hopeful. Swarna for one seemed to be calmer. Wendy had made her relive the good memories of her life over and over again.

"Where are you?" Wendy asked.

"I'm on the beach, swimming with my sisters."

"How does that make you feel?"

"Happy, safe," she sighed. "We are splashing water at each other," she smiled.

"Great. Now go to sleep, and tuck safely the feelings that day evoked in you. When you wake up, I want you to remember and feed on those emotions, let them heal your soul."

Wow, that was too cool. I was looking forward to seeing the changes in her.

As I covered a sleeping Swarna, I heard Oliver enter the room, his eyes frantically searching for me.

"I was looking for you."

"And you've found me," I said, raising an eyebrow.

"The tunnel caved in," Oliver said. "It's bad."

"I don't understand," I said. "What are you talking about?" I asked as a chilling, numbing fear crept over me.

"We don't think there are any survivors, Belle. I'm sorry, but Keith is dead."

My breath froze in my chest.

"No! I don't believe it. You're lying, where is he?" I screamed in agony. Keith was dead? No, I refused to accept that.

"I'm really sorry," Oliver said with an expression of sincere regret.

"Take me to him, now!" I told him, clutching his arm. I couldn't stop shaking.

"As you wish, but there's nothing you can do. We already tried everything," Oliver said. I commanded my limbs to move which had been paralyzed with dread and terror. Keith had to be alive; he had to be. I could not and would not believe he was dead, not until I saw it with my own two eyes.

"The Moon Goddess, help him, please," I murmured over and over again as we went to the center of the city followed by some of Oliver's men as a backup force. Oliver knelt down on the ground to reveal a secret hatch protected by a witch rebel's spell. There were no stairs, just two coiled ropes that hung down. I looked at the rope in despair, how was I going to lower my body using the damn rope? Damn it; I would throw myself down if I had to, but I was getting to Keith!

"You can fly, you know?" said a dark demon, whose name I didn't know, as he spotted my bleak expression.

Of course I could! I kept forgetting I had such powers, even if they were minimal, and now, somehow, I could trigger them on command. We both floated down as others used the ropes to climb down.

Waves of fear and panic merged into one pit of agony that surged up into my throat. I felt as if my insides were spewing out. I had fought with him last night and this morning; I had told him he was my nothing. How could I have done that? How in the hell could I have done that? He was everything to me, and I had sent him to the tunnels believing he meant nothing to me. Had he been careless because of me? Had I driven him to lose his focus, had he been absentminded thinking of the fight, of my safety in the rehab center? I couldn't bear it if anything happened to him, I simply couldn't. Tears sprang to my eyes and I brushed them away angrily. I was not going to cry, because he was not dead. He simply was not dead. As long as I didn't believe it, it wouldn't be real. I hung onto that thought.

We walked in the tunnel until we reached the cave-in. The ceiling and the walls on both sides had collapsed, creating a blockage that seemed impossible to clear.

I ran there, trying to remove the debris with my bare hands. "Keith? Keith, are you there?" I shouted over and over again.

Others came to help, for the second time that day, but nothing seemed even to budge. I beat the huge stones in frustration, my hands bleeding as I continued calling out to him. "Please, Keith, answer me," I shouted.

"Belle, I'm sorry," Oliver said, putting his hand on my shoulder. "We should go back."

"No!" I cried out. "I'm not leaving him. I'll stay here; I know he's alive. He needs to feel I'm here."

"He's dead; he can't feel anything. You know that."

"I don't believe it, not for a second," I said stubbornly.

"Please, Belle. He would want you safe. We should get back to the city. There's nothing you can do in here. You have to accept it."

"No, I'll stay here," I said, my throat constricting with the pressure of suppressed tears.

Oliver insisted. "I can't leave you here alone, Belle. You have to come back with us."

My voice firmed. "I said, no."

He sighed. "Fine, then I'll leave Kappas and Garuda here with you. They'll keep you safe until you decide to come back." He touched my elbow, squeezing it gently. "You are not alone, you are one of us now, Belle. And we take care of each other. I hope you'll remember that," he said.

I nodded, it was too difficult to form the words.

"Good," Oliver said as he and the others went, leaving me alone with my two guards. I collapsed on the floor, my face touching the large boulder, one of the many that blocked my way to him. "Keith, please come back to me," I said, no longer restraining my tears. My heart vibrated with pain. I closed my eyes in desperation; then I suddenly raised my head. How was it that it hadn't occurred to me before? Holy Moon Goddess, I had a way of reaching Keith. I had done it before and I surely could it again. I was going to help him, all I had to do was go back to sleep. How hard could that be?

It was damn hard as I found out soon enough, sleeping turned out to be a real challenge! I cursed at myself, turned this way and that way on the ground, but I was simply too excited to reach him and too frightened of failure that I simply could not relax. My brain was on the express with thoughts and emotions constantly swarming in my head. Damn, double damn! I tried breathing in and out for hours, keeping my eyes continuously closed. It took me a long time with lots of cursing, huffing and puffing, frustrated sighing and deep breathing, but eventually sleep fell upon me.

I found myself surrounded by heaps of rock. Had I made it?

"Keith?" I shouted. "Where are you?"

Before I could do anything else, I was mercilessly snatched from there, just like that!

"No!" I screamed in despair. On top of that, I couldn't breathe. I gasped for air, but I couldn't get enough of it to my lungs, I felt the terrifying pressure of fingers around my neck. I opened my eyes; he was squeezing my windpipe, his eyes looking at me maliciously. It was the dark demon Oliver had left behind to stay with me. I reflexively summoned a small ball of flame in my palm, and threw it at him. He laughed as his fire-resistant body simply devoured the fire. I tried to smash my fist at him but it didn't do any good, he batted it away as if I were a pest. He was too strong. From the corner of my eye, I spotted the other rebel on the floor whose head hung at an agonizingly wrong angle, as if loose, and the neck glistened wet, coated in a sheen of blood. I felt my life force slowly leave my body. Silent tears rolled down my cheeks at the thought that I would never see Keith again.

It's Damn Gray!

Belle

I was choking. I felt the blood rush to my head. This was it! I was dying. I closed my eyes; I didn't want his ugly face to be my last sight. Suddenly, a vicious growl wailed through the tunnel and my eyes opened automatically to see a huge beast, almost twice the size of a human, miraculously attack the demon. Its long claws pierced the dark demon's neck and blood spurted all over me. Just like that, the fingers on my throat disappeared, and I collapsed on the floor, holding my neck, coughing and trying to get precious air to my deprived lungs. As I was gasping and just breathing on the tunnel ground, the demon's head rolled in front of me. I yelped in shock! I tried to rise to my feet, but I was so panicky that I stumbled back on my bottom. I clawed backward, holding my hands up as if that would keep the beast at bay. It was completely covered with hair like an animal, but it certainly wasn't a wolf nor did it look like any animal from the geography channel. I gasped as I saw its sharp and elongated teeth which were bloodied. It must have severed the demon's head with its teeth. I was glad I hadn't seen that.

"Please," I said with a shaky voice as I finally managed to get back on my feet. Fate was merciless; it was evident to me that I was going to die today, one way or another.

The creature growled taking two huge steps to close the distance between us. He bent his large form and leaned towards me. I feared he was going to rip off my head and my hands

232

automatically closed around my bruised neck as if to fend off that attack. He growled again. I lowered my palms, trying to bring fire on them, but his claws caught me by my wrists, raising them above my head. How had it known, damn it! I could see his bloodied teeth up from a close distance as its body came closer, the heat of his breath warming my face. I felt the moment of my death upon me. I expected to feel his sharp teeth penetrate my skin any second now as he leaned in further towards my neck. And then, he freaking inhaled me. He took deep intakes of my scent, in and out, over and over again as if he couldn't get enough of it. He growled with satisfaction. Then, I felt his huge tongue lick my bruised neck, back and forth. I couldn't move out of fear, and my heart was pounding hard in my chest. Then, the beast changed in front of my eyes, his elongated teeth withdrew, the animal hair on his body disappeared, his size shrank, the claws that held my wrists turned into the beautiful hands of, well, Keith. The beast was Keith! As the realization of what it all meant hit me, I started crying.

"Let go of me," I said. I had to hug him; I had to touch him. And for that, I needed my hands which he still held over my head.

He flinched. "Belle," he pleaded.

He freed my arms. But I didn't do any of the things I had intended. The whirl of emotions in me seemed to take over as I slapped him on the face. "Don't you dare do that to me again!" I said.

"I'm sorry, Belle. I know I scared you. I know, babe. It was my berserk stage," he said. "But, I promise that you don't have to see me like that ever again."

"I don't care about that! I'm talking about you trying to get yourself killed today. Do you hear me? I'm so mad I could kill you myself right now." I said. His eyes lit up with amusement. Then, I went a little berserk myself as I threw myself at him, kissing him everywhere, touching him, holding him. Groaning, he lifted me underneath my thighs, and I wrapped my legs automatically around his waist. He kissed me deeply, running his hands through my hair, then down my back, his hands pulling my butt up as he slammed his pelvis against mine. It was then I noticed he was stark naked and he was poking me with his shaft which seemed to have a life of its own. The life and death trauma had washed away all my shyness and reservations. I was so hot; I couldn't breathe. What was he doing to me?

"I want you so fucking bad it hurts," he said, in a husky whisper, out of breath.

"I want you, too. Just as much," I said, looking deep into his eyes.

"But, not here, not now," he said breathless. "Let's get out of here," he whispered as he grudgingly lowered me down.

Now that the moment was over, I tried very hard not to let my curious and hungry eyes roam down his naked body as I asked, "Keith, what happened over there?"

He grinned in understanding. "Nothing you wanna know about, trust me," he said as he grabbed the clothes of the dead demon and dressed hastily.

"Keith," I said, raising my voice threateningly. I wasn't taking that shit from him. Definitely, not today, not after all that I'd been through.

"It was Deumus. Another dark demon. He exploded the tunnel."

"What do you mean?" I stammered.

"It was a suicide mission. He was working with Azazel, it seems. Just like our friend right here," he said, pointing at the dark demon whose body lay lifeless on the ground. "I told you so; they cannot be trusted. Oliver should have known."

"I can't believe it!" I said. "By the way, how did you get out? I tried to contact you through my sleep, just like before. But I didn't believe I could, not this time."

"But you did, Belle-mine. You did come to me. I heard you yell my name, and then I heard you scream," he said, his eyes full of rage. "I wish I could kill him all over again," he said, cursing.

"Really? I can't believe I did it. I'm mighty proud of myself," I chuckled.

"And, you should be," he said, smiling.

"But, how did you turn into that thing? " I asked.

"Your scream triggered it. Shifting to my wolf hadn't done any good. But, I was able to remove all the boulders with my berserk strength. I'm mighty proud of myself, too," he joked.

"And you should be," I said. "I didn't know werewolves could do that. But, why didn't you turn berserk when the tunnel first exploded?" I asked a little surprised.

"Other werewolves can't. Only me. Unfortunately, I happen to possess this power without the ability to use it on command," he said shrugging. "The reason I turned berserk the last two has been because of you, Belle-mine. My berserk beast is latched onto your welfare, thank the Moon Goddess."

We made our way out of the hatch, back to the cave. I was so damn happy, despite having gone through the fear of losing him and the panic of choking. I had him back, that was all that mattered! He was mine, and I was keeping him no matter what the Moon Goddess had to say about it!

When we opened the door to the underground city, we almost walked into the death trap of Oliver and his men waiting at the other side who were ready to attack us at the entrance with their swords high in the air.

"Keith?" asked a stunned Oliver as he looked at us. "How is that possible? We thought there were no survivors?"

"There are none, but me."

"How?" Oliver kept asking. "And Kappas and Garuda? Where are they?"

Keith gazed at the men gathered at the entrance. There were two dark demons among them.

"You should ask them," he said pointing at the dark demons. "It was Deumus who bombed the tunnel. And Garuda killed Kappas, and he tried to choke Belle. She'd be dead by now if I hadn't got to her. In case you failed to notice, your dark demons seem to be under the spell of their master, just as I warned you."

"What the fuck?" Oliver cursed. He raised his eyebrows silently, signaling his men to undertake some implied action. Things went chaotic afterward as his men attacked the two dark demons among them, neutralizing the threat. The two demons were sprawled on the ground, their hands tied, struggling in vain to free themselves.

"I didn't do anything, man! This is bullshit!" said one of them while the other was completely silent. "You know I've been loyal to the resistance. Heck, I hate Azazel's guts. What is this supposed to mean?" he pleaded.

I was shocked watching all of this unravel before me, unable to do anything.

"What do we do with them and the others?" one of his men asked Oliver.

"You should kill them before they jeopardize the whole organization," Keith said.

"Kill them? Are you crazy?" I said, unable to keep my mouth shut any longer. "They haven't done anything."

"They haven't done anything as of yet," stressed Keith.

"Keith has a point," said Oliver.

"No, he doesn't. You are assigning guilt by association. There is no individual guilt here. This is all wrong!" I exclaimed.

"I don't think we can wait for them to slip," Oliver said. "We don't have enough men to spy on each of the dark demons who defected to our side. There are like fifty of them, including the ones we reformed among the tormented souls."

"Tormented souls? No! This is wrong. You can't just kill them when they've done nothing wrong."

"Do you forget they tried to choke you to death?" said Keith in exasperation.

"Yes, but that was Garuda. These demons on the floor had nothing to do with it."

"Perhaps the rehab center can give them all another fine-tuning," suggested one of Oliver's men.

"I don't know what to do. We need them to increase our ranks, but they can annihilate us from within if the gamble doesn't pay off. This is fucking messed up," said Oliver in despair.

"There is too much risk if you ask me," commented Keith.

Oh, no! This was going in an awful direction.

"Why don't you just gather all of them together for the time being, keep them under surveillance? Don't do anything rash. Give Wendy and her crew a chance to work with them." I begged. "Keith, I'm not going to forgive you if you keep supporting this massacre." I turned to Oliver with pleading eyes.

"Damn, Belle!" Keith said.

"What if you are wrong? What will happen if they are the ones who do the massacre because we don't stop them right now? Will you forgive yourself then?" Keith said.

"What if I'm not wrong, Keith? How will we justify killing fifty of them just because you don't even wanna give them a chance to come clean?" I asked.

"They are supposed to be dead anyway. I'm fine with it," said Keith, nonchalantly.

"You think everything is black and white. It's not as simple as that," I said. "Keith, please. Don't do this."

"Keith, what do you say?" asked Oliver for confirmation, torn about what to do.

I turned to Keith hoping he would not insist on this nonsense.

"I'm sorry, Belle, but I need to protect you. And I can't do that if the threat is right in front of our noses," he said.

In a moment of seconds, I found myself flying to where the two demons lay on the ground, and I raised my arms in the air as flames erupted around us in a small circle, taking us into its protective cocoon. I didn't know I could do that; I was as mesmerized by this new development as all the others.

"Damn it, Belle!" Keith said. "What are you doing? Stop it!"

"I'm doing what needs to be done. I'll not stop it until we reach some kind of agreement here. Believe me; I have the will to hold on for hours, and days if needed, even if it kills me."

"Belle, you are violating the rules of the resistance here," Oliver remarked. "If you don't stop immediately, I will have to punish you for this offense; you know that," he continued.

Keith growled. "Come again, Oliver?" Keith barked. "Nobody touches Belle. Nobody. Do you get that? Not if you want your precious resistance still standing."

"She's bluffing," one of the others said.

"She's not," Keith said. "Fine, we'll gather them together and decide what to do about them later on. Isn't that right?" Keith asked Oliver.

"Yeah, okay. But, this doesn't mean we'll eventually let them go. You need to understand that, Belle," he explained.

"That's fine; I just want you to do your best to give them a fair trial. That's all I'm asking. Now, seal the deal with your blood."

"C'mon, Belle, is that really necessary?" asked Oliver.

"Heck yeah, it is," I answered. Blood was sacred for werewolves; I assumed it was the same for all supernatural beings.

"Fine, as you wish," Oliver said as he made a small cut in his hand, allowing blood to drip on the ground as he swore on the deal.

As I let the flames die, I saw the gratitude on the dark demon's face who had previously attempted to defend himself and had miserably failed. One second later, I felt hot, dizzy, and next I didn't remember anything as my vision turned black.

Confessions

Belle

I opened my eyes, stretching lazily. When the hard ground dug into my back, I knew I was back in our cave room.

"You fainted," said Keith who was sitting a few steps away, his eyes roaming over me. "I was worried about you. You don't yet know your powers, and you are overusing them. I'm scared you may be damaging yourself."

"Well, they didn't come with a freaking instruction manual," I said sarcastically. "Besides, you left me with no choice. Where are they by the way? If Oliver killed them, I swear …"

"They are all safely contained on the same floor with the rehab center."

"I'll go there," I said, standing up.

"Belle!" he said as he followed me. "You are the most stubborn woman I ever met, you know that?"

"Thank you. I'm flattered and honored to be ranked first given the long list of women you met and frolicked with in your life."

Keith's facial expression was priceless. He couldn't utter a word.

As we walked towards the rehab center, he seemed to have gotten back his tongue, unfortunately. "You see everything in a different lens, Belle. But in battle, you can't make mistakes. Every mistake costs lives. These creatures have been to hell; this is who they are, and who they'll forever be."

"Don't freaking tell me they are a lost cause. Everybody deserves a second chance, you should know that better than anyone else," I said, reminding him of how he'd previously hurt me.

He was finally silent. When I entered the rehab center, Wendy ran straight up to me and hugged me.

"What were they thinking?" she asked.

"I have no clue. So, what's the plan? Where are they?"

"They are distributed into three chambers on this floor. We'll probe their minds today to see who's guilty and who's not. Unfortunately, the guilty ones will be eliminated."

I nodded. That was fair.

"That doesn't mean the ones who pass the test won't flip tomorrow," Keith reminded us.

I looked at him, pestered.

"Surely, you can make routine weekly checks with your ability to see the truth," I said to Wendy.

"Yeah, sure. We can and we should, now that we know it happens. But that doesn't mean we should kill them. Some of them have been real good friends to us."

"That's great. You see," I said turning to Keith. "The problem is resolved to everyone's satisfaction now. I'm so glad I intervened in the first place."

"Will you be helping us today?" asked Wendy.

"Sure, I wouldn't miss it."

Keith was about to object when I stopped him with a hand gesture. "No you don't. You've already fulfilled your quota for annoying me, and this is despite the fact that I've been overly patient since your return from near-death. Let's not overdo it, dear Keith."

"Belle."

I stopped him again. "No, Keith. Let's not."

He left the room, cursing.

"So how long has it been since you met your mate?" asked Wendy.

240

"You mean Keith? No, he's not my mate," I said. "Actually, Azazel is." I liked Wendy, and I felt I could talk to her.

"You gotta be kidding me, Azazel must be crazed over your loss," she exclaimed.

"There's no love lost between us, believe me. I was as precious to Azazel as a tormented soul. He wasn't exactly reciting poems as he severed my fingers and burned me."

"Ouch! Well, perhaps that's not too surprising, he's Lucifer's right hand after all. I could swear you were mated to that hunky werewolf, by the way," she winked at me.

"I wish, " I said sighing. "I'm simply crazy over him despite everything, you know what I mean?" I said. No need to list all the faults in his personality- that would take a whole day.

"Sure," Wendy responded. "We can't change them, yet we still love them."

"Do you have someone in your life?" I asked her.

"Yes, I'm in a relationship with George, but he's also not my mate."

"Well, mates are overrated," I said.

"Indeed they are," she said, sighing.

I spent the day helping Wendy. Later in the day, Keith came back to check up on me; then we headed together towards the kitchen, hand in hand.

"Let's grab some food and go to our room. We have things to talk about. It's time," he said.

Okay, I was all right with talking as long as we didn't fight. We got some olives, cheese, and bread and headed to our room. The food was scarce in the underground city; it was mostly cheese and bread for every meal. The can of olives had been a pleasant discovery.

We sat on the ground, facing each other. I fed him olives and came closer to him each time. Soon I was sitting in his lap. I then fed him some cheese and planted little kisses along his face while he was eating it. I looked deep into his eyes as I put another olive in his mouth, he twirled his tongue around the end of my finger, and he sank it deep into his mouth, sucking it. The passion in his

241

eyes should have scared me off, but I craved him too much. His lips found mine, food completely forgotten. Another type of hunger was driving us as our kiss became crazed, our tongues slowly moving in and out. I wrapped my hands around his shoulders, digging my nails into his skin beneath his shirt. He growled low in his chest as his fingers clutched me tighter at my neck. He kissed his way down my neck, leaving a wet trail and dozens of tingling love bites, tiny stings he eased with his hot tongue. "I have this need to mark you, babe. I don't know how long I can control myself."

"I'm not your mate, Keith. How can you mark me? I asked, surprised.

"But, you are, Belle-mine," he said as his hands were traveling all over my body, taking away my breath.

His words didn't register, not at first. But then, I pulled myself away from his heavenly lips. "What did you say?" I asked him.

"Uhm. Belle, this is what I wanted to talk to you about," he said, a little hesitant. "You are actually my mate."

"No, I'm not," I said, regretfully. "You know that. I'm mated to Lasarus and Azazel."

"Yes, that's right, unfortunately, but you're also mine."

"How's that possible?" I asked. "You are not making any sense."

"You are part of a prophecy. That's what I learned when I went to visit Tannon. You are the first hybrid child to be mated to all the leaders of the night children". He added unwillingly, "That's why Lasarus, as the head of the light demons, and Azazel, as the leader of the dark demons, both wanted you. Although I'm surprised that the Moon Goddess would let a disowned child be included in this prophecy as a potential mate."

Wow, could it be true? I wanted to dance with joy.

"Are you serious, but what does this all mean? I certainly don't want so many mates," I said. "Wait, is that why you came after me?" I asked, suddenly not happy with what he was telling me.

"No, babe. That's what I was afraid you would think. I came after you before I heard about the prophecy. Please believe me,

242

Belle. I decided you were mine, damn the fates, when I lost you at that cursed door in the attic," he said as he held my face gently between his hands, his eyes piercing into mine. "Do you believe me?" he pleaded. "Do you?"

I could believe anything as I gazed at his eyes which held me captive. But, I also could see the sincerity in his eyes as he waited in fear for my response. His brows were furrowed while he searched my face for any reaction.

"Yes, I do," I said and immediately spotted his relief.

"Thank you. You don't know what that means to me". His fingers brushed my lips. "I want you to be mine, I *need* you to be mine. I want it more than anything."

"But Lasarus will always come after us; I know he won't let go," I said in desperation.

"That's the beauty of it all, sweetheart. Once I mark you, the mate bond will slowly fade away for him. He won't chase you because he'll not feel the pull anymore."

Finally, I could sense a way out of this darkness and desperation enveloping me since I first left my pack. I could be free from Lasarus. I could be free from Azazel. And I could be with Keith, just as I wanted.

"Do it," I said. I wanted him to mark me. Desperately.

"Uhm, it would be more pleasurable if we follow the M&M routine," he said, his eyes twinkling with amusement.

"M&M routine?" I asked. What did he mean?

"Mating and marking," he chuckled.

I felt my face heat as I blushed. "Uhm."

"I thought you liked my touches?" he asked as his fingers softly caressed my face. He brushed his nose against mine with a feather-like touch as he leaned in towards me, his lips gently brushing my lips.

"I do. I love your touches. But, I'm a bit scared, that's all," I managed to say, pulling back.

"You'll love it. Trust me," he said, his voice thickened with desire.

"But, we don't have privacy here. Perhaps, we should wait till we get out of here," I remarked, finding myself in the clutches of panic.

"How about the well? There will be no one there at night," he said as he held my hand. Then, he noticed my body was shaking. "Belle, I need you so damn badly, but I'll wait an eternity for you if you're not ready."

"Okay," I said, still scared out of my wits. But I knew I wanted him as much.

As we went down the stairs, I felt nothing would ever be the same again.

M&M

Belle

As we walked hand in hand towards the well, I felt more confident that I could do this. As he had predicted, there was not a soul in here. Keith put the blanket on the ground, and gently laid me down on it.

"We'll go slowly," he whispered as he stretched above me, and I felt the length of his body press against mine. "Belle-mine," he whispered with his lips only inches from mine. Then, his assault started as he pressed his lips to mine, licking and ever so slowly nibbling them. My hands immediately hooked around his neck, desperate to bring him closer to me. His kisses became frantic as he moved his tongue in and out of my mouth, sucking on my tongue, quicker and faster each time. Our heavy breathing merged into one with the intensity of our passion. "You are everything to me," he said softly as he moved to my ear, nipping my earlobe with his teeth.

His lips trailed small kisses from my cheek to my jaw and my neck, I pressed my breasts against him as a lustful hunger gnawed at the pit of my stomach. Then, he pulled up my shirt, hastily removing my bra. I welcomed it as my swollen breasts finally split free. His hands moved to my breasts, cupping them gently. He brushed across my nipples with a light, deft touch and I let a low moan escape my lips as I pulled him closer to me. He rubbed and twisted my nipples into hard peaks and pleasure twirled in my belly. Then his lips replaced his fingers as he ran his tongue across my breasts, pressing a kiss to one of my pebbled nipples, gently biting it. I sucked in my breath, giving into this incredible sensation. How was I going to survive this, I had no clue. My heart was pounding so fast, I couldn't catch my breath. He slid his palms over my stomach, his thumbs and fingers teasing my skin. His face trailed down to where his hands were, his tongue dipping aptly over my belly button, making my tummy quiver. He removed his lips for a second to remove my shirt, and he just looked at me. I tried to cover my breasts, suddenly shy with his unfettered attention.

"Don't cover yourself, babe. You are so beautiful that I could gaze at you forever," he whispered softly.

Having Keith look at my half naked body like that made me so hot. "You are still fully dressed," I said to him. "Shouldn't my eyes feast on you too?"

He chuckled, pulling off his shirt and tossing it to the cave floor. I smoothed my hand over his bare chest; he exhaled slowly as if in pain. He leaned towards me, his bare chest now touching mine. I felt a torrent of heat vibrate through my body as I kissed his skin whenever and wherever accessible. My fingernails began a delicate journey, trailing patterns over the bare skin of his back until he could hardly breathe.

"What are you doing to me, Belle-mine?" he asked as his chest heaved with each breath.

The hunger in his eyes made me purr with want, and I lifted my hips toward him. He groaned clutching me tightly by the waist. "I can't wait any longer," he whispered. His hands trailed to my pants and I helped him take them off. He then tugged off his own jeans, pulling them down to the floor, and I gasped as I looked at my monster in all his glory. He was simply beautiful. The pain was little and fleeting when his body first joined with mine. I clamped my legs onto his hips, meeting him thrust for thrust. Tears of joy streaked down my cheeks as he made love to me, his hips agonizingly slow at first and then moving faster and faster, building that exquisite pressure inside me.

Every part of my body trembled as our bodies moved together naturally, effortlessly. My moans were now a constant in the room, penetrating its silence as I sought relief from this constant ache, this pleasurable torture, this insanity. His lips found my neck just when I was lost in the throes of passion. His ascending canines grazed my skin, and he bit me, his sharp teeth easily breaking through my skin. The pain and pleasure mingled as I arched one more time and screamed in passion. As we came down from our lovemaking, he pressed his lips against my skin where he'd marked me and whispered, "Mine."

"I believe M&M was a very good idea," I said as I grabbed his face. "Can we do it again?"

It was hours later when we finally stopped, I lay exhausted, my naked body fully stretched over his, and I fell asleep within the loving embrace of his arms.

I woke up to his kisses in the morning. "My Belle," he hummed as he rained kisses all over my face. He moved my hair behind my shoulder as his nose all but connected with my neck, taking sniffs at where he'd bit me. "Mmm, heaven," he murmured. "You carry a wisp of my scent now."

We made slow love and then we got up and dressed slowly, finally ready to face reality outside.

Love making had me starved and I easily devoured two sandwiches in the kitchen.

"Keith, I've been looking all over for you since last night," said Oliver, questioningly.

Then he looked at both of us in an inquisitive manner, his gaze pausing at my neck for a second and he chuckled. "Congratulations, no wonder you were nowhere to be found," he said.

I blushed to my ears. How did he even know?

"Why were you looking for me?" asked Keith with a nonchalant attitude while his fingers drew scorching circles on my back.

"We've spotted a new bunch of kidnapped people just brought in from outside. We need to move fast today."

"How in the hell does that happen when Tannon is protecting the gate so well that we can't get out? How does anybody leave this place to bring in more kidnapped species from outside? I fucking don't get it!" snapped Keith.

"Perhaps the gate is open," I said hopefully.

"Don't think so, but it needs checking. I'll be right back," said Keith as he stormed out of the room.

"Keith, come back here. It's not open. My men would know," shouted Oliver, but it was in vain.

We waited for Keith's return. Oliver felt uneasy in my presence after what I'd done; that was evident to me. There was a tense silence in the room until Keith finally came back, very annoyed.

"No, it's fucking closed," he cursed.

"I told you so," muttered Oliver. "Now, you've appeased your curiosity, can we please make a plan on how to rescue Azazel's new victims?"

"Fine. We should go for surveillance first, see how many there are and where they are kept, et cetera."

"Okay, take Daren with you. I'll be at the rehab center all day long today checking on the dark demons' progress. Then at night, we make our move."

"I'll come with you," I said to Oliver. "I mean to the rehab center," I explained upon seeing Keith's disbelieving face. Keith opened his mouth as if to say something, but then he didn't. My clarification hadn't done much to appease his concerns, that was evident.

Keith took my hand, dragging me down the stairs to the rehab center. He pushed me up against the cave wall before the bridge; then he gave me a kiss that took my breath away. "Don't leave Oliver's side, Belle-mine. Promise me," he said.

"Don't worry about me. I can take care of myself."

"Promise me," he repeated, taking my face in his hands and looking at me anxiously.

"I promise," I said. I didn't want him worried. I certainly didn't want another tunnel-like episode. I knew he was compromising by letting me work at the rehab center, because it went against all his nature as the need to protect his mate was too strong in him. The least I could do was accommodate his request.

"Good," he murmured as he licked and kissed my mark, unable to help himself. "Now that we are mated, I want to be inside you every fucking minute," he whispered as he playfully squeezed my ass.

I simply couldn't breathe.

"Do you want me inside you?" he asked, his lips an inch away from me.

I nodded as if hypnotized.

"How much?" he insisted, still not making a move to come closer. I wanted his lips badly.

"A lot," I managed to murmur, out of breath.

"Good," he said as his lips finally met mine in a kiss of searing possession. "Save it all for the night; you are all mine tonight. And I won't let you get any sleep. That's a promise," he said as he pulled back regretfully. Then he left for the surveillance mission.

I walked to the rehab center completely dazed after what happened. This mate thing was intense; I didn't know how I'd be able to continue with daily tasks with the thoughts of him creating a dense cloud of distraction every damn minute.

The chambers were crowded with almost fifteen to twenty demons in each. The three vampires were working on each dark demon individually, so it was taking time. Twelve guards were patrolling the premises making sure the dark demons behaved. I was with Wendy as she had one demon on trial; she was interrogating him about his loyalties.

Suddenly, I was hit by thoughts of gloom and desperation. Wendy also flinched. I wasn't surprised when Shana walked in. She generally kept away from everyone in the resistance, it was sad really, but no one could be near her long enough and not be affected by the darkness she carried around her.

"Hi," she said shyly. "I heard about all that happened and I want to be tested, too. After all, I'm one of them. I don't want anyone looking at me as if I got special treatment."

Now I thought about it; it was weird they'd skipped the umbra in this treatment. I guess the fact that she hadn't drunk Azazel's blood and had rejected being in his service in the first place, not to mention her help in bringing us to the resistance, had all acted in her favor.

"Sure, that's probably a good idea. I'll take you in within five minutes. Can you please wait outside till then?" Wendy asked wisely.

I don't exactly know how it happened but the dark demon on the interrogation chair suddenly grabbed Wendy by the throat, raising her up in the air. The rest of the dark demons in the room started attacking the guards. Wendy had now survived the shock and broken loose from the demon's grip and was fighting him as her fangs elongated and her eyes turned to bloody red. The four guards in the room tried to restrain the dark demons in vain.

A dark demon grabbed me from behind. Unfortunately, I was completely useless in defending myself. Yes, I was immune to their demonic powers, but they were also resistant to mine, and they were far stronger than me. Without my powers, it all came down to brute strength which meant I was screwed.

As I was struggling, I could hear a similar ruckus coming from the other chambers. What was going on? Keith had been right I was pained to accept. This had all been my fault.

The demon grip was too strong; I couldn't free myself. I tried to kick him from behind, but he didn't even budge. I had to do something, but what? It was then I had a revelation. I stopped struggling as I shifted to my wolf form. Yep, I created an illusion. I was still there in my human form, I knew now, but I looked like a small wolf on the outside. He let me go, thankfully, suddenly startled by what he was seeing. I ran as far as I could from him. But there was no escape, the whole floor was being attacked, the dark demons were all fighting as if in the clutches of insanity.

I ended the illusion, now appearing in my human form, as I tried to find a weapon. I found a pot of soup on the ground outside the chamber room, probably just brought for lunch from the kitchen. It would do. I grabbed it with both hands, hitting one of the demons Wendy was fending off. I was satisfied when I heard the thump of metal against flesh. The hot soup also dripped down the demon's face, blinding him momentarily. I used that second to hit him again and again. But that didn't stop him; it only made him angrier. He seized me brutally by the arm before I could get away and his other hand coiled around my neck. As he was about snap it, I saw Oliver's sword descend on his shoulders.

"Get out of here, now," Oliver shouted as he killed the demon and continued lashing his sword in a vicious whirlwind assault on multiple opponents.

As if I could … There was no way out of this mess. The whole floor was a battlefield.

Then the whole game changed as Keith charged in bringing help along with him. His eyes frantically searched for me, and I could see his relief when they locked on mine. He ran towards me, lifting me up in his arms, and carrying me to the stairs that would take me out of the insane floor.

"Go to our room. Stay there till I come and get you," he ordered.

I didn't second that, I was utterly useless in this battle with only a pot as my weapon, and I didn't want to get in the way.

I threw myself on the ground in our room, shaking like a leaf. I knew they'd be fine now that Keith and the others had come to help, but how could I have been this wrong about the dark demons? I suddenly wanted to cry so badly; I was crouched in the corner filled with misery, pain, and indescribable regret. I deserved to be punished for this.

"I'm sorry, but this is the only way," I heard Shana speak.

What was going on? When had she come? Was she the one making me feel this way?

"How long have you been there? I managed to ask as uncontrollable tears poured down my cheeks.

"A few minutes," she replied. "Enough to be the source of those," she said pointing at my wet face.

"I'm sorry, I mean no offense, but can you please leave?" I said to her as nicely as I could under the circumstances.

"I made a deal, I'm sorry," she said. "Your mate couldn't carry out his promise to me; the gate closed before he could. I wanted to go out when he was searching for you, you see? But, the protector was at the other side. He killed many of my kind, and in front of my eyes, just like that! I didn't dare try to get out. Not when it was still open. He was there waiting to kill me. He then sealed it. The protector." She was rambling. "I have to go out. The master promised it to me. He said the protector is finally dead. He said he's the only one who can get me out. I had to do this. I'm sorry."

What was she talking about?

"What did you do?" I asked her.

"I discovered I could be of help when I accidentally touched Deumus. He simply went crazy in the clutches of my darkness. My vapor triggered his blood bond, reversing the work of the vampires. And he exploded the tunnels. The master relished it. Then I tried it on Garudas. That worked too. I was surprised myself; I didn't know I could turn all the dark demons back to his servitude, just like that. And today was a miracle with all of the dark demons gathered in just one place. It was simple as I just visited all the chambers one by one, floated among the dark demons, making sure they all got a whiff of my darkness. And it worked like a charm."

I couldn't even utter a word.

"But, I'm not all that bad. I didn't tell him where the city was. I swear I didn't. I said I didn't know, that my eyes had been closed. He was angry because I'm the only one who can still hear him, others had the vampire touch, and they can no longer contact the master. And, I didn't tell him anything. Not a thing. But now I have to do something else for him to deserve my reward. My master says you are not valuable anymore, not after the marking. I have to kill you, I'm sorry. It is either you or everyone else in the city. You see, I'm not bad. I don't want to kill everyone. It will be just you. It won't hurt, just relax, let my vapor of darkness do its trick, and when you are weakened enough, I'll just breathe in your energy. It won't hurt a bit, I promise. Not a bit," she said as she came closer to me, her darkness trailing right after her.

Her vapor was weaving its dark spell around me. I felt so weak, so stupid, so sad that I just wanted to crawl on the floor and let it all end. But I was resisting the pull, hell yeah I was. I had to think of how Keith would feel if something happened to me. He'd be devastated. I had to fight this thing. She wasn't a dark demon, so could my powers work on her? I didn't know, but I sure hoped so.

I opened my palms, summoning the flames. I saw blue veins of energy become visible on my arms as my palms lit with fire. I threw the flames at her blue incorporeal form with all the energy I could muster. Right in the center. But nothing happened. Damn it, was she immune?

I was going to die anyway, so why was I struggling? It was all in vain. I deserved to die. I shook myself again to overcome the savage attack of her darkness on my emotional state. I threw several balls of fire on her, at her head and her torso, but she kept coming. When she was one step away from me, I had become so weakened that I simply fell on the ground.

"It's all right, Belle. I promise. Just open your mouth, and it will be all over in a minute."

My lips seemed to be under her spell as they opened involuntarily. She knelt down in front of me, bringing her lips close to mine. When she was about to suck my energy, ending it all, I lifted my hand one last time and threw a ball of fire which didn't even hit her but bounced over her head to hit the space behind her blue form. She shrieked in pain as she stumbled back. The vapor around her seemed to be fading away. Surprised and hopeful, I threw another ball of fire in the same spot, at the vapor surrounding her. She cried out in agony. Then she just vanished in the air. Who would have thought that her survival was dependent on the cloud of darkness? I just lay down, utterly still, my energy completely depleted.

The Light

Belle

"Belle, are you okay? What happened here?" asked Keith as he came running to the room straight from battle, his clothes drenched in sweat and blood. He knelt down beside me. "Belle, talk to me," he said as he looked around, trying to detect the source of the danger. He looked utterly confused as he failed to find any.

But, he couldn't have known about Shana, could he?

"How did it go? Were you able to contain them?" I asked as I tried to rise.

"Contained? That's one way of putting it; they're all dead. Just as they should be."

"I see. How about the others? Is everybody okay? How's Wendy?" I asked, worried.

"They all have cuts and bruises, but they'll live. And that's all that matters," he said, understanding why I asked this question. I could never live with the guilt if something had happened to them.

"It was Shana," I elaborated.

"What was Shana?" asked a puzzled Keith.

"It was her who did it all. The tunnel collapse, my choking, and now this episode. She was working with Azazel. She discovered that her vapor of darkness didn't mesh well with the dark demons, it pushed them off the edge to the other side."

"Belle, how do you know this?"

"She admitted it herself when she was here. I killed her Keith. I had to. She wanted to kill me. She said I wasn't useful anymore, not after the marking," I said, my limbs still shaking from the shock of it all.

"Whoa, slow down. Are you telling me she came here to kill you?" he asked.

"Yes."

"I can't believe I sent you here to face her. I fucking sent you straight into the midst of danger," Keith said in a low voice, a muscle ticking in his jaw. "How did you kill her?" he asked.

"You couldn't have known, Keith. She fooled us all. I was feeling sorry for her being in constant isolation in the resistance. My sympathies were definitely misplaced. Perhaps Wendy should give me a fine-tuning as well," I said, smiling bitterly. "Anyway, I killed her by burning her life source which, guess what, turned out to be the vapor of darkness that surrounded her."

"That's my Belle," he said proudly. "There's nothing wrong with you," he added softly. "You're incredibly stubborn, but I love it that you find good in everyone, even if sometimes there's no good to be found. I may be angry at you for some of your decisions, and I may not always agree with the things you wanna do, but that's all because the need to protect you is fierce inside me, and I'm a cynical selfish bastard after all. But you are an amazing woman, Belle-mine. I want you to know that."

"What are you saying?" I whispered as my heart started its rapid dance.

"What I'm saying is," he said as he planted small kisses on my face. "I love you, Belle-mine. I love you very much."

I jumped into his lap, hugging him fiercely. I couldn't believe he had said the L word. Despite everything that had happened, I was feeling jubilant. M&M&L, mating marking and loving, all in the last twenty four hours, what could be better than that? "I love you too," I said back. "And as much. Let's go to the well. I can't wait for the night," I said dreamily, believing he would jump at the offer. He didn't.

"I'd love to but we can't," he said with a pained expression.

"Why?" I asked, not understanding it.

"Because I got things to do. You know I went to see who the kidnapped outsiders were".

Why did I feel there was more to the story. "Yeah, and?" I asked patiently.

"One of them happens to be Daisy."

"Daisy? You mean Daisy from the witch coven? Your ex-lover with whom you …" I couldn't finish my sentence as he palmed my mouth to stop me.

"That was before, Belle. Please listen to me. I don't have feelings about her that way. I never did. I was trying to resist your pull and she was just convenient at the time, that's all. But none of this changes the fact that I have to save her. You know that, right?"

"I do. But I don't have to like it. Not one bit." I knew I was acting like a petulant child, but the wound was still too fresh, too deep. I took a deep breath. "I'm sorry. You're right. But I don't understand how she was kidnapped in the first place, I thought she was a powerful witch."

"She is. Look there are many things we don't know about these dark demons."

"How many others were taken along with her?"

"At least ten. That's why we have to move fast before they are forced to drink from the fountain. We have a meeting in ten minutes. We'll make a rescue plan, and I'll be leaving quite soon after that. I probably won't be back before midnight. Hopefully, we'll be bringing them back with us."

"Joy, oh joy," I muttered under my breath. Then, I felt wretched. Of course Daisy had to be saved. I knew that. Yet, I didn't relish seeing her again.

"Look, Belle. I know how you feel, but this won't change anything between us. You know that, right? Nothing can ever come between us. Nothing. I love you."

I sighed happily. I could never get enough of this L word. I could just live and die hearing it on constant replay.

"By the way, your timing was perfect today," I said. "It could have all gone in a different direction if you hadn't come in time."

"It wasn't coincidence, Belle. I knew you were in danger. We were done with the mission and we were returning when I felt your fear and panic."

"You can do that?" I asked.

"Yes, we are mated now. We can feel each other's extreme emotions. I also felt your anxiety here in the room."

"I see," I said, suddenly understanding why he came running to our room just after my Shana episode.

"That's cool," I said. I loved all the added perks to being mated to a hunky and lethal werewolf. Not to mention the great love making. Mmm, having all of that in one package was great I had to admit, I'd gotten a great deal!

After Keith left, I got up to check on Wendy and the others. The rehab center was a mess; blood was sprayed all over the place but thankfully the dead bodies were removed. I found Wendy tending to a wounded George. His body was burned in several places.

"Wendy, George?" I said hesitantly. "Are you guys okay?"

"We are. Well, considering," Wendy said.

"I feel bad."

"Don't. We were with you on this, you know that. They fooled us all. I still don't believe it. It doesn't make one bit of sense to me."

I told her about Shana.

"That's why she turned up like that at the rehab. She was the switch! Where the hell is she?" she snarled.

"Dead," I said.

"Good. I now feel sorry, you know? About the dark demons, I mean. They served us well, that is, until her. But now, we have to shut down the whole humanization program. The resistance can't take the risk. Heck, I won't take it myself knowing it only takes an umbra for them to turn to Azazel slaves. I still can't believe it! All this time Oliver hoped the umbra would defect to our side, little did he know how lucky we were that they hadn't. Who would have thought?"

257

.yself busy for the rest of the day which kept me from
over Keith. The mating bond was so strong that I
help but think about him every damn minute. I helped at
u̱ nter tending to the wounded. Thankfully, there were no
humans among the hurt ones, and they would all heal. When the
evening settled in, I went to my room. I had a plan. Shana had told
me the protector was dead. I had to find out. I was going to reach
Tannon in my sleep. I had to. I was getting better at this, and I
hoped I would be able to contact him this time, if only he wasn't
dead of course. I shivered in fear, what if he *was* dead? In that case,
we were doomed. Could we ever get out? And what did Shana
mean by saying Azazel was planning to bring down the gate? This
was all giving me a headache. I covered myself with the blanket
which still carried Keith's scent, I inhaled it deeply, wishing he
was here with me. I tried to relax as I closed my eyes. I fell asleep.

I was in pitch darkness. No! Not again. Please, no! How was
this possible? Damn, why was I ending up here all the time? Did
my talents only work with Keith? I would never try this again if
only I got out of here, I promised myself.

"Tannon?" I asked, knowing full well he wouldn't answer.

Terror gripped me slowly as I inhaled and exhaled deeply. What
if I couldn't get out this time?

"Hello, someone, anyone? Please answer me." I moseyed
cautiously to find the wall. I had no intention of punching it this
time. I just wanted to lean back against the wall and close my eyes,
hoping to wake up back in the cave room once more.

"Damn," I cursed loudly. I absolutely hated this place. This
room was turning out to be my personal torment.

"Hello, who's there?" I heard someone shout as my hands
finally found the wall.

"Hello, hello, who's there? Where are you? Can you open the
door?" I asked, excited, hopeful.

"No, I can't open the door. But you can. Who are you? What's
your name?" she asked.

"Belle. My name's Belle."

"Belle, is that you? My goodness, I can't believe it. It's Alice."

"Alice, what is going on? Where are you?" I asked, slightly flipping out.

"I'm outside. I'm so excited, this is a miracle just when I was losing all hope," she said, her voice tearful.

"Alice, what are you talking about? What's going on?" I asked, feeling completely and utterly lost.

"I'll explain it all. But can you find the door? It's imperative that you find it."

"What door? There are no doors here, believe me I know. I've been here before. Why can't you open it from outside?"

"Belle, listen to me. Tannon is dying. He's been in a coma for weeks. I can't help him, I've tried. Moon Goddess knows, I've tried. But he's fading away."

So Shana was almost right. I could scarcely believe it. "What happened to him?" I asked.

We don't exactly know. Days back, Tessa went into a sudden trance, crying out for her twin. She said he was in the middle of a desert dying and his hawk needed to be saved. Apparently, Tannon's life energy was linked to a hawk who was also dying on the floor in the Alps. She asked me to heal the hawk while Tessa tried to rejuvenate his body. But, neither of us could make any progress on Tannon. We've been trying for weeks now.

But how can I help, I don't understand," I said.

"Belle, do you know where you are?"

"No, not really. But it's dark here, very dark. I can't see a damn thing."

"You're in Tannon's head. He's trapped in there and he's lying in all that darkness which is slowly taking him away. I need you to find a door, a window, an opening, anything that will let me in so that my healing can work. Can you do that?"

"I don't know. I don't think there is any door or window. I wasn't able to find it the last time I was here. It's just four walls," I said desperately.

"Just try again, please, Belle. You are our only hope. We don't have much time left. He's already too weak."

"Okay, sure," I said. Now that I knew where I was, I wasn't frightened anymore, and Alice was just outside guiding me through all this.

I splayed my hands like a lizard's against the wall, moving them all over as I moved into the room from one side to the other. There was nothing.

"I can't find it," I said, exasperated.

"One more time, Belle, please. There's gotta be something. Look for any weakness in the wall."

I started all over again, moving my hands in a wider arc than before, also kneeling down on the floor, and rising on my toes to make sure I covered every inch of the wall my height would allow. As I was on my knees trying to cover the bottom part of the wall, my fingers came across the underside of a stone which was slightly sticking out. I felt for a hold, gripped its edge and began to shimmy it out.

"What's happening?" Alice asked when she found me silent.

"Nothing as of yet, just give me a minute," I said, not wanting to excite her for nothing. Could this be the weakness Alice talked about? I hoped so. I took it out. And there was light shimmering from behind it. Alice ran to the opening as I tried to pluck more stones from the wall, but the others didn't budge. This was it, it the only opening she was going to get.

"You did it. I can't believe it, but you did it! Thank you, Belle! Thank you!"

A healing energy erupted from out of Alice's hands, and soon she was projecting it inside the narrow opening.

"Belle, you need to leave now. But there's so much to talk about. Can you find us again?"

"Yes, I believe so. By the way, Daisy is here in the underworld, so don't worry about her. Keith will bring her to safety," I said as I closed my eyes, willing myself back into the cave room. I surely hoped I could do this as waking up next to Keith last time had been entirely accidental.

I felt my body float away as I vaguely heard Alice in the distance say, "Don't…"

I woke up back in the city. Unfortunately, I was no longer in Keith's arms, and I was freaking out with the little of what I'd heard. Don't what?

Bringing them Home?

Keith

I couldn't help grinning as I left Belle's side. I couldn't stop thinking about my beautiful mate. This mission was the last thing I wanted to do right now; I still remembered her shy invitation to make love. How I wished she was in my arms right now, every step away from her was pure agony. The sooner I finished the task of rescuing, the sooner I'd get back to her. That thought made me hurry to the meeting. At the meeting, I told Oliver about Shana's treason.

"We have to be careful not to be visible to the umbra as we leave the outskirts. We can't trust them anymore," stressed Oliver. "We have to be sure not to leave any trail behind us."

"Exactly my sentiments," I said.

We made our way to the center of the underworld, making sure to hide our tracks. I crouched in darkness with the others, waiting patiently for Oliver to give the signal. The kidnapped were taken to somewhere in the underground tunnels where the tormented souls were being kept. The plan was to go in two groups of three to search the whereabouts of the victims and rescue them while the others created a diversion to distract the guards. There was going to be a blood bath; that was unavoidable. We would then use the secret hatch to the caved-in tunnel to hide and wait it out as Azazel unleashed his dark demons after us. I hoped the waiting would not be too long. I wanted to be back early enough to make love to Belle. I would kiss every inch of her body starting with her toes and then move slowly up, taking my time to worship every part of her. I growled low in my chest in anticipation. I couldn't wait.

Oliver put his finger to his lips to silence them as a group of dark demons were heading their way. In their midst stood Daisy. They entered the majestic building.

"Damn," I cursed. "They're keeping Daisy separate from the others. You should follow the plan to rescue the others; I will go into their lair to save her. I'll meet you in the hatch."

"You can't do this alone, Keith. It's too dangerous."

"I'll be less likely to be detected, and I'll move faster alone. Don't worry about me."

"Do we have to save her? Don't get me wrong, I mean every kidnapped person is precious to us, but sometimes if the odds are stacked against us, we should let it go. We'll still have the other victims to join us."

"She's too powerful to let go," I said. "Trust me on this. You don't want her on the other side. She can be very useful to us in this fight ."

"Okay, I'll take your word for it."

Oliver turned to Silius, "Okay, it's time for that diversion."

The rebels scattered around, each one equipped with explosives. Silius was a brilliant human chemist, and he'd been extremely useful to the resistance by making explosive mixtures. It was his mixture that Deumus had exploded in the tunnel. Each of the rebels equipped with explosives disappeared from view. Soon explosions were heard in the vicinity, drawing guards like a bee to a honey pot. Some demons also came out running from inside to find out what was happening. This was my cue; I sneaked into the building. It was huge inside with many floors above. The problem was that there were no stairs winding to each floor. Apparently, they were considered a useless addendum in the underworld. They must have carried Daisy to wherever she was kept. I'd have to climb the rock structure and search each floor for her. Could she open a portal in the underworld I wondered? Otherwise, once I saved her, I'd have to carry her down hoping no others were on our trail. This was going to be a pain in the ass rescue. Hopefully she'd be imprisoned on the first floor.

As I was silently climbing to the fifth floor, I was cursing. She'd better be here, I thought. I could hear the sound of demon voices coming from the upper floors which meant going further up promised trouble. I hoped it would not come to that. Thankfully, I heard her voice in one of the rooms as I kept searching the floor I'd just climbed. I'd have to get in, kill them all, and get her out. That was the plan. I shifted as I broke down the door. There were surprisingly only four demons inside; I dodged their fire as I killed the first two who threw themselves at me. One of the remaining two tried to run away, the coward! He was the first to die and then the other one threw a series of fireballs at me. The flames seared me as they came into contact with my thigh, and I cursed. I was losing my patience as I closed the distance between us. The demon tried to punch and kick me, and my paws descended on his torso, clawing a deep scratch on his chest. The demon shrieked in pain as I gave him the killing blow on his neck as I severed his artery.

I looked at Daisy who thankfully seemed to be unharmed. "C'mon, let's get out of here before we are discovered," I said as phased into human form.

"Keith? What are you doing here? How?" she asked. "Not that I'm complaining. You can't believe how happy I am to see you. I thought this was it, you know."

"Later we'll have the time to chat, but now we need to get out of here."

"I know a shortcut. That's how they brought us here on the first day. They seemed to be cautious of some rebels. I thought they were joking. You are with them, right; you must be? This is unbelievable."

"Yes, I'm with them. Where is the shortcut?"

"I believe they have one on this floor. Follow me".

"Can you later transport us out of the underworld?" I asked hoping for an affirmative answer.

"No, I can't, Keith. That's the problem. Or I would have been long gone by now."

"That's what I thought. Anyway. Where is it?"

"That door, right there. It's a secret passageway that directly leads outside. Open it."

I opened the door, but with the first step I took forward, I found myself trapped in a cage. What the fuck was going on? I beat the bars. "Daisy!" I shouted, "Don't come in, it's a trap."

I saw her appear right outside the cage after ten minutes.

"Aw, my dear Keith, aren't you sweet worrying about me?"

I was so stunned that I couldn't even utter a word.

"My hero who tried to save me from Azazel and the dark demons. How I adore you! You've always been my best lover," she said, winking at him.

"What the fuck is going on in here?" I asked even as I was getting the picture. I just needed the details.

"My love, you know what's happening here. I've been working with Azazel for some time now. Of course, he's not as hot in bed as you are. Actually, he's disgusting, but somehow I make do," she said sighing. Then she looked at Keith in a rather weird manner. "It makes me wonder, though, now that you are here, I may have it all. What do you say, Keith," she asked, chuckling.

I tried to shift. I needed to break the cage.

She laughed. "Don't even try. You see that's wolfsbane all around you. I can't create a portal on the outside, but I can create many portals here in the underworld. I have to admit creating an all-time-use teleportation door on each floor was a brilliant idea of mine given the constant threat from the rebels. The mighty army of the kidnapped ... I told my Azazel that we should be prepared in case the rebels break in. How right I was!" She seemed mighty proud of herself as she played with her hair. "But, even I have to admit that I never thought creating a portal to a cage dipped in wolfsbane potion would be much use to us. You see we have cages of various sorts, each one created to mute the powers of different species. But, so far we had never captured a werewolf from the other side. I thought this portal was utterly useless. But look at us now. We have the king of all the werewolves. I didn't even know

265

you were here in the underworld. This is such an honor, dear Keith."

"What did you do?" I growled.

"Well, I might have killed Tannon, that's all."

My face cringed in disgust.

Daisy was too willing to talk about her exploits. "Oh, I see you also knew about the hawk. How interesting given it took me many fucking years to find out what that bitch Tessa's brother was hiding. I discovered it all by myself you see. I knew his coordinates in the Alps, and I teleported myself there when he was visiting his dear sister. And what did I see, a small stupid hawk on the floor! I thought it was just a pet, but then the floor shook so violently that I was nearly thrown off my feet. This hawk stopped the shaking and answered back in Tannon's voice. Then, I suspected something of course. But it took me some more adding up to get the whole picture."

Tannon dead? It couldn't be.

"Then, last year when the dark demon incursions happened, and the council decided to take concerted action against them, guess what I did? I found a dark demon, not for the intention of killing, but instead of sending a message of friendship to his master. I made an offer to Azazel, and he accepted. This alliance has not been easy as I couldn't contact Azazel by blood, not like Tessa or Tannon. I always relied on some dark demon getting out and finding me at a portal I established at the coordinates I gave them."

"What was the damn offer, bitch?" I bellowed.

"Not much," she laughed. "Just bringing down the gate in exchange for ruling the world together. But you see for that Tannon had to die. I knew he was way too strong for me, but did you know, dear Keith, that killing his hawk would do the trick as well?" she said wickedly. "Anyway, miraculously I got my opportunity when I heard Tessa complain about Tannon going away instead of coming to the coven. I went to the Alps with the intention of killing his hawk, and coming straight back."

"Is the hawk still alive?" I asked gritting my teeth.

266

"Yes, apparently it's still alive, if you call that living. It's hanging onto life by a thread. I learned that when Tessa went into a trance feeling her twin's agony. She saw the hawk lying on the floor, gravely injured, though she had no idea it was my doing. The stupid bitch asked me to take Alice to the Alps to tend to his hawk while she teleported herself to Tannon's side. Can you believe it? And, of course, I did what she asked being her bell girl in the coven. It was another golden opportunity for me. So, I took Alice there to kill the hawk for good this time. I hit her on the head and was about finish the stupid bird when Tessa appeared suddenly, as if feeling what I was about to do. Crazy antique bitch! I got out of there, and made it to the gate and waited to get in. Thankfully, a crack appeared a few days back".

She saw my astonished expression. "Don't get overly excited, dear Keith, it's all mended back again, nobody knows how. But, don't worry, soon the whole gate will come down. I know it," she said it with conviction.

"I'll kill you," I promised.

"We'll see. A few days with Azazel and you'll wish you were dead. Perhaps I'll spare you some of that torture. Only if you are good to me. What do you say, my sweet Keith, will you be my fuck-boy?" She grinned as she left.

"Screw you!" I cursed. Tannon was either dead or dying, I was trapped in a wolfsbane cage and I definitely would miss my rendezvous with Belle. This day was so fucked up!

Finding Keith

Belle

I woke up probably towards morning, feeling utterly sick. I didn't know what was wrong with me, but there was this indescribable anxiety clawing inside my chest. I bent into two holding my stomach in pain; what was going on? I took deep breaths. Was it something I'd eaten? It was unlikely as it'd been another simple sandwich. It was then that I noticed Keith hadn't come back. Where was he? He was supposed to be back by now. I got up, restless to find where he was. Was he tending to the victims, was he at a meeting with Oliver? I had to find him; I just had to!

I was so worried that I ran to find Oliver, anyone who'd let me know where Keith was. I found some strangers in the kitchen. Aysha was distributing more sandwiches.

"I see you moved your lazy butt to help the victims," said Aysha.

"Not now," I retorted at her. "When did they arrive?"

"Half an hour ago," she said.

"Have you seen Oliver, where is he?" I asked impatiently. I felt something was wrong, I felt it in my bones.

"He's in the meeting room."

I remembered where it was. I ran there, not stopping until I was face to face with Oliver.

"Where is he?" I asked.

"Belle, I never seem to have good news for you."

No! I didn't want to hear his next set of words. I couldn't. Not again!

"Please tell me he's not dead," I begged, my voice shaking.

"No, he's not dead. At least, I don't think he is."

I let out the breath I'd been holding. Thank the Moon Goddess, he was alive! That was all that mattered for now. All else could wait.

"Belle, he's been taken."

On second thought, all else couldn't wait. "What? What do you mean taken?" I couldn't help but shout.

"We think he's been captured by Azazel. He never came to the hatch which was our safe place, and he'd gone to rescue the witch."

"But you're not sure?" I said, trying to hold onto a slim hope.

"No, but the witch he wanted to rescue was apparently working with Azazel and Keith didn't know at the time."

"Are you talking about Daisy? What, no! How do you know?" I asked in shock.

"Yes, Daisy, the powerful witch. The other kidnapped victims told us. It was too late for us to warn him. I thought he'd not be fooled, you know. It was Keith after all. I really thought he would not fall into any trap set for him. If anyone could make it out of there, it'd be him. But he didn't. We think he's captured."

"The bitch," I shrieked. My hair and body started to rise high up in the air. A fire erupted from my hands. I closed my palms to kill the flames. How she disgusted me, she had hurt my mate. I wanted to kill her. I wanted to hear her scream in pain. "What's the plan?" I asked as calmly as I could under the circumstances.

"Plan?" Oliver asked.

"When are you planning to rescue him?" I asked. I was anything but calm. My heart was thumping, and there was a huge knot in my chest. Now I knew it was him I felt when I'd woken up. It was the mating bond screaming in my heart to let me know that Keith was not safe. He was suffering, I knew it. Only the Moon Goddess knew what that bitch was doing to him. The feelings of worry and fear bum-rushed me, nearly knocking me off my feet.

"Rescue him?" Oliver asked in a hushed tone.

"Yes, rescue. How are we going to save him?"

"We can't, Belle. Not, yet anyway. He's in their headquarters. You can't go poking the bear in his lair. It's extremely well protected, it's where Azazel lives and breathes. Going there is an entirely different game than going to the tunnels or fighting the demons outside. Moreover, we don't even know where they are keeping him. No diversion will empty that building, let me tell you. I'm not saying we will leave him there, of course not. But we have to lay low for a while now, at least for a week. Our rescue of the kidnapped, I'm sure, has already led to a huge uproar. They'll undoubtedly increase all security precautions. That building will be impenetrable for some time now."

"What are you saying? We can't wait that long, he may be tortured, he may be demonized. What the hell is wrong with you?"

"Belle, we have to be rational at this. Look, Keith is the best soldier among us here. He's the king of all werewolves, the deadliest creature I've ever come across. Believe me, he'll manage until we get him out."

I tried to convince him in vain, but he didn't budge. I couldn't wait till then; Keith couldn't wait till then. I knew it in my heart. I would have to go in there myself even if it would be the last thing I did on Earth. I would try to save him. I had to use what I was good at to accomplish this mission. First, I would contact him and find out where he was. And second, well, there seemed to be nothing else as my powers were utterly useless against the dark demons. I didn't care. I would cross that bridge when I came to it. I tried to fall asleep again, but this time it was worse than in the caved-in tunnel. Every passing minute in which I remained awake was making me anxious which, in turn, was making it impossible for me to fall sleep. It was a vicious cycle, and I couldn't seem to get out of it. After I had wasted two precious hours like this, I was so desperate that I was willing to do anything. There was one thing that came to my mind, the only thing that could potentially work. I went to find Wendy who was sleeping, cuddled with George.

"Wendy," I whispered, hating to wake her up, but really needing her help.

I don't exactly know how it happened but one minute I was addressing Wendy and the next George had me pinned to the wall and Wendy's fangs were at my throat.

"Wendy, it's me. Belle," I said in a hurry before she sank her fangs deep into my throat.

She looked at me and then let me go. "Don't ever wake up a vampire from her sleep, Belle. It's plain stupid," she said withdrawing her fangs.

"I'm sorry. I didn't think; I just needed your help."

"About?"

"I need to go to sleep to find Keith. And I can't fall asleep!" I said, exasperated. "I tried but I can't. Can you do it with your mind trick?"

"What do you mean you are trying to find Keith? Where is he?"

"He was captured tonight while trying to rescue an undeserving witch."

"I'm so sorry, Belle," she said sincerely as she rubbed her eyes. "What's Oliver doing about it? I'm sure the resistance will get him back as soon as possible."

"Not soon enough," I said. "He says it's too dangerous right now, and I can't leave him there knowing he's in the hands of the witch and Azazel. By the time Oliver finally gives the green light for the rescue, it'll be too late for Keith. Trust me, I've been in Azazel's hands for one night, and I can imagine what they are doing to Keith right now. I can't, and I won't, let him go through that."

"I understand. I don't know how sleeping will help you find him, but I can assist you with that."

"Thanks, please hurry," I said in gratitude.

Wendy let me lie on the floor. She then approached me, inched her face closer to mine and looked deeply into my eyes. I felt her steely, hypnotic gaze as it drew me to her, and I couldn't look away. A sense of ease and relaxation swept through my body, her hypnosis wrapping me in a warm, protective cocoon. I closed my eyes.

271

I found myself in a closed room facing a cage. I yelped when I saw it was Keith who was chained in that cage. His torso was bare, streaked with blood. Fresh lacerations crisscrossing his bare skin were accompanied by burn marks scattered all over his body. Purple bruises, cuts, and trails of dried blood covered his beautiful face. My heart squeezed seeing him like this. I went to the cage, my hands grabbing the bars. "Keith, my love, what have they done to you?" I asked. Seeing him like this was killing me. I tried to bend the bars using all I had, but I wasn't strong enough. It was impossible.

"Belle, is that you? What are you doing here, you need to leave now," he said urgently.

"Keith, don't worry. They can't see me. Only you can," I said trying to comfort him. Actually, I had no clue. "How are you?" I asked. What a dumb question; he was tortured, beaten, burned, how could he be?

"I'm fine, don't worry about me," he said, trying to comfort me.

"Keith, tell me where we are."

"Belle, you are not going to try anything stupid, are you?" he asked as if feeling what I was about to do.

Of course I was! But he didn't need to know that. "Look, Oliver is planning a rescue mission for you. You need to tell me where you are so he can make plans," I said, blatantly lying.

"All I know is I'm in this cage which happens to be in this enclosed room. So you see, I don't have a fucking clue. I came here through a portal. That bitch Daisy set a trap for me. And I can't do anything as both the chains and the bars are dipped in wolfsbane."

Of course they were. Azazel was an expert in making cages with the ability to mute powers. "I know, Oliver told me what happened. I will shred her body to pieces," I said, spitting out the words in venom.

Keith tried to laugh, but his cuts only allowed a half smile. "My beautiful Belle! How I missed you."

I went to the door.

"Where are you going?" asked Keith in a panic.

"I'll just look around, see where we are. I'll be back in a minute."

"Are you crazy, come back here," he shouted, thrashing around at the chains, trying to break free of them to stop me.

"No one can see me, don't worry," I said as I opened the door. I could hear his muffled objections behind the door.

There was not a soul outside, thankfully. It was a long narrow tunnel with other closed rooms. I walked till I came to an opening with winding stairs to an upper floor. I took them cautiously, watching for any footsteps or voices around me. When I got to the upper floor, I gasped in shock. This was where the cages of the tormented souls were. It seemed we were in the tunnels where I was caged, and they were keeping Keith one floor below them. Apparently, they had reverted that floor to a cell-like system for all the kidnapped. I went back to Keith.

Keith was relieved to see me reappear.

"Thank the Moon Goddess, what were you thinking? How could you do such a stupid thing? I was going nuts in here."

"I'm fine, I wasn't in any danger, I'm telling you. I found out where we are. We are one floor below the tormented souls," I explained. "I'm not sure how this works, but I wonder whether I can get you out of there while I'm in this state. I was able to help Tannon after all."

"What? Did you contact Tannon again? When?" Keith asked.

"Last night. I know you didn't want me to do it again, but I had to."

Keith nodded. He knew it had been the right call on my part.

"Is he alive?"

"Now he should be. But he was in a coma and that's why I was finding myself in a dark room every time I tried to contact him. Alice was there outside the room the last time I tried to reach him, and she helped me. The darkness was fading as I left him. I have a feeling he's getting better even as we speak. Alice is healing him."

"That's great news. Daisy tried to kill Tannon. She said he was dying, I'm glad that turned out to be false information," Keith said, relieved.

"That bitch!"

We needed Tannon to get out of the underworld, but first I had to save Keith. I'd been able to touch the cage before, so that was good news. All I had to do now was unlock it and break the chains, all in that sequence. It couldn't be harder than finding a loose stone on the wall in a pitch dark room and taking it out to lett the light in, could it? I heard voices just outside the door.

"Carry that carefully, you douchebag," I heard Daisy speak to a dark demon in an angry tone.

"I'm carrying it carefully," he said.

"Don't act wise with me," Daisy shouted. "Do you want Azazel to hear about your disrespect to his mate, his beloved queen?" I heard the sound of a hard slap outside.

Just as they were barging in, I pulled my body back to the cave. I could try my chances with Daisy, but I didn't know how many dark demons were accompanying her. Even one demon was enough to guarantee my capture. I couldn't risk that. Keith's eyes widened in panic. I heard him sigh in relief as he saw my fading form.

"Are you okay, what happened?" asked Wendy when she saw me open my eyes.

"I know where he is. Guards were coming so I had to retreat. But I need to go back there."

"You were there? With Keith? How could you that? I never heard of any species possessing such a talent, even witches," Wendy said.

"I'm a witch demon hybrid, I seem to have weird abilities," I explained, slightly embarrassed.

"Still, you shouldn't go back there alone. Where is he being kept?"

"One floor below the tormented souls."

"Let us help. George and I have been talking about it since you went to sleep. We want to help."

"I can't ask that of you. And it's easier and safer for me to go to him in my state of sleep."

"Yes. But you can't get him out alone. You'll have to go out the routine way, try to make it out of the underground tunnel right under the nose of the guards who watch everything from the sky. We can help you with that, we've been there before. You know you need us, Belle."

Of course I needed them. She saw right through my false bravery. She was there when I tried my best against the dark demons. It wasn't impressive at all. The truth was I was not strong, and Keith was in a sorry state. I didn't have the luxury of refusing their help. Swallowing hard, I nodded. "Thank you," I said.

"Okay, good. I'll ask Dresner to send you back. George and I will get going immediately. We'll meet you there."

George went to bring Dresner who came to the cave room half-asleep. I was restless as I paced back and forth in the small space, simply wasting time. I had to wait to make sure Daisy and the guards were all gone, and it was killing me. It took every ounce of my will to stop myself from going to Keith immediately. I waited for half an hour but then asked Dresner to start the hypnosis. I hoped my impatience would not be costing us. His eyes quickly took me under their spell, and I fell into sleep, swiftly finding myself back where Keith was. There were no guards in the room. But most importantly, Keith was no longer chained, and the cage was unlocked. How had he done that?

"Keith, are you okay. Did they hurt you?" I ran towards the cage as excitement ran through my veins. He slowly came out of the cage. I hugged him gently, giving heed not to touch his wounds. A chilling cold entered my soul when he didn't hug me back.

"Who the fuck are you?" he asked as he pushed me away. There was no recognition in his black eyes.

275

Memory Loss

Belle

"Keith?" I said, not really grasping the meaning of his words.

"I said, who the fuck are you?" replied Keith.

His words cut through my soul like a knife. "What do you mean? It's me, Belle." I replied.

"I don't know you. I've never seen you in my life. Who are you working with, answer me?" he asked as he shook me.

What was going on here?

"She's working with Azazel," Daisy said, suddenly entering the room. "Kill her, she's going to give us away," Daisy said, faking the panic in her voice.

So she could see me too. Well, that was unexpected.

Keith looked at me. I stepped back. "Keith, she's the one who threw you in that cage, don't you remember? It was Daisy who betrayed you." I said trying to reason with him. He didn't react to my words. "What have you done to him?" I shouted at Daisy. I couldn't believe what was happening. It all seemed surreal.

Daisy was one step ahead of me in the game as he somehow seemed to know her, but, conveniently for Daisy, he remembered her before her betrayal.

"C'mon, we don't have a minute to waste, if she found out about us, the others must be nearby. We must kill her and get away," Daisy urged Keith.

Keith seized me by the collar, lifting me high up in the air.

276

"Kill her, be done with it," Daisy said again.

"Keith, don't do this, it's me," I whispered, unable to believe that my mate who had claimed his undying love for me a few hours back was about to kill me. But Keith didn't choke me, his face reflected a mixture of emotions as he kept me in the air, then he lowered my body slowly until his nose was right at my neck and inhaled me deeply, his eyes fixed on my mark. He growled low in his chest. Then, he let me go and looked at Daisy, utterly confused.

"Keith, you're not going to trust a stranger, are you? I'm the one who freed you from your chains and the cage. I'm the one who came back for you so that we could get away from Azazel." Daisy said. "You know she and her lover kidnapped me, tortured me. You know me, Keith, we have a past together. Don't let her get away," she cried out.

Keith looked torn with indecisiveness.

"Fine, if you can't kill her, I have to do the deed for both of us. Step away," she said as she took out the gun tucked in her back pocket.

The bitch was about to shoot me. Would my powers work in this state? I raised my palms to find out and was thrilled to see the flames in my hands. I threw a ball of fire at her which hit her right in the stomach. She cried out and bent over with a groan. That felt so good.

But then she rose so suddenly, firing the gun so fast that I couldn't even dodge. Keith threw himself at the bullet which tore through his chest, exiting out at his back. I almost cried out, but I held myself with an iron will as my scream lodged in my throat like a rock. I couldn't afford to do anything that would attract the guards. Keith just let out a deep breath as his already tortured body suffered through the bullet wound and the damage to his organs, but he was still standing.

"Keith," I whispered, touching him, wincing as if feeling his pain.

"Look, what you've gone and done now," shouted Daisy. "Are you insane, she's Azazel's bitch. Get out of the way."

When Daisy raised her hand again, I was ready this time. I threw a fireball at her wrist and she cried out, dropping the gun. I then raised my arms, and let her body be surrounded by flames by creating a wall of fire that rose up to the ceiling, making her the target of my new neat trick. There was no way she could get out unless I released her and I had no intention of doing that. I nudged Keith by the elbow, and said "Let's go." Of course, he would have to kill her once I put down my arms.

"Keith, she's taking you straight to Azazel. Get me out of here, they'll find me, and Azazel will torture me, you can't leave me here," Daisy begged from inside the flames.

"Release her," Keith ordered me. "I said, release her!"

The plan where Keith killed her was not an option, it seemed. "Are you kidding me, Keith, I'm seriously losing my patience with you right now."

The door opened, I turned around in panic expecting the guards, but it was my friends. I was tremendously relieved to see them. I seriously needed some help here.

"Come on guys, let's go," Wendy said. "The floor is empty." Then she noticed the flames. "What's with that?" she asked.

"I trapped the witch inside."

"Aha! Okay, let's get going, the clock is ticking," repeated Wendy.

"Guys, Keith does not remember me. I'm having a tiny bit of a problem here convincing him to come with us," I explained.

"Are you telling me they've already demonized him?" Wendy asked in shock.

"I don't know. Oh, that never occurred to me. Do you think so? No, no, that can't be," I said, feeling a trickle of dread worming its way through my body. "Please tell me it's not so," I pleaded, my voice shaking.

"We'll figure it out later," Wendy said. "Now, we have to go. Is that what I think it is? A wolfsbane cage?" asked Wendy.

"Yes," I said, not understanding where she was going with this.

"George, upon my count?"

George nodded in understanding.

"One, two and three." And both Wendy and George jumped at a battered, wounded and now utterly confused Keith, trying to drag him inside the cage. I couldn't help them as I needed to keep the flames around the bitch.

Keith was growling in rage, struggling to free himself and he almost did it, despite his condition, punching Wendy around the ribs, kicking George on his burned thigh. But, once he was in the cage, the fight was over. Wendy sat on his bloody chest while George held his hands and simply looked at his eyes, "You are coming with us, no questions asked," he said.

"Screw you!" Keith spat at him.

"Damn, he's one stubborn werewolf!" George cursed.

"Try again, George," shouted Wendy. "We don't have any time to lose."

George leaned in much closer than before, his eyes only an inch away from Keith's and repeated the words. This time around, it seemed to have worked.

"You're lucky that he's extremely weakened and the cage was right there, or else this was a lost cause; he'd have blocked me out repeatedly," George said.

The relief I felt was beyond words. They'd convinced Keith to come with us, albeit unwillingly.

"And now for the bitch," I said. "Once I put down my arms, she'll be free."

Wendy nodded.

Catching up with the game, I counted. "One, two, three."

Wendy jumped to sink her fangs into Daisy's throat the moment I lowered my arms. But, Daisy was gone.

"Where is she?" Wendy asked, confused.

"She must have opened a portal to somewhere else. We need to get out of here fast. She's probably alerting the guards as we speak," I said, cursing.

We rushed out of the room. It was all going well until we were almost about to reach the stairs that would take us outside. We heard footsteps coming our way. And then voices. The guards were coming! Where could we hide? All we had were some empty cages in an open passageway. They wouldn't do. They were moments away, they were coming.

"The Queen said she was here somewhere. Scatter around; we have to catch her."

Wow, all these guards were just for me. I'd be flattered if I wasn't scared out of my wits.

Hundreds of guards were searching the premises. Daisy had sent an army after us. Slipping away unseen was not an option. Wendy closed her eyes in dismay. I didn't know how many of them were coming our way, but there was no way we were getting out of this alive. Keith was not himself, and only Wendy and George had the strength to fight with dark demons. I could do an absolute nothing. This was it. I saw Wendy mouth the words 'I love you' to George. She was saying goodbye. I looked at Keith, wanting my last exchange of words with him, but all I received in return was a look of indifference.

I wasn't willing to give up. I didn't want anything to happen to my friends, and I wanted my forever with Keith. And, hell or heaven, I was going to have it.

I turned to Wendy and whispered, "I'll try something. I'm not sure it'll work, probably it won't. But I need all of you to be absolutely still." Her widened eyes reflected her surprise, but she nodded as she put her fingers to her lips to signal the plan to George. He nodded. Keith was like a puppet anyway, so he'd pose no problem.

"Hold hands and don't move," I whispered. We took each other's hands and stood immobile.

I closed my eyes. I knew how to create an illusion of a wolf; I had done it so naturally and for such a long time that it had never occurred to me I could do anything else. Now was the time to try it. Since I could create a fireball, there was no reason why my other skills shouldn't work in this state. I didn't have a choice; I had to give it a shot. I imagined all of us as free spirits, roaming around bodies that were invisible. I erased the contours of our bodies, over and over again in my mind, imagining, seeing, creating the empty space where we stood. My heart was pounding like crazy, and I had no clue as to whether it was working or not. I kept my eyes closed to keep from freaking out which would ruin my concentration, and any chance of getting this right. I heard footsteps approaching our way. The dark demons marched into the passageway, and scattered out looking for us. I knew we were right within their sight. I heard them speak.

"Look inside each cage, make sure they are not hiding inside one of them," one of them instructed.

I held my breath as I heard shuffling footsteps all around us. I expected them to attack us any moment now. Then, miraculously nothing happened and in what seemed like hours, but was only minutes, the sounds in the room faded away.

"I don't know what you did, but it worked," whispered Wendy. "They're gone. I can't believe it. They looked straight at us but didn't see us. You're wonderful, Belle. I thought we were dead." She hugged George, and they kissed quietly to savor their togetherness. I wanted to do the same with Keith, but he had no clue as to who I was. Instead, I grabbed his hand, and he let me like a little child. I had to be content just by touching him under the circumstances.

"What did you do?" asked George.

"I created an illusion. I believe that's what I did. I think I made us invisible."

"That's incredible. Can we also get out like this? It would make it incredibly easy to get away," George said.

"I don't know, I guess so, I can surely try. We need to make sure we don't bump into anyone, and we need to walk without making any sounds. I've never tried anything like this before."

George reset Keith's mind not to make any sounds, just to make sure, before we went any further.

We walked hand in hand towards the stairs, keeping Keith in the middle. The guards had no intention of leaving, so we had to be extremely careful when we ran into them. There was a group of demons keeping watch by the stairs, we walked forward step by step, tiptoeing as we passed right beneath them, taking the stairs one at a time, taking heed to make no sound whatsoever. I was keeping the lead as I tried to create a blanket of invisibility linked individually to everyone in the group. Just before I reached for the door that would take us out, it opened from the other side revealing Daisy and Azazel. Now we were doomed! Every second was precious as they were about to go down the narrow stairs where we all stood. Azazel and I stood face to face. I stood frozen in my spot, not daring to move, not daring to breathe.

"What's that smell?" asked Azazel sniffing the air where I stood. He stretched his hand towards me as if sensing my presence. I reflexively dodged to the side, almost losing my balance. If it hadn't been for George who held me with a firm grip, I would have rolled down the stairs. Thankfully, Azazel withdrew his hand. That had been so close; I had barely avoided his touch.

"It's your stinky demon army, that's what it is," said Daisy sarcastically. Thankfully, they gave each other icy stares before heading down the stairs which gave us enough time to get away.

I nudged George, who nudged Keith, who nudged Wendy, who had already turned around, and now was coming down the stairs as silently as she could. Once we were down, we waited it out as Daisy and Azazel disappeared, still arguing heatedly.

Thankfully, we managed to get out of the tunnel completely undetected. Afterward, it was a lot easier as the guards above could not see us. We didn't stop until we came to the cave that would take us to the underground city.

"I'd better get back to my body," I said as I pulled myself back to my sleeping form and woke up looking at a worried Dresner.

"I thought you'd never wake up," he said.

"I'm fine, thank you," I said without making any further explanations as I hurried to meet the others. I ran into them on their way.

"Where do we take him?" asked Wendy.

"To our room, please," I said as I led the way.

"You know what will happen to him if he's demonized. Oliver will not be forgiving, especially after the episode with the dark demons," George said.

No, I didn't even want to think about that. All I knew was there was no way I would allow anyone to hurt him. "Please end the hypnosis," I said.

"Are you sure, perhaps you should rest a bit before you deal with him."

"Yes, I'm sure," I confirmed.

"Okay, as you wish," George said, snapping Keith out of the hypnosis.

Keith looked puzzled for a few seconds. He looked around, disoriented.

"Where the hell am I? Where is Daisy?" he asked.

Moon Goddess, help me. This was a nightmare.

"Keith, sweetheart. Daisy was our enemy, you remember, right? We brought you somewhere safe."

Keith seized me suddenly, burying his nose in my neck. He took deep breaths which seemed to soothe and relax him.

"Are you a witch?" he asked. "Why do I feel you are my mate? What the fuck have you done to me?"

Oh no! I was having a deja vu. It seemed we were back at square one in our relationship.

Patience

Belle

I didn't even know how Keith managed to stand.

"Please lie down," I said to him. He needed some medical attendance immediately. I went to fetch some clean clothes, bandages, alcohol and water which was pretty much all they had at the resistance. I had to clean his bullet wound, cuts and burns to prevent infection, not that there was much I could do to heal him. I couldn't even give him my blood the way he gave me his as it wouldn't do him any good. I was no leader, my blood didn't matter. I was relying on his super healing abilities to mend his body. His face already looked better.

Still, he looked so weak and confused as he lay on the ground.

"Stop your spell, witch," he said.

"I'm only a half witch and spells are really not in my skill set, Keith."

"Why do I …" he started saying and I cut him short.

"Let me guess: Why do you feel I'm your mate? Because we are. We're mates. You even marked me, see?" I said showing him my neck. "What happened to you? What's the last thing you remember?"

"I don't remember marking you. That's for sure, witch," he said narrowing his eyes.

I cleaned and bandaged his body and changed his clothes which turned out to be a huge task as he did nothing to help me. All the while he just looked at my face.

"I want to fuck you," he said when I was finally done, sweaty and exhausted from the effort.

"Vulgarity doesn't become you, Keith," I said, still trying to adjust to this new Keith and desperately failing.

His hand grabbed my head. "You are so beautiful," he said out of breath as he dragged my face closer.

That was better. My heart started pounding as my body reacted to his nearness. "Keith, do you remember me?" I asked, excited and hopeful.

"Love, let me kiss you," he said as his lips came closer.

"I told you never to call me that," I said, suspicious this time.

"As you wish, Bella," he murmured sexily as his lips sucked mine greedily.

"Damn you, Keith. It's Belle, not Bella. You don't remember," I said pushing him away in frustration.

"Whatever, what's the difference? Look, you already think we're mates. And, I want you so damn badly, I can't seem to draw breath to my body. So, you want it, I want it. What's the damn problem?"

I slapped him in the face. "You can't breathe? Perhaps that's because there's a bullet wound right in the middle of your chest. Look, my patience is wearing thin, Keith. You better stay the hell away from me until you get your memories back."

What if he never did? I didn't even want to imagine.

"I don't have a problem with my memory. It's your spells I have a problem with. I remember Daisy quite fine. By the way, what have you done to her, witch? Where is she?"

"Have you forgotten she's the pure-blood witch, not me! Your precious Daisy set the hounds on us, Keith, we barely got away. Trust me on this, everything she told you was a lie. She's the one who set a trap on you and erased your memories."

285

"Maybe, maybe not," said Keith, shrugging his shoulders. "Besides, she can't erase memories."

"She can't, but her lover Azazel can. Remember Azazel, the lord of the underworld?" I said. "Remember his Fountain of Lethe? Did you drink from that, Keith? Did you?"

"What bullshit, I didn't drink a damn thing! You're a good story teller."

Moon Goddess, give me strength!

"You better get some rest to heal. And, I certainly need to be away from you for a while," I said. I needed to find what happened to him and I needed to keep him away from Oliver until I did. But when I was about to leave the room, his voice stopped me.

"Stay," he said quietly. It hadn't sounded like an order, more like a prayer. I saw him wince as he tried to breathe. He was suffering, my poor Keith, my poor mate. And, he didn't remember me. I was going to kill that bitch!

"Okay," I stammered, not used to seeing him helpless like this.

He tapped on the empty space on the ground as if beckoning his lover. He wanted me to lie down next to him. It was extremely hard to love him and want him this much knowing that none of what I felt was reciprocated just because that bitch stole his memories. His arms came around me, he buried his nose in my neck and kept inhaling my scent as he fell into a peaceful sleep. His arms felt so familiar; a giant sized lump settled in my throat, and my eyes prickled with the salt of unshed tears. How was I going to get him back?

I slept next to Keith, completely unaware of how exhausted I'd been. I woke up when I heard someone speak in the room.

"Belle ..."

I looked around, confused. There was no one in sight. Keith rose suddenly as he clutched his wounded chest. He growled while he tried to detect the intruder in the room.

"Keith, is that you?"

Keith continued growling.

"Have you come for your woman, Azazel? Show yourself!" bellowed Keith.

"Azazel? It's Tannon. What's with him?" asked Tannon.

"Tannon? Are you okay, I'm so glad Alice was able to heal you".

"Yes, I'm fine and all thanks to you," Tannon replied.

"I heard so much about you," I said. "As to your question, it's rather difficult to explain. He was imprisoned by Daisy, and I think she did something to him. He doesn't remember, well … some things."

"I see."

How come I couldn't see him? "Uhm, Tannon, where are you?" I asked.

"I can contact you with blood. But it's more like a phone conversation. I heard it's different for you."

"Yes, I guess so," I said. "Do you know what happened to Keith?" I asked immediately.

"I think so."

"What? Please tell me he's not demonized."

"Not yet," Tannon replied. "How long did he stay with Daisy?"

"Several hours."

"They must have given him a dose or two, starting the process. But that would not be enough to demonize him, his blood is too ancient to be diluted. But it must have erased all his recent memories."

Now I remembered the conversation Daisy had with the demons when I was with Keith in the room. She was cautioning the dark demon to carry something carefully. That something must have been the vial of blood from the fountain. It was then that I had left the room which must have given them enough time to pour it down his throat. And, that's why he didn't remember me when I had made it back to him. It all made sense now.

"Can he recover his memories?" I asked in worry.

"Hello, I'm right here," said Keith. "Stop talking about me. And stop flirting with my mate whoever you are, asshole."

Wow! Now, I was his mate?

"I'm Tessa's twin. Do you remember her?" Tannon asked.

287

"Yes, I remember her. I'm not an imbecile you sneaky mate thief, show your ugly face!"

"Keith, please! You are acting like a little child. Stop acting like a jealous mated werewolf when you can't even remember my name."

"Is that so?" asked Tannon.

"No, that is not so. Mind your own business! I remember your name fine, Bella," Keith bellowed.

I let out a frustrated sigh. "You are so paying for all this when you get back your memories," I said. "Tannon, I hate to ask this but can you get us out of here?"

Keith continued growling. "I can get us out of here wherever we are, I don't need his help to protect my mate!"

I couldn't take it any longer. He was driving me nuts.

"Yes, I can. I'll give you the details. I need to leave now. But I'll ask you a favor, Belle."

"Ask away," I said.

"I didn't want to set eyes on you, ever. But, knowing what I know now, I need to see you, to be sure. Can you come to me in your sleep?"

"Do you want me to kill you, huh? Is that what you want? I may not remember why or how, but she's fucking mine! And I keep what's mine, do you get it?" Keith raged. "Find your own mate!"

"I'm sorry, I didn't realize Tannon" I said, feeling extremely embarrassed. "I thought the mate bond between us was supposed to fade away after Keith marked me," I explained. Tannon apparently had feelings for me, poor him!

"Are you also mated to this asshole?" Keith asked. "She's seeing you over my dead body, you bastard! What part of it don't you understand, she is mine!"

"Belle, I had no clue of your existence, I wish I did. Everything would have been different," Tannon said.

"Uhm."

"But, I want you to know I already love you," Tannon said. "Even if I never set eyes on you," he continued. "You are so special to me."

Keith was raging, and I fidgeted with my hair, unsure of what to say. This was really awkward.

"But, there's someone else who loves you and would love to see you very much."

"No, I don't want to see Lasarus," I said to Tannon.

"Who the hell is Lasarus? Do you have a death wish, Tessa's twin?" Keith snarled. "I'll fucking kill you! I'll kill him, too," Keith said as he began to punch the cave wall.

Tannon completely disregarded Keith and continued addressing me. "Not Lasarus. I'm talking about someone else."

"Who?" I asked, confused.

"Tessa."

"Tessa? I don't understand," I said.

Keith intervened. "Yes, we'll see Tessa about this fake mating bond that seems to be driving me crazy. Look at how real it feels, I want to rip your heart out." Keith said. "But, that's for later. Now, Tessa's twin, I want you to leave us the hell alone!"

Some things never changed, he still wanted to take me to Tessa to get rid of the bond.

"Shut up, Keith," I shouted at him. "The bond is real, accept it!"

"You see, the prophecy said: mated to many rulers not all the rulers of her children. I should have realized long ago," Tannon muttered.

"I'm sorry I don't understand?" I said.

"I told Keith that the prophecy said you were also mated to me."

"I know."

"But the prophecy had a loophole. I know that now."

"What the fuck are you rambling about, man. Spit it out!" Keith barked.

"Keith, I'm not her mate," Tannon said.

I was perplexed, but Keith still seemed agitated.

"Then who the hell are you? What do you want with my mate?" Keith asked.

"I'm her great-uncle," Tannon said. "I believe Belle is Shea's daughter."

New Memories

Belle

"Tessa's granddaughter?" asked Keith.

"Excuse me?" I asked, stunned.

The priestess who annoyed the hell out of me was my grandma? The idea of listening to her chuckles for a lifetime filled me with dread. She'd better revisit the visitation fee if she wanted me to come for holidays, or else she had to forget about seeing me. A giggle erupted from me on that thought. I was losing it; this was all so crazy. She almost looked as young as me, for Moon Goddess's sake, how was that for an eccentric grandma?

Keith was silent. At least he was no longer in the clutches of jealousy, punching the walls or ranting on.

"I'm sorry, you caught me by surprise. I mean are you sure, this is so sudden, so unimaginable." And so preposterous, but I didn't say that. "How do you know?" I asked Tannon.

"He can feel and sense images that leave a trace on you," explained Keith. And then he said," Oh, wait, how do I know that?"

"Did you get back your memories?" I asked him, forgetting about all else.

"No. Not really," he said, but he no longer seemed to be disputing his memory loss.

"Yes, I can feel Shea all over you. And, this also explains the mystery of you."

"Mystery?" I asked.

"Your talents, Belle. The ability to create an illusion is given to a few only. Shea could do it. And only ancient witch blood can procure long distance contact. You have it, too," he explained. " I have to go now. But, I want to see you, Belle. And Tessa will, too. We lost Shea, but now we have you."

"Wait!" I said after him. I wanted to say, 'this is your lucky day, buy one get one free,' but he was already gone without giving me a chance to tell him about Gregory.

"This is some news indeed," I said.

Keith was looking at me very intensely. "I don't know what to make of all this," he said with obvious frustration. Then he sighed, and sat down leaning on the wall, his long legs stretched on the floor. He raised his hand towards me, his palm open in silent invitation.

I loved him so much; I would take every crumb he threw my way like a starving kid. I walked towards him, my hand taking his as I lowered my body next to him. He suddenly lifted me and placed me in between his legs which were now spread wide open. He pushed me up against his body, and when he saw my hesitation, he leaned me back against his chest with one hand.

"Shh, just relax. We'll talk," he said.

"But ..."

"Well, I don't know what has happened to me. But my instinct tells me there is truth in what you've been saying," he said, exasperated. "Look, I don't know who you are, my mind is completely blank about you. But my body recognizes you. Your touch sears me to my core," he said.

Aww, I was melting all over.

"I don't have memories with you; that's true. But, there's no reason why we can't create new ones. What say you?" he whispered in my ear.

"But, you called me a witch. You said this mating bond was fake?" I asked, surprised. It was like I was on a roller coaster ride with him. As always, it was impossible to comprehend his mood swings.

"I know, I'm sorry. I was confused and I unleashed my anger at you".

Hell yeah, I accepted his apology. But what next?

"Look, I don't know lots of things right now, but I know one thing," he said, pushing my hair away as he inhaled my scent.

"What is it?" I asked as my heart beat wild in my chest.

"I'm addicted to this scent; I can't seem to get enough to it to my lungs. And that can't be faked. So?"

Was he hypnotizing me? I was so lost wrapped in his arms. I felt I was dying as I savored the melting warmth of his mouth against mine, it was so tender, so soft, so sweet that I wanted an endless supply of that, all wrapped and gifted to me for eternity.

"So, what say you?" he asked again as his lips left small kisses at my neck.

My heart did a somersault inside my chest, and I could swear that my heart skipped a beat or two. "Hmm," was all I was able to say. What was he asking, I had no clue? I was irrevocably lost, and I wanted more of all he was doing to the power of infinity.

"You wanna create new memories?"

"Yes, please," I said, completely acting like an idiot. All my limbs had melted, the cells and nerves in my body were burning, and desperately begging for his touch.

"Okay, great," he said as he pulled back, heartlessly withdrawing his hot lips and sweet touch, all at once.

"Huh?" I managed to say, having a hard time drawing breath to my lungs.

"Let's talk then and get to know each other once more."

Damn, was this a joke?

"Talk?" I croaked, crying inside.

"Yes, talk. So tell me who Belle is."

Well, he'd gotten my name right this time. But, I wouldn't even have cared if he'd only continued kissing me, my body ached for him.

I sighed. He looked resolute. I took a deep breath to silence my wildly beating heart. "Well, let's see. I've just turned eighteen.

I've lived with a werewolf pack until you came and fetched me. I love my adoptive parents, and I have an older brother, Sean," Then I gasped, remembering. "Oh wait, I have a twin, brother, too. His name is Gregory."

"So you lived among werewolves, and you liked that?" he asked, concerned.

"Yes, I loved it," I admitted. "I've lived among them all my life. I thought I *was* one until you told me otherwise."

"Are you close to your brothers?"

"I've been very close to Sean all my life; you see I didn't know that I was adopted. Sean's always been very protective of me. But I knew Gregory only as Sean's best friend. Lasarus was the one who told me about Gregory when he took me to the demon island. Apparently Gregory was keeping tabs on me in the pack, and he'd gone to live with the demons once I left. Oh, did I say our father was a demon?" I said.

Keith was listening with undivided attention.

"Am I hurting you?" I asked suddenly remembering his chest wound. I tried to pull away, but he stopped me. "No, please don't. I seek your closeness. It helps me heal," he said giving me a quick brush of his lips on my head.

"Well, anyway, I was angry at first, but then Gregory and I started mending our relationship. Now I miss him too. And I worry about him; I don't know what Lasarus has done to him now that I'm gone."

His body tensed at the mention of Lasarus. "So Gregory is also Shea's son?"

"Yes. All of this seems unreal."

"All will be well, Belle. I promise. Tell me more about yourself. How did you spend time in your pack? What do you love and hate? What's your favorite color? I want to know all about you," he said.

"I mostly spent time goofing around with Joshua and Daniel, my two best friends. They are a bit crazy, you know. They don't take life seriously but they are incredibly fun to be with. I loved hanging around with them all the time in the pack. We got into lots of trouble together, eavesdropping on pack meetings, pulling pranks at school. Well, I'm not sure whether you'd like them actually. You are a kinda serious guy, their complete opposite in that way," I muttered, my forehead now wrinkled with concern. "But, they are extremely loyal friends. Did you know they came to the demon island to save me?"

Keith flinched. "And I didn't?" He didn't remember, my poor Keith. The idea he hadn't come after his mate enraged him.

"You didn't know where I was, silly. They had found me accidentally by following Gregory."

I looked at him; he looked disgusted. If I knew him, he was blaming himself for not accidentally finding my trail.

"That's no excuse," he said, angry at himself.

"It's okay, Keith. You've saved me when it mattered; you saved me from Azazel in the underworld."

"What did he do to you?" he asked, his two hands which were previously clasped on my belly now fisted.

"It doesn't matter, Keith. I'm fine; you gave me your blood, and I healed," I said looking at him deeply, my eyes begging him to lean in and kiss me. But he didn't. Instead, he continued asking questions.

"And, what else?" he said.

"Well, my favorite color is black." Duh, it was the color of his eyes and hair.

"What do you hate and love?" he asked.

I started listing it all. "I hate broccoli and cauliflower. I hate change. I hate Azazel. I hate manipulative bitches." And I wanted to add, 'I hate that you don't remember me,' but I didn't. "I love chocolate and especially chocolate chestnut cake. I love reading mystery novels. I enjoy watching fantasy and science fiction movies. I love everything about science. I love nature. I love my family and friends." I then looked at him. "And I love you." He looked grieved. "I don't expect you to respond," I said to him, fidgeting. "I'm sorry; I didn't mean to put you on the spot. It may have looked like it, but that wasn't my intention at all. I know you don't have feelings for me now because…"

He put his forefinger on my lips, stopping me.

"Your soul just whispered to mine. And my chest ached right here," he said, placing his hand over his heart. Then he added the magic words, "Belle-mine."

He remembered!

I grabbed his head and pulled him to me, kissing him as if life depended on it. I didn't know, at the time, that it really did. He turned me around and settled me back on his hips. "I'm so sorry for hurting you like that, I'll kill that bitch myself," he muttered as he left kisses all over my face, his hands traveling sensuously up and down my body. I clasped my hands around his neck before finding his lips again. My fingers brushed back and forth through his hair as I continued kissing him with full passion. My fingers came across a hard lump at his neck, a piece of information I immediately ignored as his hands were unzipping my jeans. I cupped his face, kissing his jaw, going down and letting my tongue savor his skin along his nape like he always did to me. He was pulling down my jeans; I lifted up my hips to help him as my lips and hands continued their exotic journey at his neck. My finger brushed against the hard lump again, and this time around, I paused. I trailed my fingers on and around it, turned his neck a little and looked at it.

"Belle, babe. I need you, please," Keith was begging as he felt my withdrawal.

"Keith, what is this?" I asked, trying to hold off his lips which were hovering over mine, seeking access.

"Later, babe. I want you now."

"Keith," I said in a panic. "Stop, what is this on your neck?"

The dread in my voice seemed to penetrate his lust as he stopped. "What?" he asked in a voice thickened with passion.

"Keith, there is a hard lump here. It looks as if there's something inside."

He touched the spot for a few seconds, then he cursed. "Fuck! Fuck that bitch."

"What is it?" I asked in fear. I didn't like what I was about to hear. This wasn't good. I knew it. What was going on?

He moved me off his lap and said, "I need to take it out," he said as he half shifted until his paws emerged. "It's not gonna be nice, you better not look."

"Take what out? What's going on Keith?"

"It's a magic tracking device. Daisy must have planted it on me in case I got out before she erased my memories."

"Why?" I asked, my voice shaking.

"To open a portal of course. We need to get out. They're coming," he said as he dug his sharp claws to his neck, digging deep to grab the device as blood spurted out.

Despite his warning not to look, I couldn't turn away as my eyes got transfixed on what he was doing. All I could do was scream.

Uninvited Guests

Belle

I screamed, unable to help myself. I felt faint with the horror of the scene unfolding right before me. I focused on breathing in and out as Keith took out his claws holding firmly the small tracking device that was previously planted in his neck. The hole on his neck continued to bleed profusely. I forced myself to move and rushed to put pressure on it. My poor Keith, my poor love! First the torture, then the bullet wound, and now this. How would he survive all this? There was so much blood!

Keith saw my face which, I'm sure, was as white as a sheet. He stilled my shaking hands, covering them with his. "It's okay, Belle. I'll be fine," he said as he tore a piece of his shirt and wrapped it tightly around his neck. "But we have to warn Oliver; we have to evacuate. We don't have any time to lose. They could be here any minute," he said trying to snap me out of my shock.

I was so shaken I didn't know what to do. I looked at my bloodied hands. Breathe in and breathe out.

"Belle, I have to get rid of this device. Can you find Oliver?"

"What will you do?" I asked as I grabbed him tightly to keep him with me.

There is a small chance they haven't fixed on our location yet. It's unlikely, but I have to take this somewhere else, even if just to gain us a few precious hours."

"Throw it into the well," I cried out.

"It won't help. They won't get any coordinates in the water, so they'll just create the portal based on the previous one, which will be right here, right in this room. I have to do this, Belle."

"You are in no condition to do anything, look at you. Let someone else do it," I begged him.

"No one can run as fast as me, you know it. Besides, we brought this on them. You know that. Look, we've already lost enough time. You need to contact Tannon, see if he can get us out. I'll find you at the gate. Meanwhile, tell Oliver to put explosives everywhere. We need to bomb the whole place. That will hold them back."

I remembered well how fast he could run when he shifted, I'd been barely able to hold onto him when he'd taken me from my pack. I knew we had no other choice; I had to let him go.

"I love you, Keith. Please be there when we leave," I said.

"I love you, too. I'll make it; I promise, Belle-mine."

We left going in different directions, my heart aching for him. I watched as he disappeared out of my sight. I was so scared with all that was happening that I remained immobile for a precious few seconds. Then I willed my legs to move, and with a humongous effort I turned around and ran, my knees barely holding me up, my throat dry with fear. I found Oliver in the kitchen, having breakfast, enjoying himself, and joking around with his men. Little did he know that all that was about to end.

"Oliver, the dark demons are coming. We have to evacuate the city," I said, out of breath.

Oliver, who didn't even know Keith was rescued, was looking at me as if I was crazed. But he had stopped eating. I had his full attention.

"Come again?" he said. The befuddled expression on his face said it all.

"I rescued Keith this morning. But we found a tracking device on him."

"Whoa, what?" he asked, again stupefied.

"Look, I'm sorry we brought this to you, but we didn't know."

'You didn't know?" he said almost inaudibly, his voice chilling.

"I know you are angry, but this is not the time to discuss this. What is done is done. Now, we have to act to save our asses. Keith said we should bomb the city to hold them off."

"Is this a joke?" he asked, cursing.

"No, I'm sorry. I wish it was." I was about to strangle him, quit the dramatics and act, please!

"But, how will they open the door to the city? They won't know about the switch."

"They don't need it. Unfortunately, the witch who betrayed Keith is powerful enough to open a portal that can take them directly inside."

"Damn, Belle, what did you guys do? Where is Keith?"

"He's gone to get rid of the tracking device. But it'll only gain us minimal time, they'll eventually find us here. We spent enough time in the room for them to get our location."

"Screw it," said Oliver. "Where will we go? We'll have to fight," he ground out, desperation taking hold of him. "It'll be suicide for us; there are so many of them and so few of us."

"No, we don't. I can get us out."

"Out where?"

"Out of the underworld."

"How? The gate is closed," Oliver said, frustrated.

"Leave that to me; you just handle the rest."

"Are you kidding me? There's no way out!" he yelled.

"There is. Just trust me."

"Trust you? Why should I?" asked Oliver bitterly.

"Because you don't have any other choice," I retorted, unable to bear his whining any longer.

Oliver blinked. Hesitation and hope jockeyed for first place in his eyes.

"You get us out, Belle, and we'll be even," he eventually said. "C'mon guys, you heard her. Let's get everyone out," he said to those around him. "Someone fetch Silius. Now! Let's go," he said clapping his hands.

I went to find Wendy; I needed to be put to sleep immediately. "Wendy," I yelled as I first ran to her room, and then to the rehab center to find her.

"What's going on? Is it Keith?" she asked when she saw my face.

"No, it's bad. Really bad. Keith had a tracking device on him. They are coming. We have to leave. I need to find Tannon to get us out. I have to sleep. Fast."

"Got it," she said as Wendy approached me. That's what I loved the most about her; she had a quick wit, and she didn't waste any time arguing, she was all immediate action at the moment of need. As always, worry took me in its grasp; I couldn't help it. I was so worried about Keith not making it, about me not finding Tannon, about Tannon not getting us out, about Oliver not evacuating quickly, about everything. Just when all of these disturbing thoughts were swirling inside my head like a hurricane, her gaze was already making my eyes droop heavily.

I realized I was in a cabin and Tannon was just sitting, simply staring into space. "Tannon? Is that you?" I asked.

He was startled when he heard me say his name.

"Belle, you're here," he said, a small smile quirking his lips. "I can see Shea all over you. I can't believe you're here, niece. Let me look at you."

"Tannon," I addressed him. Somehow calling him uncle felt weird. "I need your help. We need to get out. They are coming for us. Please, help us. Please open the gate."

"Of course I will help you, Belle. I'll get you out," he assured me.

"But, there are at least two hundred of us, maybe more," I said in dismay.

"Hmm, that is a problem," he said thoughtfully. He looked at my horrified facial expression and was driven to correct his previous assessment. "But not impossible. You have to put everyone in a line; it will take some time to get all of them out. I'll bring Tessa to help me hold the line. Be there in half an hour. Go now. It will be all right, Belle."

301

"Thanks, Tannon," I said as my eyes filled with tears of gratitude. "I owe you."

"You don't owe me anything, Belle," he said.

I forced myself to wake up. "Half an hour. We got only half an hour; we gotta hurry," I said to Wendy.

I ran back to Oliver as Wendy and George, who had now heard it all, tagged behind me. I could feel the rush in the air as people were being put into a long line, their expressions worried and scared. I couldn't blame them; they were about to lose the only security they had in the underworld and while the journey ahead promised freedom, it could also deliver death or, worse still, their capture by Azazel. Oliver had assigned teams of ten to twelve men on each floor to make sure there was no one left behind. They were placed in each aisle and passageway from one end to the other, constantly urging people to join and keep in line. From time to time I could hear them yell, "come on people, hurry up!" or "make it fast!" or "faster!" to expedite the process, their hands poking people to hasten them along. The evacuation had already started on the top floor and was moving down to the others. It was an expedient system; I had to give Oliver that. They were also taking sacks of food from the storage in case things went in an unexpected direction, and we were left to survive back in the underworld. Lastly, Silius and ten others were planting bombs on each floor which were to be triggered once the evacuation was complete.

"We need to be at the gate in half an hour. Tannon will be getting us out. What can we do to help?" I asked Oliver.

"We don't have much time. My men are covering each floor in general, but we need to make sure there is no one left behind. Just double check each floor to make sure everyone's with us when we leave."

We nodded.

I heard Oliver's voice, "Guys we need to wrap up in twenty minutes, tops."

"I'll take two floors below," I said as I knew the area well. Things seemed to be working fine, the line here was already moving towards the upper floor as it was being emptied. I passed the line of people, going to the other end of the floor to search for those who may still have been in remote parts, uninformed of the recent events.

I took all the passages winding right and left, running as I yelled to find somebody undetected. Thankfully, I was unable to find a soul. It seemed Oliver's men had already gathered everyone on this floor. My last stop was the well. I found it to be empty; I smiled remembering the magical moments I had spent here with Keith. If I could take the whole room and carry it with me in my pocket, I would. But I just had to be content with the memories.

Satisfied, I turned around to leave. The floor had already emptied on my way back. I ran up the stairs easily catching up with the last bunch of people who were leaving. Once we were outside the city and the cave Oliver asked, "Please look around you, and if there is anybody you find missing, this is the time to alert us."

"Sasha is missing," I heard Aysha shout. "Where is she?"

People asked around, but she was not to be found.

"Where was she last?" Oliver inquired.

"She was sick, she had left the kitchen early to rest and get some sleep," said Aysha.

"She asked me to put her to sleep cause she had a splitting headache," Dresner said, suddenly remembering.

"Where is her room?" I asked.

"It's a few rooms ahead of yours," said Aysha.

"I'll go," I said. I couldn't help but assume responsibility for what was happening, and I wanted to make sure nobody got hurt for what we unintentionally brought on them. "I'll catch up with you guys. You should go, Tannon is waiting for you at the gate."

"Someone should go with you," said Oliver.

"I'll go with her," said George. I thanked him silently.

"You've got twenty minutes to get out, the bombs are set to go off afterward," warned Oliver.

We ran back inside the underground city; we knew exactly where we were going as we headed towards Sasha's room. Once we passed my room, we started looking around. She was supposed to be close by.

"Sasha," I shouted, not really expecting her to hear me. I assumed she was in a deep sleep.

George suddenly hissed, his fangs elongated. I turned around to see what had brought this change and came to a standstill. There it was, Daisy and her army of dark demons coming out of the portal in the room we had just passed.

She saw us too.

"Look what we found boys," she chuckled throwing her blonde hair over her shoulder.

She walked lazily towards us as the dark demons suddenly circled us.

We were outnumbered.

"Don't kill them. Just tie them up real good until I come back and bring Azazel and the others. Apparently, we found the city," she said. "Look at how I've changed everything in the underworld, and just in a few days. Wait and see what I can do in a month," she said. She looked around, suddenly noticing the silence. "Where are they?" she yelled at me.

"I don't know what you mean," I said.

She slapped me on the mouth so hard I tasted blood.

"Don't lie to me, girl," she said. "Cover the bitch's mouth too. I don't want to hear her babble until, well, until I make her talk. I'll enjoy that. I still remember the pain of your fire, bitch! You'll feel a thousand times more pain than what you gave me, I promise you that," she said as she turned around.

George fought, trying to protect me, but it was no good. I couldn't even try the invisibility illusion as they knew we were right within the circle. Soon, we were tied around two beams, our wrists held behind our backs. They tied an extra rope around our waists which fixed our hands tightly against our backs. They made sure my palms were fisted and immobile, killing any chance of bringing fire to them. Nevertheless, I tried, but the fire burned down inside my fist. Our mouths were also covered with a piece of cloth.

I looked at George, silently apologizing to him. We both knew what this meant. He smiled, shrugging. The whole place would

304

explode in about fifteen to twenty minutes. We were as good as dead. At least we would take them down with us.

***

Keith

I was running to the gate with all the energy I could muster given the condition of my body. I had thrown the device somewhere far away. I felt restless which scared the hell out of me. I had to see Belle as it was the only way I would ever calm my heart. Was she okay? I needed to know. I felt her anxiety, but I didn't know whether it was because she was simply worried about me, or if it was something else. I saw the long line of people at the gate, waiting for Tannon to open it.

"Where is she?" I asked when I spotted Oliver.

"Man, I hope this gate opens or else we are screwed," Oliver said.

I held him by the collar, "Where is she?" I asked one more time, my voice chilling.

"She and George will catch up, they went to find Sasha who was left behind," he stammered.

"And you let her go?" I said. "When you have so many warriors here? You let Belle go, a girl who's powerless against the dark demons?" I asked, my voice so threatening that Oliver gasped.

"I sent her with George; I wouldn't send her alone," Oliver stammered.

"Did you set the damn bombs?"

Oliver nodded, swallowing hard.

"You set them to go for when exactly?" I growled.

Oliver kept his silence, his eyes widened with the ramifications of what might happen. I let him go; I didn't have a minute to waste with the bastard. "You better pray she's all right, or I'm coming back for you," I promised. I shifted back, running towards the underground city. I had just reached the cave when it exploded right in front of my eyes, destroying everything in its path as the fire and explosion threw me far away.

"No! Belle!" I screamed, feeling the pain right in my heart. "Belle!"

Expect The Unexpected

Belle

Fifteen minutes before the explosion...

Most of the dark demons had left to explore the underground city to find some trace of the rebels. Only two remained behind to guard us, not that we needed any guarding as we were securely tied to the beams and, according to my calculations, the bomb was about to explode in ten minutes. I was only thinking about Keith. I wanted my mind to wander to happier moments when the explosion happened.

Everything happened so quickly afterward that I had trouble distinguishing dream from reality. One moment the two guards were standing up and chatting, and in the next, they were down, their heads severed by a sword held by another dark demon. Where had he come from? I shrank back as much as I could given my bound state, expecting him to kill us viciously too, but the dark demon lowered the blood-covered sword. There was something familiar about him, but I couldn't exactly put my finger on it.

"We need to hurry," he said as he started untying us.

"Molloch ... I don't understand," George said. "I thought you were dead like the rest."

"I wasn't there when it all happened. The dark demons were being taken one by one to the well to wash under the supervision of a guard. It was my turn. But, when we came back, it was all chaotic up there. I had no idea what had happened. The guards were fighting the dark demons; it was as if a virus of insanity had taken hold of everyone. I escaped, but there was nowhere else to go. I didn't want to serve Azazel. I've been hiding ever since, scavenging every night just to survive, fearing discovery, fearing for my life."

Suddenly, I realized who he was. He was the dark demon who had objected to the idea that he was working with Azazel, the one whom I had encircled with the protection of my flames, the one who had looked at me with gratitude in the end.

My goodness, this was nothing short of a miracle, but we'd have enough time to get the details later on. Now, we didn't have a minute to lose. "The bomb," I reminded George.

"We need to get the hell out of here, fast! The whole place is about to explode," he exclaimed. "How will we get out? Belle, can you do your cool trick?"

"Yes, but first we have to get Sasha," I reminded them. "She must be somewhere here."

George said, "Wait here; I'll be back in a minute."

As promised, George was back with Sasha whose hypnosis he had ended prematurely. She looked utterly confused waking up to a city that was emptied. She had no idea what was going on but was following George meekly.

"Thank the Moon Goddess! Let's hold hands. Come on, quick now," I urged them.

"What are you going to do?" asked Molloch.

"I'll make us invisible," I said.

Molloch looked at me as if I was crazy, but he held Sasha's hand, and Sasha held George's. I concentrated on turning us into spirits like before, imagining our bodies to be incorporeal and fluid.

"Did it work?" asked Molloch.

"I've no clue. Hopefully it did," I said. "Let's go; we don't have any time to waste."

First, we started walking as fast and as silently as we could. But I looked at the time, we had so few minutes left. We began running until we came face to face with a group of dark demons Daisy had left behind. We dodged around them as if we were participating in a running race with hurdles. But the demons heard us even if they couldn't see us.

"What the hell?" asked one. They started running around as if chasing ghosts based on the thumps our steps made. The dark demons extended their hands in the air as if to seize unseen forces while they came full force at us with legs running at full speed. One of the demon hands came into contact with my back; his fingers twisted around my invisible shirt and within seconds he was holding me by the waist. I kicked him, but I couldn't free myself. I was holding onto the illusion of invisibility, but it no longer mattered. The demon was holding my solid body even if he couldn't see me. George, who was leading the group, had already opened the city door to the cave. Molloch was tugging me towards the exit, but the demon wouldn't let go. I saw others were also coming now, fixed on the invisible targets their friend had brought to their attention. Within seconds, all of us would be caught, and our bodies would explode right afterward. I tried to unclasp my hand, but Molloch let go before I did as he raised his sword and let it fall it on the demon's elbow. The demon and I shrieked at the same time, him from pain and me from horror, as his severed elbow fell on the ground. I was finally free to go, but the others had already caught up with us. "Go, leave me and go," shouted Molloch as he turned around to confront the others. "There is no saving me," he said regretfully as he tried to hold them back to allow us the time to escape.

George nodded.

"No," I cried out, but George lifted me over his shoulder and simply ran from the open door towards the cave, and then outside, as we left Molloch behind. There were a few dark demons behind us but they didn't make it out as the cave exploded, blowing them all to pieces. We barely made it out alive. We lay on the ground a few meters away from the deafening explosion. I covered my head as the explosion ejected chunks of rock and other types of debris from the cave, hurling them all over us. I lay down, utterly still from the shock. Suddenly, even with my ears still ringing from the thunderous explosion, I heard Keith's desperate scream, "No! Belle!"

Keith's cry of agony pierced the darkness as he howled in pain beating his chest. The pain, the hurt, and the broken soul were clearly evident in his voice as he yelled "Belle" one more time in a heartbreaking plea. He then shifted right before my eyes before I could even get to him. His body and face became unrecognizable as they both grew in size, turning him into a humongous beast, just like in the caved-in tunnel, leaving no trace of Keith behind. The transformation shook me out my stupor as I tried to get up. "Keith!" I shouted. "Keith, I'm here." But he was far too gone to hear or see me. He was in the mood to destroy everything in his path. I was a bit scared as I slowly walked towards him to bring him back. George tried to stop me, but I shook him off. "Get back," I said to George.

"Are you crazy? He's a berserker!" he said. "He'll kill you; he'll kill us both. We need to get the hell outta here."

"Get back," I said to George again. It was then Keith saw us and he snarled and howled, waving his massive paws at us.

"Fuck! We barely got out of there alive; now we'll die here," said George as he brought out his fangs, stretching them long in his mouth. Sasha had retreated far back and was hiding in the corner.

Seeing George increased the fury on the beast's face as he growled and bared his teeth, he then started charging towards us with his paws extended at the same level as our throats.

George hissed, but he knew the inevitability of it all. Just when the beast's paws were about to pierce his throat, I threw myself in front of him. The berserker stopped the descent of his paws an inch from my face as he continued looking at me ferociously. He leaned forward as he inhaled my face, my neck, my hair and my chest. I stood immobile, allowing him to rub his nose all over my body. There was complete silence in the air except for the sounds of his sniffing and then the low satisfied growl rumbling in his chest. His huge tongue came as his lips parted and he licked me from one side of my neck to the other. "Mine," the berserker hissed, growling at George. I rose up on my toes and patted his face which calmed him down a lot. "Mine," he continued saying as he licked my palm.

"Whoa, okay man. She's yours, she's a hundred percent all yours," George said, holding up his hands, as he slowly retreated. He was amazed at the power I held over this huge wild beast. I was, too.

The beast's face relaxed as it slowly changed to the features so dear to me.

"Belle?" he croaked. "Moon Goddess, help me, but it's you. I saw it all explode. I thought you were inside," he whispered as he wrapped me so tight in his arms that I had a hard time breathing. "Belle" he kept repeating as if he couldn't believe it, all the while he kept kissing me anywhere and everywhere his lips willed.

"Keith, I'm all right," I said, lifting my face up and looking him deep in the eyes.

"I don't know what I would have done if something had happened to you," he said, his voice laden with unabated apprehension. "I once told you I had no weakness, ever."

"Keith, it's okay," I said, trying to comfort him.

"I lied. It's you. It's been you all along. You are my weakness," he whispered.

My heart was thumping so wild that I couldn't speak. I swallowed hard, shaken by the pressure of overdriven emotions. I wanted to kiss him, hug him, laugh, even cry.

"Man, you scared the crap out of me," said George, ruining the moment. "I thought, you'd kill us for sure."

Keith turned to George, his eyes still set with an intense burning within them. I saw him swallow hard, and unlike me, it was a sign he was gaining control of his emotions again. He took several long, slow breaths and then said "Sorry, but you were holding her."

"I see," muttered George.

"We should get going; Tannon must have opened the gate by now," Keith reminded us as he held me tightly by the hand. He shifted, putting me on his back. Unlike the past, I savored riding him this time. I flattened my body on his back, my hands firmly clutching his fur as I enjoyed his warmth and scent while he carried me towards the gate like precious cargo. When we arrived, we saw no one in sight, except for Tannon whose eyes were desperately roaming around. It was hard to miss the sign of relief on his face when we came within his eyesight.

He looked at me as I got off Keith's back. "Niece, I'm glad you're fine."

"Thanks, Tannon. Did everybody make it?"

"Yes, they're all outside. Let's go. I need to seal the gate before others flood in."

"Finally it's happening," I said. "But, we still have to wait for George and Sasha who are a little behind."

After the two had joined us, we all slipped through the gate towards our freedom.

Though only a desert, the view that greeted me at the other side was the best one I'd seen in a long time. As Tannon started sealing the gate, I felt the satisfaction of achievement. We had done it. We were safe from Azazel; we were safe from the underworld. All the rebels had mixed expressions of disbelief, awe, and happiness as they looked around. Time spent rebelling and suffering in the underworld had not abated their connection with the world they once knew. Some of them were crying, others were hugging each other and laughing. Some were simply touching the desert sand and splashing it all around them as if it was a beach resort. There was an undeniable joy in the air.

"Child," I heard someone say to me, and I turned around. It was Tessa. She was standing right behind me with her arms wide open, her eyes teary.

"My dear sweet grandchild," she said, apparently expecting me to walk into her arms.

I knew I had to. She was my grandmother after all. Putting my past feelings aside, I disentangled myself from Keith's embrace and walked towards her. The moment her arms came around me, I felt an excruciating pain in my head. I screamed and screamed in agony with the feeling that my head was splitting into two halves. I heard Keith's frantic voice in the distance, although his words were inaudible. Then everything became dark around me, and I blacked out.

Back To The Coven

Belle

I slowly opened my eyes, my head still causing me some pain though it was now tolerable.

"Belle, are you awake? Are you okay, sweetheart?" Keith asked, his face anxious. Tannon and Tessa had similar facial expressions as they stood above me.

I tried to get up but Keith held me down. "Whoa, slow down. You should just lie down for a while until we know what's going on."

"I think I'm okay now," I said.

"What happened?" Keith asked.

"I don't know. I suddenly felt this extreme pain in my head; I thought my head would just burst."

"I'll heal her," Tessa said as she knelt down.

"No, don't touch her until we know what's going on here. It might be your touch that caused her pain," Keith said. "Nobody touches her from now on, but me," he warned as he slowly lifted me under my legs effortlessly.

"Then we should take her to Alice," Tessa said, not debating him. "But she needs a healer."

"Fine, but it won't be you," grunted Keith.

"Don't worry, Keith, I won't do anything to risk my granddaughter's health," she assured him.

Would I ever get used to hearing her call me her granddaughter?

"I'm okay, Keith. You're exaggerating," I said, but he had no intent to listen, his face was taut with determination.

"What about the others? How will they get back?" I asked.

"Damn, Belle, we just got them out of the underworld. Surely they can get back home on their own."

"They are in the middle of a desert, Keith," I reminded him.

"Belle, you just fainted from the pain. Don't you think you should start thinking of yourself a bit?" Keith spoke wearily.

"Tannon, can you help them get back to their homes?" I asked, disregarding Keith.

"My Shea was like that," said Tessa, smiling. "She was always thinking of others."

"Sure," Tannon replied.

"Thanks," I said. As Keith carried me through the portal Tessa created, I saw a shadow spirit float under the shining sun. It was probably Oliver, finally enjoying the powers the constant darkness had deprived him of during his unwilling stay in the underworld. He looked at me, nodding his head in acknowledgment. Then he disappeared from my sight as the portal closed from behind me right after Tessa.

"Oh, my sweet Moon Goddess," shrieked Alice as she saw me in Keith's arms. "What happened?" she asked.

"We don't know exactly, I hugged her, and then she was overcome with extreme pain and fainted. Can you check her?" Tessa said.

"Of course," Alice said. "Where was the pain, Belle?

"My head," I explained. Keith put me down on the sofa and Alice knelt down next to me, touching me on the head as she closed her eyes. A magical light erupted from her palms as she moved her hands up and down over my head.

"What is it?" asked Keith, concerned.

"Unfortunately, I don't see a thing. Whatever that was, it's all gone now," Alice said.

"Great, then I can get up. It's my first day on Earth after a lifetime in the underworld, and I want to enjoy it."

"Of course, my dear. We'll show you to your room, bring you some hot food, and you can take a long warm bath after you eat. How does that all sound?" Tessa asked.

"Wonderful," I said, and I meant it. Food, bath and lots and lots of cuddling with Keith in a real bed in a private room. Hmm, I loved the thought of it.

"I see that you marked my granddaughter, Keith. I hope you are happy, child?" she inquired.

I felt my face flush but nodded.

"Lovely," she said. "Alice, can you take them to the blue room, please? They should be comfortable there," Tessa explained giddily.

"Sure thing," Alice said as she showed us our room at the end of the hall on the second floor. The bedroom was a spacious, comfortable and attractive room with blue painted walls. There was a large twelve-foot square beige Persian rug on the floor, a mounted LCD television on the wall, a giant king sized bed covered in a navy blue comforter in the center and a small beige sofa overlaying the window with tossed pillows snuggled all around it. Before she left us, Alice hugged me and said "I'm so glad you're all right, Belle," and then we were alone.

Keith stared at me intensely, his steady and penetrating gaze was turning my knees to Jell-O. His stride towards me was graceful, solid, yet powerful, and dangerous like a hunter going after its prey. The corner of his mouth curved into a smile as he held my face in his hands and pulled my chin up. His face was only inches away; my heart stopped as his perfect lips came closer and closer. My eyelids surrendered when his lips touched mine, his arms pressing me against the hard contour of his chest. My hands traveled over his body, memorizing every muscle, every inch of him as I kissed him deeply, losing myself in his mouth and delicious scent. Then we heard the door knock.

"Screw you! Go away whoever you are, witch," Keith cursed, continuing to kiss me.

"I brought some food, children," chuckled Tessa. "Be good and open up for grandma."

"Damn!" I'm hungry for something else," Keith said, sighing in frustration as he reluctantly put some space between us. There was a louder knock on the door. "Fine, bring it in," Keith said, finally giving up.

Tessa and two other witches brought us piles of warm food, and a small folded table which they set in front of the sofa. Wow, Tessa certainly was treating us as honored guests. I was enjoying the perks of being the grandchild of an ancient priestess up until I saw the others leave, but not Tessa. She simply sat down with us.

"Belle, do you remember anything about your mother?"

"No, I don't."

Uhm, how was I supposed to refer to her? Grandma? Tessa?

"How about your father?" she asked

Did she remember her previous words about the union of a witch and demon, I wondered.

"No. But Lasarus confirmed he was a demon."

"I wonder how they met. It must be right after she traveled through the door of destiny. It's hard to imagine my Shea with a demon," she murmured." Apparently she did remember her previous words.

"I heard they met accidentally as she was trying to find a way to get back to you. They fell in love immediately but couldn't live among the demons, so they chose to live in exile until they were chased, we don't know by whom. She died in childbirth, and father was wounded, probably protecting us. That's all I've been told about their story."

"I see," she said thoughtfully. "Anyway, my dear Belle. You can't imagine how Tannon's news has thrilled me. I can't believe I didn't notice it myself when I first saw you. It's true that Tannon has always been better with past images. But, I should have detected something, anything! I guess I've been locking every memory about Shea to a safe place in my mind for so long now that I simply chose to ignore the signs. You see that's been the only way I could deal with her loss up until now. I thought she was gone forever. But now I have a piece of her. It's you, my child," she said tenderly. "I can't wait. We'll get to know each other. You'll stay here, and I will train you properly. I've heard you've got an interesting set of talents. They need to be nurtured properly."

"Are you fucking kidding me?" Keith asked, interrupting her rudely. "Belle is coming back with me. She's so not staying here. We'll be here for a few days, but then we are getting the hell outta here."

"But, Keith. Belle is a powerful witch, an honored member of our coven, my only grandchild."

Oh, wait! That reminded me, I had to deliver her the news.

"Actually, I'm not your only grandchild. I have a twin brother."

"Excuse me?" Tessa said.

"His name's Gregory. He was staying at the demon island the last time I was there. He was supposed to escort my friends and my adoptive brother back home from there, so he should have been back by now. Our father apparently took Gregory to Lasarus while he left me at the werewolf pack because of the prophecy when Shea, I mean our mother, died. They were being followed and my father was wounded. And, he died shortly after he left Gregory. That's all I know."

"What a miracle! I can hardly believe it. I've got two grandchildren. I've got to fetch him right away. Tannon!" she shouted as she left the room in a hurry.

"Thank the Moon Goddess, I thought she would never leave," Keith said, locking the door behind her. "Now, where were we?" he asked as he continued from where he left off by stripping me slowly of my clothes. He filled the tub with hot water and carried me there in his arms. He picked up a sponge, dipped it in the warm water, then lathered it with soap and started washing me. Using the foamy sponge, he drew delicate circles over my naked flesh, massaging every inch of my body slowly and erotically. Then he joined me in the tub after washing me, and sat behind me, cradling me in his arms. I lay my head on his chest as he started kissing me. I moaned as he slid his hand down to caress my breasts. After torturous minutes of kissing and touching me, and turning my limbs into a mush, I returned the favor as I first used the sponge, then my fingers and my lips, on his body, mercilessly exploring him to my satisfaction. When the water was getting cold, he got me out. He patted me dry with a large fluffy towel and carried me to the bed where we continued our lovemaking. Hours later, our hunger for each other now temporarily appeased, we were lazily lying in bed and feeding each other the now cold, but delicious, food Tessa had previously brought us.

"Do you want to stay here?" Keith asked as he fed me a piece of the veggie crepe. "I know I told Tessa we would go soon, but you know I'll do whatever you want. You're everything to me."

I kissed him, my sweet, adorable beast, my very own. "I want to stay here for a while if they are fetching Gregory. I really wanna see him and make sure he's okay," I said to him as I ran my fingers through his hair.

"Sure, babe. I understand. And we should invite your family to the castle; I know how much you care about them. It's time I got to know them better," he said, capturing my hand and kissing my fingers. "Holy crap, I will have to apologize to your dad," he said, suddenly remembering. "He may not have good memories about our last interaction," he said, wincing.

"Yes, you will have to do some groveling even though you're a king," I said, smiling.

The grimace on his face said it all. My poor mate was already in pain thinking about it! It was time he learned some humility in life.

Our fingers intertwined under the soft sheets. "It's all worth it. You're all worth it," he whispered, his kiss was sweet and tender as our lips locked together, making every thought in my head completely disappear. Just when his touch was stirring the embers of lust in my body all over again, there was a knock on the door.

"Belle! Belle, open the door. C'mon sweetie, I have excellent news for you," I heard Tessa shout from the other side of the door.

"I swear this woman will be the end of me. Why doesn't she let us be?" Keith cursed as he got up from bed.

"Keith, you should put something on, "I reminded him as he walked to the door stark naked.

"Damn!" he cursed again as he wrapped a towel around his hips.

"What?" he snapped at Tessa.

"Keith, I see you are enjoying yourself. But, step aside. I have news for my Belle," she chuckled as she entered the room.

I pulled the sheets modestly up about my neck when I saw Tessa move towards the bed. My grandma walking in on me in bed while I was naked with my mate wasn't my idea of fun. This was quite awkward and inappropriate despite her being cheerful about it.

"Don't you dare touch her!" yelled Keith.

"I won't, Keith. Relax," she replied as she looked at me. "Belle, Gregory is here with us downstairs, and he's anxious to see you."

"What?" I exclaimed in excitement. "Is he all right?"

"He is, now that he knows you're here with us. He said he'd been looking all over for you."

"I can't wait to see him," I said. But Tessa wasn't leaving. "Uhm" I muttered, not knowing how to get rid of her.

"Get the hell out, Tessa. Give us a minute to put on some clothes," Keith said.

"Of course my dearies. There should be some clean clothes for you both in the closet."

"Thanks," I replied.

"You can call me grandma, you know. I would be euphoric."

Oh crap, now I was trapped. I nodded, faking a smile. I just needed more time before I could make her happy the way she wanted to be.

"Okay, then, I'll let you be," Tessa finally said as she left.

"I hate sharing you with anyone today," Keith said when he came back to bed and pulled down the sheets I've been clutching at my neck ever so slowly as his eyes feasted on my body.

"I know, but I want to see Gregory," I said in a low husky whisper.

"Well, then Belle-mine, I guess we'll be seeing Gregory," he said giving me a quick peck on the lips and got up reluctantly.

I dressed as quickly as I could and went down the stairs with Keith. They were all in the living room, chatting. Tessa was sitting next to Gregory, her hand patting him on the knee as if he was a little child.

"Gregory," I exclaimed, so happy to see him.

"Belle, thank the Moon Goddess! I was so worried. You scared the hell out of me," he said as he stood up and hugged me, his usual shyness completely forgotten.

The moment I felt his arms around me, I screamed. A searing pain had me in its clutches; it was as if it were a vise squeezing my temples to crush my skull. The darkness seized me again.

Humans

Belle

He was kissing me softly on the forehead. Mmm, it felt good. "Sweetheart, please open your eyes," he pleaded. "Alice, do something," he then yelled.

"I'm sorry, but she has no physical sickness, I don't know how to help her, " I heard Alice say vaguely.

What was happening? I opened my eyes to find myself cozily tucked in Keith's arms, perfectly fitted against him. I sighed in happiness.

"Baby, what's happening to you?" Keith asked, desperately. I yearned to brush the creases of worry away from his forehead and the fear from his eyes with a kiss. My poor love, he was so scared.

"I don't know; perhaps I'm coming down with something. But, I'm fine now," I said smiling at him.

My words and smile did nothing to appease him.

"We are leaving right away; we are not staying here where there is this unseen force that's hurting you. You are not safe with anyone but me. I'm the only who'll ever touch you, ever," he said, suddenly becoming possessive with the implications of his words, squeezing me tightly in his arms.

He was so damn sweet, even the possessiveness he couldn't help was appealing to me. Moon Goddess, help me, I was so in love with him!

"And perhaps Alice," Keith later added on.

"Yes, but I haven't had the time to talk to Gregory yet or spend time with Alice or Tannon." And then I felt compelled to add, "or Tessa."

"Tannon actually left right after he brought in Gregory," said Alice sadly, averting her suddenly blushing face. "He conveyed the message that he'd be very happy if you visited him with Gregory in the Alps."

"Well, the family reunion can wait. First, we have to get you well, and it's very apparent to me this is not the place for that. You've fainted twice now. I'll not have you faint a third time," Keith asserted.

"Oh, I know what may be wrong with her," Tessa exclaimed as if suddenly reaching a certain wisdom. "Can she be pregnant?" As the first hybrid girl, the symptoms of pregnancy may be different, I mean painful, for her."

I caught the expression of awe and hope on Keith's face. Suddenly, his tense face relaxed into a grin.

A child, were they kidding me? I was too young to be a mother.

"Alice?" asked Keith, his voice giddy with excitement.

"I don't know. I've always checked her head up until now, let me see," she said as she touched my abdomen. She moved her hand around and down my stomach to my ovary, drawing circles with her palm all the way through.

She made us wait for a minute which seemed like hours to me as I held my breath for the news that would change my life forever.

"No, I'm sorry. She's not pregnant," Alice declared.

"Are you sure?" Keith asked, clearly disappointed, but trying desperately to hide it. I, on the other hand, was vastly relieved.

"Yes, I believe so. There is no evidence of a fetus in there."

"Then, we are back to square one with no fucking clue of what's wrong with Belle," Keith said. Then, he turned angrily at Tessa, "What happened to your skills as a seer? Where's your damn intuition when you need it? How come you can't help your granddaughter?"

322

"I don't know, but I'm completely blank right now," Tessa admitted frankly. "How about Tannon? He might be able to help; his senses are sharper when it comes to Belle."

"That's an excellent idea, we'll spend two days in here, and then we'll visit Tannon before we head back home. This way, I'll have spent time with everyone, just the way I wanted," I said.

"But…" Keith tried to intervene.

"No buts, my sweetheart. This is how we'll do it, won't we?" I asked sweetly.

"As you wish," he muttered unwillingly, despite the clouds of worry thundering his face.

"Gregory, tell me what happened. Were you able to leave the island? Did Lasarus keep his promise? Did everything go as planned? How are my parents? What about Sean, Joshua, and Danny? Tell me all about them," I kept bombarding him with questions.

"We left that night, just as Lasarus said. It was a challenge dragging Sean along with us; we had to hit him with a piece of wood on the head to knock him down and put him forcibly on the plane. It was hard going back to the pack, seeing everyone who had no clue why I had left in the first place. I decided to come clean to them all," he said, embarrassed. "I owed it to them."

"And?" I urged him to continue.

"They were quite understanding. Your dad assured me I was still part of the pack. Sean was hard on me, but I felt like I could mend our friendship in time. Right then, Lasarus contacted me, frantic over your loss," he said gulping. "I didn't know you were gone. He asked me to come immediately. I didn't say anything to others as I had a pretty good idea about what had happened to you. It's what we've feared from the start. I knew Lasarus's enemy, his twin brother Azazel, had you. We knew from the start he'd do anything to hurt Lasarus. You see, that's why our father had left you with the werewolves and why Lasarus hadn't fetched you until you were eighteen. We'd been scared of Azazel getting his hands on you," he explained.

"But, what changed when I was eighteen?" I asked, confused.

"Once Lasarus marked you, he would have been able to protect you better."

Keith cursed, the muscled cords of his neck stood out with rage. "I'll fucking kill him if he lays even a finger on you," he barked.

"Behave," I said to Keith as I patted him on the cheek. "But this doesn't make sense. Did you know I was also Azazel's mate?" I asked Gregory.

"No, are you serious? You were? No, I didn't know that. That's weird. But then why did he hurt you? I saw your severed fingers, Belle. We were so helpless. We didn't know how to get to you."

Keith growled like a wounded beast. I turned to him with a questioning look. His face was red, impotent with pain and rage as his body trembled like a roaring lion.

"I'm fine, Keith. See, I'm alright," I said, this time kissing him on the lips.

Gregory seemed perturbed with our intimacy. "But," he said. "What about Lasarus?" he asked, his gaze intense on my neck.

"I have a feeling you were kept in the dark, bro. Lasarus wasn't my only mate like he led us to believe. Besides Azazel, I was also mated to Keith."

"And probably Samuel, the Vampire King," added Tessa. "That's what the prophecy implied anyway."

"But, I don't understand?" said Gregory, apparently confused.

That's probably why Lasarus left me with the pack in the first place; a place where he thought Azazel would never think of looking. He must have feared Azazel would want me for himself. That's why he brought me in only when he knew he could mark me. Because the prophecy deemed that, once the marking was done, the mating bond would fade away for others, including Azazel, who would then presumably have left me alone." I shivered, remembering my time with Azazel. "Little did Lasarus know that marking was the last thing on Azazel's mind. But how did Azazel know about the prophecy I wonder?"

No one had an answer to that.

"I'm sorry Belle, I didn't know. I thought he was your mate and the only one who could protect you from Azazel," Gregory admitted.

"I know. It's not your fault. And, I have Keith, now," I said, and my beast immediately growled with satisfaction beneath me. I chuckled. How easy it was to appease him!

"We've looked everywhere for you. Lasarus had always been keeping constant tabs on his twin and the dark demons, getting intelligence from Tessa from time to time despite his hatred for witches. But, he didn't see this coming. And Tessa, I mean grandma, wouldn't tell us how to get you back. Lasarus, well… it wouldn't be wrong to say he's not been himself since your disappearance."

"I didn't know where Belle was, not until she contacted Tannon in his coma state," Tessa excused herself. "And, I had no clue as to where the gate to the underworld was until Tannon was wounded and The Moon Goddess showed me where his body lay," Tessa said, trying to justify her actions.

"Well, I think this much apologizing is more than I can handle for today. I want to spend an average day away from all of this, the underworld, the light and the dark demons, and everything else that's crazy in this world," I said.

"What are you saying, baby?" asked Keith, confused.

"I want to purify my body and soul with lots of regular shopping. It's still day outside, and I'm going to the mall. I've been wearing other people's stuff for such a long time now. I want to buy myself some clothes for a change."

Keith looked disappointed; it was evident he wanted to go back to our room and spend the whole day in bed with me. As much as I wanted that, we had a lifetime to spend together, but the two days I would spend here were for others. "Alice, do you want to join me?" I asked.

"I'd love to," replied Alice, elated.

"How will we get there?" I asked.

"Oh, the usual way," she said.

Please do not say the portal, I thought.

"We'll take the car," she smirked as if sensing my thoughts.

"Yes!" I exclaimed; we were definitely on our way to spending a normal day. I was so damn excited.

"I don't like this," complained Keith.

"Come on, Keith, don't ruin this for me," I said. "What can possibly go wrong?"

"Fine, but I still don't like it," he grumbled.

We took the blue Mercedes in the garage. Keith gave me a limitless credit card and some cash. I looked at him puzzled, how had he come up with all that?

"We all keep a small storage of cash and a pile of credit cards at each other's house for occasions like this, it is part of the council rules," Keith explained.

Aha, kill each other but then make sure you keep each other's stuff for emergency situations. I would never understand the diplomatic relations between these species!

I took what Keith gave me without objections. We drove a good half an hour along the country road, and then another hour on the highway until we made it to a relatively busy mall with many cars parked outside. The mall was crowded, as expected, but it felt good to be one of the humans as we wandered around the stores, trying out clothes, checking out prices, and buying whatever we liked. Within an hour, I had bought jeans, underwear, shirts, shoes and a fancy black dress accompanied by sexy lingerie to appease my growling beast. We then sat down to drink some coffee and have dessert. As I took a large bite of my raspberry cheesecake and sighed in happiness, I couldn't help but ask "So, anything happening between you and Tannon?"

"No," she said, embarrassed. "I'm not sure he's even aware of my existence."

"Well, didn't you heal him?" I asked, surprised.

"Yes, but Tannon is always so detached emotionally, you know? It's completely hopeless. Can you believe he already left?" she said, clearly disappointed. "But, Belle, you got what you wanted, I can't believe Keith marked you."

"How in the hell does everybody know that?" I asked.

"Alice laughed heartily. "Did you look at yourself in the mirror girl? You have a large eye tattooed on your neck; it's Keith's eye."

"Huh?" I said as I reflexively touched my neck. "Are you serious?"

"Yes, of course."

"But, I've never seen that in any of the marked werewolves before. My mom doesn't have it, for one."

"Of course she doesn't. But in your case, it's the king marking his queen. Have you no idea that the leaders of the Moon Goddess's children always leave a trace behind when they mark their mates?"

"I had no clue," I admitted frankly. "Wait, do you have a mirror with you?" I asked Alice, suddenly impatient to see the tattoo.

"I should have a small one," she said as she searched her bag for it, finally taking out a small rounded mirror.

I held it at the side of my neck where he'd marked me. There it was, one large black eye, a replica of Keith's. I gazed at it in amazement; it was simply beautiful.

Then, all of a sudden a plate hit my head. "Damn!" I said as I held the small lump forming in my head. When I was about to turn around and reprimand the guilty person, other plates and cups started flying in the open cafe as if we were in a food fight. Before I could even understand what was happening, people had begun punching each other. The waiter dumped the tray he'd been carrying on one woman's head, while a man who was passing by grabbed a chair and hit another with it. Things got uglier as the security guards came with guns, but instead of restraining violence, they started shooting at people. Bullets began flying inside the mall, ricocheting off walls, smashing windows and hitting unlucky shoppers.

Hell On Earth

Belle

We were hiding under the table waiting for things to calm down. Then the tablecloth that was hiding us was folded up to reveal a smirking bulky man who held a gun to my face. "Look what I found," he said, as he waved the gun at me. "It's my Christmas gift," he said, nonsensically. Then he pulled the trigger. I gasped in pain as the bullet entered my shoulder. Just when I was grateful that he was a bad shooter, he pulled the trigger again, shooting me right in the chest. I was hurting badly, but I managed to throw successive balls of fire at him before he was able to pull the trigger a third time. He yelped in pain, falling back towards the ground, clearing the way for us to get out. But I couldn't move. The gunshot wounds, especially the one on my chest, hurt like hell, and I had difficulty breathing.

"Let me heal you first," Alice said as she saw the blood soaking my shirt. I was grateful that she was with me right now as I was still unsure how and when I was able to heal myself. She used her palm to heal both my chest and the shoulder wound. I watched as her palms extracted the two bullets from my body and then mended my damaged cells and organs. I was still sore but I could definitely move now.

"Thanks. We've got to go now," I said to Alice who nodded. I tucked the lingerie inside my pants, but I sadly looked back at all the other packages I had to leave behind as I needed my hands free. We crawled on our knees and stood up. The sight that greeted us was drastic. People everywhere were beating and killing each other. I saw a teenager who was banging his own head on the wall, a child who was strangling her dog, and an old couple who were beating the hell out of each other. The sounds of punching, kicking and choking all meshed inside the mall with the screams and cries of humans.

What was going on?

"We need to leave. Fast!" I told Alice.

I held my hands up, throwing balls of fire to open our path. Alice was clutching my shirt at the back. We went down the escalator, pushing through the crowd of people who had simply gone wild. Was it the same outside? Had the whole human world gone crazy? We managed to get to the exit despite the prolific violence which placed hurdles in our way and we finally opened the door outside. The sound of police and ambulance sirens echoed through the street outside as they were racing towards the mall. It looked totally normal outside I saw with relief. Hopefully they would be able to contain whatever craziness lurked inside, but we wouldn't wait to find out.

"Let's go," I pushed Alice and we ran to our car and drove away fast, leaving all that craziness behind. Katrina, the child witch, greeted us at the coven.

"Finally, you're here," she said.

"Why?" I asked. Did they know?

"Two hours ago, Keith kept saying something felt wrong and then we saw the news on TV."

"Where is he?" I asked.

"Keith, Gregory, and Tessa all went to find you," Katrina explained. "Tessa opened a portal right inside the mall."

Wow, a rescue mission by the Werewolf King, the priestess, and a witch/demon hybrid just to save us from a bunch of crazed humans. "I can't believe they dived straight into all that!" I said.

Thank goodness I had the time to take a hot shower and throw out the bloody shirt before Keith came back and flipped seeing me like that.

"Belle," Keith shouted the moment he stepped inside the coven. He found me in the living room and lifted me in his arms. I winced when he held me too tightly. "Are you okay? What happened?" he asked as he put me down and slackened his hold.

"Some crazy guy shot at me. But I'm fine. Alice was there to heal me," I said to him. "It was so weird, everyone around us in the mall just went nuts." I snapped my fingers, "Just like that."

"I know, we saw it all on the news. A lot of people died and many more were wounded. Others were arrested; nobody knows what happened. The cops were already cleaning up the mess when we were there looking for you," Keith explained.

"Well, that completes my quest for an ordinary day. I guess normalcy is not my thing," I said forcing a smile.

"Are you sure you are okay?" he asked, kissing me on the forehead.

"Yes," I said, nodding.

"Belle, did you see anything out of the ordinary in the mall, anything weird?" Tessa asked.

I thought for a few seconds, but nothing came to mind. "I don't think so. Did you Alice?"

"No," Alice said,. "What's going on?"

"I don't know," said Tessa. "Let's sit down and have a cup of tea, dears, and calm our nerves."

Keith held my hand as he squished his huge body next to mine. I could feel the heat from his body and it made me feel excited yet peaceful at the same time.

"By the way, what happened to Daisy?" Tessa asked.

"Well, we don't know. The last time I saw her, she had opened a portal to the underground city, tied me up, left some demons behind, but then had gone back to bring Azazel. The ones inside the city positively exploded when the bombs went off, but I can't be sure whether she was there when it all happened," I admitted.

"No," Tessa said, sadly shaking her head. "I don't think she's dead, and neither is Azazel. I fear she's still breathing. I sure would like to get my hands on her."

"Damn," exploded Keith. Then he added, "Get in line, she's all mine!" he snapped, remembering all Daisy had done.

"Something's boiling, I can feel it in my bones, and it's not good," Tessa said, her eyes closed.

"Tell me about it," Keith said sarcastically.

"I wish I could get a better frequency on what's looming," Tessa remarked, exasperated.

There were no other weird incidents reported on TV that day, and we relaxed on the sofa, just chatting about random stuff.

"I meant to ask you both, what kind of powers do you have?" inquired Tessa.

"So far, I can only do a lousy illusion," said Gregory in dismay. "I watched Belle use her demonic powers, though; it's really impressive."

"Uhm. I'm not sure, but I think I'm getting pretty good with flames," I joked.

"The illusion was Shea's thing. She couldn't contact by blood, however. I heard that you possess a different version of that talent, Belle. One that's far superior. You can actually move yourself in your sleep, can't you? What happens when you do? Can people see you? Can you use your talents? Is it you that you are transporting or a projection of you like a hologram?" Tessa asked.

"My body remains behind, but it's almost like I take a replica of it with me wherever I go. I was visible to everyone when I went to find Keith, and I was able to touch things, throw a ball of fire at Daisy or do an illusion. So, I guess I was physically and mentally there."

"Very impressive. But, that's not completely a witch skill, Belle. I wonder..." she said, pausing. "The prophecy says you possess at least one talent from each of the Moon Goddess's children. You certainly display skills from demons and witches, but what about vampires and werewolves? Can you do mind control?" she asked, curiously.

That took me by surprise. Keith had told me about the mate part in the prophecy, but not about my potential talents. It seemed I still had to be filled in on the prophecy. "I don't think so," I said.

"Have you ever tried?" Tessa asked.

"No," I admitted.

"Try it on Gregory, cause it won't work on Keith or me."

"Are you serious?" I asked. This was too crazy.

Tessa nodded.

"But, what do I do?" I asked.

"Just concentrate and give him a command. It'll come naturally to you."

"No, you can't touch him!" shouted Keith as I approached Gregory. "Have you forgotten?" he asked.

"You don't really need to touch him," Tessa said.

"Hold very still," I said to Gregory as I approached him. I remembered how Wendy had done it. I extended my hands close enough to touch his temples if I wanted to, but I didn't. And, I looked him in the eye, commanding him to go to sleep. I did this over and over again, concentrating as I locked my unblinking eyes on his. "Gregory?" I asked him. He seemed to be awake, but perhaps he was sleeping with his eyes open.

"Yes?" he asked. "When do you start?"

"Uhm, I'm already done," I said. That was settled then; I couldn't do the hypnosis.

"Perhaps, it didn't work with me?" asked Gregory.

"It should have," said Tessa.

"Well, I don't have fangs or vampire strength and speed. Nor do I have the ability to do mind control. It seems to me that the prophecy got it wrong," I said. "I've got absolutely no vampire skills."

"That's not true," Tessa said. "You have mind control dear, it's just you can't use it on others, but only on yourself, possibly because it's not a direct gene passed onto you by your parents. This talent of contacting others is a mesh of vampire and witch skills."

"Excuse me?" I asked, confused.

"You utilize the talent you got from our witch genes to contact others telepathically. Then using the mind control you possess, you can send yourself physically and mentally to that location while your body freezes back home, turning into a doll-like being. The power of the mind is simply incredible," Tessa said. "Brilliant!" she added on, expressing her awe. "Shea would have been so proud of you, of you both."

"Thanks," I said, uncomfortable with so much undeserved praise.

We kept talking for another hour or two, but then I felt fatigued. The day was certainly taking its toll on me. Keith seemed to have felt my exhaustion as he pulled me up and we headed back to our room. I immediately locked myself in the bathroom, took a quick shower and put on the lingerie I had rescued amid all that danger. I was tired, but not too tired to skip lovemaking. I was indeed wearing that lingerie; I couldn't wait to see Keith's eyes pop out of his sockets when he first saw me.

"Sweetheart, are you okay?" Keith asked, worried when I took my sweet time preparing myself for our coming session.

"Yes, I'm coming out," I announced as I opened the bathroom door and posed for him, feeling utterly silly. I did it anyway.

The lust in his eyes said it all as they roamed my body from top to bottom. "Belle-mine," he said, his voice thickening with the intensity of his passion. He came towards me like a panther ready to jump at his prey. But before he could even touch me, I held my head in sudden pain and screamed.

"Tessa!" I heard Keith yell as he jumped to catch my falling body.

The Pain

Belle

"Do something, she's suffering," Keith shouted at Tessa and Alice.

"I don't know what to do," Tessa cried out.

I had passed out like this before, but the pain didn't seem to be abating even after I'd woken up.

"Just kill me," I screamed, unable to bear it any longer. "Please," I begged.

Keith's face was also contorted in pain seeing me like that. He was probably feeling my distress through the mating bond.

"My healing doesn't work," Alice said in distress as her hands inspected my body. Tessa also tried, saying her touch couldn't make it worse. But, it did, and she let go immediately.

I kept moaning, but thankfully after ten minutes of wanting to die, the pain was no longer constant. Despite flinching with sudden spasms of pain, I had moments of peace in between. I kept breathing in and out as if I was in labor while Keith held me in his arms, caressing me, kissing me each time I was hit by a new wave of pain.

"Belle, try healing yourself," Gregory suggested. "It might work."

"I don't know how," I croaked as my fingers pressed my temples.

"Belle, you have to trigger your demonic powers, what heals Lasarus and other light demons is their scalp. The scalp excretes a unique healing substance in demons. When demon hair spikes up, it applies pressure on the roots which increases the rate of excretion. While theirs is a constant state and is automatic, you may have to trigger that state. I've seen your hair rise before, just like theirs. I guess I'm more like mom as I heal fast but probably it's the witch way, not the demon way. But, for you, I think it's different."

Wow, would have thought Gregory would be the one to shed light on how I managed to heal myself? I was too exhausted even to move, but what he said made sense to me. I had healed myself as I was trying to escape from Azazel. My severed fingers had reappeared miraculously, or that's what I had thought at the time. All my demonic powers had been unleashed then. I had to try it. I felt the blue veins pop up on my arms and I let my hair defy gravity. I waited for precious minutes, but there was little improvement on the pain level. Apparently, this was not a sickness I could heal. I fell into an exhausted sleep as the pain finally started ebbing away after another hour of suffering.

When I opened my eyes, I was my old self again. I was in bed held firmly by Keith; my head rested on his chest, and I found comfort in the rhythm of his beating heart. He woke up when I shifted in bed. "Belle?" he said.

"I'm fine, Keith, go back to sleep."

"What's happening to you? I don't know what to do," he whispered to me.

"I know, it's all right, Keith. It's gone now," I said.

He looked so forlorn. I knew how to take away his worry for me. I cupped his face in both of my hands and kissed him. He responded passionately as he took control, his hands roaming the curves of my body, making me shudder at each touch. His hands snaked around my back, brushing my skin with his fingertips until he found the clasp of my bra. Wait, what? Don't tell me I still had the lingerie on! I looked at my bra and panties, and yep, there they were: a set of laced black see through lingerie!

"No!" I exclaimed. Keith stopped, in shock.

"Did the pain start again? Are you hurting?" he asked.

"Keith, don't tell me everybody saw me like this!" I said pointing at my body. "Oh, the shame of it! How will I ever look them in the face again, my twin brother, my very own grandma!"

I heard him sigh in relief. "Well, they might have had a tiny peek, baby. But, it's your family after all," he teased. "Seriously, I had you covered most of the time, baby. C'mon, don't fret over it," he said when he saw I wasn't amused after all. He kissed me on the neck, his lips trailing to my mark, as he did his best to take my mind off it.

"I love it, you know," I murmured.

"What," he whispered as he gently nibbled on my earlobe.

"The tattoo you left behind when you marked me. How come you didn't tell me?"

"You didn't know?" he asked, surprised.

"How was I supposed to know, nobody in my pack had anything like it."

"I'm sorry, babe, I assumed you knew. I love seeing it there, you know. It's my biggest pride," he said, smirking.

"Do you, now? And yet you doubted I was your mate? How else did you think I'd acquired this?" I said reminding him of the time he'd lost his memory.

"I'm sorry, I know I was an asshole. I could see it right in front of my eyes; I knew you had to be my mate. And yet I still couldn't accept it. I thought it was part of your witchcraft if it's any consolation."

He sounded so very guilty, my poor beast! I had no intention of making him suffer more for that bitch's crime, so I said "where were we?" as I held his hand and brought it back to the clasp of my bra. The world ceased to exist just for us in the throes of passion, and we fell into a peaceful slumber in each other's arms, our love chasing away all the worry and pain of the day we slowly left behind.

The next day, I woke up freshened.

"Hmm, you are finally awake," Keith said, kissing me. He pushed a hard thigh between mine and his hand slid down my chest, down over my belly, curling at my waist, and then down over my hip, all of this happening in slow motion. I grasped his hair in my hands and arched my hips backward towards him as an undeniable desire knotted my belly.

"I can't get enough of this, of you," Keith murmured.

My sentiments, exactly! It was another hour before we could go down for breakfast.

Gregory was there eating pancakes.

"Morning, bro," I said to him.

"Morning," he smiled. "When are you guys visiting Tannon? If you don't mind I'd like to join you," he said.

"Sure, that would be great. I think we should leave today. Afterward, I'd like to go back home," I said, looking at Keith. I didn't want to prolong our stay any further. I didn't miss the expression of joy and relief on Keith's face upon hearing we were going back home. Poor him, he absolutely hated it here.

I spent the whole day with Tessa listening to her talk about Shea. In the late afternoon, Tessa opened us a portal to the Alps. Tannon was expecting us; he hugged Gregory, but before he could hug me, Keith stopped him.

"Don't touch her! Don't you know? She is pained when she's touched."

"Pained?" Tannon asked. "You mean that's still ongoing?"

"Yes, she keeps getting these excruciating headaches. You were there when it happened with Tessa, and then later we got a repeat of that when she touched Gregory."

"But the last time it happened she hadn't touched anyone," corrected Gregory.

"Let me look at you, Belle," said Tannon.

He looked at me intensely as if he was a doctor examining his patient, his silence scaring me.

"This is impossible!" he said, shaking his head.

He was freaking me out.

"Speak up, man. What are you talking about?" bellowed Keith.

"I'm sorry, Belle, but I have to touch you," he said, his voice low.

"Why?" Keith asked, scowling. "You think your touch won't affect her?"

"I know it will."

"Are you insane? The hell I will allow you to touch her!" Keith growled.

"I'm sorry, Belle. But I have to see what happens when you are pained. It's the only way."

Silent tears rolled down my cheeks; I didn't want to. I didn't want to feel that pain again. But I took a step towards him. Keith stopped me, "What are you doing," he asked, puzzled.

"I need to know," I said, knowing exactly what the next few minutes would bring me.

"Fuck, " he said punching the wall. "Fuck!"

Tannon opened his arms, and I walked right in. Pain shot through my head; I felt my head bursting with an undeniable pressure, a force so powerful that I was left with no coherent thought as the pain simply took over my whole body. Thankfully, I didn't remember the rest.

Keith was rocking me in his arms, " Screw this! I shouldn't have allowed him to touch you," he was berating himself.

Damn, this was turning into an everyday event, a nice dose of excruciating head pain sequentially followed by fainting and Keith's helpless outcry.

I touched my head, my temples were still throbbing, but what I felt was more like a migraine pain now, definitely bearable.

"I'm sorry, Belle," Tannon said. "But this was unimaginable, I needed further evidence to confirm my suspicions."

"Tell me this wasn't for nothing, tell me you know how to cure her, Tannon. Or else, Moon Goddess help me, I'll beat the crap out of you!" Keith barked.

"I don't know how to cure her, Keith," he said. "But I have an idea about what's wrong with her."

"Do I have a brain tumor?" I asked.

"No, Belle. You don't have any physical sickness."

I was perplexed.

"Then what the hell does she have?" asked Keith. "Don't tell me this is all psychological!"

"No, the pain is real," Tannon said.

"Tannon?" Keith urged.

"It's hard to explain."

"You know, Shea left a mark on you from birth. I could feel traces of her all over you when I first came to you in the underworld. I can see them on Gregory, right now."

"Yes."

"Well, the images are as it should be for Gregory. But, for you, they have changed. Before, they were faint because they belonged to the past. Now, however…"

"Now, what?" interrupted Keith.

"Now, they are sharper, clearer, as if they belong to the present."

"I don't know what that means," I said.

"Neither do I, what the hell are you saying man?" snapped Keith, impatiently.

"It means Shea is alive."

"Huh?" I uttered in shock.

Aliens?

Belle

"I'm afraid you lost me," I said frankly.

"And me," added Gregory.

"I'm not sure I understand it myself. But some of the images on you are quite current which means she's projecting them in the present time. I think she can tap into your mind. When you hug someone who's connected to her, whether it's Tessa or Gregory or me, it becomes easier for her to do this. But, apparently, she has become strong enough to do it without requiring an additional connection lately."

"What's she trying to do? Does she want us to rescue her? Is she trying to communicate with me?" I asked.

"I'm afraid I don't know," Tannon said.

"How do we stop it?" asked Keith.

"We can't. Only Shea can," explained Tannon.

"This is bullshit. What, we'll wait for her to come to her senses and realize she's hurting the crap out of her own daughter, and that's it? That's the damn plan?"

"Keith, she may need my help," I said.

"Belle, be reasonable! Shea has not talked to you so far, has she now? Thrice now, all she's done is hurt you. The pain is getting more frequent and random, you don't even need to touch anyone to get it now. What will happen when you get it twice a day, five times a day, heck, twenty times a day, for all I know, huh? How will you bear it? Your brain will burst just from the pressure, just like that! We need to find a way to stop it, that's the only solution!"

"Well, if she's alive, we should be able to contact her," I suggested. "I can do it, I can find her."

"No, it's too dangerous. If somebody hurts you while you are there, I can't save you. If anybody's gonna do it, it should be Tannon."

"I agree," said Tannon. "Let me prepare for the ritual. I need the moonlight, so we need to go outside."

We went outside where it was freezing cold. Tannon drew a circle on the snow and sat inside it, folding his legs beneath him in the style of a warrior. A ray of moonlight streamed through the dark sky, illuminating his face. He nicked a vein in his right wrist with his belt-knife and let a few drops of blood fall onto the snow as he mumbled an almost inaudible chant. The air around us stirred with the power of chanting while Tannon's eyes closed. We watched in silence the subtle muscle changes in his face. Minutes passed agonizingly slowly as first an expression of awe and then a deep, almost unbearable sorrow, marred his features. Then he opened his eyes, breathing deeply through his nose only to exhale in a huff of frustration before he spoke.

"She is alive."

"That's amazing news!" I exclaimed. But why was Tannon not sharing the joy?

"Where is she?" Gregory asked.

Tannon rubbed his eyes and temples silently. "It's bad news. Really bad news!" he said.

"I don't understand?" I said.

"She didn't recognize me. I couldn't get to her."

"Where is she? What's wrong with her?"

"I don't know, she wouldn't say and I couldn't see. But it was obvious she didn't want me there." He looked at our puzzled faces. "I know because she called the guards on me," he clarified.

"That was unexpected," I murmured. "Nevertheless, we gotta help her."

"I'm afraid we can't do anything until we know where she is. And since she has no intention of telling me, our hands are tied, unless ..." he said, pausing as he looked at me.

"Unless I contact her," I said, understanding his implication.

"Absolutely not," Keith yelled, throwing up his hands in the air.

"What other choice do we have?" I said, trying to appeal to his good sense.

"We'll let Tessa contact her, the mother-daughter bond is more likely to snap her out of her state, whatever that might be. It seems like she has some kind of amnesia, but apparently she's not held against her will," he commented. He held me firmly, "Promise me, Belle, you won't do anything reckless."

"But..."I muttered.

"Promise me, Belle," he insisted.

"Fine," I said, giving up. He was one overly protective stubborn mate!

Tannon asked Tessa to come. She entered from the portal she'd just created, not knowing exactly why she was summoned. When Tannon told her Shea was alive, her face was utterly emotionless. She simply looked at Tannon who firmly held her stare, and then she knew. Her violet eyes lit up with a hint of hope.

"I can't believe it, how is she alive? Why hasn't she found us?" asked an ecstatic Tessa. "The Moon Goddess has been extremely kind to me; first I found my grandchildren and now my daughter. It's too good to be true."

It was indeed. That was the problem.

"She doesn't remember, Tessa. She didn't know who I was," Tannon explained sadly.

Tessa's face fell.

"We are hoping she may recognize you though," Tannon said.

Tessa rushed outside immediately and conducted the same ritual Tannon had completed a while ago, with exactly the same outcome. She was crying when she was done. "She doesn't know me, she just doesn't. My Shea is alive and I have no clue where she is because she won't tell me," she said, her voice laden with pain as tears strolled down her cheeks. "She told me to go fuck myself. My beautiful, kind Shea. What have they done to her?" Great gulping sobs wracked her body and shook her like a rag doll until she couldn't breathe. "Not again, I can't lose her again," she cried.

"Can you?" Tessa asked me as she looked at me, teary eyed.

I knew what it was she wanted. "You know I have to do this," I said to Keith who opened his mouth to object. "I know you don't like it, but we have no other options left."

"You are going to sacrifice your granddaughter? What kind of a deal is that?" Keith roared. "Do you know that should they kill her there, she'll be dead here too? How can you ask me to approve this?"

"Keith, please. She's my mother, too."

"Please, baby. Don't do this," he said, his eyes pleading.

"I have to," I insisted.

Tessa stared at me hopefully. Keith left in anger, banging the door behind him as he entered inside the cabin.

"But we have to wait for the night. I can only do this in my sleep," I explained.

Tessa nodded, taking deep breaths to stop the gush of emotions racing through her body. "Thank you, Belle," she said, trying to assuage the guilt holding her in its grip.

We found Keith staring into space with clenched teeth when we entered inside. I was aware that he'd been trying very hard simply to respect my decisions since the episode of the dark demons in the underground city. And he was on edge, barely hanging onto his composure as the urge to protect his mate seeped its way deep into his brain and penetrated his whole being.

I rubbed my hands to gain some warmth, my face red from the biting cold. Nobody spoke, and an uncomfortable silence engulfed the room.

After half an hour, Tessa took us back to the coven. Keith kept scowling. We eventually turned on the TV in the living room to watch further news on the mall episode as we waited for the night to settle in.

The news on TV was shocking; the mall disaster had been repeated in a few other places. The reporter on the news channel was slowly building the tension by saying it was an alien invasion and that they had the shots to prove it.

Alice snorted. "What utter nonsense!" she said.

They were showing people going crazy in a movie theater, punching, beating those around them, tearing down the projection screen and the seats.

"There it is," said the reporter as he pointed at a blurred image in the corner of the screen.

"Here is our alien from outer space," the reporter continued while they froze and zoomed in on the image.

As the image filled the screen, a collective gasp rose around the room. What he referred to as an alien was floating in the air and it was blue.

An umbra. That's what it was.

"How is that possible?" I asked in shock. How had the umbra come out? And how many of them were out there ruining mankind?

The Convention

Belle

"What the fuck?" Keith shouted. "Did we let them out while we were using the gate?"

"No, we didn't. I was keeping a close watch on the other side. I'm pretty sure of it," said Tessa. "This is not our doing."

"They are driving the humans insane," I said. "Their darkness is as effective on humans as it is on the dark demons."

Keith became silent; his face froze as his eyes looked into space. I knew that look by now; he was communicating with his men using the alpha command. After a few minutes, he was back with us.

"It's worse than I thought. Humans have attacked several werewolf packs with clubs and knives. Obviously we are not dealing with a few umbra here. We have to convene the council," Keith stated. Then he looked at Tessa and said, "You have to do it."

Tessa nodded.

Keith explained the rules to me when he saw me puzzled. Apparently, the head of the council was elected among the supernatural species every four years. Tessa had been elected two years ago, and it was her responsibility to convene a meeting in an emergency situation like this.

"I'll send the missives right away," Tessa said as she left the room.

"Keith, can you make sure my pack is okay?" I asked, concerned.

"Sure, babe," Keith said as he contacted my dad. I cracked my knuckles in worry as I waited for his conversation to end and his stony expression to soften. The conversation took longer than expected.

"What's going on? Is everything all right?"

"Yes, Belle. They're fine," he said, giving me a quick assuring kiss.

As we waited for Tessa, I rested my head on Keith's shoulder and closed my eyes briefly. He curled his arm around my head, giving me brief kisses on the head as he stroked my hair softly. I opened my eyes when I heard Tessa enter the room.

"We are gathering tomorrow; everyone is informed. This is worrisome," Tessa briefed us. "I also heard from the witches in London of events of a similar nature. I don't know how many of those we are dealing with in here. We need to hunt them one by one. This is gonna be one difficult mission."

"Can I come with you guys?" I asked. I had never been to a council meeting, and I didn't want to be left behind.

"No, that's not a good idea. All the others will be there," Keith said immediately. I didn't need to be a wizard to know whom he meant. My other mates of course! My face fell in disappointment.

"You already marked her, Keith. The bond the others feel with Belle must have been weakened by now," Tessa said.

"Please?" I pleaded, using the puppy-eye look on Keith.

He hesitated, then sighed in defeat. "Fine, but don't you dare leave my side when we are there!" he warned me.

"Great!" I said, hugging him tightly and burying my head in his chest.

We had some light dinner and I wanted to watch a movie which I thought would help me fall asleep. Every time I was on a mission to contact someone, falling asleep was turning into a challenge. We started watching a very long and not so exciting science fiction movie. After an hour into the film, I finally fell asleep snuggled up to Keith.

I woke up in bed, not remembering much of the previous night. I felt drained despite having just woken up.

"I failed to contact Shea," I said remembering.

"It's okay, baby. Apparently, you were too exhausted," Keith said, smiling. It was obvious he was happy with the outcome.

"I still feel exhausted," I said yawning.

"Wait," Keith said suddenly touching my forehead. "You have a fever. How come I didn't notice?"

"I'll call Alice," he said as he left the room in a rush.

I managed to get out of bed and go to the mirror in the bathroom. I pulled back my shirt and looked at my wounds. Though my chest wound was healed, the one on my shoulder seemed to be mildly infected.

Alice walked in with Tessa, both of them heading to the bathroom. Alice saw the infection with dismay. "I'm sorry, Belle. It's all my fault. I rushed it all in there in the mall, but I should have checked it at the coven last night. I completely forgot with all that was happening."

"It's okay, Alice. It's nothing to fret about. I've had worse," I said, trying to smile.

"Did you find Shea?" asked Tessa, excited.

"No, I'm sorry. I believe I just slept. It must have been the fever. I'm sorry. I'll try again tonight," I said, shivering.

"That's enough about Shea. Belle is sick, and she needs to be in bed, she needs healing," Keith yelled, lifting me in his arms and carrying me back to bed.

"Of course, I'm sorry. There's no rush," Tessa added, but it was impossible to miss the sad expression that settled on her face.

My whole body was shaking by the time Keith lay me in bed. Alice placed her hands on my shoulder again, I felt her hands weave their magic as my shiver slowly disappeared, and I felt the heaviness of my body and the pain of my bones ebb away. A wave of energy swept through my body, lifting my weakness as she swept her palms all over my shoulder. She also checked up on my chest wound just to make sure.

"I think you are fine now. I'm so sorry again," Alice said when she was finally done.

"No wrong done, Alice, don't blame yourself for nothing," I said, trying to assure her.

Keith wouldn't let me out of bed even though I felt completely fine. He brought me breakfast in bed. I had nothing else to do so I just read a book in bed wasting time until we were ready to leave for the meeting. Finally, Keith entered the room.

"Babe, we will leave soon. You need to get ready if you are insistent on coming with us," he said, hoping that I would just prefer to stay in bed.

I got out of bed in a second and changed my clothes. I was as giddy as a small child visiting Disneyland.

"Belle, are you sure you're fine? Perhaps you should just stay and rest," Keith said, trying his luck again.

"I'm fine, Keith. I was fine an hour ago, heck I was okay even two hours ago," I said, humphing.

"Okay, if you say so," murmured Keith. The disappointment was written all over his face. "You need to pack a few things. We'll stay the night," he added.

I prepared a small bag for the convention. We followed Tessa through the portal; I had no idea where we were going, but I was damn excited.

When we walked out of the door, I gasped in shock. We were inside a fancy hotel. The lavishly decorated foyer had an extremely tall ceiling with the statues of the Moon and Sun Goddess greeting us right in the center. I saw a group of ifrits walk to the hotel and check in at the reservation center. I spotted Derek and a bunch of shadow spirits standing in the lobby chatting idly.

"Derek," I yelled, and he turned around.

"Belle?" he said, completely surprised at my presence.

Keith tensed beneath me as Derek walked towards me.

"What are you doing here?" asked Derek. "I thought you were with Lasarus?" he said as he recognized Keith standing next to me. "Keith," he said, greeting him with a subtle nod.

"Derek," said Keith, acknowledging him in return.

"I'm not with Lasarus. It's a long story," I said.

"I'm glad things have turned well for you. I thought about you often," he said.

I noticed the muscle tick on Keith's face. He was extremely jealous by the looks of it, but he kept his silence. He settled his arm around my waist just to display his ownership. Derek didn't miss the warning gesture.

"I felt really guilty for turning you in, I hope you can forgive me for that," said Derek.

"Forgotten and forgiven," I said. "What about Oliver, how is he?"

"How do you know him?" asked Derek, puzzled.

"Oh, didn't he tell you? We were in the underworld together," I filled him in.

"I didn't know," Derek said.

"Perhaps that's because he didn't want to confess how he let her walk into a place about to explode to save his own fucking ass."

"I think we need to go now. It was nice seeing you Derek," I said as I tugged Keith in a different direction.

"What's wrong with you?" I asked Keith.

"Nothing," he pouted.

I let it go as we checked ourselves in and settled in the room. It was stylishly decorated inside, with a blend of comfort, elegance, and luxury.

"Xavier is here, baby. I need to see him. Are you coming?" he asked.

"Sure," I replied. Now that I had Keith, I didn't mind Xavier's early transgressions.

"Where are we going?" I asked as we left the room.

"We are going to the conference room on this floor."

"Well, that's convenient. I thought they only had bedrooms here," I said.

"No, every floor has conference rooms, cafes and restaurants, a fitness center and a pool. This floor belongs to us," Keith explained.

"Us?" I questioned him.

"The werewolves. Every floor belongs to one supernatural species. This is ours. Any werewolf I bring with me stays here on this floor."

That was cool.

I followed Keith as he opened the door to the conference. And, someone jumped at him.

"Surprise!" Zena said as she wrapped her arms around him, lifting one leg around his hip and grinding her pelvis against him while trying to pull his face towards her lips.

"I missed you so," she murmured.

I couldn't help it. Nope, it really wasn't my fault, call it the mating bond or the Goddess of Jealousy possessing my body, but I found myself throwing a giant ball of fire at her auburn hair before Keith even had a chance to push her off his body.

"Aah," she yelled as she ran to the sink to put out the fire on her sizzling hair.

"I will kill you, bitch," she came back a few minutes later, her long hair on the right-hand side was all burned up to her shoulder. I caught the smell of burned hair on her which reminded me of the smell of singed chicken feathers. She threw herself at me viciously.

Keith separated us, dangling Zena from the back of her belt. "Why did you bring her here?" he asked Xavier in frustration.

"Well, could it be because I always brought her here before and you always appreciated it?" Xavier asked, grinning.

"Not anymore. Damn, with all that was going on, I forgot to announce that I found my mate."

"Your mate?" Xavier said in shock. Then he looked at me. "You mean Belle?"

"Yes, of course, it's me. What did you think?" I answered, smirking.

"No, it can't be. I won't accept it," said Zena, suddenly wailing.

"Take her back," Keith said in anger. "I don't have time for this nonsense in the middle of all that's been going on, and I don't want her upsetting Belle."

"Okay, he said as he grabbed Zena and dragged her outside the room.

"I'm sorry, Belle, I didn't know she'd be here. She won't bother you again, I promise."

"You got me all wrong; it's you I don't want her bothering. Believe me, next time I will scorch her entire mane," I swore vehemently.

He looked at me. "I love you, you know that right?" he said.

"I do," I said. "But it doesn't change how I feel about your previous lovers."

"Fair enough. I need to go to the meeting now. I'll see you later?" he said.

"Wait. Hold on a minute, I thought I could attend the meeting too. Can't I?" I asked.

"You can, babe, as my mate. But why would you want to? It'll be boring," he said, again trying hard to dissuade me.

"I want to. I've spent so much time in the damn underworld. What is happening now concerns me too."

He grunted but held my hand and we took the elevator to the top floor. It was a restricted area, and the elevator worked with a palm recognition system. Only the leaders of each species could take the top floor. Keith pressed his palm on the elevator wall and pressed the button. It started moving. We got out of the elevator into a rugged hall and entered a round room. There were seats allocated to each leader, the Sun Goddess's children were seated at the right side while the Moon Goddess's children were seated at the left. I followed Keith to a comfy large luxurious leather sofa and squeezed right next to him. I saw Tessa sit in the center of the room. I tensed when I saw Lasarus enter the room. The one moment of surprise in his eyes turned to hurt when he saw me, but instead of walking to his seat, he chose to stroll towards me. Keith growled next to me as Lasarus stood right in front of me, completely ignoring Keith.

"Love," Lasarus said. "I was so worried about you."

Keith stood up so fast, grabbing Lasarus by the neck. "You don't get to call her 'love.' The next time you do, I'll snap your neck and leave your remains out in the open for dark demons to find. You get it?" he roared.

"Stop acting like kids," Tessa said. "Lasarus, please go back to your seat. My granddaughter is mated to Keith, and I hope you'll respect that. We have more important things to discuss than the matters of the heart in this council," she said with a commanding voice.

Lasarus looked at me again so sadly I almost felt bad for him. "Why, Belle?" he murmured as he finally walked away. I took a deep breath, a catastrophe was averted, but just barely. Tessa, as the chairman, started the meeting when all the leaders were seated. She talked about the emerging threat of umbra and gave information on what they could do.

"How can they be eliminated?" asked a handsome man. I had never seen him before; he had black hair like Keith's, but his eyes were green.

"Samuel, I talked to Tannon who had the opportunity to kill one. The umbra affects people with the cloud of darkness they carry around them. That's also their weakness. Tannon has scattered their cloud with a dispersion spell."

"But we can't do magic. Is the sword effective as a weapon? What about fists? You want us to hunt them with no explanation whatsoever on how to eliminate them?"

"Excuse me," I said raising my hand.

"Belle, do you have anything to say," asked Tessa.

I felt Samuel's scrutinizing gaze on me as I started talking. "I have killed one, too. The cloud of darkness can also be dispersed with fire. " I said, feeling very awkward from all the attention on me.

"Thanks, Belle," muttered Samuel as his eyes pierced me. "That is very helpful," he said with an intensity that somehow disturbed me.

"We need to establish hunting teams in each territory, specifically in those areas where disturbances have been reported.

The meeting went for another hour. I felt exhausted with all the bickering that went on among the leaders. It was incredible how the strongest of all the supernatural beings were gathered in this room, yet these creatures had no skills in diplomacy. They had a hard time finding common ground on anything they discussed. Just when we were leaving, Samuel interrupted us.

"I'd like you to know that I made an appeal," he said to both of us.

"Excuse me?" I said, confused.

"I was given no chance to win your heart as your mate. You spent time with every mate of yours, except for me. I've been deprived of a fair chance to win you over. I felt the pain, the void right here in my chest when he marked you, and I didn't even know why. It's not fair."

"What the fuck, Samuel?" Keith shouted.

"I have appealed to the Moon Goddess for her mark to be erased. I demanded a week with her before she made her choice. She accepted my plea. I just wanted you to know," he said.

It was then I had this extreme pain in my head, and I screamed, which is exactly why Keith chose to catch me rather than kill Samuel. I fainted.

Revelations

Belle

"I can't bear this any longer," I heard Keith say. "How do we help her? I don't know how much longer her body can tolerate this."

"I'm okay, Keith," I said opening my eyes and patting his cheek. He leaned his forehead on mine and we stayed like that for minutes, not saying anything, just inhaling each other's scent, basking in each other's warmth. He finally lifted me in his arms and carried me to our room.

"I have a surprise for you, Belle. It'll cheer you up."

We heard a knock at the door. "And here they are," said Keith smiling as he opened the door.

"Oh, my goodness," I exclaimed in joy as I saw my dad walk in with Mom and Sean. I jumped out of bed to hug them. How I had missed them! "I can't believe you didn't tell me anything," I said to Keith. My tone was affectionate in its joking reprimand.

"It was a surprise, baby. If I'd told you anything, it would not have been a surprise now, would it?" he smiled.

"How, when did you arrange it?" I asked as I savored my family's presence in the room.

"It was when I talked to them the other day to inquire about their well-being," he said, winking at me.

Aha, that's why that conversation had taken so long.

It was awkward between my dad and Keith. Dad kept averting his eyes, and Keith, well, he just ignored Father.

354

"I'll leave you alone with your family," Keith said as he left the room as if Satan was after him.

Men! They were as weak as a newborn puppy when it came to emotional stuff such as apologizing.

"Are you happy, Belle?" Dad asked me.

"I am. I really am," I assured him.

"How come he didn't mark you?" Sean asked, judging.

"He did, see the tattoo on my neck?" I said turning my head and pulling back my hair.

"There's no tattoo there, Belle," my mom stated.

"Of course there is."

"No, there's not," repeated Sean.

I rushed to the bathroom to look at my neck. It was gone! My tattoo was all gone. Then I remembered Samuel's words before the pain had hit me. I was going to kill the fucking bastard myself. Of course, if Keith did not beat me to it. Asshole! Did the Vampire King think for a second I would feel any affection towards him after this? What a joke! I would make that week hell for him. I swore I would!

"I can't believe it. It's been annulled because of Samuel's appeal," I explained to them. "He wants an equal chance with me; he claims he didn't get it."

"Samuel, the Vampire King?" asked my brother, his eyes widening in confusion.

"Yes, the one and only one."

"You are mated to him, too?" my dad asked, joining the herd of confused family members in the room.

Poor them, they had been completely kept in the dark about everything. I told them about the prophecy, about Lasarus and the underworld. They listened in utter shock and horror. I watched as emotions of confusion and worried realization hit their faces.

"I can't believe I wasn't there to protect you from any of this. I should have killed Lasarus when I was there," Sean said, rage making his humongous body shake like a leaf.

355

"Look, what is done is done. And after Lasarus, Keith was there with me most of the time; I wasn't alone." I assured them.

Keith came back after half an hour, bringing Tessa was with him. Oops, I hadn't had the chance to tell my family about Tessa or Shea.

"This is my real grandmother. She's a witch," I said, introducing her to my family. I apparently skipped the part about her being an ancient priestess.

"I just found out," I added when I saw their expressions bearing another wave of shock.

My mom gasped, but then she shook off her stupor and extended her hand for a shake. "Nice to meet you," she said kindly. My dad and Sean joined her in the gesture.

"Likewise," Tessa chuckled. "I'm so grateful that she was raised in a loving family. You see, I didn't know about her existence. Otherwise…" she said, stopping in mid-sentence.

She didn't need to add that she would have fetched me long before had she known. Everybody in the room got the message. The air suddenly became tense. Who would have thought my old and new family would turn this into a fierce competition?

"Keith, your mark is gone. He wasn't bluffing," I said as I tried to divert everybody's attention. I showed him my neck.

Keith roared like a wounded animal. "I'm gonna kill that bastard!"

Well, perhaps I should have selected another topic.

"Look, Keith. This is beyond you, this is beyond me," Tessa intervened. "Only the Moon Goddess has the power to erase the mating mark; you know that. This is obviously her doing. And you won't get it back, not unless you abide by her rules, you know she will not allow a new marking to stick," she said calmly. "Why don't you allow her to go with Samuel and we'll fetch her right back in a week. Why do you hesitate, don't you trust her?" she asked, baiting him.

"This is fucking wrong," Keith said punching the wall. "How can I trust Belle with him when she keeps getting all this pain? Who will hold her, comfort her? Who will look after her? And now she's fair game for others as well; she'll be a fucking target for Lasarus, too. How could the Moon Goddess have done this?" he snapped. "No, I won't let her go with him; if he wants to spend time with her, he can do it at my castle. And that's my fucking stipulation."

"That's not a bad idea," I said agreeing with him. That sounded fair to me. And on what grounds would Samuel object to that? I couldn't think of any.

Keith warned us not to leave this floor. He was scared Lasarus would simply kidnap me. I gave him an assuring kiss, and let him deal with business. I spent time with my family the whole day. I was simply thrilled to be with them again. We chatted for hours after a wonderful dinner. It was past midnight, and as I was drinking my second glass of red wine and I felt extremely sleepy. We were all leaving tomorrow, so this was it. I hugged my family one more time, feeling the sadness of saying goodbye. I got their promise to visit me at Keith's castle, and I headed to our room. Keith was not yet in bed. I let my body sink into the softness of the sheets. Sleep was imminent.

I found myself in a strange room. It was dark inside, but it looked to be someone's bedroom. I could see the lump of a figure beneath the sheets. I moved hesitantly towards the bed. Who was that lying in bed? Could it be Shea?

"Shea?" I shook the figure softly.

She opened her eyes but didn't seem to be surprised at seeing me.

"Are you Shea?" I asked the woman.

"Yes, who's asking?" she said.

I tried to see what she looked like, but the darkness prevented me from seeing her features clearly. Did she look like Tessa?

"I'm Belle. Your daughter," I explained with a shaking voice. This was my mom, and I didn't know what to say to her. My heart started pounding as the reality of the moment hit me. I was in a state of wonder, amazed at this chance encounter.

"Finally. I've been waiting for you, daughter. I thought you'd never come," she said as she suddenly seized me with a viselike grip.

What in blazes was going on? "You're hurting me," I said, desperately trying to shake her off me, but failing. She held onto me with the grip of death.

A laugh emanated from deep within her throat. She was doing something to me as I felt my energy drain. "Let me go!" I yelled, but I couldn't move. I tried to withdraw to my body at the hotel, but I couldn't move my limbs. A massive exhaustion now held my body in its impenetrable grip.

The door opened, and somebody turned on the switch. I finally saw Shea's face. She had long dark black hair matching perfectly with her dark skin. This was impossible! My mother had turned into a dark demon.

I didn't even have the energy to look behind me and see who the newcomer was. But I didn't have to, her voice was as familiar to me as my secret place in the pack. My body shook with tremors of disgust as I heard her ask, "Is she finally here?"

It was Daisy! I was in the underworld, drained by my mom who was now a dark demon. And there was nothing I could do about it. Whatever magic Shea held over me was strong, and I couldn't free myself from it. I felt my eyes close and I embraced the darkness.

***

Keith

I came to their room at 3 am in the morning. I had talked to my men, and then to Tessa, sketching in detail the plan to get rid of all the umbra. We'd decided that the werewolves and the witches should act in unison, producing teams of both species and attack together. I was tired, and I had missed my mate. I sank into bed, wrapping my hands around Belle's waist and drawing her to me. She was sleeping so deeply that she didn't even stir. I was disappointed; I hoped I'd have the chance to show her how much

I loved her despite the disappearance of my mark. I simply enjoyed inhaling her scent as I grudgingly fell asleep. I opened my eyes as the morning sun bathed my face. I stretched in bed, kissing Belle softly on the cheek. My hands traveled the length of her body, exploring the places that pleased her, searching out those very secret parts of her that made her emit those helpless moans I adored so much. I always drank her moans like wine, loving every sound that she made when she was consumed with passion. Except this time, she was completely silent. It was as if she was completely immune to my touch.

"Belle," I said in fear. I touched her forehead and was relieved to see she didn't have a fever. I shook her as she lay utterly still in bed.

"Belle," I said, again. Now I was frantic as I tried to wake her up. "Wake up," I yelled.

After minutes of countless attempts, I accepted the truth. She wasn't waking up. What had happened? Was it the pain which had pushed her to this state? I had no clue as I could no longer feel her.

"She's in a fucking coma," I said punching the wall. "And I can't even feel her distress because that bastard had her mark erased," I roared, fisting my hands so tightly that the veins in my arms popped up visibly.

"Please wake up, baby," I said, in one last desperate plea.

Turned

Belle

Where was I? I had no clue as I looked around, desperately trying to understand what had happened to me.

"So you're awake," she said. The moment I looked at her dark eyes, I remembered. It was her. I refused to call her mother.

"What did you do to me?" I asked.

"I tapped into your powers," she said, smiling.

"What are you planning to do with me?"

"I'll keep draining you until I have enough."

"Enough for what?"

"Enough to open a constant portal to the other side, of course."

Not only had she crossed to the dark side, but she had gone crazy.

"You see, dear Belle. That's your name, right? Well, I managed to open a temporary portal, but I couldn't keep it open. Only the umbra at the outskirts could get out. And then the portal closed. I've been trying to tap into your powers from the underworld since then, but I could only get a few sips. I needed you here to get what I required. I kept giving you small doses of headaches, and you walked straight into my room. Imagine my joy at this mother-daughter reunion."

Now, the excruciating pains in my head made sense. Those were the times Shea had tried long distance draining me. How naive we were in thinking all she wanted was communication and help.

"How? How can you tap into my powers, how is that even possible?" I asked. Though the fact that I could hardly move my limbs confirmed her words, what she said seemed so surreal, so impossible!

"Lucifer is the key to everything. Did you know he's the rebellious brother of your dear Moon Goddess? Everybody thinks she just has a sister, but nobody talks about the brother. He's not offended, our Lucifer is very humble, always forgiving of his jealous sisters. He just wanted to tip the game a little by allowing me to keep my powers after I was demonized. But my powers were not enough to open a portal from the underworld. As ancient as my blood may have been, it was not good enough. I needed to bolster it by stealing yours. Your powers were almost an exact substitute to mine, a beautiful mesh of dark demon and witch powers. I needed them to enhance what I had, but I wasn't sure I could do it, " she said. "Who would have thought I could? It even took me by surprise. I guess there's something special about a mother-daughter bond, after all; you turned out to be the perfect vessel," she said, her chuckle reminding me of Tessa.

"How were you even demonized?" I asked remembering Tannon's words about ancient blood.

"It took me eighteen years to demonize her, eighteen long years," Azazel said as he suddenly entered inside. "It was damn hard to dilute her blood. I didn't give up, though. I fed her my blood every day until she finally stopped struggling. Can you believe she still retains some of her memories? The power of ancient blood … it's simply amazing."

I flinched seeing him.

"Don't worry; you are safe from me for now. I need you strong," he said as he saw my reaction." How is it going, Shea? Will you be ready soon?"

"Yes, I need a few more days. You just keep your army ready to go."

"Lucifer also sent reinforcements; we'll be okay. I'll leave you to it," he said, and left.

"How did you end up here? Father thought you were dead after the birth. Did Lucifer reincarnate you?" I asked.

"What nonsense, child, what kind of gibberish paranormal books are you reading? There is no such thing as reincarnation. I wasn't dead, and your stupid father didn't wait long enough to make sure. He just grabbed you both and got away from Azazel who was chasing us. You see Lucifer had already leaked the prophecy to him and he was after you. Guess what; he ended up having me instead. I was so weak that my heartbeat was barely audible. Azazel took me to the underworld; I guess it was a lucky exchange," she said.

"Enough of this chit-chat, we got work to do, dear Belle," she said as she held me just like the last time. I felt so faint as she drained me. I collapsed in her arms.

Every day she woke me up and kept transferring my energy and my powers as she called it. I tried a few times to get back to the convention hotel, but I couldn't manage to. I felt so weak that my body felt like an empty shell. Daisy came a few times to watch the process.

"I want her after you're done with her," she said to Shea, her eyes twinkling.

"She will be all yours," said Shea. "Of course, if there's anything left to do with her." She stretched lazily in her seat. "This feels so damn good, so invigorating. I believe I'm ready now. I feel so damn good. She opened her palms. The flames that rose from her hands reached the high ceiling. "Call Azazel," she ordered. I caught the flicker of rage on Daisy's face, being the recipient of this order, but she managed to conceal it. It was obvious the two women were in severe competition and disagreement over their rank in the hierarchy of the underworld. But Daisy relented in the end as she left the room.

I couldn't allow my mother to open the portal; I crawled on my knees to stop her, my hands grabbing her ankle. She looked at me pitifully and kicked me in the chest so strongly that I lost my breath. I just lay there, unable to move.

"Bring her with us in case I need more," she said to the dark demons, and they carried my limp body to the gate.

362

What I saw when we got there escaped my understanding, there were thousands of dark demons ready to march in a solid array. This was the end of the world! How could their advances be stopped? It defied logic! Not with the Vampire King worrying more about his fair chance with me, not with Lasarus worrying over not giving his enemy, the witches, an inch, not with Tessa caring more about her precious daughter. How would any of these species stop their bickering to act united against this threat? They were so unprepared for what was awaiting them; everyone would be slaughtered on Earth. The alliance of the insane humans and the dark demons would bring life to an end. And I could do nothing about it. I couldn't even give my friends a warning.

Shea stood with her eyes closed. I could hear the hum of her chanting as her body lifted up and was surrounded by a shield of dark energy. With an abundant energy, she spun around the room in little orbits, her dark eyes shining, her hair floating around her shoulders like a black cloud. She raised her palms upward, and a dark mass began to rise from the ground slowly taking the shape of a solid door. She continued her chanting and the door slowly opened, revealing a sunny meadow outside. Where was she transporting the army? It surely wasn't the desert outside the gate.

"This is going to take a whole day," she said, finally opening her eyes and lowering herself back to the ground.

"March in a solid line. Hold the line," commanded Azazel as he led the army outside. I watched in dismay.

The army was still marching through the portal after hours and hours had passed. When only a bunch of demons were left behind, Daisy walked towards me, grinning maliciously. "I guess it's my turn with her now, isn't that right?" she asked Shea.

Shea turned to Daisy, "Yep, that's right," she said smiling. "But, first it's my turn with you," she added as she bombarded her with flames so strong that I had to cover my ears to stop hearing her painful shrieks. The smell of burning meat filled the air and then she was silent. I surely had not expected that.

"I never liked her. She was overrated," Shea said, shrugging her shoulders. "Call it a parting gift from your dear mother," she said as she left through the portal.

Wait, what? It took me only seconds to catch up with this new development. I crawled on my knees as that was all I could do with what was still left in me. I used the portal to get to the meadow outside. I could see the army moving ahead. How was I going to get out of here and how was I going to let Keith know what was coming?

The Return

Belle

I dragged myself along the ground, my body feeling like dead weight as though it was in a sandbag that had been immersed in gallons of water. I crawled on my knees for what seemed like hours; my jeans were torn, my knees and palms were scraped and bloody. I continued on all fours until I could no longer do so. I collapsed on the ground as though I had no working muscles left in my body. I lay immobile like that, my energy completely depleted.

"Mommy, look what I found," I heard a child squeak as I tried to lift my eyelids. "A pretty girl. She's lying on the grass, Mamma. Can we take her home?"

"Oh my goodness, what has happened to you, darling? Hold on; we'll help you," the mother said, and I felt her shadow as she leaned in towards me. Her face blurred right before me, I closed my eyes. The next time I opened them I was lying on a soft bed in a hospital room.

"Good, you are awake. The doctor said you were feeble, but nothing else seems to be the problem. He put you on a drip, be careful when you move your arm," the woman who'd found me said.

I looked at my arm. Indeed, there was a needle tied to my vein.

"Do you want some TV, dear? Let me put it on for you," she smiled as she turned on the TV. "Is there anyone we can contact for you?" she asked.

Yes, can you please contact the witch coven? I had to get out of here, but how would I contact Keith or Tessa? I had no clue. Their numbers were certainly not listed anywhere. What about Dad, I knew his number. I could call him, or Mom or Sean. I grabbed the phone and dialed their numbers one by one, over and over again. Each time, I was taken to their voice message. Where were they? As a last resort, I tried Daniel's phone.

"Hello," Daniel said. "Who's this?"

"Oh thank the Moon Goddess, Daniel it's me. Belle."

"Belle, it's so nice to hear from you," Daniel said as if we were having our daily chit-chat. "How is everyone at the convention? How was the surprise? You didn't expect to see your family, did you now?" he asked, chuckling.

"Daniel, I need your help," I said, cutting him off.

"What's going on, Belle, are you all right?" he asked.

"No, I'm not. I need to contact Tannon or Tessa or Keith. And I don't know how."

"Huh? You mean our king? I have no idea who the others are, but I can guess. Belle, it's not as if I have access to any of them. Basically, they are royalty."

"Is Father back?"

"No," Daniel stuttered.

"Good, can you contact him? I'll give you the directions to the hospital. I need Tannon. Tell him to find me."

"Hospital! What happened to you?"

I knew he was worried, confused and curious. But the end of the world was near, and I felt that was the moment's pressing obligation, particularly being the only one who knew about it. "Daniel, please hurry," I said giving him the directions I took from the woman.

What was I to do? My body was lying back there, how was I going to get back to it? I had no idea. I hoped Tannon would have the divine knowledge to share with me.

"Okay, Belle. Just hang on," Daniel said and hung up.

"I'm glad somebody's coming for you," the woman said and thankfully left the room before things got awkward with Tannon's non-physical visit.

Minute after minute dragged by as though time sunk its claws in, resisting any budge.

Finally, the moment I waited for was upon me when I heard Tannon call my name.

"Belle?"

"Tannon, I'm here."

"Belle, what happened? We thought you were in a coma."

"I went to find Shea. Listen, Tannon! We don't have time. She tapped into my powers, don't ask me how. Shea's turned into a dark demon, but she's also still a witch. She drained me for days and opened a portal from the underworld to let all the demons out. They are advancing as we speak. Thousands and thousands of demons, Tannon." My tension was becoming high and shrill, as was my voice. " I don't know where they will strike, but they will," I said frantically.

"I see, so I'm protecting the gate for nothing," Tannon remarked. "First things first, can you return to your body?"

"I don't think so; she said she took all my powers, and she was damn convincing. Let me see," I said as I tried to bring fire to my palms. I couldn't. "Yep, I have no powers, I just checked," I said, confirming my previous point.

Tannon paused for a few seconds which scared me. Then he spoke. "Belle, listen to me. You said it yourself that Shea's now a hybrid like you. I don't know for sure, but she could have tapped only the powers you both shared, like the ability to create illusions or fire. It's like, you can't compliment something you don't have. You see?"

"Aha," I muttered. "Not really," I then confessed. This was not the time to lie.

"Shea never had the skill to contact anyone by blood, let alone do what you do."

"What are you saying?" I asked, still confused.

"She couldn't have stolen your ability to go back to your body. That power still resides somewhere in you."

"Tannon, what you say doesn't make sense. She told me she needed my powers to create a portal. That was not a power I ever had."

"It probably was, you just didn't know. Did you ever try it?

"No," I admitted. "I wouldn't even know how. But, I tried going back to my body when she was draining me and it surely didn't work," I reasoned.

"Of course it wouldn't, you must have been too exhausted at the time from all the drainage," explained Tannon.

I felt hopeful for the first time. And, just when the nurse entered the room with a tray of food, I started the process of withdrawal. I pulled myself inward, feeling my body become incorporeal and merge with my soul in perfect unison and harmony. Then I felt the familiar feeling of dizziness that always accompanied my withdrawal. I heard the fall of the tray and the scream of the nurse as I disappeared from the room and returned to my former self.

Keith's huge body covered mine the moment I opened my eyes. I briefly noticed we were back in our room at the coven. Just as I felt the weight of his body, I hugged him back, forgetting about all else for a second, like the looming war with the dark demons. I had thought I'd never see him again!

"Belle," Keith said in agony as he expressed the same sentiments. "Belle-mine, I thought, I'd never get you back. Do you know what I went through?"

I filled my lungs as I took a deep breath to get back to the unpleasant business. What I had to say was going to be hard.

"Keith, they are marching to war," I said, trying to shake him off my body. "We need to hurry, get ready."

"Who, Belle? What are you talking about?" Keith asked as he kissed my face. He tried to kiss me on the lips but I dodged him. It was evident he thought whatever I had to say could wait. Well, it couldn't.

"Keith, listen to me," I shouted. "The underworld is no more. They are all here now, seeking war."

"What the fuck?" he said, and it was then that Tannon entered the room, having just finished his ritual outside. Tessa came in a few seconds later.

"Now, Belle. Tell us all about it," Tannon said.

I explained all that had happened. Tessa was a mess as she listened to what Shea had become.

"No, my sweet darling. What have they done to you?" Tessa cried as if Shea was right in front of us. "I will save her. I'm sure I can save her," she murmured over and over again.

"Can we focus here?" I urged them. "What do we do?" I asked.

"We'll fight, Belle. That's what we'll do." Keith said.

The War - Part I

Belle

Minutes passed like a blur as preparations for war continued at full speed. Tessa visited the children of the Sun Goddess, the Fae King, the leader of the shadow spirits, and Ifrit King while Tannon went to see the children of the Moon Goddess, the Vampire King, and the Demon Lord. Though I didn't know how anyone had reacted to the news, I could imagine how Azazel's marching army must have distressed Lasarus. Keith ordered every abled person in each werewolf pack to gather at his castle and wait for his command. We still didn't know where the army would attack. Keith and Tessa spent a long time looking at the world map, keeping in mind where the army had landed and trying to predict where they were headed towards, but they came up with no clue about their destination. The anchorwoman on TV kept reporting news on the human massacres all over the world, but there was no trace of the dark demon army. I was the only one who could find out, but Keith was adamant that it was simply too dangerous after what Shea had done to me.

"What if somehow she steals your ability to get back this time, huh?" What will happen then? Or what if she simply kills you the way she killed Daisy?" Keith said, sternly. "You have no way to protect yourself. I'm not taking that risk," he insisted.

"I have to agree," Tannon said. "They'll eventually reveal their location. We are not in a hurry to fight."

Katrina commanded all the children to lock their parents at home. With the umbra doing its worse, Tessa hoped we could

370

contain the damage this way. She wanted to avoid fighting on two grounds, both with the demons and the humans.

There was still a point I wasn't clear about.

"The humans under the influence of umbra seem to be attacking everything and anything," I said watching the news which reported a supermarket raid by a herd of crazy humans who had broken everything and then had killed the workers. In the end, when there was nothing else to do, they had turned against each other. "Are you sure they can be commanded to do Azazel's work?" I asked, finding it hard to believe they could listen to anyone's orders. "They just seem uncontrollable to me."

"It's Azazel himself who has created the darkness of the umbra," Tannon explained. "Believe me, when the time comes, they will be under his full influence."

I nodded in disappointment.

"Can you use a gun?" Keith asked me.

"Uhm, I believe so," I answered.

"Tessa? Do you have the special bullets?" Keith asked, raising his eyebrow questioningly.

"Of course," said Tessa. "It's the damn demons; you always have to be prepared." She snapped her fingers, and there it was, a huge case landed itself on the floor.

"Special bullets?" I asked, surprised. And then the horrid memory in the underworld resurfaced. "You mean the bullets include copper, don't you?"

Keith nodded hesitantly.

"Okay, that sounds good," I said, smiling. "Let's get those demon bitches."

Keith grinned and knelt down to open the heavy looking case. He grabbed a few of the weapons and tested each in his hand, finally settling on the one he thought I could handle. Before he handed it to me, he illustrated the basics of using it.

"You pull back the safety latch on the pistol like this," he said as I heard a loud click. "And then you pull the trigger, see?" He fired a test shot. "Look, you'll only use this to protect yourself. You will not fight. It's just a precaution," he said. "I want you to

371

stand far away at the back, got it?" he asked. His eyes turned to mine as if delving into my very thoughts.

I nodded to appease his frantic worry. He also gave me a small knife to slip into my back pocket and a dagger to sheath on my belt. It was evident he was worried about my safety. I held his hand, "It'll be all right. I can protect myself," I assured him.

"I'll not let anything happen to her," said Sean. "I'll not leave their side, I promise," he said referring to Alice and me.

"Right," approved Keith. He looked at me deeply, his gaze wistful, yearning. His eyes lingered on my mouth; then his lips plunged onto mine. He kissed me so slowly, ever so tenderly as if this was it, the only moment to cherish, the only moment to love, the only one worth remembering. It felt like he was putting his whole heart and soul into that kiss.

And then it happened, right there, right then, when I was still immersed in his kiss.

The sky outside lit with a blaze of fire as dark demons flew above, throwing balls of fire to signal their arrival. Hundreds of humans were slowly gathering in the background as if they were joining a protest movement, their expressions dull and blank. The fires shooting from the sky rained on the infected humans who were there to fight alongside the demons, their wails of agony piercing the sky as the fire burned their skin. The demons simply didn't care who went down among their allies in this display of power and intimidation.

"They are attacking my castle right this minute, too," Keith explained as he mind-spoke with Xavier whom he had sent back home. "They are attacking all the targets simultaneously."

Apparently, the demons had marked the houses of all the supernatural leaders.

I gasped as I looked outside. We'd all be burned. Yep, that also included me since Shea had stolen my powers.

"Lin," shouted Tessa. "It's your turn."

The lean blonde woman went outside and raised her hands to the sky. Suddenly the sky roared with the sound of thunder and multiple bolts streaked beneath the clouds. And then there was rain. We saw the first drops of rain fall like the tears of a giant monster which soon became a steady downpour and then hail. The rain poured over the burning fire, putting it out where it fell while the wind Lin had generated cut across the demons' speed. The rain and hail had lowered the utility of shooting fire from the night sky as they flew like fire dragons, and left them with no choice but to continue the fight on the ground. Soon they all lowered their bodies to the ground, thousands of them mixing along with the army of humans who were just programmed to be on terminator mode. Shea stood in all her glory as the leader of this army.

We were all gathered outside at this point, waiting for them to strike.

"Shea," Tessa exclaimed as she took a step towards her.

"That's not your daughter," Keith said.

It was Tannon who managed to hold on to her as she struggled to run to her daughter. There were thirty five to forty of us in the coven, and Tessa was not herself. What chance did we have of defeating them? My heart sank as I looked at my family, my friends and my mate; everyone who was dear to me. How could we ever get out of this alive?

"Tessa, we need you here. You have to focus," Tannon warned her.

"Don't hurt her. Please don't," Tessa whispered in crippling emotional agony.

"Tessa, come to your senses." Tannon shook her.

"Promise me, Tannon. Promise me you'll not hurt her," she begged.

"I promise," Tannon said. "But you have to help. I can't do this alone." Surprisingly, Tannon and Tessa walked to each one of us and touched us on the shoulder. I had no clue what was happening when I felt Tannon's hand, but I felt the power of his magic seep right through me. I was amazed to see a small black mark appear on my right shoulder as his hand left my skin. "What's this for?" I asked in shock.

"It will protect you from the portals," he said.

"I see," I muttered. Needless to say, I didn't. But the war was upon us, and this wasn't the time for explanations, so I didn't push for one.

Gregory had returned to the demon island but other family members were here with me. I saw Keith, Sean, and my parents shift. I wished I could join them, but alas all I had was an illusionary wolf, and it was utterly useless in this war. Tannon was fully sheathed with swords. Most of the witches carried many daggers and knives. Alice and I, the only two who had no battle skills, held our guns tightly.

The war began when Shea raised her hand and brought it down, and all the dark demons advanced at once. The witches with daggers and knives lifted them magically and threw them across the demons, stabbing them in their jugular veins. Dad took out various demons as they kept coming. And Keith was a lethal beast, his movements were nimble and quick, his attacks powerful, savage and precise. He soon disappeared as he advanced in the midst of war. Tannon and Tessa chanted. I saw them create portals at each side with the energy to draw anyone inside who was within the orbit of the door. When I saw Keith approach one without being pulled inside, I could appreciate the mark on our shoulders. It was a protection spell to save us from the portals' magical pull.

Humans attacked with clubs, some of them used just fists, but mostly these possessed humans didn't stand a chance against the supernatural creatures. They were called there just to mess things up. Their purpose was to create a diversion, nothing more. The witches basically pushed them towards the portals, sending them far away to an isolated part of the world. Unlike the dark demons, there was a hope that they could be salvageable if and when the umbra left. What would then happen to the demons transported possibly to Siberia or Antarctica? I had no idea. Apparently that was to be decided later.

Unfortunately, human victims also turned out to be unavoidable as they simply got in the way. Still, our sole focus was the demons. Tannon kept creating more portals which worked their magic on these creatures. It was unbelievable how the demons who were running towards us were sucked inside the portals as if hitting a black void in space and simply disappeared. I watched the shock on their faces the minute they realized they couldn't withstand the magical force. The ones who managed to escape were hit by bloodied knives and daggers which flew through the air, and the few werewolves who kept charging at them. Alice and I tried to contribute by shooting at targets. At first, Sean did not leave our side as he kept lifting the demons that somehow made it close to us as if they were little children and threw them across others, knocking them all out. Slowly and unwillingly, though, he was pushed further away from us until he was no longer within sight.

I was so intensely involved in shooting every demon that moved around us that I failed to watch over Alice. I noticed something was wrong when I heard her cry. She was surrounded by three demons who were almost upon her. Worse yet, she had lost her gun. I shot two demons one after another, but the last one was fast enough to grab me by the wrist. The good news was he was no longer interested in Alice. I dropped the gun in agony as he squeezed my wrist. He was grinning as he seized me by the neck. I saw Alice jump at him from behind, but he knocked her away so hard that she went tumbling backward. He was so close that I could feel his heat. As he raised his sword above me, his eyes rolled upwards and then closed. I tried to throw him off my body, withdrawing the dagger I had pushed towards his neck in the last second. He hadn't seen it coming, the arrogant jackass! I wiped my dagger with his shirt.

"Are you okay?" I heard Alice ask frantically as she crawled towards me, still dizzy from the blow.

"I'm fine. Let's find your gun. Unfortunately, we don't have any time to rest," I said as my eyes roamed the ground.

"I got it, "she said as she spotted her gun on the ground where she'd dropped it. And then, it all began for us again as we went back to shooting mindlessly once more.

Except for Tessa, Alice and I who were holding the line, everyone else had disappeared from sight, advancing deeper into the field. The battlefield was soon strewn with the bodies of dark demons and, unavoidably, humans. But, the war was nowhere over. Everybody was fighting with all they had, but the dark demons kept coming. Just when I thought we did not stand a chance of seeing the end of this, a miracle descended upon us. I saw Shea's form rise above the ground. As if on cue, her army of dark demons disappeared beneath the veil of darkness in the sky. And then there were only humans, but they started running away from the coven as if their asses were on fire. Nobody cared to chase them. The dark demons were the problem, not the humans.

I looked around frantically, still holding the gun firmly in case of a surprise attack. While I was still searching for dark demon targets in my dazed state, I was lifted high up in the air by Keith who'd just come running to find me. He buried his head in my neck and held me like that.

Soon, others had joined us. "Daughter, are you okay?" asked my dad taking a quick step towards Keith, and then he came to an abrupt stop, his hand stretched towards me. He was obviously fighting the urge to grab me, his little daughter, from the arms of what he still saw as a stranger. I'd always been Daddy's girl, and he was struggling to come to grips with the idea that now I had somebody else worrying about my protection.

"What just happened?" I asked as I lowered my body from Keith's. I saw no reason to tempt a mini family war here on the premises while the outcome of the one that mattered was pretty much undecided.

"They'll be back," said Keith. "I need to check on my men."

After a minute or two of watching him use his alpha voice, I was relieved to see his stoic facial expression disappear. Unfortunately, what replaced it wasn't any better. "The battle has also come to an intermission with the werewolves." Keith's stern voice shattered the silence.

"What does this all mean?" I asked again.

"They are planning something, but the question remains: what?" commented Keith.

Almost as if triggered by Keith's words, Tessa entered into a trance. She looked as if she'd jumped straight out of a ghost story with her white iris and incorporeal form, the shape of her ghost-like body shaking uncontrollably until the retrieval of information was completed. Her form slowly took a solid mass as the color of her eyes settled into normalcy.

"The clue is Shea. She'll be the end to all of this," Tessa said, sighing. "I knew it! I knew she wasn't all gone. I can reach her; I know it."

"You don't think she will allow a chat session over tea, do you?" Keith asked. "Tessa, I never thought I'd question your sanity," he remarked. "Is there actually any vital information in here we can use?"

"Yes, the Moon Goddess said their mission was to kill all the leaders, and Shea was sent here to kill Tannon and me," she said, her voice screaming the unsaid emotions, the disappointment, the pain, the despair Shea's betrayal left behind. "You were not in the equation, Keith. You were meant to be in your castle. They apparently confronted more surprises like that. They are reorganizing the units to be directed to the location of each vital target, and Shea is the only one who can send demons across space. Azazel has called her back. That's why they all retreated."

Great! There was still more to come for the evening!

"Let's go back inside," Keith said as he wrapped his arm around my waist. "We need to make preparations too."

"Like what? What else can we do? We can't retrieve your men because they are also fighting. This is the summation of all we have, right here, right now. This is it!" I uttered in complete exasperation.

"Baby, it's not the quantity that matters, it's the quality," Keith said, his assuring and confident tone doing wonders in dissipating my fear and panic. "You know, nothing will happen to you as long as I breathe," he added.

Yeah, but I was not worried about myself as much as I was worried about him. He was the Werewolf King and, apparently, he was one of the three targets in here. How could he fight with so many? It defied any logic.

We went inside; there were only minor wounds on everyone as if to confirm Keith's point. We had a handful of fighters in the coven, but each seemed to be extremely capable. But would that be enough?

Keith, Tannon, and Tessa stayed awake discussing strategy and tactics while the rest of us took light naps to refresh our bodies for the second stage. I lay my head on the couch next to Mom. We closed our eyes, embracing the few moments of togetherness before the darkness of the unknown unfolded.

Sometime in the night, I felt Keith lift me in his arms, placing me on his lap. I simply buried my face in his chest, his smell lulling me to a pretense slumber.

I opened my eyes the moment I felt Keith shift.

"They are coming," Tannon said as he looked in space.

It took us very little to switch to war mood as none of us had completely snapped out of it. Within a few minutes, all of us were out, waiting for the second session of battle to begin.

Just as Tannon had predicted, the sky filled with dark demons in the sky. This time, though, Shea was not the one who was leading them. It was Azazel himself. He'd come for Keith. Not only was that surprising, but it was alarming as well. I would assume he'd be after his arch-nemesis, Lasarus. Why was he here? Had he already killed Lasarus and moved on here?

"I'll draw him away from here," Keith said. Tannon nodded. It was evident they'd already discussed this possibility.

"But," I stammered.

"I'll be okay, Belle," Keith voiced. He looked at me with such intensity, such hunger that it was as if my limbs melted into thin air. Then he shifted and ran in the opposite direction, away from us, away from me. Just as expected, Azazel was following him in the sky, keeping him within close distance. I felt the thud of fear as I glanced at his slowly disappearing form. I could still spot him despite the unexpected return of humans who started filling the battlefield from a distance. Other dark demons lowered their bodies to the ground once more, and it all began again.

The War - Part II

Keith

I ran as a werewolf while I continued eyeing Azazel flying in the sky, towering just above me. I darted among the herd of mindless humans who simply didn't care enough to stop me. When I came to the clearing, I stopped running and turned around to face Azazel who'd now landed his dark body on the ground across me.

The two of us circled each other for some time, just eyeing each other. Azazel slowly unsheathed his sword, then he let the flames surround his body and the sword as he lifted it high up into the sky. Despite his fearsome look, I was not moved. Werewolf King or not, I would burn all right, but I was not a timid boy who would shy away from a burn or two. My tolerance for pain was extremely high, my healing abilities fast, my instincts sharp as cut glass.

I felt an abysmal rage and hatred in my veins against this being who'd hurt my Belle. I emitted a rumbling growl, letting the anger take over my body. The rumble shook the leaves on the trees, echoed, and rang through the quietness of the clearing. Azazel smirked as if to rattle the beast in me.

"So, the girl has chosen you, huh?" he said. "Too bad, I had so much more planned for her, so many more souvenirs to keep from her body," he said, testing my reaction.

I jumped high above to intercept Azazel who suddenly rose in the air, planning to attack me from high up. We collided in space. I gripped him tightly despite the scorching heat that enveloped my skin. I didn't feel the pain, pushing it deep down to a secluded

379

section of my brain to be chained and trapped until the time I'd allow it to rise back to the surface. Only then would I permit myself to feel the pain. My control was perfect, firm, unrelenting. I felt my paws pierce Azazel's skin, lopping off a junk of his neck at first attack. Blood gushed forth and Azazel leaped backward, screaming in pain. But, since I did not let go, Azazel gravitated towards the ground with my additional weight, and his body hit the bottom with a loud thud.

Azazel tried to push me off his body, the wound in his neck weakening him. Unlike me, the king of torture seemed to be sensitive to pain as he lost his concentration, and the flames around his body switched on and off intermittently as if following a random pattern. I relished those moments the flames ebbed as they gave me reprieve from the pain and helped me initiate healing. Azazel threw a ball of fire at my face, almost loosening my hold on his body. I hissed in pain, feeling the tight pulling and shrinking of my skin after the transmission of the heat, but I didn't let go. Azazel then raised his sword hand from the ground, his fingers firmly grasping the weapon. My sharp paws severed his hand from the wrist. Azazel's agonizing scream filled the space, accompanied by the sound the sword made when it rapidly whirled in the air and then fell back with a clang while still being clutched by Azazel's severed hand. I grabbed Azazel's neck, my claws bringing deep punctures in his skin. I raised my other paw up high and was about to deal the final lethal blow when I shook to my core with the distant cry of Belle. I was up in a second, Azazel completely forgotten, and I ran back to Belle with all the energy and force I could muster in my burned body. I felt the waves of desperation tighten my chest, take away my breath, my will to live. Where was she? What was happening to her? I ran with no other thought than to save Belle. I prayed I'd make it in time. I would accept no other option.

***

Belle

380

A few minutes before…

My mind was constantly on Keith. I prayed he was okay.

I was continuously shooting at the dark demons, but the clue to winning the war was to bring down Shea and Azazel. While I had no idea how Keith scored against Azazel, the worst was knowing that nobody had any intention to confront Shea, neither Tessa nor Tannon.

I moved closer to the demons to take a better shot. Perhaps my minuscule efforts of killing a hundred dark demons or so would urge Azazel to retreat? Yeah, if only. I raised my hand and pulled the trigger one time after another at the demons who were running towards me. I suddenly dropped the gun when I yelped with the heat of the fire on my hand. While Lin's magically generated rain to immediately cool my hand, my neck was gripped, and I felt the touch of a sharp knife at my throat.

"Dear Daughter, we meet again," I heard Shea speak.

Damn, now I was doomed. She pressed the knife, grazing my skin as blood dripped down my neck.

"Don't do it, Shea," I heard Tessa say.

"But, I will do it, Mother. You know I will," she said.

"Shea, please Daughter. This is not you. I know the good in you," Tessa insisted, and I could see from her expression that she was unwilling to harm her daughter, not even at the expense of saving her granddaughter. She acted as if this was the moment where she would convince Shea to change sides, and the tide of the war would automatically turn in our favor. I pretty much suspected we were far beyond the talking stage, and I was not comforted by Tessa's perseverance.

I heard Keith cry in the very distance. He ran back to me, trying to make it in time as his sharps paws attacked right and left at the dark demons in his path. I had no hope he would make it. I heard his agonizing yell as he turned berserk, massacring all in his path. I looked at Tessa, she looked desperate but remained frozen where she stood, making small talk to get to Shea. Tannon wasn't even around.

I felt the pressure of the knife on my skin. The moment I sensed Shea's hand move, I leaned back and stretched my hands way back. I aimed to locate her eyes, and apply pressure in a clawing out movement to loosen her grip on the knife. But instead, I found myself grabbing her temples and then I heard her scream. I didn't know what was happening, but I held on for life. I didn't exactly know why and how, but I started taking it all back, the powers she'd stolen from me. I pulled them all into my body, feeling rejuvenated with the potency of all that was flowing back to me. Shea shook all over, dropping the knife. She was as helpless in loosening my grip as I'd been when she was the one doing the draining. It was as if an invisible force was holding the two of us glued together. I kept taking and taking until there was nothing else to take and she simply collapsed. What happened afterward was shocking. The demons using Shea's portal simply vanished into thin air as the magic that sustained the portal was gone along with all of her other powers.

"Shea," Tessa screamed, finally freed from her frozen state. But before she could get to her daughter, Keith in his berserk state, leaped in the air inches away, somersaulting as he went and landed stretched over Shea's body, and simply snapped her neck.

"No!" screamed Tessa. "No! It wasn't supposed to be like this!"

I held my beast tightly. I wouldn't allow him to hurt anyone else. My touch helped him shift back. He took a deep breath when he was himself again and embraced me. He was stark naked in the battlefield and I almost laughed.

"No," Tessa cried. "How could you do that? She was redeemable."

"Belle almost died because of you. You just stood there and stared," Keith raged. "Shea was no longer your daughter," he said, a bit more calmly now.

It was then I noticed the burns on Keith's skin, and I gasped in shock.

"Keith," I exclaimed.

"I'm all right, the berserk stage accelerated my healing," he said, grinning, although I could spot the grimace in his face.

How could he be so calm about this? My thoughts were diverted as I saw Tannon walk towards us.

"Belle, are you okay?" Tannon asked.

I nodded.

"Did you do what I thought you did?" Tannon asked.

"It was accidental," I said. "I didn't know I could do that," I apologized, uncertain about how he felt about all this.

He looked at me with a barely visible grin as an indication of his silent approval.

Keith talked to Xavier and Tannon contacted the others. The demons and the umbra had all disappeared. Azazel was also nowhere to be found. Our best guess was they were back in the underworld. The remaining humans were looking around at each other with no remembrance of where they were or what they were doing here. They slowly scattered.

"I guess, it's back to protecting the gate for me," Tannon said.

I didn't know how I felt about Tessa, but I was going to keep in touch with Tannon, that was for sure. He hugged me lightly as he sent my family and us back to Keith's castle. I asked Tannon to check on Gregory and was relieved to hear he'd also made it out without a scratch.

As I was taking a shower in our bedroom, letting the water wash away all the fear, worry and stress of the day, I couldn't help but think about Shea, the mother I had never got the chance to know and love. Though what she'd done was unpardonable, I also couldn't help but sympathize with Tessa. An ancient priestess she might be, but she was also a mother, a mother who refused to accept her daughter was long gone. As I was drying myself and combing my hair, I yelped.

Keith entered the bathroom in a hurry. "What's wrong?" he asked in a panic.

"Look, Keith, my mark is back," I said showing him the eye on my neck. Moon Goddess, how had that happened?

"I know. I felt you when I was fighting Azazel ..." He didn't go on as if not saying the words would take away the horrid memory.

"But, I don't understand," I said.

"The Vampire King is dead, Belle. Tannon said so. Apparently, Azazel killed him in the first round."

"Huh?" I uttered. The Vampire King was taken down? That was shocking. The news made me thankful that my family and friends were all safe.

"The decision must have been revoked upon his death," Keith said, reminding me of why we were having this conversation in the first place.

"I'm sorry he died," I said. "What about the others? Derek, and Lasarus?" I asked, cautiously.

"They seem to be among the living," Keith said.

That was good. "I sure am thrilled to have your mark again," I remarked.

Keith grinned cockily, and I just adored seeing him like that. He was my very own beast. He would always be mine.

We lay in bed, not touching each other. His burns still needed more healing. But we didn't need to touch to feel the flow of love between us. I looked at him remembering the journey that brought us together. What an adventure it had all been with all its ups and downs. But, in the end, it had all been worth it. He looked at me affectionately as he brought his lips to my hand and whispered "Belle-mine." The heat in his eyes stole my breath away and made my skin burn.

Yep, I thought, it had all been worth it as I closed my eyes smiling.

Epilogue

Belle

A year later…

"Hmm, what's that smell? It's so damn good," I said waking up in bed.

"What smell?" Keith asked.

"The smell of newly baked apple pie of course," I said inhaling deeply again.

"Baby, are you serious?"

"Yes, why?"

"You can actually smell that?"

"Yep. And I want it. Badly," I said trying to get out of bed.

"Not so fast," he said holding me.

I kept sniffing.

"Well, I'll be damned."

"What?" I said, crossly.

"Belle, you always said the prophecy had got it wrong. That you had not inherited any powers from the werewolves."

"Yes, and I stand by my word. Not that I need any more powers, not with the boost I got from Shea, but it's true. I never got anything from your kind."

"Sweetie, it's no longer true. That pie is in the kitchen, and you can smell it from a great distance."

385

"Oh," I said, my face falling. "I got your sense of scent? That's it?"

"Are you disappointed?" Keith asked, smiling.

"Well, I'd hoped I could shift like you."

"You can't, Belle-mine. But perhaps the baby you are carrying can."

"What? This is no joking matter," I said.

"But I'm not joking. I can hear his heartbeat," he said as he put one ear on my belly. "And that's why you've been craving the pie," he chuckled. "While I've been craving you," he added as he draped his body over mine, his need for me apparent in his eyes.

"Are you disappointed about the baby?" he asked, concerned.

I thought about it for a few seconds. Yes, it was early, but what the heck? Everything in my life had been on a roller coaster since the day I had met Keith, and I had loved every minute of it.

"No," I said, and I meant it.

He started kissing me, his fingers tracing the line from my neck up to my ear so lightly, making me shiver.

"Keith," I said before I was too lost in passion.

"Yes, Belle-mine?"

"I've been meaning to ask you for some time now," I managed to say. A gasp and a moan escaped my lips as I felt his kiss and hot breath on the nape of my neck. "How old are you exactly?"

"Seven hundred, give or take."

"What?" I croaked.

"I love you, Belle-mine," I heard him say.

Was he joking?

Probably.

He then attacked me with his scorching lips, making me forget about everything else. "I love you, too," I managed to mutter before the erupting fire of passion consumed me.

Bonus Chapter: The Moment is Upon Us

Months later...

I shifted in my bed uncomfortably like a restless child and took a long deep breath before slowly turning myself sideways, my body mimicking the awkward incremental movements of a robot. I looked at Keith, but within moments, the smile I had plastered on my face evaporated like a puff of mist. I let out a deep, exasperated sigh. It didn't take long for Keith's expression to change from happy to alarm to worry within seconds. I held him back with a raised hand before he could move. I didn't need his help; I could do this, damn it! I started turning in bed again, reversing back to my previous position until my body was leaning back against the soft cushions piled up against the bedpost.

"Is this normal?" I asked Keith. "I mean to be this big when carrying your pup? I look like a whale," I complained, creasing my forehead in distaste. "I know I look utterly disgusting."

I caught an almost imperceptible flicker of panic on his face, but the wide grin, which suddenly stretched upon his lips, washed away all the potential evidence. I was left with thinking I had imagined it all.

"Baby, you are beautiful," Keith attempted to assure me as he brought his body closer to mine, his hands reaching out to caress my belly, which happened to be his all-time favorite hobby now. "You are simply stunning," he whispered as he raised himself on one elbow and leant forward to capture my lips.

"Mmm..." I murmured in between his scorching kisses, forgetting all about my insecurity in those blissful moments.

"Are you sure?" I asked hesitantly. I simply couldn't help it, pregnancy and raging hormones had been taking me on an emotional roller coaster for weeks now.

"Always. You are my addiction; don't you know that Belle-mine?" he asked with such a depth of conviction in his tone that I shivered. I could feel the swirl of emotions pouring out of him to embrace me in a cocoon of warmth and love, fending off the ferocious attack of suspicions and self-doubt. I felt much better. Yep, that had done the trick. Well, at least for now.

I smiled. "Okay then... if you are sure," I murmured as I suddenly clutched my stomach in pain. "Holy shit, this hurts," I gasped, trying to catch my breath.

"What's wrong?" Keith exclaimed in horror. "Shall I fetch Alice?"

Thankfully, Alice had come to the castle a month ago with the intention of staying with us till the birth, and I suspected, perhaps for even longer. Apparently, living with Tessa, who was now a hollow shell of her former cheerful self after the death of Shea, was turning the Coven into a nightmare for all. I had the feeling my friend needed to be here as much as I needed her here with me.

"No!" I said, slapping his hand as he attempted to rise from the bed. "She must be sleeping; it's the middle of the night. I'm fine now. It's passed. See, all is well," I said.

He put his cheek on my belly; his palm spread wide as if he could touch his child beneath the skin. "Stop hurting your Mommy," he whispered, as if the baby could hear him. Worried and frustrated lines stretched across his forehead as he fixed his black eyes on me. His deep gaze was heart stopping and I felt it penetrate the depths of my soul. He was so very beautiful in his concern.

"Belle..." he sighed. "I want pups, but I want you more. I won't let anything happen to you. I won't let you hide your pain from me. I need to know when and how much you're hurting. I can feel that you're still uncomfortable, despite what you say."

I laughed. "I'm always uncomfortable. Look at me! I'm carrying pounds and pounds of extra weight. But, the pain is gone, Keith. I mean it." I smiled. I was becoming an expert in faking my smiles. "I want to sleep now. I'm rather tired."

I had said the magic words, the ones that my poor Keith waited for so patiently each and every night. It was becoming more and more difficult to find a comfortable enough position to sleep. So, each night, Keith kept me company, his hands working miracles as they massaged my body to take away the exhaustion and the heaviness of my limbs until the moment he was sure I'd finally surrendered to sleep. But today sleep was going to be difficult. Despite what I had said earlier, and as much as I was doing my best to ignore it, I still had patches of burning pain here and there, making relaxation an unattainable goal. Nevertheless, I closed my eyes.

"I love you Belle-mine," he whispered as he laid his body next to mine, wrapping one arm loosely around my chest.

"I love you, too," I said. I lay in bed, faking a soft rhythmic breathing as if claimed by sleep, for at least an hour. Just when I was finally falling asleep, I screamed in a burning pain at the pit of my stomach like my insides were scorched with a hot iron. Keith got up in a second, ready for action.

"Belle... baby. Fuck this! You're hurting, what the hell is going on?" he raged. "I'm bringing Alice, and that is final," he said. His face became stern; it was evident he was waking Xavier in alpha command and probably ordering him to immediately bring Alice to our room. Within five minutes, Alice rushed into our room followed by Xavier, who had been in my good graces since his bitch sister had left the castle to live with a relative in a far away pack. Good riddance, she was now somebody else's problem. Apparently, she was now sleeping with the alpha's son in that poor pack.

"Is it time?" Alice asked, rushing to touch my belly with her stretched palms. When she unrolled my shirt, she gasped. Keith cried out in agony. I was so stunned with what I was seeing that I was rendered speechless.

"What the fuck is this!" Keith shouted in exasperation. "How in the hell is this possible? Is this some sort of witchcraft?"

"No, it's not witchcraft," Alice said, calling the light to her fingertips to heal the second-degree burns that had emerged on my belly. "It's your child burning her from the inside out. Apparently, he has some of Belle's demonic powers. We need to start the birth before he burns her alive, thankfully she was due in two weeks anyway."

"But, how is that possible? I couldn't create fire until I was eighteen," I said, utterly stupefied. Keith was not faring any better than me, his face was deadly serious and his jaw rigid.

"But, how can fire do this to Belle?" Keith asked. "She's fucking supposed to be immune," he cursed.

"I don't know. Maybe the impact of the fire is bigger from the inside, or the pregnancy is making Belle vulnerable, muting some of her ability to protect herself. Whatever it is, she won't last."

"Okay, let's start the process then," he said, determined. He touched Alice lightly on her shoulder. "I want her safe at all costs. Is that clear?"

"Well, hello. I'm right here, and I do not like the sound of that. You are so not sacrificing my child. I want him safe at all costs. Is *that* clear?" I said forcefully. While all the supernatural species, possessed with the powers to defend themselves against danger, and the ability to heal fast, had long life tenures compared to humans, birthing was one freaking exception that didn't discriminate much among the living beings. Actually, death by birth was more common among the supernatural beings than it was among the humans. That was a fact.

"Dear friends, it won't come to that. I know what I'm doing," said Alice in a confident tone. "But, I want everyone out."

"No way, I'm staying here with Belle," said Keith, as stubborn as a mule, while Xavier left the room without much ado.

"I will help you with the process, Belle," my friend explained to me. "I will now induce your labor by opening up your cervix, and I will initiate the contractions. But once you feel those, I want

390

you to push with all you've got. Do you understand?" she asked as she brought the healing light to her palms.

"Yes," I managed to utter.

"Are you ready Belle?" asked Alice.

I nodded, unable to form any more words as a knot of fear welled in my throat. I felt Alice's palms upon my bare belly; her magic spreading a feeling of warmth to my skin. I looked at Keith whose face was ashen, as he stood immobile in the middle of the room. I had never seen him like this; this desperate and helpless. Not when we were trapped in the Underworld, nor when we had to confront the dark demons who were unleashed upon us from the sky, not even when he finally had to apologize to Dad for his forceful and rude intrusion when he'd come for me. Then I suddenly felt them, the contractions, starting slowly at first, but then gaining pace and severity with each breath. Keith was forgotten as I was left with no other thought, but to end the damn pain.

"Push," Alice reminded me.

I pushed, and pushed more, and then again repeatedly with all the force I could muster.

"Good girl," Alice cooed. "More, Belle," she said.

"Aagh," I screamed out as I felt uncontrollable fire erupting from my hands, shooting flames all over the room.

"Whoa," Alice leaped back as one came close to burning her to ashes.

"Damn it, you need to tie my hands," I said, exhausted and damn disappointed that my baby was still inside me.

"She's right," said Alice. "Or else, she'll burn the whole room," she said, smiling. I extended my hands as Keith tied them to the bedpost, with palms facing down.

"Push," Alice said again. If I heard that word one more time, I was gonna vomit. But, I pushed regardless; did I have any other choice?

Keith was sitting next to me, urging me, soothing me to give one more push, always one more push. "C'mon baby. You can do it. I love you so much. It'll soon be over. One more time, now," he said, holding my hand dangling from the bedpost. And I squeezed his hand real good as I gave one almighty push. I didn't care whether I burned him or not.

"I can see the head," Alice shouted in joy. "The baby's coming!"

Those words, lies or not, urged me to continue until I felt Alice pull the baby from my womb and I heard my baby's first cry. Tears poured down my cheeks in a torrent as I felt the exuberant joy of hearing his voice. My lovely sweet baby had arrived...

Alice cut the umbilical cord. But just when I was about to relax, I heard the shocking words.

"There's more Belle. You have to push again," I heard Keith say calmly.

"What in the blazes are you talking about?" I said, utterly confused and depleted.

"He's right, you've got another baby coming. You are having twins," said Alice as she handed the newly born baby to Keith. "It's a girl," she added.

"You knew, and you didn't tell me?" I said, my voice etched in disbelief. No wonder, I'd been that huge. "Screw you, you are so dead," I shouted at Keith. But, the sudden contraction halted me right before I could let it all out, the fury, the pain, the fear and the joy which, by now, had molded into a gigantic ball of emotions wrecking me from deep inside. Then, I was shaken by another worry. We had picked a name for the boy; it was to be Aidan. And we hadn't even had the time to think of a girl name; I was so gonna kill him.

"Didn't want to scare you, my heart. You were already so worried about being a mother of one, I'm sorry. I was torn between telling you and not telling you every damn day."

That explanation and poor apology had not calmed me down one bit.

"She's coming, Belle. C'mon love, you can be angry with me later on. But now push," I heard Keith say. I redirected all the pent up anger I felt for Keith to delivering my baby girl. Soon, her shrill cry was added to that of her brother's. I lay in bed exhausted and disgustingly sweaty, with all my frizzy hair plastered to my face, yet I'd never been happier. Keith placed a soft kiss on each wrist as he finally untied my hands. "I'm very proud of you. I love you, Belle," he whispered.

"Congratulations, Belle," Alice said with moist eyes as she lifted the squirming bundle to my arm. Keith also placed our son on the other arm as his lips grazed my forehead.

"Aren't they the most beautiful babies you've ever seen?" I asked Keith, having already forgotten about the labor, the pain and the tremendous effort put into this miracle.

"Indeed, they are," he confirmed proudly, his voice deep with emotion. "Thank you Belle-mine."

The cries of the two babies brought me to my senses; I knew what they wanted. I bared both breasts, first helping Aidan find my nipple and suckle, but before I could even attend to my baby girl, who was crying like a banshee, I saw her body lift up in air. With her wails continuing to shake the room, she was desperately trying to find the nipple she sought with grave hunger. Keith caught her in the air as she tried to lower her body with a ninety-degree angle straight down on baby Aidan's body. Keith's expression was all telling; he was utterly shocked.

"I think we may have a slight problem with our baby girl," he said in disbelief. "How is this even possible?"

Alice was chuckling. "You may be right, my dear Keith. I'll let you discover the answer to that on your own," she said. "Well, I'm done with the birthing and both the babies and the mother are fine. So, if you'll excuse me, I will take my leave and let you adjust to your new wonderful life. It should be interesting. I'll check up on you in the morning, Belle," she said, grinning as she left the room quietly.

"What shall we name her?" Keith asked, still in shock as he placed the baby on my other breast.

"Kaia... I want to call her Kaia."

"What about me, did you forgive me? Are we good?" Keith asked; his tone laced with worry.

"Of course not, you're grounded! No sex for you for at least six months," I said.

It was damn hard, but I was holding myself not to crack up, his face had turned greenish, like the color of demon blood. We had stopped any physical intimacy for the last two months, and I knew he was looking forward to starting it at the most convenient time after the birth. I had just sunk all his ships, and I saw his shoulders stoop, as he conceded whatever point had just been lost. I would let my poor horny Keith suffer and sulk for a few more days before I would let him in on the joke and allow him to find his bliss again. That was the fitting punishment.

***

Belle's adoptive mother opened the door quietly and she sighed happily at the scene that greeted her. Tannon had just brought them in through the portal and the whole family, including Tessa, was now gathered in the castle to meet the new babies. Belle and Keith were both asleep. There was saliva on Keith's naked chest from the drooling baby that was lying contentedly on his body. The smell of sweat and milk permeated the room. It was a mess and Belle and Keith were a mess. Their exhaustion was apparent from the way their breathing deepened into soft snores, yet there was happiness and joy in the air as well. She could tell by the way their lips slightly slanted into a grin, by the way their faces were completely relaxed into a peaceful and content calm, and by the way Belle and Keith's hands clasped tightly and lovingly in the middle of the bed.

There would be ample time to get acquainted with the babies in the morning, Belle's mother thought. Smiling, she left the room quietly.

Bonus Chapter: Trouble brewing

"Kaia, stop scorching uncle Xavier's hair," I shouted, looking at the small trail of smoke rising just above Xavier's head.

"I swear, I've got no hair left," complained Xavier, trying to remove her from where she was seated behind his neck, her legs dangling from each shoulder and her little hands tightly clasped around his head.

"Please Uncle Xavier, it was an accident. I swear on my favorite chocolate ice cream," she said, her voice shaking with tears, which threatened to roll down her pink cheeks.

I looked at poor Xavier who stood little chance of resisting her charms. I knew what was next to come, a scene that I had witnessed at least a dozen times before. As much as he'd complain, Kaia had him wrapped around her little finger.

"Well...okay then, just this once. But, make sure you fist your hands. I mean it, Kaia,"

"Yes, of course. See I've done it, Uncle Xavier. Thanks, I love you so," Kaia said, kissing him on his temple.

"I love you, too little pumpkin. Only the Goddess knows why, as you've scalded me too many times to count and left me bald for good. My poor mate will not have me when I find her," he sighed, trying to insert a dose of reprimand in his voice; a futile attempt judging by the soft and loving tone in his voice which immediately gave him away.

Kaia's expression was serious for a few seconds; it was obvious she was contemplating the problem she may have caused, which was not sitting very well with her. Then her cute chubby cheeks poked out in a wide a grin as she said, "Don't you worry Uncle Xavier. I'll burn her hair too, so she'll have no choice but to like you."

"Moon Goddess help me," I heard Xavier sigh in utter desperation.

I laughed, and then I remembered why I'd come to find Kaia in the first place. "Baby, Kathildon has arrived," I said. Kathildon often came to visit and stay with us, to the dismay of Keith who had no idea why his daughter would want to be friends with the weird Ifrit boy. Not only were they friends, but they were best friends ever since the Ifrit King had paid a diplomatic visit to us, bringing his son along with him last year. The two had been inseparable since then. Kathildon often asked Kaia to stay with his family too, but Keith was adamant in rejecting his invitation. He stood his ground with his infamous words, "No, thank you. I refuse to send my daughter to a house harboring a horde of dangerous and unpredictable freaks." And that was that. He would not budge and refused to change his mind. My sweet Keith was so damn predictable! Despite all my attempts to change him during the six years in our relationship, he had not wavered an inch in his overbearing and overprotective manners, the only difference being that his urge to protect me now had extended to the twins whom he loved as dearly.

"Yuppie! Kathi is here, Uncle Xavier. C'mon, let's go," she shouted in excitement, pressing her legs around his neck and squeezing her already fisted small hands to his temples, urging her make-believe horse to trot.

At hearing Kaia had somebody else to play with the rest of the day, Xavier's face suddenly relaxed, a hint of joy and relief flickering over his expression. He didn't even second her request as he suddenly shifted and took off, carrying her towards what he believed to be his salvation. I could hear the sound of Kaia's giggles fill the air as she shouted, "Run faster, faster Uncle Xavier. As fast as papa."

I followed them slowly from behind, my eyes searching for Aidan's whereabouts at the same time. The twins were different from each other like ice and fire. While Kaia was impish, playful and a trouble-maker, Aidan was too serious, studious, and responsible for a five-year-old child. I worried about his proclivities, which so resembled his father's, as much as I worried about his sister's potential to make mischief. I guess that was the definition of being a mother, and as I was a a young and inexperienced one, I struggled with this constant worry for my kids as I watched them grow every day in this dangerous world, which I'd been thrown harshly into myself a few years back. It was at these times that I found consolation in Keith's strength and love.

I sighed with relief, amidst my thoughts, as I spotted my baby boy in the garden. He was thrusting a wooden sword, one taller than his height, with the expertise of a grown up as he advanced towards a boy twice his age. The boy I recognized to be the young pup of one of Keith's warriors. Despite being only five, Aidan had shifted a few months back, a miracle, as Keith put it, in the world of werewolves. And his strength was scary, as scary as the ability of his sister to fly and make fire since birth. We had learned that the one who had burned me from inside during my advanced stages of pregnancy had been Kaia after all, and not Aidan. So far, the kids' talents seemed to be perfectly divided across gender lines, with Aidan having taken over the genes of Keith, while Kaia took over mine. We did not know what the future would bring, however, and that scared the hell out of us. The twins were already a challenge with their unprecedented talents and the thought of them developing others prematurely threatened to push us to the brink of insanity.

"Belle," Keith roared the moment he spotted me.

"Yes, sweetheart. What is it?" I asked, knowing full well what rattled him.

"What is he doing here again?" he said pointing at the Ifrit boy. "Are we adopting him or what? I swear. Lately, I seem to be seeing him as often as my own kids."

"Hush, be nice," I said laughing. "He's staying the week with us, so you better take the wind out of your sails."

"I don't like this at all. Not one bit," he said as he looked at the departing figures of Kathildon and Kaia, who had already started their game of hide and seek as they were flying out of the room, speeding to outdo each other.

"Ouch," we heard Kaia cry out as she hit her head on the wall she was trying to climb to catch up with her much faster friend. "I'm all right," she hollered, rubbing her head as she disappeared from sight.

"I swear she will be the end of me, I already have gray hair," Keith mumbled. " I have a series of pack related fights to judge, I'll see you at dinner?" he asked as he gave me a quick peck on the lips, which left me wanting for more. He knew this, the asshole, as he winked and said, "Later, babe."

I nodded, grinning, before I made my visits to a few households. Afterwards, I went to oversee the construction of the health clinic that had started a month back. With the werewolves doing the manual labor, the building was almost finished. While werewolves, like other species, had overly developed healing abilities, they were not immortal. My goal was to minimize the risks for younger children, pregnant women and also those harboring graver injuries. The idea had come to me when Alice had tended to me during my pregnancy. I had the damn urge to replicate the process for others. So, with the help and intervention of Alice, we had hired the services of a healer witch who was to start next month at the castle. I was lost in my thoughts of this, which is why it took me a few precious seconds for me to hear Aidan's cry.

"Mommy, I can't find Kaia. She's gone," Aidan shouted as he came running towards me.

"What do you mean she's gone? I'm sure she's around," I said, trying to remain calm.

"No, mommy. She's not!" he said, trying very hard not to cry. Despite the differences in their character and talent, the twins were very close to each other. I lifted Aidan up, wrapping my arms tightly around him, as I started looking for Kaia. After half an hour of searching every room and asking everyone I ran into without finding a trace of my baby girl, I had no other option but to interrupt Keith at his work.

I opened the courtroom in a hurry, not even bothering to knock. Keith's relief of getting a short break from the boring job of deciding on pack disputes was short-lived when he heard why I was there.

"Are you sure she's not around?" asked Keith.

"I don't know. Maybe. All I know is I can't find her," I admitted.

"Okay, let's not panic. Xavier?" Keith commanded.

"You gotta be kidding me. How many times has she been lost in the past? No, let me answer that, zillion times... It's Kaia we're talking about; she must be hiding in a closet even as we speak," he said.

"Xavier," Keith urged him again, curtly.

"I've turned into a babysitter, great. Just fucking great," he said as he leaped to his feet in a hurry to find her. We all knew his words of indifference and frustration were a mere cover-up for his love for Kaia.

"Thanks, Xavier. Sorry for interrupting," I apologized to the disputants as I left.

"Xavier, let me know the moment you find her," shouted Keith.

We yelled her name all over the castle grounds with a search team of ten people, but when another half an hour passed with no news of her, I sat down on the stairs, utterly defeated, my whole body shaking with tremors. Xavier was shaking his head as he mind-spoke with Keith. Within minutes, Keith was by my side, his face grave.

"I knew nothing good would come from that Ifrit boy. If they've kidnapped my girl, I'll kill them all," he said, punching the wall. "Belle, take me to that asshole Ifrit King, now," he said.

As Tannon had predicted, I had soon discovered that I was able to open portals, just like my real mother, Shea. Thankfully, Tannon had trained me, helping me develop the talent that lay latent in me all this time. I brought my hands together and tried to concentrate, despite being mangled with a wreck of emotions ranging from despair to a heart-wrenching panic. I brought my palms upward as I focused on the Ifrit dwelling, which I had the misfortune to visit last time when I was fulfilling one of Daisy's challenges to get to the Wiccan Coven. A door began to emerge as I continued chanting the words that would take us to the Ifrit cave. Once the door solidified, we all rushed inside, only to be confronted with the sharp dank musky smell of the cave. I had certainly not missed this place.

Soon, we were facing the Ifrit King sitting at his magically elevated throne; a chair gifted to him by Tessa, I was later informed.

"Welcome. You staying for dinner?" asked the king cheerfully. "Are the kids with you?"

"Where is she?" bellowed Keith. "If you think you can kidnap my daughter and get away with it, then think again. I will bring this whole place down; I will end your species. Right now, right this minute, do you understand? You have five seconds to tell me where she is!"

It was the flicker of confusion that flashed in his eyes, which alerted me to his innocence. While Keith was too far gone in his rage to notice, and the Ifrit King was too stubborn to stop and ask what was happening, things were soon spiraling out of hand.

"This is war," the Ifrit King declared. "Where is my boy, you savage beast?"

"This is your last breath," Keith raged as he began to shift. Xavier was also beginning to shift, getting ready to fight as his fisted hands started to turn into claws.

"Stop it, stop it all of you," I said, crying. "Don't you see, somebody has kidnapped our babies while you are fighting here like mule-headed kids."

There was a moment of clarity on their faces as they suddenly grasped the gravity of the situation. Worse than thinking that Keith had Kathildon, or that the Ifrit King had our Kaia, was having no idea who had our kids. That was exactly where we stood now. At square one.

"Oh, for Moon Goddess' sake, what will we do?" I asked in sheer panic.

"Belle." I heard somebody call me. It was the voice of Tannon.

"Not now, warlock," Keith said, impatiently.

"This is not a social visit, dear Keith. I have something that belongs to you. I figured you'd want it back."

"What the hell are you babbling about?" Keith roared.

"I have Kaia and her friend here with me. Did you know she could open a portal? Amazing how she ended up opening one to my cabin. Simply amazing!" he said. "No, my dear boy. I do not have human eyeballs in demon blood sauce. You will have to eat the meat sandwich I just made for you," he said, obviously talking to Kathildon. "Do you guys mind if they stay the night here? I must say I'd missed the kids. This was a nice treat for me. I wish Aidan had come, too."

I started laughing. It was a simple transition as my tears of panic miraculously transformed into tears of joy. "Not at all," I said. "Thanks, Tannon."

"Young lady, you are in so much trouble when you get back," Keith said with obvious relief. Xavier had also started grinning.

"Well, then... It was good seeing you. We'll take our leave now," said Keith to the Ifrit King as if nothing of import had happened in between them.

"You, too," said the Ifrit King in exactly the same manner. "Let's do this again sometime."

Welcome to the world dominated by men, men who never owned their mistakes and where ignorance was so much better than acceptance. I chuckled, creating a portal that would take us back to the castle.

"I'll be in an early grave because of her. I know it," murmured Keith as we lay in bed that night. "I just hope she finds a mate to protect her before I take my leave."

"You'll be fine. We'll be fine. As long as we are together," I said, my hands caressing his naked chest. "You are not regretting us, are you?" I asked hesitantly.

"How can you say that? You and the kids are everything to me. Look at all the excitement you've brought to my boring life. I do not regret one moment of it," he said, laughing. "I cherish it all, Belle-mine. I love you. I always will. For an eternity."

"For an eternity," I repeated his words. "Hmm, I remember you promised me something today. I believe it has arrived. Am I wrong?"

"No, you are right my dear Belle. You are so very right. And, I always keep my promises," he said as his lips descended on mine.

Alternative ending

Outside the castle door stood a hunched figure, listening to the sounds and whispers of the still night, thinking, deliberating on this day of discovery. "She can open a portal, interesting. Very interesting indeed," the figure mumbled, disappearing from sight.

Printed in the USA
CPSIA information can be obtained
at www.ICGtesting.com
LVHW040421210224
772425LV00024B/178